"IF PRESENT TRENDS CONTINUE . . ."

How many business forecasts have you read that contain the above phrase?

Count them up, and you will know how many business forecasts you can't trust.

To plan on present trends of any kind continuing is to construct a blueprint for disaster.

Although this book cannot tell you what is going to happen in the future, it can show you how to figure it out for yourself, and make inevitable change work *for* you, not against you!

MASTERING CHANGE

"Rationally based and uncommonly sensible."
—*Minneapolis Star*

LEON MARTEL is the co-author (with Herman Kahn and William Brown) of *The Next 200 Years* and the author of *Lend-Lease, Loans and the Coming of the Cold War*. Formerly Executive Vice President of the Hudson Institute, he is currently a lecturer and consultant on issues of management and strategic planning to major corporations and professional associations in the United States and abroad. He holds a B.A. from Dartmouth College and an M.A. and Ph.D. from Columbia University.

MASTERING
CHANGE

LEON MARTEL

A MENTOR BOOK

NEW AMERICAN LIBRARY

NEW YORK AND SCARBOROUGH, ONTARIO

Copyright © 1986 by Leon Martel

Library of Congress Catalog Card Number: 86–63904

MENTOR TRADEMARK REG. U.S. PAT. OFF. AND FOREIGN COUNTRIES
REGISTERED TRADEMARK—MARCA REGISTRADA
HECHO EN CHICAGO. U.S.A.

SIGNET, SIGNET CLASSIC, MENTOR, ONYX, PLUME, MERIDIAN and
NAL BOOKS are published in the United States by NAL PENGUIN INC.,
1633 Broadway, New York, New York 10019, and in Canada by
The New American Library of Canada Limited, 81 Mack Avenue,
Scarborough, Ontario M1L 1M8

First Mentor Printing, June, 1987

1   2   3   4   5   6   7   8   9

PRINTED IN THE UNITED STATES OF AMERICA

For Marilee

Contents

Acknowledgments

This book grew out of studies of the future first begun while I served on the professional staff of the Hudson Institute. My initial gratitude, therefore, is to that unique institution for the opportunity it provided for wide-ranging and uninhibited speculation on all matters bearing on the future of mankind and, above all, to its late founder and director, Herman Kahn, who brought new insights and great wisdom to every subject he examined. The ideas of Herman—as he was fondly known to all who ever met him, from presidents and prime ministers to hotel doormen—are sprinkled throughout this book, acknowledged in notes when they could be traced to published sources but just as often—so pervasive and enduring was his teaching—embedded in my own thinking and writing.

Two other of my former Hudson Institute colleagues have influenced important parts of the argument presented here and deserve special mention. One is William Brown, whose forecasts of energy and raw materials—heaped with scorn by many when they were first made more than a decade ago—have continued to prove remarkably prescient. The other is Patrick Gunkel, from whose prodigious knowledge of human physiology and the natural world has grown a provocative forecast of the future which is both awesome in its imaginative sweep and convincing in its conception.

Others have helped importantly with their assistance and counsel. Robert P. Walker has been a steady and welcome source of support for this project since its inception, and it was because of his efforts to bring it to the attention of others that Roger Jellinek saw an early outline and made the important suggestion that mastering change be its central focus. Arnold Dolin, a valued friend and a talented editor, reviewed early drafts of the first two chapters and

ix

made very useful suggestions for the organization and development of the entire book.

Esther Newberg, who has believed in this project and encouraged it from the moment she first learned of it, has been the perfect literary agent. Not only did she build the bridge between concept and contract, but she followed the writing of the manuscript with just the right mixture of support when it was most needed and occasional prodding when that, too, was needed. At Simon and Schuster Alice Mayhew's wise recommendations have helped give this book life and form and have added its author to the large and growing list of those who have been the grateful beneficiaries of her fine editorial hand and unwavering support; Ann Godoff has attended to the entire editorial and production process with a rare and welcome combination of skill, patience and good humor; and the copy editing of Edward Johnson has carefully brought order to the stylistic variations that randomly populated the original manuscript.

My greatest debt is to my family. My two sons, Christopher and Jonathan, have again patiently endured the long hours of my enforced absence for research and writing and, with growing awareness and interest, have inquired regularly of my progress. Even more, they have been useful sources of information and unfailing deflators of errant trial balloons hoisted in their direction. Most important has been my wife, Marilee. Her suggestions and emendations have guided this book on every step of its journey from initial outline to publication. Each page has benefited from her astute critical judgment, both substantive and literary, and the volume now stands completed only because of her constant encouragement and support. I am grateful indeed.

All of the above have helped make this a better book. The faults that remain are mine alone.

Preface

We live in a world of change, yet we act on the basis of continuity. Change is unfamiliar; it disturbs us. We ignore it, we avoid it; often we try to resist it. Continuity, on the other hand, is familiar; it provides safety and security. Thus, when we plan for the future, we prefer to assume present conditions will continue. But they rarely do. As a result, we experience unnecessary losses and miss unseen opportunities. If we could learn to anticipate change and to prepare for it, we could make it work for us, not against us. Alvin Toffler, in the book that made him famous, warned that the future would shock us. In order to avoid that shock we must learn to master change.

This book has two purposes: to explain the major changes likely to occur during the next twenty years, and to show how to make use of them. Its central argument is that the best way to prepare for the future is to understand change. To do so, it proposes a new approach to the future and a new strategy for dealing with it.

The new approach is to recognize that change is natural and to be expected, and that continuity is unnatural and to be suspected. Because of change, a great deal of what is happening today will be different tomorrow. But though different, much can be known, for change is not random, not the chance outcome of a roll of dice. There are distinct kinds of change; and these have patterns—with dimensions of direction, magnitude, pace and duration that can be seen and measured.

The new strategy enables us to identify those changes that will affect our businesses, our occupations, and our personal lives; it helps us determine their kind and see their dimensions; and it assists us in making use of them. If we make this strategy a conscious ongoing activity, change will become familiar and we will welcome it, seeing in it not cause

1

for alarm but reason for action. And as we come to understand and use change, we will be better prepared for the future, increasingly able to make tomorrow's world the world we want.

CHAPTER 1

THE NEED
TO MASTER CHANGE

THE GREAT ATLANTIC AND PACIFIC TEA COMPANY—despite its grandiose name—had a modest beginning: a small business buying tea at dockside in New York in the 1870s and selling it by mail at price far below the $1 a pound it fetched at local retailers. So successful was this initial undertaking that by the turn of the century the A&P had two hundred stores around the country, selling not only tea, but also coffee, spices, flavorings, and a full line of basic groceries. For the next sixty years, building a reputation on low price and dependable quality, it was the undisputed national leader in grocery marketing. By 1961 the A&P had over 4,500 stores and more than twice the volume in dollars of Safeway, its nearest competitor; among *all* U.S. firms it ranked fifth in total sales.

But two decades later the Great Atlantic and Pacific Tea Company was a shrinking floundering giant, great in name only. Pared down to just over a thousand stores, it had lost $400 million in the last ten years and its fiscal 1981 sales were 38 percent of those of Safeway, which, along with Kroger, had long since passed it in total volume. Among the twelve major U.S. food chains that year it stood dead last in both sales growth and profitability.

J. C. Penney also had a modest beginning, as the Golden Rule Drygoods Store, established in Kemmerer, Wyoming, in 1902 by James Cash Penney. During the following half century, through changes in name and new store openings, it slowly established itself as a merchandiser of dry goods and staples, mostly to lower-middle-income and low-income families. But twenty years ago, at about the time A&P was peaking, J. C. Penney began a rapid climb; by the early 1980s it was third in total sales of all major chain stores, grocery and retail, with more than twice the volume of A&P.

What was the difference? Why did Penney prosper while A&P floundered? The answer, very simply, is that A&P ignored and resisted change, while Penney acceptd it and made use of it.

World War II made Americans mobile, and the unleasing of pent-up demand and stored-up liquidity that followed the war made them affluent. When they moved to the suburbs and to new homes, and to the West and Southwest, Penney moved with them. A&P stayed behind, in dying urban neighborhoods. When Americans became more choosy about what they bought and more aware of the surroundings in which they bought, Penney expanded its line and modernized its outlets. A&P continued to give pride of place to its own brands, stacked on plain shelves in spartan stores. When automation revolutionized retailing, Penney installed computers while A&P still made do with pens and pencils; and when new attitudes toward work developed, Penney responded by structuring greater group participation while A&P doggedly stayed with "Papa knows best."

J. C. Penney prospered because it made change its partner; the A&P floundered because it fought it, and lost. For A&P the failure to master change has been very costly, but happily the story may not be over. Another chapter is being written, by a new chairman, James Wood, who has acknowledged the changes occurring in the supermarket environment and has started making use of them. By boarding up profitless processing and retailing facilities, creating new store formats, and introducing an imaginative bonus compensation plan for employees, Wood has begun the process of returning the "Great" to the A&P. In mid-1982 the chain finally ended nine consecutive quarters in the red, and for the entire year it showed a modest profit, its first since 1977 and a base on which it is continuing to rebuild.

But it is not only the economic system that provides examples of failure and success in mastering change. The political system, too, offers abundant illustrations, often of even greater consequence since its effect is more encompassing.

Social security was begun in the United States in 1935, in the depths of the economic depression, as a measure of the compassion a great democracy could feel for its people. It was designed as a contributory pay-as-you-go program to provide a minimum income for those who could no longer work. Since its inception, conditions have changed greatly.

As a people, Americans have prospered. Per capita income has increased enormously, in both nominal and real terms; the total assets of the average family are now over $100,000. Life expectancy in 1935 for males (by far the majority of the workforce at that time) was below sixty; now for all Americans it is over seventy-five, and for women (43 percent of today's workforce) it is over seventy-eight, dramatically increasing the number who will receive social security benefits. At the same time, population growth is slowing, dramatically reducing the numbers who will be paying the taxes to provide those benefits. Also, the United States is shifting from a higher-growth industrial-activity-dominated economy to a slower-growth service-activity-dominated one, meaning a decreasing rate of growth of real tax revenue at current rates.

What these changed conditions mean in sum is less need for social security benefits by many Americans, a growing number of beneficiaries who will be collecting longer, and a shrinking base—in numbers and revenue—from which the benefits must be provided. Clearly such changes—visible in some measure for almost thirty years—have required a major restructuring of the program, along with lines of changing eligibility rules to reflect increased life expectancy and reducing benefits to reflect both greater affluence and a more slowly growing revenue base. Yet just the opposite has occurred. For almost fifty years successive Congresses have lengthened eligibility and enlarged benefits, most notably in 1965 by adding medical care, and thus blindly ignored trends indicating that the real outcome of their actions will be either to imperil future beneficiaries or impoverish future contributors.

It would be manifestly unfair today to cut present and near-term beneficiaries, and very foolish economically to increase payroll taxes severely; so the near-term crisis (of the mid-1980s) has been "finessed" with a combination of new rules and emergency measures permitting borrowing by one social security trust fund from another, accelerated tax collections, and delayed benefit increases. Fortunately, revenues are likely to be sufficient during the 1990s to fund the relatively smaller pool of retiring "Depression babies" with the peaking earnings of the postwar "baby-boomers"; but a new and far more serious crisis will arrive ten to fifteen years later when the latter group begins retiring.

What is pertinent here is that these future changes are all clear now, *fully a quarter of a century before their effects will be felt*. So far, all Congress has done is to reduce total future benefits modestly by slowly raising the retirement age to sixty-seven by the year 2027, a first step in the right direction but only a very small one. Will it do more, now when it can, to manage the changes to come?

While politicians collectively provide numerous examples of failure to master change, individually they have had some notable successes. The career of George Wallace provides an unusual example of one. When Wallace was first elected governor of Alabama in 1962, there were in the whole state less than seventy thousand blacks registered to vote, a figure deliberately kept low through the efforts of unyielding segregationists like Wallace himself. Twenty years later, when Wallace was reelected for the fourth time, there were 437,000 registered blacks, and it was their votes that provided the margin of his victory. Wallace understood the change that had occurred in those twenty years. He had done his arithmetic well and he knew that to win he needed the votes of those he had once spurned, and so he sought them. It is ironic that late in his political career Wallace should be returned to the statehouse with the support of those whose way to the schoolhouse he had once physically barred; but it is also indisputable evidence of his ability to successfully master change.

But not everyone masters change as well as George Wallace. In fact, change is often ignored, and even when it is perceived it is frequently resisted. The failure to recognize and use change leads to three common errors.

Error No. 1:
Believing yesterday's solutions will solve today's problems
American automobile makers have for years been noted for their sophisticated technology, high earnings, and well-paid workers. But today they are not yet able to build a small, high-quality, low-cost car. The reason is that they are still following a manufacturing philosophy and a marketing strategy that is almost fifty years old! Their philosophy, first enunciated by Alfred P. Sloan in the 1920s when he was president of General Motors, is based on what Sloan called a "mass-class" market, built on the "mass-market" foundation erected earlier by Henry Ford. Through the use of

used-car trade-ins and installment buying, Sloan reasoned, Americans would be able to "upgrade" their cars regularly. To encourage this, General Motors produced a full line of automobiles, each with a bit more power, comfort, and style (the familiar progression: Chevrolet to Pontiac to Oldsmobile to Buick to Cadillac) and introduced model changes each year in the entire line. Since each higher model could use many components of lower models (for example, a Pontiac could be built on a Chevrolet chassis), the "mass production of automobiles," as Sloan himself put it, "could be reconciled with variety in product." This meant that with only marginal increases in production costs far larger prices could be charged in the marketplace.

This was a brilliant strategy, eventually duplicated by both Ford and Chrysler, each of which developed its own full line of annually changed models. The only problem was that it could not be run in reverse. That is, while it was economically feasible to make a profit by "upsizing" cars, it was virtually impossible to do so by "downsizing" them. Thus, when demand began to build for a small, economical high-quality car—accentuated by the rapid rise of oil prices in 1973–74 and again in 1979–80—Detroit could not meet it, and Americans turned in droves to foreign car makers, especially the Japanese, who had just the products they wanted. By blindly staying with Sloan's philosophy, long after the conditions that made it appropriate had begun to change, U.S. car makers lost—perhaps permanently—a large and growing segment of the American automobile market.

A variant of this error is what has been called the "sailing ship phenomenon." When steamships were first introduced it was apparent that they had the potential to revolutionize the ocean freight business. But because the first models were slow and broke down frequently, conventional shipbuilders responded by building more efficient sailing ships. When the steamship revolution finally occurred, their strategy of sticking with yesterday's solution left them out of it.

RCA Corporation provides a perfect example of the sailing ship phenomenon. Having developed and successfully sold vacuum-tube technology over many years, it responded to the invention of the transistor by trying to develop still more sophisticated vacuum tubes. When solid-state technology finally proved faster, cheaper, and more reliable, RCA found itself way out front in an old technology, but left far behind in the race for position in a new one.

A future example could well occur in the photography industry. In 1982 Eastman Kodak took traditional chemical imaging one step further with the introduction of the Disc camera, a technically sophisticated new format for exposing film for still pictures; but the miniaturized negatives produced by the Disc have proved too grainy when blown up for prints and sales have been extremely disappointing, so poor that *Forbes* labeled the new camera "a flop—a humiliating Edsel of a product." In the meantime Japan's Sony has leapfrogged to an entirely new technology by inventing and producing a filmless camera, the Mavica, based on electronic imaging. Still photographs from Sony's Mavica are as yet inferior to those produced by chemical imaging, but it may well be that while Kodak was laboring to achieve marginal improvements in yesterday's film technology, Sony was gaining a commanding lead in tomorrow's electronic technology.

Something similar happens when a company stays with an old product or technology because it is unaware—or ignores—changes occurring that eventually will reduce demand for what it is offering. In the early 1980s the International Harvester Company (now known as NAVISTAR) tottered on the brink of bankruptcy largely because of continuing losses in its farm equipment division, an activity it finally sold off in November 1984 in order to concentrate on the more profitable manufacture of trucks. International Harvester's losses in the business in which it was founded eighty years before were due in large part to its failure back in the 1950s to foresee the post–World War II trend toward fewer and bigger farms, betting instead on a boom in demand for small tractors. However, Deere and Company, Harvester's main rival, correctly saw what was happening, invested heavily in research and new product development, and in the mid-1950s—with its larger and more powerful tractors—overtook Harvester as the foremost producer of farm equipment. Today, it not only retains that position, but given the weakness of its competitors, it has an excellent opportunity to strengthen it.

Eastern Air Lines dug itself a similar hole when its longtime chief, World War I flying ace Captain Eddie Rickenbacker, refused in 1958 to introduce newly developed passenger jet aircraft because he believed they were underpowered and inferior to propeller planes. Eastern's rival, Delta Air Lines, not only sensed that the public would quickly take to jets, but also understood that the new planes would be more efficient to operate and hence more productive. As a result, Eastern found itself playing catch-up, forced to wait as others who had ordered earlier received delivery of their new jets. Delta, on the other hand, following a policy of regular modernization of its fleet, moved quickly ahead and today still ranks near the top among all airlines in total profits, well ahead of Eastern, which has succumbed to a takeover by Texas Air.

Not only are the products and technology of yesterday out of date for the tasks of today, but so too are many of yesterday's procedures and practices. This is especially true in information-dominated service-sector activities, many of which have spent heavily to create electronic "offices of the future" only to discover they now have less productivity than in the past. The advantages of new information-handling equipment are many, including speed, efficiency, cost reduction, and even improved employee morale and satisfaction. But these will be realized only if it is understood that optimum use of the new equipment usually requires major changes in work organization and work flow. Avoiding errors by mastering change requires more than just replacing yesterday's equipment; it calls for reexamining and restructuring the entire organizational and procedural context in which that equipment is used.

Error No. 2: Assuming present trends will continue
The Global 2000 Report to the President of the United States was three years in the making (two more than planned), cost $1 million to complete, and fills over a thousand pages in its three volumes. It begins with the words "If present trends continue . . ." and it goes on to make forecasts of dire consequences should trends in population growth, resource utilization, and pollution accumulation continue at recently reported rates. There is no point in reading further. Resting on such an assumption, the forecasts of the report are virtually useless. The continuation of present trends—as the following chapters will show—is the *least* likely possibility for the future. If history teaches anything, it is that present trends rarely continue for long in the same direction and at

the same pace. They may go up or they may go down, and they may go faster or they may go slower; but seldom do they go on as before.

No better example of the costly consequences of assuming the continuation of present trends can be found than the actions which followed the quadrupling of oil prices during the Arab oil embargo of 1973–74. This sharp rise led, naturally, to a proliferation of new forecasts of future patterns of demand and supply for energy sources, especially oil. Yet in most of these forecasts little account was taken of the effect on them of the very rapid run-up in prices that had prompted their creation. Some downward adjustments in demand were made, to be sure, but these were only marginal reductions in a pattern that had been showing a steady drop over time in Energy-GNP ratios as industrial countries, without much deliberate effort, simply became more efficient in their use of energy resources. They were not the dramatic drop that a fourfold increase in the price of oil could be expected to bring.

Exxon, for example, in 1977 saw the average annual growth rate in energy demand for the free world dropping a modest .7 percent, from 4.6 percent during 1975–80 to 3.9 percent during 1980–90. The Organization for Economic Cooperation and Development (OECD) predicted a somewhat lower annual increase, slightly over 3.6 percent from 1975 to 1985, for its more efficient industrialized members. And for the United States, the Department of the Interior projected that from 1973 to 1990 energy consumption would increase 2.7 percent annually.

These estimates meant, of course, that total demand for oil would continue to increase, pressing on a finite nonrenewable supply. The CIA projected in 1977 that by 1985 world oil consumption would climb to 75 million barrels per day, with about two-thirds being met by production from the Organization of Petroleum Exporting Countries (OPEC), and that by the early 1980s the USSR would be a net importer of oil. The widely acclaimed MIT Workshop on Alternative Energy Strategies (WAES) Report, "Energy: Global Prospects 1985–2000," concluded that "world oil will run short sooner than most people think. . . . Petroleum demand could exceed supply as early as 1983 if the OPEC countries maintain their present production ceilings because oil in the ground is more valuable to them than extra dollars they cannot use."

Forecasts such as these meant in turn that oil prices could go only one way, and that was up! Believing this trend would continue, apparently indefinitely, the oil industry went into high gear. Exploratory activity was stepped up, rigs were purchased, pipe was ordered, keels for new supertankers were laid, and plans were made to increase refinery capacity. Banks fell over themselves supplying credit to companies that sprang up literally overnight, and venture capitalists and growth stock funds rushed in with bundles of cash. Oil-exporting nations, too, caught the fever and, with expectations of greatly increased revenues, commenced orgies of foreign spending and vast new projects at home.

But present trends never continue. Instead of climbing steadily higher, steep oil prices had two much more logical—if less readily discernible—consequences: They sharply slowed demand because they forced conservation and more efficient use of petroleum products (as well as because of the worldwide recession to which they contributed) and they greatly increased potential supply as previously marginal sources became economically exploitable. As a result, oil demand worldwide *declined* over 15 percent from 1979 through the end of 1984, and by early 1986 OPEC—instead of straining to produce the 50 million barrels per day that had been forecast less than ten years before—was struggling to enforce a production ceiling of 16 million barrels per day (less than a third of world consumption) and watching helplessly while the price of a barrel slipped to below $10 on the spot market, tumbling nearly $20 below successive "official" prices it had set following earlier drops in the spot price.

Within less than a decade after the original embargo, countries, companies, and banks were paying the price of their naive straight-line projections. In all of the OPEC nations dollar surpluses have dwindled far below projected totals, and most now find themselves borrowers instead of lenders. Outside of OPEC, optimistic forecasts also went awry. In Canada, where steady economic growth had been predicted for the 1980s on the assumption that energy prices would increase each year at a rate about 2 percent higher than inflation, the decade opened with a deepening recession which forced major adjustments in economic policy. And Mexico, having incurred large foreign debts to finance an ambitious development plan with the expectation of re-paying with steadily increasing oil revenues, found itself instead facing falling revenues and the need for stringent belt-tightening to avoid becoming the debt-burdened Poland of Latin America.

The oil companies and their financial backers have fared no better. Dome Petroleum, which invested heavily in technology to explore and develop oil resources in the hostile environment north of the Arctic Circle on the forecast that demand and price would rise fast enough to cover the high cost, has had to sell assets and weather several elaborate financial rescue missions just to stay alive. Even giant Exxon, which projected steady rises of oil prices in real terms, was forced to shelve its massive synthetic fuels project and cut back its retail operations. In Oklahoma City, oil-boom fever caused the collapse of the Penn Square Bank and seriously weakened the financial condition of other banks, such as the Continental-Illinois Corporation (saved only by federal takeover) and the Seattle–First National Bank, which had eagerly bought its loans. By mid-1986 total losses from Penn Square's failure were nearing $2 billion and still growing.

Examples abound of companies, communities, and even whole countries seduced by expectations that present trends will continue. To add just a few:

- Airline executives in the 1960s, caught up in the euphoria of growth, affluence, and a rapidly increasing class of jet-hoppers, forecast a traffic rate expanding at a constant 15 percent a year and blithely ordered squadrons of the new jumbo jets to accommodate their expectations. Years—and several bloody fare wars—later they are still trying to fill them.
- When gold soared to over $800 an ounce in the spring of 1980 and a weak dollar accelerated the currency exchange business, Deak & Company responded with a rapid expansion of its chain of Deak-Perera retail outlets. It was at the peak of that expansion when the price of gold slipped back to the $300–$400 range and the dollar strengthened against all foreign currencies, sharply reducing gold buying and the foreign exchange business in the United States. Partly as a result of its miscalculations, Deak & Company was forced to file

for reorganization under the U.S. Bankruptcy Code in December 1984.

• When interest rates, having risen sharply in the mid-1970s, later tumbled a few points, savings and loan associations were quick to offer eager customers familiar fixed-rate mortgages at lower rates. Later, when rates rocketed back up, they were stuck with large portfolios of loans earning less than the cost they then had to pay for money, and only slowly and painfully are they now learning the hard lesson that long-term lending solely on the basis of fixed rates may indeed be a fixture of the past.

It is easy to make the assumption that present trends will continue, especially when the trends are favorable; but such an assumption runs against the deeper wisdom that it is change that should be expected, not continuity. A bet on the continuation of present trends is almost always a losing wager.

Error No. 3: Neglecting the opportunities of future change
For six years, from 1943 to 1949, a patent attorney named Chester Carlson made the rounds of America's major high-technology firms trying to interest them in a new process he had developed for making copies of manuscripts, drawings, and printed materials. He visited IBM, NCR, 3M, DuPont, Eastman Kodak, and many others, but none of them saw any potential market for his new copying machine. Finally a small, struggling Rochester, New York company named Haloid decided to take the risk. Today Haloid is the multibillion-dollar Xerox Corporation.

Chester Carlson and Haloid both understood that two changes occurring in the late 1940s—postwar normalization and expansion of commercial business activity and advances in electrochemistry and photochemistry—constituted important alterations in current conditions; and they saw in these alterations an opportunity that could be exploited by developing a faster, cheaper, more efficient way of making paper copies.

It is this fundamental quality of change—the alteration in some way of present conditions—that creates opportunities. Since future change is the measure of the difference between what exists now and what will exist at some later time, it can be likened to the potential stored in a charged battery. When that potential is released it creates energy and accomplishes work. In the same way change has a potential which can produce gain. This can occur with many kinds of change, including scientific discoveries and the development of new technologies, the growth of incomes and the expansion of markets, the evolution of new demographic patterns, and alterations in attitudes, preferences, and priorities. Those who perceive such changes and act to make use of them will find opportunities for gain; those who do not will be left behind, to struggle later to catch up or to be permanently consigned to second place.

Today the future development of the technology of low-cost microprocessors—introduced a little over a decade ago—provides just such an example, since it heralds a whole generation of new products as well as major modifications for many old ones. The capability of microprocessors to monitor and control ongoing functions will mean new uses in factories, offices, and homes—for purposes that range from product design to medical care. New equipment, such as robotics for automated manufacture, will be built around microprocessors; and old technologies, for transportation and appliances, for example, will incorporate them for greater efficiency. Simultaneously there will be a need for more operators, trainers, and technicians for the increasingly specialized electronics and communications equipment spawned by the development of microprocessors. The U.S. Department of Labor expects employment in computer-type occupations in the United States to rise almost 50 percent by 1990, nearly three times as fast as the expected rate of growth for all occupations in the economy.

Yet even this projection is likely to severely underestimate future growth in the information science industry. The computer revolution has just begun, and is only now starting to ascend its curve of growth. It will be decades before it reaches maturity, both in the United States and abroad. Those intervening decades will see new materials for storing, processing, and transferring bits of information, new applications for microprocessor-based devices which—because of improved technology and automated manufacture—will continue to fall in price, and, above all, new means of enabling people to relate to, and make use of, the full range of information science technology.

In any true revolution, it is institutions that are replaced first; new relationships to those institutions take much longer to develop. In just a few years the computer revolution will have provided us with a completely new suite of electronic equipment for accomplishing many basic tasks now done mechanically; but it will take many more years—and the creation of an information science industry that will dwarf the present one—to develop the full range of man-machine relations to complete the revolution.

Other developments in technology will provide still more opportunities. The materials industry, for example, is developing new fibers, plastics, ceramics, and metal alloys that not only exceed natural materials and current synthetics in such basic qualities as lightness, hardness, strength, and durability, but also possess improved special properties such as insulating against cold or conducting electricity.

- A single hair-thin glass fiber can carry as much information as thousands of copper wires.
- A plastic battery can store two or three times as much energy as a lead-acid one weighing the same amount and can give up its power twenty-five times faster while requiring less time to be charged.
- High-grade ceramics exist which are harder than diamonds, stronger than steel, and more heat-resistant than metal.

Increasing median income—and especially the rise in the numbers of those with substantial discretionary income—has created new opportunities by opening and enlarging markets for leisure services and luxury goods. Howard Head seized just such an opportunity. In the early 1950s he saw rising incomes, increased leisure time, and a growing population of well-educated upwardly mobile young people eager for a vigorous recreational activity that had both status and a built-in social life. The activity was skiing, and Head was ready with a technological innovation that saved hours of learning time and sped the achievement of competence on the slopes: metal skis. In 1950, with six employees, he turned out three hundred pairs; in 1955 output reached eight thousand; and in 1965 it passed 130,000, with profits of almost $400,000 on sales of $8.6 million.

Today, a different set of trends in income and demographic change presents new and different opportunities. Median income is continuing to rise, but more slowly in the

United States and other advanced nations as they become service-activity-dominated economies. At the same time, average interest rates, passing through a series of cyclical changes, have attained a plateau several points above their traditional levels, raising the cost of purchasing big-ticket items, like homes, with long-term loans. Birthrates have slowed, reducing family size and increasing the average age of the population, a figure also being raised by lengthening life expectancy.

To find the opportunities in these present and future changes, businesses and professions must change, too; and not just in how they operate, but in what they offer as well. Thus, in the housing business and in the industries closely connected with it, there has to be greater thought and planning for the kinds of future changes in products and services that will respond to a still-growing demand from clients who are older, have smaller families, are affluent enough to want and afford a variety of amenities, but still have definite limits on the percentage of monthly income that can go for mortgage and other installment payments. That this is indeed possible—in a slower-growth, high-interest economic environment—is illustrated by the case of the Arvida Corporation, a 1984 acquisition of Walt Disney Productions. Its carefully planned residential communities offer a wide mix of sizes and styles of homes, with energy-saving features and ten-year warranties, accompanied by elaborate contemporary recreational facilities. With such offerings Arvida regularly has more than enough customers, many of them willing to wait in line for days to be sure to get a home in a newly opened area.

Changes in attitudes, preferences, and priorities also provide opportunities for gain that should not be neglected. Increases in per capita income and family net worth in post–World War II America have meant greater interest in the protection and preservation of what has been acquired. Risk avoidance has surpassed risk taking, and growing emphasis has been placed on the importance of health, comfort, and safety. This shift in attitudes has led to strong backing for environmental causes and to greater demands for product safety and reliability.

Since these changing attitudes affect preferences and priorities for almost all goods and services, they present numerous opportunities for those who understand them and act on them. In 1980, the New York–based advertising firm of Backer and Spielvogel, capitalizing on growing concern about the nutritional content of foods, suggested that Campbell Soup shift from a campaign that had for years emphasized taste ("Mmm, mmm good!") to one that focused on health benefits to the consumer ("Campbell Soup Is Good Food"). Its efforts with this campaign in an initial trial on the West Coast were so successful that Backer and Spielvogel eventually won the entire $20 million Campbell account.

Similar concerns about sugar and calories have meant a fall and rebound for Tic Tac, the small candy breath mint. Tic Tac had prospered when first introduced ten years ago as a tiny mint packed with a lot of flavor, some sugar, and no claims concerning its caloric content. But during the 1970s public concern about calories grew, and because most people assumed sugar meant calories, Tic Tac's competition (Dynamints, and then Velamints) was able virtually to drive Tic Tac off the market by claiming that its products were sugar-free. Tic Tac finally understood the change in attitudes occurring in the United States and repositioned its product, pointing out that sugar-free is not necessarily calorie-free. It began stressing its low calorie content compared to its competition, giving calorie information on the package; and it successfully regained market share by focusing on young female adults rather than more fickle children.

Dentists, too, stand to both lose and gain from changing trends. Improved hygiene, and especially the widespread use of fluoride in toothpastes and public water systems, has reduced tooth decay among school children by roughly one-third in the last ten years, according to a survey by the National Institute of Dental Research. Thus, dentists specializing in conventional "drill and fill" practices are finding themselves with fewer and fewer patients. However, with greater affluence has come greater interest in maintaining and improving personal appearance and hence an increase in the practice of cosmetic dentistry. More and more adults are wearing braces and improving their smiles by having their crooked teeth fixed. One clinic in San Francisco, enjoying a flourishing business in cosmetic dentistry, has even advertised itself as "a dispensary of ideal images."

All of these examples indicate that those who make the error of neglecting future changes—in technologies, markets, and attitudes—that will affect their businesses and professions, and their personal plans, too, do so at their own peril. On the other hand, those who make a conscious effort to understand the changes that are coming, to anticipate them, and to make use of them, will find new opportunities for gain.

Change must be mastered.

Managers—whether of their own or others' business or professional activities—have many responsibilities: to keep up with the state of the art of their industry or profession, to preserve their plant and resources, to maintain adequate liquidity to overcome any crisis or take advantage of any opportunities, to serve well their customers and clients, and to increase earnings. Their ability to fulfill these responsibilities will be greatly influenced by the way they manage the changes affecting their activities, and as these changes increase, the importance of their management of them will increase too. In fact, their capability in managing change will have to grow faster than the changes themselves, for when there is little change its management largely can be ignored, but when change is pervasive and frequent—as it is today and will be even more in the future—its management will be their most important task.

This task requires a wholly new way of dealing with the future. It often requires going against advice that is rooted in experience. It means questioning the "tried and true" and discarding precepts that have provided guidance in the past. It calls for opposing what passes as the "common wisdom" and overcoming the temptation to fall back on habitual remedies. It requires, in short, a revolution in thinking, away from past continuities and toward future changes.

In mastering change we have to begin by assuming that the factors that affect our activities will not remain the same but will change, and we have to ask how these changes are likely to develop. We have to inquire about their direction, their magnitude, their pace, and their duration. Then we have to resist the impulse to tame or to "ride out" these changes. Instead we must think how to use them, how to exploit them, how to make them our partner. We must think of change not as presenting problems but as offering opportunities.

To do so we need to know what kinds of changes are occurring today and how these changes are likely to evolve during the next generation. The first step is to understand the basic characteristics of contemporary and future change.

CHAPTER 2

A SIMPLE
THEORY OF CHANGE

THE HORSE WAS DOMESTICATED around 2500 B.C.. but the stirrup—very helpful in mounting the horse and absolutely necessary for fighting from it—was not invented until A.D. 500, three thousand years later. Gunpowder, too, was slow in making the transit from discovery to efficient application. Five hundred years passed between its first known use in the tenth century by the Chinese and the earliest rifles in Europe; and so little progress was made in rifle development over the next three hundred years that Benjamin Franklin—certainly no technological slouch—proposed to the Continental Congress during the American Revolution that the new American army be equipped with the longbow.

In numerous cases in the past, inventions and their applications have been ignored by whole populations who had known about them for years. The Arabs, for example, must have been aware of the technology of the printing press from the books of the Jews and other religious communities they ruled, yet they made no use of it until three centuries after Gutenberg's invention. Similarly, as recently as the nineteenth century, seed broadcasting (a method which results in considerable loss to wind and birds) was still widely utilized, even in areas where far more efficient seed drills had been known for over two hundred years.

These examples illustrate the slow pace of change in the past. They show long lead times between discovery and utilization, the ignoring of inventions in other lands, and little effort to make use of them when they were known.

This is no longer true. Lead times have shrunk to years, even months, as witness the rapid application of such recent inventions as transistors, solar batteries, and new plastics and other synthetic materials. Word of new technologies and products travels quickly, in professional meetings and proliferating scientific journals and through the worldwide reach of radio, television, and the press. Utilization is widespread, often for reasons that have more to do with status than any rational calculation of what will assist development and growth—as with the acquisition of steel mills and national airlines in newly developing countries whose infrastructures have neither need nor support for them.

In past times change took place occasionally and irregularly, in a few activities or in a few locations, leaving others untouched for long periods; it affected a few people in various places or large numbers in one place, but never everyone everywhere. In earlier centuries a person could usually count on ending his life in the same environment of institutions, practices, and values in which he began it. There were changes, to be sure, but except for such rare and cataclysmic events as a foreign invasion or the overthrow of a regime, they occurred so slowly or so remotely as to be virtually imperceptible.

This pattern was profoundly altered with the coming of the Industrial Revolution, bringing changes eventually affecting the lives of every person in England and Western Europe. By the second half of the twentieth century, aided by the enormous advances that have occurred in communications and transportation, these changes have spread to every part of the globe. In more and more areas, patterns unchanged for thousands of years are breaking down within a single generation. "The world alters as we walk in it," wrote nuclear physicist Robert Oppenheimer, "so that the years of man's life measure not some small growth or rearrangement or moderation of what he learned in childhood, but a great upheaval."

Today, this great upheaval signals nothing less than the beginning of a new era in the history of the world, for with our recent changes we have reached and begun to transcend the heretofore ultimate limits of nature and the earth itself. In the past, change was isolated, infrequent, and limited; today it is becoming ubiquitous, continuous, and universal. We now have the capability of communicating simultaneously with every person on earth (already in the summer of 1982 nearly half the earth's population could at the same time watch the World Cup Soccer finals); it remains only to complete the networks that can link us all up. We are now able to produce enough food to feed everyone on earth; it is necessary only to spread the technology for growing it and assure the funds for purchasing it. And we are on the verge of efficiently tapping the energy of the sun and the earth's heat, thus assuring that our own energy resources will be illimitable and inexhaustible. And so, too, can we destroy the earth, for we have created weapons which if used in sufficient number might extinguish all life upon this planet.

This is indeed a profound moment in human history. Up to now we have been the earth's wards, kept apart by its distances, subjugated by its elements, nourished by its riches. But now, with the changes we have made, we have domesticated our planet, shrunk its dimensions, and tamed its forces, turning them to our own use. Today the earth is our charge; its very existence is dependent on us.

But change does not stop, nor have we, its authors. Already our changes are carrying us beyond nature and earth; we are bursting our integument. Until this century we used the energy nature gave us, in wind and falling water, and in animals and the long-since-fossilized plants of earlier millennia of photosynthesis. But now we have split nature's largest atoms and fused its smallest, boldly claiming equality with the sun and the stars as producers of energy. We have accelerated our movements on this planet, impatiently seeking to travel faster and faster—with horse, carriage, sailing ship, steam locomotive, motor car, propeller and jet aircraft, and rocket ship—until we have reached the limit compatible with remaining in its gravitational field, twenty-five thousand miles per hour; and we have passed that limit, escaping orbit and slipping from Earth's grasp. Finally, we have begun the conquest of natural selection itself. We have cracked the genetic code that controls all living things, and in a supreme act of blasphemy (to our eternal glory or our eternal folly) we have taken life out of God's hands and put it in our own. Faust's bargain pales by comparison.

This generation is crossing a threshold, from a time of penury to a time of plenty, from an age of limited power to one of power without limits, from an era when change was the exception to one where it will be the rule. We are passing beyond the physical limits of our own planet and the constraints imposed by its resources and its natural order, and we are entering a realm of new discovery and new learning that will change us far beyond our current imagining. The world of tomorrow will resemble the world of today even less than today's world resembles yesterday's.

But while change itself is ever increasing, becoming limitless and infinite, any particular change has its own pattern, with a discernible direction, magnitude, pace, and duration. If we understand the pattern we can anticipate the change, prepare for it, and make use of it. In order to discern the patterns of change we need to know first that there are two basic kinds of change: structural and cyclical.

STRUCTURAL CHANGE

Structural change is a fundamental transformation of some activity or institution from a previous state. Usually the transformation occurs because of alterations which are in some measure quantitative—such as a considerable rise or decline over time in amount, size, or range—and which in turn prompt other alterations. The net result is a change in the essential quality, or structure, of the activity or institution. For example, a new form of society arises during the process of industrialization which is in turn made possible by a great increase in scale of manufacturing. Almost always such structural change is permanent; that is, there is no return to the prior level or state. Finally, just as the change is permanent, so too must be the adjustment to it.

In brief, then, structural change is a considerable quantitive rise or decline which results in a change in essential quality; it is nonreversible; and it requires permanent adjustment.

Quantitive change results in change in essential quality. The speed of communications increased only slightly as messages went from human runners to horseback and carriages. But the telegraph, telephone, and radio caused a dramatic acceleration. And now, today, with physical limits all but reached, we have nearly instantaneous communication. In the future, change will be in the amount and format of transmissions, not in their speed. This is, typically, the pattern of a great deal of structural change: it begins slowly, accelerates rapidly, and then, finally, levels off, usually as it reaches some physical or economic limit. The same pattern is seen in social changes, as for example in the growth of literacy, which typically begins slowly, speeds up, then tapers off at a level below the maximum theoretically possible.

In these and other changes, magnitude, pace, and duration vary greatly, but almost always there is the attainment of a new level resulting in a change in the essential quality of the activity or institution. The shift now underway in the guiding and controlling force of society—from energy to information—provides an especially dramatic and comprehensive example.

It was the use of inanimate forms of energy (at first the burning of coal, later oil, natural gas, and other fuels, to produce heat and make electricity) that greatly increased the power to run machines for the manufacture of goods. This large increase in the quantity of energy available changed manufacturing processes and required the building of large permanent installations—factories and warehouses—near sources of power and main transportation arteries. To these factories came the people needed to run them, leaving their small towns and villages and forming new larger communities adjacent to their places of work. This opened an age of permanent workplaces and mobile workers, a profound change in the essential quality of society.

Today, the increased production and use of another resource, information, is bringing a further major structural change in the essential quality of society. In the rapidly oncoming postindustrial era, an era dominated by service activities, the principal resource will be information. But this resource, unlike the raw materials and fossil fuels needed for manufacturing, can be distributed cheaply and swiftly to literally any point on earth. At the same time many people—achieving a level of prosperity and comfort made possible by the rapid economic growth of the industrial era—have acquired a stake in place and property and are less willing to move on to new locations, even for evident economic gains. Thus a new age is opening, one of transient workplaces and immobile workers, again transforming the structure of society.

A qualitative change of even greater import has arisen from the immense quantitative increase in the destructive power of weapons of war. Until the era of nuclear weapons, war was regarded as a viable means for defending national interests and pursuing political goals. It was, to be sure, usually the means of last resort, and those who pursued it sometimes failed to achieve their goals and instead suffered losses which proved to be irreparable. Nonetheless war was considered, in Clausewitz's famous phrase, "the continuation of political intercourse by other means," and nations who resorted to it did not believe they would be extinguished by it.

However, since the explosion of the first atomic bombs in 1945, the increase in the destructive power of weapons has grown so much that the nature of military doctrine and the course of international relations have undergone a profound qualitative change. Since the use of these weapons can cause damage far greater than any ever inflicted before, a whole new theory of warfare has developed around perceptions of the circumstances and targets of their use. The characteristics of these weapons, their modes of deployment, and declarations concerning their intended use have become themselves "means of political intercourse," and in the international politics of the future the acquisition and manipulation of these "means" will play a role analogous to—and in addition to—the more traditional means of diplomatic exchanges, economic sanctions, and military battles fought with less apocalyptic weapons.

In the future, quantitative changes will bring more changes in essential quality.

- In agriculture the increasing success of food production in controlled growing environments, such as in large greenhouses and in hydroponic media, as well as the development of manufactured food (especially for animal feed), will mean less and less farming on the land. Eventually, the increased yields, reduced waste, and cost efficiency of such techniques will move almost all food production off the land, revolutionizing the structure of agriculture.
- In the production of energy the coming on line by the middle of the next century of a sufficient quantity of eternal sources (some combination of geothermal, solar, and fusion) for the generation of electricity and other power needs will herald the beginning of the end of the era of fossil fuels and will fundamentally change the essential quality of energy as a basic need. Thenceforth the availability of energy will be a matter of adequate distribution and quality, no longer one of nonrenewable supply, possible cutoff, and rising prices.
- In medicine, continued understanding of genetic structure and of the body's creation of antigens and antibodies will radically change the nature of preventive care.

Instead of public health systems based on the notion that everyone is exposed to the same hazards, preventive medicine will recognize that each individual is unique genetically and biochemically. The net effect of this quantitative increase in knowledge will be to change completely the essential quality of health care delivery.

Structural change is irreversible.

Structural change means that what has changed has undergone a permanent transformation and attained a fundamentally new state. There may be stability in the new state for some time, or there may be fluctuations of shorter-term cyclical changes, or there may be a continuing evolution to yet another new state; but there is no going back, no return to the prior state.

This is true because what is learned or discovered today—once it is made known and disseminated—is unlikely to be lost. It is also true because structural changes work together and reinforce each other, creating still further structural changes. Parts of the whole may stagnate or erode, but such developments will not undo the whole, which will continue to evolve.

Thus, new knowledge once acquired cannot be unacquired. It exists, whether we use it or not. It may lie dormant for some time, awaiting the circumstances of its use, as did knowledge of the antibacterial properties of penicillin following its accidental discovery by Sir Alexander Fleming in 1928. But once its use has been demonstrated, it is available forever after. To our eternal benefit we will not unlearn what is known about the human body and the cure of its diseases and the care of its injuries, though our knowledge may pose new awesome and controversial possibilities, as is likely with our further understanding of human genetic structure and its manipulation. It is the same with new inventions and processes. They are part of our scientific heritage, passed along from generation to generation, usually for the betterment of mankind, though in some cases putting it at greater risk. We cannot uninvent the atomic bomb. We are stuck with it for all time.*

---

*The extreme possibility exists that this very knowledge may someday be used to create such destruction that virtually all knowledge will be lost to the few who might manage to survive, including that of the

This irreversibility of structural change is also true for the new processes of production we have developed and the new products we have created. These are improvements on past processes and products. There is no sensible reason—and no likelihood—that we will revert to what is less efficient and more costly. We may collect Model Ts as antiques, but we will commute in new Fords.

We may yearn to experience some of the characteristics of an earlier, simpler time, and we may even occasionally pass a few weeks living a far more primitive life-style than we usually do, in an environment—like a raft ride on a wild river in a wilderness area—that is virtually untouched by human civilization. But we are likely to reach our jumping-off point traveling at high speed on a smooth superhighway, in a modern automobile with tinted windows and comfortable temperatures. The food for our trip will be carefully prepared in a government-inspected factory to provide high nutrition and maximum efficiency in packaging, and in our passage down the river we will have the assurance—in the event of emergency—of instant contact with the outside world by modern radio communication. We will, in the evocative title of Leo Marx's book, have the benefit of *The Machine in the Garden*. Would most of us want it any other way?

The passage to a service-sector-dominated postindustrial era—with the many changes it implies—is also irreversible. We are rapidly leaving the era where energy has been the guiding and controlling force in society and entering one where that role will be played by information, and we shall not return to the former. The implications of this are indeed enormous, for they affect how we will educate ourselves and our children, what industries and jobs will grow and diminish, what life-styles we will seek, and even how long we will live.

In addition, the general path of future population growth is set. Barring possible migration at some future time to other habitats in space, we will not again increase at exponential rates. Population growth will continue in many still-

---

building of atomic weapons. The corollary possibility, suggested by the late Harrison Brown, is that our depletion of readily accessible nonrenewable resources has threatened the prospect of restarting industrialization following a nuclear catastrophe.

developing nations before it finally slows there, too; and in the developed nations, like the United States, now experiencing a permanent slowing of rates of growth, there are liable to be baby booms and succeeding baby "boomlets," prompted by short-term economic and attitudinal changes, but the combination of prosperity-induced preferences for fewer children and improved technology to facilitate family planning will inexorably work their will on the populations of the developed nations today and the still-developing tomorrow. For the world as a whole the population bomb is being defused, permanently.

These are changes that will not be undone. They describe movement from a past to which we will not return. They depict situations that in the future will have a new form. They make clear that the engine of structural change has no reverse gear; it moves only forward.

Permanent adjustment is required.

Not to respond to change is to be out of step, to fall behind, to be at a growing disadvantage, and thus to do less well; and because structural changes are permanent and irreversible our responses to them also must be permanent and irreversible.

The discovery of new knowledge and the creation of new techniques and new equipment make the old obsolete. Those who do not keep up become obsolete themselves. New tools and new materials provide better ways of doing things and making things. Those who do not stay with "the state of the art" will be less efficient and will lose out to the competition.

In the same way, when populations change and when they become involved in new activities (for example, the growth in the number and per capita income of Hispanics in the Southwest of the United States or the huge increase in voter registration of blacks in the South in the last two decades) permanent adjustment must be made by those who want to survive economically and politically.

Changes in the structure of attitudes, priorities, and preferences, such as those that come with increasing prosperity, also require adjustments by those who produce, distribute, and advertise products and services. Those who fail to anticipate and respond to such permanent structural changes will lose customer interest and market share, while those who do adjust will find new opportunities for sales and growth.

Since structural changes are irreversible, and frequently ongoing, we must also not delay in adjusting to them. If we do, not only will we pay the price of falling behind, but we may also increase the cost of catching up. It is important, therefore, to recognize early the structural changes that are underway and to track their progress, for often such changes, beginning slowly, can advance rapidly. Such has been the case, for example, with the increased number of women who have entered the labor market in the United States. This change began toward the end of the postwar baby boom, accelerated rapidly in the sixties and seventies, and is slowing in the eighties as the upward limits of its expansion are reached.

We also must take care to respond strongly enough to structural changes. In responding to change there may be a temptation to hold back and make only a preliminary tentative adjustment. But if changes are permanent and irreversible, corollary responses are required. If at first we respond timidly and tentatively, we are likely to raise the cost of responding more positively later. For instance, those who hestitate to acknowledge the coming of information as the guiding and controlling force in society and who fail to make the appropriate adjustments in hardware and software not only will fall behind but may find themselves unable to continue.

Finally, it is necessary to recognize that structural change often requires the dismantling of old institutions, relationships, and procedures and their replacement with wholly new ones. We cannot expect to move successfully into the future burdened with the baggage of the past.

CYCLICAL CHANGE

Cyclical change is temporary change in a certain measure or condition from a level or state to which it is likely to return later. Over time, cyclical changes follow a discernible pattern in their fluctuations, returning regularly to prior states. They usually do not cause any alterations in the structure of the institutions or activities in which they are occurring, and because their durations are limited, adjustment to them is usually temporary. Cyclical changes are therefore repeating, nonstructural, and limited; and they require only temporary adjustment.

Cyclical changes recur.

Cyclical changes describe measurable movements, usually of up and down, or more and less. They represent the occurrence of a quantitative change, but one that indicates the attainment of only a temporary level in a certain indicator or measure, not a permanent new stage.

Economic growth rates, for example, depict such changes. When the value of a country's output is proportionately larger than the value of the capital and labor creating it, the country usually is enjoying high annual rates of economic growth. However, during a downturn, when productive capacity is idle and a significant number of workers are unemployed, the country's economic growth rate falls. Over time, growth rates will rise and fall, influenced by both internal and external factors, including policies taken by the country's government. It is highly unlikely that they will continuously drop or continuously increase, although over a long period of time their average annual rates may be increasing or decreasing in response to structural changes.

Other economic indicators display similar cyclical changes. Unemployment rates rise and fall, usually tracking economic growth rates and often returning to prior levels. Inflation rates rise and fall, influenced by a variety of factors, including economic growth. Like economic growth rates thay may tend lower or higher over an extended period of time responding to long-term structural changes, as they did when they rose at the end of the sixteenth century because of the influx of large quantities of precious metals from the New World, and as they again have done in the second half of this century, in part because of the worldwide creation of demand in excess of productive capacity.

Short-term cyclical changes may also be driven very explicitly by the feedback of information about the prior state of a particular measure. This is typically the case in changes of supply and demand and the prices associated with such changes. In a commodity like copper, for example, strong demand in the late 1960s and early 1970s raised its price and stimulated efforts to increase the production of copper from raw ore and its recovery from scrap. So successful were these efforts, combined with a worldwide slowing in the rate of demand for copper, that supply greatly exceeded demand and price fell sharply. Even though demand is likely to continue to slow—as new uses require more versatile materials and technological improvements reduce traditional uses of copper—supply eventually will fall back to the level of demand and price will again rise. But supply and demand will never be in perfect equilibrium, and price will continue to fluctuate in a cyclical pattern.

The supply and demand of those in various professions and occupational skills exhibit similar cyclical changes. If at any time there is a glut in the supply of, say, lawyers, computer programmers, or lion tamers, demand will be low, salaries will weaken, and applicants to graduate and training schools will drop. A shortage in supply—or a sudden increase in demand—will produce the opposite effects. It is also true that over time the demand for a particular skill—for example, stonemasonry*—may fall to practically zero; but this is a reflection of structural changes and not cyclical variations in supply and demand.

Cyclical changes also occur in phenomena of organizational and social behavior less susceptible to quantitative measurement. One such phenomenon is the periodic swing that occurs in any large organization between the opposed tendencies of centralization and decentralization. After a long period during which an organization has tended toward the pole of decentralization the disadvantages of that tendency become more and more manifest: weakening of control by the center, difficulty in coordinating operations, delays in transmitting communications, duplication of efforts, and the possible rise of rivals to central management. The remedy will be a swing toward the pole of centralization until its defects begin to arise: excessive growth of staff at the center, bureaucratic inertia delaying the formation of plans and the promulgation of instructions, increased costs in travel and communications to and from the center, less direct contact with operations, and reduced morale at peripheral locations. Eventually the reorganizational momentum will move again, in the opposite direction.

Changes of this kind occur in many large organizations:

---

*When construction recently was resumed on the Cathedral of St. John the Divine in New York City after a forty-one-year lapse, new stonemasons had to be trained by an elderly craftsman—one of the few still living—brought in from England.

- Major corporations regularly reorganize to avoid the pitfalls of excessive movement toward one tendency or the other.
- The administrative history of the United States also reveals such swings in the efforts of successive administrations to alternately strengthen the federal government in Washington or increase the domain of state and local governments.
- In the USSR, similar centralization-decentralization swings have occurred in both the Soviet administrative system and the apparatus of the Communist Party.

Cyclical changes are not structural.

What is common to most cyclical changes is that they rarely involve any changes in structure. While the successive accumulation of knowledge or population or income will often result in an entirely new configuration of an industry or a community, the same is not true of changes that recur within ranges that are physically limited or well established by prior history. Just as fluctuations in the temperature of the air at the Equator or Arctic Circle do not alter the basic climates of those areas, in the same manner fluctuations in the price of a commodity do not alter the basic structure of the industry which produces it or of the economy of the country of its origin.

Cyclical changes, as defined here, are changes that occur in the operation of institutions rather than in their form. The creation in the last decade of new forms of credit instruments issued by financial institutions represents a change in the structure of those institutions, because it enlarges the scope of their operations, but rises and falls of the interest rates of these new credit instruments do not create changes in the structures of the institutions.

In the same way, major changes in laws and procedures often constitute structural changes, while the pattern of actions in response to them is cyclical. Crime rates, for example, fluctuate up and down, while penal institutions and procedures for dealing with criminals evolve in wholly new ways.

Similarly, over a long period of time, attitudes, preferences, and priorities undergo fundamental changes because of higher per capita income, improved standards of living, and increased possession of property; but changes in fads and fashions come and go without fundamentally affecting the development of underlying attitudes. Like other cyclical changes they may leave memories, but they create no noticeable alterations in structure.

Duration is limited.

Since 1790 there have been forty-three recessions in the United States economy, and in turn, forty-three recoveries. These phases of upturns and downturns have varied greatly in length and intensity, but each complete cycle has followed a similar pattern of reduced, then rising, business activity, accompanied by analogous patterns of employment and price and wage activity. Like all cyclical changes these forty-three business cycles have had limited durations, evolving in patterns they have displayed before.

Similar patterns have been followed by other cyclical changes. In goods and services subject to the forces of the marketplace, changes in supply, demand, and price have always been limited in duration. There is no record of a traded commodity the real price of which has continuously risen or continuously fallen; there is no profession or skill the number of whose members has not changed over time in response to demand, and vice versa.

While the durations of cyclical changes are always limited, patterns of their occurrence often do vary; thus while it is possible to say with considerable certainty when the real price of a particular commodity is falling that it will eventually rise, it is very difficult to say exactly when and how much. Here the history of past cycles may give some guidance, but it must be read in conjunction with other changes occurring, both structural and cyclical. Blind faith in past cycles—such as, for example, the current attention being given to fifty-year "Kondratiev waves" in business cycles (to be examined later)—may simplify decision making, but unless the faith can set in motion forces that will make the forecasts of the cycles self-fulfilling (a possibility always to be considered), they will still be uncertain guides to the future.

Finally, it is necessary to note that the same activity may be behaving simultaneously in accordance with several cycles of change, each of varying duration. Interest rates in the United States, for example, respond in short-term cycles to perceptions of future rates of inflation, present and anticipated demands for credit by public and private institutions, and actions of the Federal Reserve Board. But in the last decade and a half they also have been behaving according to a longer cycle in which through each successive shorter cycle their average rate has steadily risen, a movement which appears to track and be influenced by other cycles in the economy. This same pattern of multiple cyclical behavior is also seen in cycles of natural phenomena, such as periods of climatic warming and cooling which annually change in cycles measured in decades, within longer cycles lasting centuries, within evolutions that extend over millennia and include the extremes of ice ages and continental floods.

The most important point that can be made, however, about cyclical changes concerns the kind of response that must be made to them.

Adjustment is temporary.
Cyclical changes are of limited duration and do not involve basic alterations in the structures of what is changing. Adjustment to them is therefore temporary, and not the permanent adjustment made to long-term structural changes.

During a period of recession, for example, a manufacturer faced with slackening demand cuts production, slows the growth of inventory, and perhaps even closes down lines and lays off personnel. But because he knows the recession will be temporary he does not make any of these actions permanent. In fact, during a downturn he may even make additional reductions in other parts of his business in order to spend more on promotion to maintain or to try to increase market share. Still in the recession, he may then make plans for the expansion his actions will bring once the next upturn is underway.

Similarly, it is inappropriate to make permanent or irreversible decisions on the basis of cyclical changes. If, for example, one decides that the practice of medicine has good long-term prospects, one should not be dissuaded from entering medical school because at the moment there is a glut of physicians. Only if structural changes indicate that the profession of medicine is dying out—a highly unlikely possibility—could it be argued that the glut will continue. It, too, will disappear, to be followed eventually by a shortage.

Not only are responses to cyclical changes usually temporary, but they are often repeated and very similar in each succeeding repetition. The actions a manager takes during an economic recession or a shortage or a glut may vary depending on the timing and dimensions of the particular cycle, but over successive recurrences they are likely to be of the same kind concerning fundamentals such as production, prices, and personnel.

Managing cyclical change also means understanding that responses to it are never final; instead they are temporary, and they will have to be made again and again. In planning a reorganization toward centralization or decentralization, for instance, managers must not think they have solved finally whatever problems prompted the new arrangement. Instead they must realize that they have just completed one phase in an ongoing process that at some future time they may be almost completely redoing. In fact, as they put together whatever new evolution they are creating, they would do well to design it with a ˙ew as to how it can be reversed, altered, or undone at some future date. At the time this may not sound like good sense, but it will make for good management.

These, then, are the two basic kinds of change which occur:

- Structural, nonreversible change, which requires permanent adjustment
- Cyclical, repeating change, for which the response is temporary and recurrent

In order to know how to prepare for them, we need to understand the specific changes of each kind likely to occur during the next two decades.

CHAPTER 3
STRUCTURAL CHANGES

THE BLINDING FLASH of light that turned night into day early in the morning of July 16, 1945, on the desert of Alamogordo, New Mexico, announced a major structural change. In a few instants the nature of warfare was profoundly altered, and with it the future course and conduct of relations among nations. The old order was gone, unlikely ever to return.

But such clearly identifiable moments of change are rare in history. Most structural changes are like the erosion that alters the course of a river. They do not occur suddenly, in a few instants, but very slowly; and they can be seen only through many observations made at many different moments over a long period of time. Yet it is just such changes that must be seen and must be understood, for they require major alterations in the way we do business, in the products we make, and in the services we deliver. Structural changes mean the future will be different, and only those who understand how it will be different will know how to prepare for it.

What, then, are the major structural changes of the decades immediately ahead? They concern:

- The resources we use to transform things
- What, when, and where we learn
- How we communicate with each other
- The goods and services we produce and deliver and how they affect the rates at which we grow
- The numbers of us and the numbers of years we live
- How and where we work
- The incomes we receive
- The attitudes we have and the goals we seek

These changes indicate fundamental alterations in the organization and operation of society, changes that are permanent and irreversible, that are creating in our time a world now rapidly evolving from the long era of post–World War II reconstruction. For us to survive in such a world—and better, to succeed—we must respond in ways that are new and different from those of the past.

INFORMATION

When twenty-two-year-old Nan Davis took six slow short steps in Dayton, Ohio on November 11, 1982, her achievement made headlines. What made her brief walk so remarkable was that she was paralyzed from the rib cage down. Nan Davis was able to move her legs—holding on to parallel bars—because of a computer programmed to order bursts of electrical stimulation in the correct sequence to electrodes taped to her skin over major muscle groups in her thighs. Information made her walk possible. Detailed information about the muscles of the body and how they act to make the legs move enabled her doctors to calculate how much stimulation should be applied at exactly which places on her body. With this information, and with information of the responses of her muscles fed back to it, the computer was then able to calculate the amount and timing of successive electrical bursts and deliver them at the correct moments to continue her steps.

Nan Davis's computer-assisted walk is a dramatic illustration of the dimensions of the increasing power of information today and in the future. It shows that we have more information than ever before, that we have enormously increased our ability to classify, store, and retrieve it, and that we can use it for precise and discrete control of an ever-growing number of activities.

Information is the value-adding resource of tomorrow. It is the building block of knowledge, the spawning ground of new products and new services; and increasingly it will be the most important tool in making and delivering those products and services. It is revolutionizing agriculture, remaking the assembly line, and restructuring every service activity from education to retail trade. It will be the major business of the future and the most important part of every other business. No structural change will be as important and none will affect as many others.

Information is the new transforming resource of society. For most of history, human labor was society's principal resource. Assisted by the power of animals, and to some extent that of wind and falling water, it was human labor that transformed things, that when applied to the soil, forests, sea, and other animals created goods of value—food, clothing, and shelter. Later a new transforming resource was developed, a much more powerful one, the resource of energy. Created mainly through the burning of fossil fuels, the energy of steam and then electricity made possible factories and the large-scale production of goods, and it created modern transportation for the rapid and widespread distribution of those goods.

Today information is rapidly replacing energy as society's main transforming resource. Now, and increasingly in the future, information will add value to products and services by increasing the efficiency of the labor and capital used to create them. In extractive activities like mining it will speed the discovery of minerals and reduce the cost of their removal; in industrial activities like manufacturing it will provide new materials, more sophisticated equipment, and improved processes—all leading to better goods made more cheaply; in services like health care it will mean improved diagnosis and better treatment, reducing pain and lengthening life.

But information is more than just a new, more powerful transforming resource. It has qualities that set it completely apart from the transforming resources of natural power and created energy it is replacing. Natural power is limited; and created energy is finite and expendable—once used it is gone. But information is not used up and does not disappear. It is always available, to be called on again and again; and for this reason it continues to accumulate, becoming an ever-increasing resource.

Thus, critical to the success of those in postindustrial societies is their ability to store this ever-increasing transforming resource, to process it, and to retrieve it when it is needed. These tasks are accomplished by the electronic computer, itself a product of increasing information about the properties of materials, and a product whose capabilities continue to expand as that information grows.

It is this combination of a transforming resource that is imperishable and continually accumulating, and the equipment available to store and process it, that makes the expanding role of information the most important structural change of our time. Johann Gutenberg's invention of movable type enormously increased distribution of the printed word, making possible widespread literacy; but the means to electronically store and retrieve information is a far greater structural change, comparable only to the invention of writing itself, for it has created a wholly new form of preserving, manipulating, and displaying information, with capabilities which completely dwarf that of the printed page.

Information is the begetter of other changes.

The expanding role of information and our greatly increased and rapidly growing capability to handle it mean structural changes in virtually every activity in society. In fact, it is no exaggeration to say that every industry and profession should begin immediately to reassess its goals, its organization, and its operations in the light of the major changes that are occurring in our ability to store, process, and use information. Mastering this major structural change means understanding how the role of information is being altered in each of the three dimensions in which we need and use it: What has happened? What is happening now? What is scheduled or likely to happen later?

Researchers of all kinds now have a large body of past information available far more quickly and easily than ever before, and new data banks are being created almost daily. In Israel, for instance, an IBM 3081 computer has just completed "learning" the entire thirty-six-volume Babylonian Talmud, making possible the instant retrieval of references to particular topics that before took scholars years to master—and so creating a structural change in Talmudic scholarship.

Physical scientists can avail themselves of information-handling equipment which can greatly facilitate ongoing experiments. Chemists, for example, can use information about molecular structure stored in a computer to examine the properties of materials in various combinations. Such methods are far superior to the old-fashioned manipulation of primitive models built with sticks and balls, and also save the time and cost of blindly synthesizing compounds in a laboratory.

For every type of scholar and scientist, electronically stored information offers an opportunity to investigate, compare, and experiment in ways that are literally a quantum leap beyond earlier, far more costly, and far more time-consuming methods. It represents no less than a new "method" for the scientific method.

Students in educational institutions are beginning to experience structural changes in their learning activities because of accessibility to computerized information. The computer, in fact, is rapidly attaining the status of required equipment for many college students.

- Dartmouth College, which has been teaching with computers since 1964, assigns an identification number for their use to every student and staff member.
- Drexel, Stevenson, and Clarkson universities require their students to purchase computers.
- Brown University and the Rochester Institute of Technology make them available at substantial discounts through special arrangements with manufacturers.
- Carnegie-Mellon University plans to equip every freshman with a computer by the fall of 1986.

Computers, with their stored programs, communications capability, and access to outside data banks, give college and university students substantial new capabilities. When effectively used they can enrich students' contact time with their professors and accelerate and broaden their learning.

But it is not only students in higher education who can benefit from the structural change in information. So, too, can their younger brothers and sisters, even in the very earliest grades. In the traditional classroom, students are in a group, exposed to the same teaching at the same pace. But no two students are identical. They come to class with different backgrounds, stores of knowledge, and learning skills; and at any particular moment they have very different attitudes toward the tasks presented them. With computer-assisted instruction each student can proceed at his or her own pace, adjusted for all of the above differences; and because computers can be programmed to operate interactively, students can get instant feedback—correcting, reinforcing, and rewarding their learning. The computer will be the major educational tool of postindustrial society, and since information will be the transforming resource of that society, the sooner the better the exposure to the computer, starting with the very first day in school.

Doctors require information about both the past (research and medical histories) and the present (patients' symptoms and vital signs). The structural change occurring in the collection and display of information is vastly increasing capabilities in both categories, especially the latter. Computer-assisted diagnostic equipment such as CAT (computerized axial tomography) scanners produce cross-sectional images of the body that reveal details often impossible or difficult to see in conventional X rays. An even newer computer-assisted technology—which epitomizes the trend toward diagnostic techniques that do not invade the body—is ultrasonics, in which images of the body's organs are generated by bouncing sound waves off them. Many other diagnostic techniques, such as blood testing, now can be done with less expensive equipment using microprocessors. This will mean more such testing in doctors' offices, thus speeding results and improving patient care.

With sufficient information about diseases and symptoms, pure computer diagnosis also becomes possible. Internist I, a program to do just that, has already been developed at the University of Pittsburgh and, in its initial trials, has given creditable results. While it will be a long time—if ever—before a patient will want to trust a computer entirely with the diagnosis of his or her ills, information technology may soon routinely be providing "second opinions."

The reduction in size and cost of microprocessors will also mean a major change in the monitoring of a patient's vital signs. Today, continuous monitoring is usually done in a hospital, most elaborately in an intensive-care unit. But eventually much of it will be done remotely for patients who are ambulatory. The same pacemaker used to steady a heartbeat can be equipped to transmit signs of weakness or dangerous irregularity; and with the advent of personal satellite radio transmission, it will be able to do so from literally any point on earth. Small inexpensive microprocessors are also hastening the advent of implantable drug dispensers that will give medication regularly, in the appropriate doses, and more directly to affected organs. Eventually, the combination of computer-assisted monitoring and drug dispensing to a patient whose biochemical and genetic makeup is precisely determined will mean a genuine revolution in the delivery of health care.

Current information monitoring and appropriate feedback will bring major changes in other areas too.

- In the automobile, onboard computers are already used in many models to monitor and improve fuel efficiency. In the future other functions will be added in a single integrated system that will monitor engine speed and adjust timing and choke control for different temperatures, keep track of tire wear, provide navigation assistance, and even warn of impending collisions.
- In "smart houses" of the future, today's simple systems for heating, cooling, and lighting will become highly sophisticated, making the most efficient use of energy and responding to the presence and programmed requirements of their occupants; electronic recognition devices will replace keys and sense efforts of unauthorized persons to gain entry; remote monitoring will eliminate the need for on-site meter reading and flash warnings of smoke and intruders to fire and police departments.

Information about what is scheduled to happen in the future is especially important to travelers, vacationers, and those simply planning an evening out. Normally one consults schedules, makes telephone calls, requests reservations, and, often, stands in line for tickets and boarding passes. For airline travel—in the years since the industry was deregulated and subsequently buried in its own blizzard of schedule changes and promotional fares—getting on board at an advertised fare often has been as chancy as buying a lottery ticket. Help is on the way, however, as more and more home computer services (like CompuServe, Viewtron, and TravelScan) are being developed to track schedules and fares and make reservations. Eventually, subscribers with an auxiliary printer also should be able to obtain tickets and boarding passes.

An illustration of the improvement possible in transportation through the use of information about scheduled public conveyances was provided by a recent two-year trial in a transit system in suburban Toronto, Canada. Buses in the system were tracked electronically by a central computer linked to a voice synthesizer that could be accessed by telephone. A caller wishing information about arrival times at a particular stop merely dialed a number indicating the route and stop and was immediately given the expected times for the next two buses. So successful was the test that after one year ridership for the tracked routes increased 23 percent. The experiment clearly shows the savings in time, energy, and money available through the efficient management and use of information.

> *Information will revolutionize the production of goods and services.*

All productive activities can be reduced to three kinds: extractive (principally agricultural), industrial (principally manufacturing), and service. Each kind will be fundamentally and irreversibly changed by the increased availability and use of information.

In farming and animal husbandry the most important new information derives from the discovery of the double-helix structure of DNA and the subsequent deciphering of the genetic code. DNA, with its imprinted genetic data, is really the biological analog of the silicon memory chip. It contains information that can be copied and duplicated. Using that information, farmers soon will be able to develop crops with more resistance to disease, insects, salt water, heat, cold, drought, viruses, and other adverse factors. Genetic engineering also promises cows that give more milk, hens that lay more eggs, and sheep that yield more wool.

New information technology will give farmers more complete and precise data about the status of their crops, as well as improved forecasts of future weather, and it can guide them in utilizing their machinery and in determining—and even directing—decisions on planting and the application of inputs such as water, fertilizer, and herbicides. Finally, with more complete information about economic conditions and the status of crops in other areas, farmers can be assisted in deciding when to plant, when to harvest, and when to go to market. It is ironic, yet true, that the first real domestic occupation—tilling the soil—has potentially the most to gain from the increased availability and accessibility of information.

Manufacturers also have much to gain, and much to change, because of the coming of information as society's transforming resource. In drafting rooms engineers now have a sophisticated new tool: computer-assisted design (CAD). Using an electronic stylus or keyboard, or a combination of both, a draftsman can try designs of different sizes and shapes, keep track of what stays the same and what is redesigned, and either preserve the results in the computer's memory or have it printed out as a finished drawing. Linked to other computers, CAD systems can test designs under simulated stress conditions, help schedule production runs, and even order parts. Costing hundreds of thousands of dollars and requiring a long period of training just a few years ago, CAD systems are becoming cheaper and simpler to operate, and at the same time faster and with improved capabilities, increasing the potential number of firms that can make use of them—low-tech as well as high-tech.

On the production floor itself, information is playing a vastly expanded role as more and more procedures become automated. The now familiar term for much of this activity is robotics, from the Slavic word *robot*—work. But the robot of the factory is a far cry from the anthropomorphized versions of fiction and film—most recently the winsome C3PO and R2D2 of the *Star Wars* series. Although robots have been designed to dispense ice cream and mix cocktails, and the Japanese have even built one that makes rice patties for sushi, their principal uses to date have involved tasks that are too dangerous, too tiring, or too boring for human workers; and these they are able to do rapidly, with unvarying accuracy, and with time off only for maintenance.

But this is only the beginning for automation and robotics in manufacturing. We are quickly passing beyond the stage of wanting robots designed principally to mimic as wide a range of human activity as possible. We are now starting to think of them as task-specific and task-sensitive, able to use information about their environment and continually adapt to it, and able to interact with a real world (and the humans in it) which is not totally precise. When Henry Ford perfected the assembly line to turn out a continuous stream of unvarying Model Ts, he created what became known as "economy of scale" production. In the future, using programmable machine tools, it will be possible to produce efficiently in very small batches to suit the diverse tastes of modern consumers, thus creating in effect "economy of scope" production.

In service sector industries the management of information not only can bring larger earnings but in some low or fixed-margin businesses may even mean the difference between profits and losses.

- Grocery stores, using automated checkout equipment, can now keep track of sales and replenish inventory; as they become more sophisticated they will be able to track the demand for different products and package sizes and project the success of different sales promotion efforts.
- Retailers that link sales data to specific purchases—as with sales that are charged—can then target advertising and other followups to those customers. Sears Roebuck, for example, by keeping track of appliance purchases by its customers can regularly remind them to renew maintenance contracts, thereby generating a continuing service income.
- Financial service firms of all kinds will continue to benefit from more rapid collection and distribution of large amounts of information. Banks and brokerage houses, for instance, can give customers faster service on transactions, move money quickly among their accounts, and design financial programs responsive to particular—and changing—needs.

What these and other companies are discovering, and what all producers and professionals will have to discover to survive, is that the fundamental change created by the shift to information as the transforming resource in society means an equally fundamental change in the way they structure and conduct their businesses. The question they must ask themselves in the future is not "How can I fit this information resource into my present operations?" but instead "How do I restructure my operations to take maximum advantage of this basic change that is occurring?"

Information will be the major business of the future. When the first digital computer became available for private use a few years after World War II, forecasters claimed that no more than a dozen would ever be needed. IBM, fully absorbed in the task of responding to a booming demand for new office equipment, decided that the market for computers would not be large enough to warrant their sale.

Today, little more than a third of a century later, the number of digital computers in use—from microprocessors to mainframes—exceeds the number of people on earth. But even such a staggering total soon will be surpassed several times over. The postindustrial era—with information its transforming resource—has only just begun, and the electronic information business, already huge, is still in its infancy.

The major industries of advanced developed nations—automobile, oil, and steel—are still those connected with energy, the transforming resource of the industrial era. But information-related industries are catching up, and the gap is closing rapidly. During the 1970s the value of computer shipments as a percentage of automobile sales doubled, rising from 20 to 40 percent, despite the fact that the price of cars was rising while that of computer power was declining. In the decade of the 1980s sales of computers will exceed in value those of automobiles, symbolizing the shift from energy to information.

Like the automobile, computers spawn a number of related industries. One which is growing even faster than computer sales is the industry which provides the "software," or instructions that run the computers. Because so many different kinds of instructions can be written for most computers, and because their writing is labor-intensive and not susceptible to economies of scale, the rate of growth of the software component of the industry is certain to grow far longer and far greater than that of the hardware component. Today it is already a multibillion-dollar industry, with over three thousand vendors, many of them working out of shops no bigger than a small garage.

Retailers who sell computers and software will grow right along with their producers. At first the business was an adjunct for traditional hobbyists' and electronics stores, but soon specialized stores were springing up, and in 1976 Computerland, Inc., of Hayward, California, started the first nationwide chain. With so many vendors and so many new products coming on the market, the next retailing mode had to be supermarkets and shopping centers, and these have recently become a reality in the Dallas Informart and the planned Boston Computer and Communications Mart, or Boscom, each with a million square feet and showroom space for more than three hundred companies. Not far behind in growth are a number of related businesses. Instruction in the use of computers, already a part of the curriculum of many public and private schools, has moved into the marketplace in almost every major city, with both new and traditional business training centers offering courses in programming, wordprocessing, and graphics creation. And maintenance and repair facilities, the automobile mechanics of the information age, are quickly setting up shop, both as small entrepreneurs and nascent national chains, in what has exploded into a multibillion-dollar business in just a few years.

Two factors ensure that all of these activities represent only the very beginning of the structural change that will make the information-handling industry the major business of the future, first in the United States and other developed countries, then in the rest of the nations of the world as they proceed on their own paths of development. One factor is the unbounded nature of information technology; the other is the virtually limitless demand for it.

The automobile, the energy-era industry that will be displaced as number one by information handling, is bounded by obvious design constraints. Its speed is limited, and so, too, is its size and carrying capacity. Furthermore, successive technological advances have done very little to reduce its real operating cost per passenger mile, and only a combination of legal fiat and market pressure have improved—within a fairly narrow range—its energy efficiency.

None of these constraints applies to the design of information technology. The capacity of the computer, in terms of bits of information its memory can hold, is for all practical purposes unlimited. Robert Jastrow, the scientist who founded NASA's Goddard Institute for Space Studies, has estimated that as early as 1995—perhaps sooner—an electronic computer the size of a human brain will match the brain's storage capacity, approximately ten billion bits of information, a capacity already exceeded in physically larger disk-drive memories. Size, too, has steadily decreased. What filled a large room, weighed thirty tons, and required eighteen-thousand vacuum tubes in the ENIAC computer of the late 1940s is now available in integrated circuits on silicon chips a quarter of an inch square; and as these chips, now commonly with a 64K capacity (containing 64,000-plus transistors) are widely succeeded by ones of the same size with a capacity of 256K (already in use), and then by one-megabit chips (one-million-plus transistors, now operational), several more orders of magnitude of effective size reduction will have been achieved.

Speed of information transfer and access is increasing almost as rapidly. Successive evolutions of large-scale-integration technology have achieved speeds measured in nanoseconds, or billionths of a second, like the speed at which electricity moves. But now a new medium with a faster speed, light, promises computers in the relatively near future that can reduce switching time to picoseconds, or thousandths of a billionth of a second, thus resulting in a capability of a trillion operations per second. Beyond this technology lies the possibility of computers based on molecular components ("biochips"), which could be grown rather than manufactured and would be much smaller than the tiniest circuits that can be etched on a silicon chip. Along with these rapid increases in capabilities come reductions in cost and energy requirements per information bit of equivalent orders of magnitude.

However, even more important with regard to information technology is the fact that the whole is far greater than the sum of its parts; that is, these rapidly increasing capabilities taken together have resulted in machines with powers of a far higher order than those with lower capability levels. Machines with these powers are usually referred to as "supercomputers," capable of processing so much information so rapidly that with appropriate programming they can mimic many activities of the human brain, such as comprehending speech, making logical inferences, answering questions, and responding in spoken language. Supercomputers with these capabilities exhibit what is called "artificial intelligence," and the race to produce such machines with a thousand times the power of today's—and thus with more humanlike reasoning qualities—is known as "fifth-generation" computer development (the first generation was the vacuum tube, the second the transistor, the third the integrated circuit, and the fourth the very large-scale integrated circuit, or VLSI).

In 1981, a fast lead in this race was taken by the Japanese when they announced a ten-year $500 million fifth-generation computer project to create a new class of superintelligent computers. Shortly thereafter, the newly formed Microelectronic and Computer Technology Corporation, a nonprofit consortium of twelve major U.S. electronic industry corporations until recently headed by former Deputy Director of Central Intelligence Admiral B.R. Inman (USN, Ret.), announced its own ten-year program aimed at new developments in computer architecture, software, and artificial intelligence.

Which side will win the race is not known, but the overall outcome is clear. It will enlarge still further the capabilities of information technology, blurring even more the distinction between machines and human minds. Whether a machine can ever be designed to mimic *every* function of the human brain, and thus in effect become human, is still very much a matter of speculation, resting on such complex neurological and philosophical questions as: How do we recognize things, often with only the barest suggestions of what they are? What makes us forget, then suddenly—perhaps years later—remember what we had forgotten? And by what means do we know that we know? It is clear, however, that like automobiles, the human brain has its own design limitations, but the limits to the development of machine intelligence are not known, and development is likely to continue far further before we do know them, if ever. We must begin, therefore, to adjust to a world in which we will be regularly creating not only machines that can think, but also machines whose thinking capabilities in many respects will grow greater and greater than our own. In short, we must begin to rethink what it means to be human.

The other factor ensuring that information technology will be the dominant industry of the future is the demand for it. That demand is signaled by all the activities described earlier that are experiencing major changes because of the greatly enlarged availability and accessibility of information. In each of these cases information is a vital input, and performance depends more and more on the amount, speed, and quality that is available.

In other areas, growth of demand is also likely to continue, though more erratically. One is the typical middle-sized business office, be it industrial or service-based, profit or nonprofit. The first wave of enthusiasm for the "office of the future" has swept in, and with it has come principally new word-processing equipment (a short but very efficient step beyond sophisticated electric typewriters) and in some cases "personal" computers with programs for tasks such as payroll, accounts payable and receivable, and inventory control.

Now, in the long trough behind the first wave, there is doubt and hesitation. In such offices electronic mail is mostly a glimmer on the horizon, strategic planning is still done only with paper, and remote data base retrieval is largely unknown. But a combination of newer equipment—with more capabilities and at lower prices—and growing awareness of the tasks that can be accomplished will bring a restructuring of office organization and a retraining of personnel to take advantage of the new information technology.

- The first step, now slowly being taken, will be a "ganging" or "networking" in offices with several terminals and other associated peripheral equipment to facilitate tasking and communications, and to better integrate work.
- Second, the availability of more sophisticated programs will encourage simulating alternative solutions to problems and developing financial, operational, and other kinds of planning.
- Finally, the development and growth of compatible interactive capabilities—via landline and satellite transmission—will provide more access to data bases in large mainframe computers elsewhere, and wider use of these capabilities finally will make widespread use of electronic mail a reality.

Today, for most small and middle-sized businesses, the "office of the future" is still very much in the future, but the future *is* coming.

Slower, and even more erratic, will be the growth of demand for information technology in the home. In the mid-1980s, the number of computers in home use has been increasing rapidly. *Fortune* magazine estimated seventeen million microprocessors in U.S. homes in early 1985, up from ten million in 1984 and five million the year before. But most of these computers have limited capacities, usually to provide some type of purely in-house information service, the most common being entertainment through the playing of videogames. Slowly other in-house services will be added, such as record-keeping, security monitoring, and environmental controls; and some systems—depending on needs and interests—will be used for more specialized functions like homework problems, word processing, and financial planning. But the real boom in home information systems will come with the development and availability of accessible services outside the home.

Some growth will occur because of the increase in "teletext" services. Teletext is basically an inexpensive one-way system that sends digitized information over regular broadcast frequencies to a computer-controlled storage unit connected to a TV set; the viewer, using an included guide or index, can call up particular pages or graphics for examination. Much more important, however, will be the development of "videotex" systems. These are far more sophisticated two-way—hence fully interactive—systems, using a computer with a display screen or a combination of a computer and a TV screen that allows the viewer to directly access a main information bank; they are more expensive, usually requiring—like the telephone—monthly hookup charges plus the cost of time directly on-line with the system.

It is these systems, but especially videotex, that will cause information technology to take off in the home. With videotex it will be possible to develop the much-heralded services that computer enthusiasts have long been touting: home banking, reservations, shopping and bill-paying, data base accessibility (for selected news and customized information packages), and eventually more esoteric services such as some forms of employment at home, electronic mail, and interactive game playing.

In France and England, regular videotex services have been created on a limited basis, and in the United States, limited systems with differing capabilities have been established both nationally and locally. What is required to make them widespread is the overcoming of both public unfamiliarity and uncertainty with a new technology and a "Catch-22" situation that makes it difficult to begin a new service because that service is not yet visible and operating and consequently there is no demand for it.

A number of factors eventually will overcome this dilemma and make home information equipment as commonplace and indispensable as the telephone. Among them are lower cost of equipment and services, the establishment of widely accepted standards, and greater ease of operation ("user-friendly" in the current parlance of the technology).

But even more important will be increasing public familiarity with information technology as it pervades all levels of our educational systems.

EDUCATION

Historians are likely to record for the early 1980s a major turning point that has gone largely unnoticed. In these years, for the first time ever, school enrollment for the world's population aged six to twenty-three climbed past the 50 percent mark. The attainment of education is a structural change of major importance, both for those who achieve it and for the societies in which they live. It means, first, knowledge and skills for a variety of occupations, and these not only improve the individual's income, purchasing power, and standard of living, they also add to the wealth of society. Education contributes even more. It increases awareness and facilitates participation; it provides the opportunity to end apathy and submissiveness; it means seeing the world as a place of achievement, not just of acceptance. In a very real sense, in this decade, for the first time in history, more than half the world's young people have the means to step from darkness into light.

The structural change in education occurring today and certain to grow still further in the decades ahead has several aspects. Collectively these are changing the way people think and act, and they will change even more what people will need and want in the future.

- For those in the developing nations who are being educated for the first time, there is the acquisition of reading and writing, the skills of traditional literacy.
- For those already able to read and write, there is the acquisition of a new kind of literacy—of electronically formatted information.
- For both of the above, there is need for change in the content of education—away from emphasis on preserving the past and toward preparing for the future.
- For all being educated there is change in the times and places of education—no longer solely during the earlier years of life in formal classroom settings, but in a variety of settings and throughout life.

All of these aspects of structural change in education amount to a recognition of its central role in conveying the information and knowledge that will constitute the transforming resource of the future. No other activity will be as important in preparing us to deal with changes to come.

Traditional literacy soon will be nearly universal.
For centuries, knowing how to read and write was the special skill of a privileged few. Gutenberg's invention of the printing press did greatly expand their number, but still they remained a distinct minority. In Western Europe, that minority was enlarged first by the Protestant Reformation and its emphasis on the reading of the Bible, then given a further stimulus by the efforts of the social reform organizations that sprang up in the wake of the Industrial Revolution. By the beginning of the twentieth century, literacy was considered virtually achieved (90 percent or more of the adult population) in most of the nations of Western and Northern Europe, in the United States, and the countries of the British Commonwealth. The Germans even stopped keeping statistics in 1913 when the percentage of illiteracy among army recruits was found to be only .5. In Soviet Russia in 1919 Lenin made the eradication of illiteracy a major goal, and forty years later it was largely achieved. In China his ideological followers have embarked on a similar campaign and are evidently meeting with equal success.

For the world as a whole there are few reliable statistics on literacy before recent times, and even current data have to be understood in the light of widely varying definitions as to what constitutes literacy. Nevertheless, it is clear that since the end of World War II, by whatever definition is used, there has been a substantial reduction in illiteracy, notably in the newly independent nations of the developing world. The United Nations Educational, Scientific, and Cultural Organization (UNESCO) has estimated that at the middle of the twentieth century 44 percent of the world's adult population fifteen years and older was illiterate. The highest percentages were found in Asia and Africa, which at that time accounted for 90 percent of the world's adult illiterates. Through a combination of economic development, expanding communications media, and public policy programs these percentages have been sharply reduced. UNESCO estimates that by 1970 the percentage of illiteracy worldwide had fallen to 32.5 percent, and it projects that by 1990 it will stand at just over 25 percent, with no continent over 50 percent. Thus, in less than half a century, an important, irreversible, structural transformation will have occurred. More than half of those in the developing world will have achieved the essential condition for a more abundant, more satisfying life. With education they will have the means to become better producers, and as better producers they will acquire the wherewithal to be more regular consumers— structural changes important both to themselves and to those who produce goods and provide services for them.

The new literacy will be as important as traditional literacy.
Beyond traditional literacy lies the "new literacy," the literacy of electronically formatted information, a wholly new way of storing, processing, retrieving, and displaying data. Acquiring this new literacy will be as important to success in the postindustrial world as traditional literacy has been in the industrial.

Traditional literacy deals with the expression and comprehension of information presented word by word, line by line, page by page. It must be accessed in a predetermined order, at a speed ultimately limited by the pace at which pages can be turned. An index to information arranged in this manner is usually entered alphabetically, involving a scan of some number of other words before finding the one desired. This is then followed by turning back to another page, or to another journal or book, elsewhere in the room or in the library or in another library or even in another city or country. The retrieval of traditionally formatted information often can be a long, slow, tedious process.

Electronically formatted information is stored very differently, as a series of charged particles or chemical transformations ("bits") on a silicon chip or a disk or a tape or some other medium. It is retrievable only by means of an electronic intermediary—a computer—whose inner instructions can translate the stored unintelligible "bits" into intelligible displayed, printed, or even spoken words. Access to electronically stored information—potentially located in any part of the world and in virtually unlimited quantities—is by appropriate commands and keywords, and its retrieval is practically instantaneous. The new literacy involves, at a minimum, understanding the following:

- How information is stored in this new format
- What kinds of ways it can be processed
- How it can be transferred among components in a system, and to other systems
- How it can be retrieved and presented in usable fashion

Only when equipped with the skills of the new literacy can one make appropriate use of the large and varied quantities of information that are becoming the transforming resource of contemporary society.

Teaching the new literacy must start at the very beginning of a child's education. It cannot be an afterthought, another "elective" tacked on toward the end of one's formal education; instead it must begin, hand-in-hand with traditional literacy, with the beginning of formal education.

Today this is being understood in a few pioneer private schools. The Lamplighter School in Dallas, Texas, in a program conceived by the Texas Instruments Company and the artificial intelligence laboratory of the Massachusetts Institute of Technology, is introducing students as young as three years old to the use of the computer. In Provo, Utah, the 120 students of the Waterford School from kindergarten through fifth grade spend three twenty-to-thirty-minute sessions per day on computers that both aid in teaching and permit communications with computers in several other countries around the world. Even in public schools, where bureaucratic inertia often slows innovations and funding decisions have to cross many desks, the imperative of the new literacy is making itself felt. According to the National Center for Education Statistics, a third of all U.S. public elementary and high schools have one or more microcomputers or terminals available to their students. But often it is just *one* piece of equipment, and most of the users are still high school students.

To manage this structural change effectively, the pace of introduction must quicken and accessibility must move to the lowest grades. Falling prices of equipment will help, and so, too, will the enthusiasm of those teaching and learning with computers. Even more important will be the reaction when word filters back from those who have graduated that increasingly the most rewarding and satisfying jobs are going to those who are familiar with current technologies of information handling and management.

White-collar and blue-collar have been the traditional groupings of labor during the industrial era. Admission to the white-collar group has usually required the credentials of additional years of education, and one of its rewards has been higher pay. But with the waning of the industrial era the division has become less significant and the pay differential has narrowed. Thus the premium gained by additional years in school is much smaller, and the perceived lesser value of education is surely one of the reasons for lower teacher salaries and declining performance in many contemporary American schools.

The postindustrial era will bring a new structural change in our workforce, a new division of labor, between the "information-rich" (those creating and controlling information) and the "information-poor" (those controlled by information). Since it is the information-rich who will hold the better jobs and receive the higher salaries, there is a new opportunity for U.S. schools—and for schools in other nations in the same situation—to provide the instruction in the new literacy that will prepare students for the better jobs in society. Doing so is their best hope to regain the value and the esteem they have lost; if they do not, others will step in—private institutes and training facilities, and corporations themselves—and the status of traditional teachers will fall still lower.

To prepare students for the future,
the content of education must change.

Increasing change means increasing obsolescence, and this is just as true in education as it is in technology. Most people receive their formal classroom education in their early years, as children and adolescents, from teachers who themselves were educated perhaps ten, fifteen, twenty, or more years before. A large part of what these teachers impart is what they learned then, from teachers who themselves were taught still earlier. There is, therefore, in our schools a tendency to carry from the past what was learned in the past, to bring along what served past generations. Much of this is undoubtedly of value, particularly in conveying to students the vital awareness that they are part of an extended historical human family to whom they are indebted for much of what they are and have today. Yet the heritage of the past is not sufficient preparation for the years of life which lie in the future, and as that future brings wider and faster change it is less and less adequate.

In our schools and educational administrations there is a need to make a conscious and deliberate effort to ask what students of today should be taught to be prepared for life ten, twenty, and more years in the future. Such an effort is certainly not easy, but just making it will give teaching a new perspective, and out of that perspective will come curriculum content designed more to prepare for the future than to perpetuate the past.

The first insight to be gleaned from such an effort is that since information is the transforming resource of the postindustrial future, the various fields of knowledge in which information is organized will be the most important assets of that future. More than ever before, knowledge will be the key to the comforts traditionally associated with enjoying a good life.

The structural changes discussed in this chapter suggest several fields of knowledge that will be important in the remaining years of this century and well into the next. Clearly science and mathematics head the list. Not only are these the core subjects for the rapidly growing information technologies, but they are also prerequisites for a large number of specialty and subspecialty fields, some of which are already well developed, some of which are still in their infancy, and all of which are likely to expand widely and steadily. Among these are communications, materials sciences, robotics, alternative energy sources, environmental protection, and the various engineering and medical specializations sheltered under the large umbrella field of bioscience.

For these fields there will be a steadily increasing need for scientists and engineers for research and technology that in some areas has only just begun. There also will be a need for more vocational training for the operation, maintenance, and repair of the equipment used in these fields. But by far the largest need—in terms of the numbers to be served— will be for the education of all the nonspecialists who in their own careers, and in their daily lives as well, will need knowledge of the concepts, capabilities, and operations of the new products of science and technology. A quarter of a century ago the flight of Sputnik, a grapefruit-sized satellite flung into orbit by the Soviet Union, spurred the United States to create new programs to expand the study of science and math in the classroom. In the wake of subsequent American successes in space and the antiscientific attitudes that were part of the legacy of the turbulent sixties, these programs have languished in the United States. Today they must be reinvigorated, not for a one-time effort to catch a rival, but permanently, for the changes they must address are permanent and increasing.

Also increasing are contacts among peoples and among nations, and with these growing contacts have come new cooperative ventures and new competitive challenges. Both require attention to another field of knowledge, one that has never had a strong priority in the United States, but that must have one now. This is the study of other nations, their accomplishments, their people, and their languages. Protected by two oceans, richly endowed, and self-sufficient in so many areas of industry, the United States has paid relatively little attention to what the rest of the world is achieving. We Americans have taken sides in other nations' quarrels, traded some products and services with them, and often given generously to assist them in emergencies and catastrophes; but for the most part we have remained blissfully ignorant of their methods and their operations, only to find ourselves shocked and surprised when their superior performance has suddenly punctured our myopic self-assurance. How much better off, for example, might many of our industries be today if twenty years ago we had given Japan the attention it is receiving now?

Structural economic, political, and social changes—already underway and to evolve still further—require that we give a higher priority to the study of other nations, that we add an international dimension to education throughout our society. Fortunately, in higher education we already have superbly qualified resources for doing so, and several of these—Johns Hopkins University and the University of Pennsylvania's Wharton School in a joint project, and Columbia University's School of Business—have recently announced new programs and emphases in international subjects. But the effort has to go deeper, to elementary schools, to scientific laboratories, and to more businesses. The future indicates a thickening network of international communications, trade, and mutual resource dependencies. With it must grow, too, our knowledge of those with whom we share this shrinking planet.

Finally, equally important to the future, and especially deserving of our attention because of the threat that it will be given short shrift in the emphasis on science and technology, is the area of the humanities. Our greatest need in dealing with change will be the need to innovate, to creatively make use of what is new and different. In the humanities, above all, is found the creativity of mankind—sometimes in a carefully ordered way, as in a sonnet or a fugue, at other times in an almost uncontrolled surge of emotion, like an expressionist painting or a frenzied religious dance; but always with a message, or in a form, that arrests our attention and places in our minds something that was not there before. It is this quality of creativity that we will especially need in order to master future change.

The humanities do even more for us. At a time of widening and accelerating change they remind us of what is constant—our human nature and the natural world about us. Science and mathematics school us in the calculation and analysis of quantitative data; but the application of the technology they make possible raises qualitative questions and requires judgments about values. It is these matters that are central to the humanities. To approach future change equipped only with quantitative skills would be to severely limit the hope aborning in the technology we have created.

When and where we are being educated is changing.
Educating the young in classrooms is rapidly being supplemented by a new practice: educating people of all ages in many different environs. For centuries we have considered education to be an activity that takes place mainly in the early years of life—during childhood and adolescence, and in the structured setting of schools arranged in three levels commonly called "elementary," "secondary," and "higher," with appropriate recognition (certificates, diplomas, degrees) for the completion of each. This educational activity usually has been continuous, the main occupation of those participating in it, and—once completed—not resumed. We usually go on to other things, to jobs and the "real world." Today this long-standing pattern is changing, and in the future it will change even more.

Many of those who go on to higher education now pause for a year or more to work, enter military service, or engage in other acitivities. Others go to college part-time, extending their education for a bachelor's degree beyond the traditional four years. An increasingly popular alternative to the usual four-year college program, particularly for those who in the past in the United States would not normally have attended college, has been the two-year community college leading to an associate's degree. From 1960 to 1980, enrollment in U.S. community colleges increased tenfold, from 400,000 to four million; in the last several years, graduates from these colleges have been growing at an annual rate of 40 percent, compared to only about 2 percent for those from four-year schools.

The pattern of elementary and secondary school—from kindergarten through twelfth grade, ages five to seventeen—has remained largely intact. But strong suggestions for change are being heard, such as those of New York State Education Commissioner Gordon M. Ambach to start children in school at age four and have them graduate after completing the eleventh grade. While the reasons for his plan are partly economic and resource-oriented (eliminating a year of high school and compensating for a future teacher shortage), they also seek to encourage learning at an earlier age and take advantage of the more rapid maturing of today's students. Eventually, schools may be restructured even more dramatically—reflecting the reality that children develop at different rates and in different ways—by making chronological age less important in assignment to particular grades and even by introducing variations to the traditional formula that one grade equals one year.

Closer at hand is the demise of the notion that formal education ends with adolescence. Retraining and continuing-education requirements—usually state-mandated—have existed for a number of years for many professionals, including optometrists, pharmacists, and certified public accountants. Now, however, and increasingly in the future, similar education programs—*not* legally required—are being made available in other fields.

- The Graduate School of Business Administration of the University of Colorado at Denver has developed a part-time two-year "executive M.B.A." for people who want to update their degrees.
- The Columbia University School of Business and the University of Pennsylvania's Wharton School are offer-

ing "post-M.B.A. updates" of varying lengths in specialized subjects such as productivity, marketing, and financial management.

As more structural change takes place in more fields the demand for updating and retraining will grow, occasioning structural changes in the schools themselves. Already faced with declining enrollments from their traditional younger population, schools of higher education will welcome the opportunity to fill their classrooms and occupy their faculties with educational programs for adults. As changes—in occupations and demographics—continue, it is likely that in many fields and in many schools the number of students seeking retraining eventually will exceed those just beginning their studies. At Harvard University, the continuing-education program—steadily growing—now enrolls ten thousand students, two-thirds the number in its traditional degree programs.

A similar increase in continuing education will develop in nonprofessional fields, stimulated by the obsolescence and elimination of many jobs as well as the creation of others in new industries. Automation in factories, for example, a major structural change that will affect still more industries, will eliminate many traditional manufacturing jobs. Those displaced will need retraining or the further development of skills which might have played only a minor role in their previous jobs. In Wyandotte, Michigan, where the recession of the early 1980s and automation have dealt a double blow to workers in the auto industry, a consortium of sixteen towns called the Downriver Community Conference has been created to retrain recently unemployed workers for jobs in industries likely to have a continuing future requirement for skilled labor. Many more such programs will be needed, demanding the cooperation of business, labor, schools, and the government, before the transition to the postindustrial era is completed in the United States and other advanced developed nations.

Education beyond the adolescent years also will be in greater demand as more and more people seek retraining for midlife career changes. Twenty percent of American workers now change jobs every year, a proportion that has risen steadily since the early 1970s. These changes occur for a number of reasons: technology-induced obsolescence of some jobs, unemployment or reduced opportunities in certain fields or industries, early retirement from public service careers or from companies promoting such plans, women returning to the labor force after a lengthy period at home, and—in many cases in what is a more affluent and mobile society—simply the desire to try something new. In the future, career changes for all of these reasons will increase, and so, too, will the demand for education to prepare for them.

A final category that will contribute to the restructuring of educational programs supplementing those designed primarily for the early years of life will be the need to accommodate people who in their later years again will be seeking schooling. In a population that is living longer, with more available time and more discretionary income, and is also better educated than previous generations, many will turn to education as a way of filling post-retirement years. For these students the goals will not be retraining or preparation for new careers, but instead mainly enlightenment and entertainment at a time in life when education can be pursued simply for the satisfaction it brings. Elderhostel, for example, conceived in 1975 to offer citizens over sixty some of the intellectual and physical stimulation of university campus life, has grown at the rate of 50 percent a year. It now numbers over 100,000 participants at locations all over the world and consistently has more applicants than it can accommodate.

The structural change underway in the timing of education has been matched by a structural change in the locations where it is occurring. Businesses have fast become major competitors of colleges and universities, offering more and more courses usually found in the catalogs of traditional degree-granting institutions. Their motives vary. Many feel that colleges have not done an adequate job teaching students basic skills, and they have sought to fill the gap with remedial instruction, especially in mathematics and communications skills. Others have had special needs to meet and have not been able to find adequate courses in the curricula of traditional institutions. So extensive have the programs of some businesses become that they have earned the right to grant degrees, and in a few cases have even gained accreditation for their programs.

- Wang Laboratories in Massachusetts has created the Wang Institute, which offers a master's degree in software engineering, mainly because so few similar programs can be found elsewhere.
- The Arthur D. Little Company, also in Massachusetts, offers advanced degree programs and has been fully accredited by the New England Association of Colleges and Secondary Schools.

Altogether U.S. business and industry spend over 30 billion a year in education and training, nearly as much as is spent by the nation's publicly financed colleges and universities; the biggest business educator, the IBM Corporation, boasts that it runs the largest educational system in the country, bigger than even the biggest big-city public school system.

Vocational training also is no longer provided mainly in community trade and high schools. Training has become a growth industry, and large private companies, like the National Education Corporation with annual revenues of over $100 million a year, are offering a variety of courses in highly marketable skill areas and enjoying better than 90 percent placement rates for their graduates. Companies are also acquiring training facilities, or entering cooperative arrangements with them, to train their own employees; and even associations are sponsoring courses.

- Hilton Hotels has eighteen full-time trainers, designing programs for everyone from hotel managers to dishwashers.
- W. R. Grace, a highly diversified company, has turned to Harbridge House, a management training organization, to train its own people.
- The National Automobile Dealer Association has inaugurated a two-year degree program for aspiring auto mechanics.

Many colleges and universities, sensing a growing threat to their traditional market at a time when the number of eighteen-year-olds is falling, have responded with innovative programs of their own. Some have even sought collaboration with major firms. In New York City, Pace University and the New York Telephone Company have jointly developed an M.B.A. program, and in Philadelphia, the University of Pennsylvania and INA Corporation have launched a project to enable the company's employees to take courses toward a liberal arts degree without leaving corporate headquarters. Others have turned to imaginative locations to offer their educational wares. The University of Pittsburgh has made it possible for students to do some of their course work at Kaufmann's, a stylish downtown department store—an arrangement that obviously offers the possibility of increasing the store's sales; and on Long Island in New York, Adelphi University for a number of years has taught degree-credit courses to commuters in specially equipped cars of the Long Island Railroad, a location which offers the bonus of extended hours of instruction when the trains run late, which they often do.

These aspects of structural change in education have several important implications. They mean, first, that more of the world's people—eventually virtually all of them—are learning to read and write, enabling them to become more fully participating members of today's society. They also indicate the need for more people to acquire quickly the skills of the new literacy—of electronically formatted information —to enable them to become fully participating members of tomorrow's society. And they show the necessary reorientation of the content of education, from the past to the future, and its accelerating evolution from an activity that mainly involves young people in schoolrooms to one that occupies people of all ages in all kinds of places. Much of this change derives in turn from structural change in another important area—communications.

COMMUNICATIONS

In the financial district of New York City, for every one person calling another person there are five computers calling five other computers. In fact, so explosive has been the growth in advanced communications devices using telephone numbers as electronic addresses that in expectation of the supply of available numbers running out, a new area code was created for three of New York City's five boroughs starting January 1, 1985. In addition, in order to maintain its position as a major world center of financial services, New York City has approved and promoted the construction of a "Teleport" on the borough of Staten Island. A joint venture of the Port Authority of New York and New Jersey, Merrill Lynch Pierce Fenner & Smith, Inc., and the Western Union Telegraph Company, the Teleport is a 220-acre office park with space for communications clients plus seventeen earth-station antennas that can receive and transmit to domestic and international satellites, all linked to Manhattan's financial district with an underground network of fiber optic cables. When finally completed the system will provide customers with a variety of forms of communications, including voice conversations, computer data, facsimile transmissions, and video conferencing.

New York City is not alone. Financial and commercial centers all over the globe are experiencing a sustained surge in electronic message traffic that is flooding present facilities and requiring the construction of new ones. All of these activities are part of a major structural change in communications, one paralleling the growing role of information in modern postindustrial societies.

When human labor was the principal transforming resource in society, the media of communications were also human, in the person of singers, storytellers, and scribes. Following the invention of movable type, and especially the development of sources of energy to power large printing presses, the major media of communications became mechanical, in the form of books, journals, and newspapers. Today, as information is rapidly replacing energy as the principal transforming resource of society, electronic media—wired and nonwired, including telephone, radio, television, and computer networks—have become the major means of communications. Thus, just as the industrial revolution spurred the growth of cities along major transportation arteries and their crossroads, and concurrently the building of such arteries by cities, the information revolution will prompt the development of new kinds of arteries and crossroads, those of electronic communications networks.

Secure and reliable communications, able to handle required volumes of traffic efficiently, have always been important in commerce. But in the future, as information itself becomes the most important value-adding resource in society, the capability to communicate rapidly, in a variety of formats, will be the single most important asset of more and more businesses and organizations. Being able to have needed information in usable form at the right time will be important not only where instant decisions have to be made (as in many kinds of financial service companies), but also where decision-making is usually preceded by more extended examination and analysis. Complete information will mean better decisions made with greater confidence; timely information will mean decisions that beat the competition.

Structural change in communications is affecting what we know, how we conduct business, and the way we relate to each other, and it is fundamentally altering the two major forms of communications media, print and electronic.

The growth of print media is slowing.

Rarely does the victim salute his executioner, but in January 1982, *Time* magazine named the computer as "Man of the Year," acknowledging the ascendancy of electronic media and, by implication, the eventual demise of its own medium, print.

Nevertheless, print media still appear to be very much alive. The number of book titles published worldwide has grown over 150 percent in the last twenty-five years. In the United States the rate of growth has been almost twice as fast, and has been accompanied by a steady increase in retail bookstores and a growth in circulation at the nation's public libraries since 1941 at more than twice the rate of population growth. The number of periodicals has increased also, rising over 50 percent in the last four decades; and although the number of daily newspapers has fallen slightly during the same period, their total circulation has increased from 42 million to 62 million.

However, a closer examination of these figures reveals the dimensions of the structural change in print media and suggests its future direction. The print medium whose content is most time-sensitive and perishable, newspapers, is now growing only very slowly, or, by some measures, not growing at all. Although total newspaper circulation in the United States has increased, as a percent of total population it has been steadily falling. Many large American cities which once supported several major newspapers now have just two, one morning and one afternoon, and most of these have survived only because of an exemption from antitrust regulations (passed by Congress in 1970) that allows them to combine such business functions as advertising, printing, and circulation while continuing to compete in editorial content; and even with this extraordinary arrangement many may still fail.

What is happening is simply that the main function of newspapers—to report the latest news quickly—can be done faster and more dramatically by the electronic media, especially television. With their principal function rapidly being usurped, traditional newspapers now must move in one of two directions to succeed in the future. For a few that direction is toward a much broader audience—albeit selective and dispersed—using satellite technology and multiple printing plants for a number of simultaneous editions. Three major U.S. papers illustrate this strategic direction:

- The *New York Times*—aiming at those of the public attentive to a wide range of national and international events
- The *Wall Street Journal*—targeted for an American and increasingly multinational readership interested principally in business and financial news
- *USA Today*—attempting to attract a mobile, relatively affluent audience with a colorful neo-television format of short news items and comprehensive statistics on the nation's weather, sports, and economic and entertainment news

For most other papers the direction is narrower and more selective, focusing on the interests of a particular group or a particular area, often suburban, stressing "soft" features such as "Life-Style," "Living," or "Style," and in some cases converting from daily to weekly circulation.

The next print medium to feel the impact of the electronic media will be periodicals. Sensing the trend, the companies that control the two major general-interest U.S. news magazines have already diversified to other nonprint activities. Since the late 1970s, Time, Inc., has expanded rapidly in the video area, building the largest cable TV system in the country (American Television and Communications) and one of the largest cable services (Home Box Office). The Washington Post Company, owner of *Newsweek* and already heavily involved in broadcasting, has recently diversified into computer data bases and cable television and has applied for licensing to operate cellular radio systems in over a dozen major U.S. cities.

In the meantime, all of the other general-interest weekly magazines that were once the staples of newsstands and living rooms across the American countryside—*Life, Look, Collier's, Saturday Evening Post*—have long since passed from the scene. In their wake came a surge of mass women's and men's magazines; but these, too, are experiencing stagnant or declining circulations. Today the audience for periodicals is increasingly narrower and segmented, seeking magazines focused on particular fields; and with automation making printing and distribution cost efficient for smaller numbers of copies, the audience's demand can be met. Such periodicals now number over twenty thousand, including trade and professional journals, and their audiences range from farmers to physicians. The pervasiveness of electronic media is illustrated by the fact that the fastest-growing field of the magazine industry in recent years has been publications specializing in computers (over two hundred titles at latest count, with a growing number supplemented with—or available on—computer disks or "diskettes"), while the sole remaining true mass-market weekly in the United States is *TV Guide.*

Books have the longest and strongest future among the print media, but they too are being overtaken by the long-term structural shift to electronic media of communications. Although the total number of book titles produced in the world has increased steadily in the last twenty-five years, the number of titles per million inhabitants peaked in 1970 and has been falling since, as figure 3.1 shows; during the same time, the number of radio and television sets per thousand people has continued to climb rapidly. Furthermore, as the price of electronic publication continues to fall relative to that of traditional mechanical publication, more and more books will appear first—and eventually solely—in electronic format. Telephone directories, encyclopedias, statistical yearbooks (which will no longer have to be "year" books) will all be simple to update and cheaper to publish electronically as equipment-based demand crosses cost thresholds that make such publication feasible. Already in certain districts of Paris, computer terminals, called minitels, are being offered in place of the annual two-volume edition of the city's telephone directory, part of a project that the French expect eventually to entirely replace phone books. Other publications that contain schedules, lists, prices, and other data that change regularly will increasingly appear both in print and electronically until finally when enough customers have electronic access print publication no longer will be economical and will cease.

FIG. 3.1.   Book Titles Published per Million Inhabitants, World-wide, 1955–1983, Radio and Television Receivers per Thousand Inhabitants, Worldwide, 1965–1983.

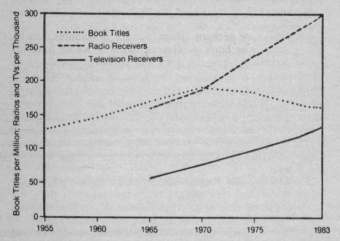

Source: UNESCO, *Statistical Yearbook 1985* (Paris: UNESCO, 1985). Tables 6.1, 6.9 and 6.11, pp. vi-11, vi-20 and vi-22.

The next step will be print publication of books on demand. It is easy to imagine a retail facility displaying bindings, paper, typefaces, and even illustrations—along with a catalog of titles and a few sample volumes—and producing books customized to the purchaser's specifications with the use of a laser printer and an automated binding machine. Eventually, as prices of electronic equipment continue to fall, a simplified version of such a printer could be available for home computer use.

Beyond this lies purely electronic publication; and it is not so far away as many may think. Each day the Library of Congress of the United States receives some seven thousand books and other textual materials. Most are printed on acid-based paper that will not last more than a century, and each item can be used by only one reader at a time. To save space and overcome these limitations, the library has begun recording new accessions on twelve-inch disks using laser optical technology. Approximately three hundred books with their illustrations, normally requiring forty feet of shelf space, can be recorded on a single disk one-sixteenth of an inch thick. The resulting record is virtually indestructible and its contents can be retrieved for display on viewing screens simultaneously by as many people as there are terminals available.

Such disks, or perhaps "chips" for single volumes, can be manufactured by book publishers, many of whom have already established new divisions for "software" publication. Purchasers can then insert them in their own terminals, reading from viewing screens—and reviewing and rereading, enlarged if necessary for the sight-impaired—at whatever pace they desire. Little of this will occur, of course, until enough equipment is in place to create an economically viable market, a condition perhaps still a generation away. But once that condition exists, the era of electronic books is likely to come on with a rush, much as the first phonograph records did once instruments to play them were widely available.

For those who will still like to curl up with a good book, it is quite possible to forecast a small hand-held battery-powered computer, bound—if desired—in soft leather, in which to display, page by page or paragraph by paragraph, one's own "chip" book. (The late Christopher Evans even suggested projecting the text on the ceiling as the ultimate comfort for reading in bed!) For those who fancy the sound of the prose they are reading or the rhythms of poetry (with even a choice of accents), their computers could be programmed with speech synthesizers. Students who might like to underline or annotate in the margins could have instruments equipped to do so. In short, not only will the electronic word eventually replace the mechanically printed word, but it will do so with a greater variety of capabilities.

The growth of electronic media is accelerating.
Radio, the first electronic medium of mass communications, was invented by Guglielmo Marconi shortly before 1900. Since that time it has undergone considerable structural change, and it is continuing to do so. Television was

invented several decades later and did not come into wide use until after World War II; thus for this medium structural change is only just beginning. However, because television is basically a technological extension of radio (augmenting a broadcast sound with a broadcast picture), its evolution will be similar, in many ways, to that of radio.

In the early years of radio, both transmission and reception equipment were relatively large and relatively expensive. These circumstances contributed to the growth of the major networks (which had the resources to afford the equipment and sufficient staff to do programming) and limited the number of receivers in the hands of the public. Under these conditions radio (the networks especially) set out to provide entertainment and news that would interest the broadest possible segment of the population, and since—in the pre-TV years—it enjoyed a broadcast monopoly, it did whatever it felt like doing. In most areas of the country the listener had essentially two choices: listen to broadly targeted programming or turn off the set.

Technology has changed all this. The cost of sending out a signal has fallen, and the equipment for receiving it has become portable, small, and—at its cheapest—less expensive than lunch at a fast food restaurant; at the same time, with the advent of television, radio has lost its broadcast monopoly.

Radio, at first shaken by this technological change, has now begun to take advantage of it. While there is still a lot of "broad" casting (and there always will be a large audience for national election returns, major sports contests, crises, and other special events), there is now much more "narrow" casting—programming for the specific interests of narrower segments of the radio audience (like formats exclusively for news, interviews, talk shows, and different kinds of music).

Radio will go even further, however, for it is beginning to understand that the electronic transmission of an audio signal (locally, and now much more easily—through satellite distribution—nationally and globally) can be used for more than just providing news and entertainment to a broad audience. Radio signals can be used to page people, to remind them, to warn them, eventually even to administer their medicine. Very specific information can be sent to very specific groups: advertising to motorists in tunnels (as is being done in Boston and elsewhere with "Tunnel Radio"), or information about traffic on specific routes being traveled, or the latest prices for a preselected list of stocks, or schedule changes for planned flights, and so forth.

Radio can also make use of other rapidly changing technologies. For example, cellular radio promises an enormous expansion in mobile phones (in Chicago, for instance, the two thousand who until recently often could not get an open line now will be able to increase to as many as 350,000 who will always be able to get one). This suggests a form of "dial-up" or "call-up" radio through which a mobile listener could request a specific type of programming from a central service, paid for either by advertising or by subscription, using for access a positive identification system like a voiceprint—a security technology that is just over the horizon.

By reducing the cost of radio transmission and reception, technology has reshaped radio's audience, changing it from an undifferentiated mass to a variety of special groups with distinct interests. Because radio has developed competence in concise quality programming, it is well prepared to take advantage of the structural changes occurring in its communications medium, and it is beginning to do so. Television, however, is not there yet. It is still in the throes of its technological changes, not yet experiencing their maturity, as radio is. These changes are altering both the reception and the transmission of television signals.

Since the widespread introduction of color, almost two decades ago, there has been little fundamental change in the quality of television receivers. Now, however, advances in metallurgy, picture display technology, and especially the development of integrated circuits are improving picture definition, adding split-screen and freeze-action capabilities, bringing stereo sound, and creating small, portable, ultralight sets.

Just as dramatic are advances in signal transmission. These include, first, two new forms of wireless transmission:

• Direct Broadcast Satellite (DBS), which uses a satellite to relay powerful TV signals to the small rooftop antennas of subscribers, can reach rural and out-of-the way areas that receive few or no ground-broadcast line-of-sight signals and cannot economically be wired for cable reception.

- Low-power television, which is broadcast over normal VHF and UHF channels with signals that are far weaker and travel much shorter distances than those of regular stations, is cheap to build and operate and thus particularly attractive for small communities, nonprofit organizations, and special-interest groups.

Even more important than new means of wireless transmission is the large and continuing increase in wired cable installations. In the United States these include, as of mid-1986, almost 50 percent of all television homes, a figure that in the mid-1980s has been increasing at a rate of 1 percent every two months. In addition, over 70 percent now have access to over 6,600 local cable systems, indicating the potential for further increase. In Europe, growth has been slower, with only about 15 percent of homes wired, and these mostly in rural areas of Belgium, the Netherlands, and Switzerland; but cable is now beginning to catch on in the more populous nations of England, France, and Germany, and since these nations have higher population densities than the United States it can be expected to grow there even more rapidly.

The advantages of cable as a means to transmit television signals are considerable. A very large number of channels can be provided (many systems now number over one hundred), picture quality is consistently high and usually free of interference, and since large urban areas typically are wired first, the potential audience grows very rapidly. Also, cable installations can accommodate interactive communications, the next major structural change in electronic media.

Clearly, technology is rapidly changing television, both in the size and quality of receiving equipment and in the number and variety of channels available to an ever-enlarging portion of the public. Yet today the television industry is in turmoil, confused about its audience, unable consistently to satisfy its advertisers, and uncertain of its future. The problem is that it has failed to understand the structural changes taking place in electronic communications, changes that in many ways it instigated. While the world about it has moved forward, the television industry has stood still, paralyzed by the notion that the purpose of transmitting visual signals is principally (if not exclusively) to provide entertainment and news. Thus, networks have agonized over falling audience ratings (and created statistical smokescreens to convince skeptical advertisers otherwise) and cable operators have fretted about their ability to match the quality of network programming; and both have failed to understand that television—in the beginning, like radio, principally a medium of entertainment and news—is now being used for many other purposes, and in the future will have still more.

The way out of the turmoil is for television—as radio is now doing—to perceive the changes that are occurring and set out to make use of them. Entertainment and news *will* continue to be major functions of the television medium, but it will serve other functions, too. We have passed beyond the time when a turned-on TV set commanded our continuous and full attention. For some programs (new feature films, special events, national and international crises, etc.), it may still do so. But more and more, it serves as background, as a companion for the elderly or lonely or ill, as security for the anxious, as an object for occasional attention when something heard or briefly glimpsed catches our attention. It is as commonplace as a piece of furniture, as accessible as the latest magazine or newspaper—equally available for a few quick glances or an hour of concentrated viewing.

Even more important, television is becoming—and will become—more of a means to an end and less an end in itself. We will use it as a tool, as an instrument to aid our occupations and satisfy our interests. Television will soon have channels that can reach a small number with the same interests scattered over a large area (via satellite) or most of a small number concentrated in a fairly small area (via low-power TV) or various combinations of the above, up to virtually the entire population of a nation or several nations. Thus, it can be used to teach (formally and informally), to respond to interests in self-improvement or health or safety, to advocate and to rebut, to coordinate and to organize, and to market products and services using a variety of techniques other than spot commercials.

Structural change in television does not mean an end to programs with broad appeal, but it does indicate an increasing opportunity to provide programming with *narrow* appeal, responding to the specific needs of a viewing public that will support such programming. Above all, it means understanding that television has new and growing capabilities and that these give it the opportunity to play new and different roles. Among the newest of these is expanding the scope of interactive communications.

> *Interactive electronics is the next major*
> *structural change in communications media.*

In December 1983, Chemical Bank in New York included a small flier in its monthly mailing of statements to checking account customers. The flier announced a new service called "Pronto," which enables customers to make use of a number of banking services, including paying bills, directly from home, without ever entering the bank. To do so, the bank advised, the customer would need a telephone, a home computer, and a TV set. These three pieces of equipment, used in various combinations, will revolutionize interactive communications—a structural change that will alter the way almost every service industry conducts its business and many manufacturers market their products.

Use of the telephone has increased steadily since its invention over a century ago; but in the last few years a number of advances have occurred which soon will dwarf all the progress of the past hundred years.

- The number of telephones in use in the world has doubled in the last decade, meaning as many were installed during that period as in the previous ninety years of the telephone's existence.
- The recent development of cellular radio not only will increase greatly the number of phones in automobiles, but also will mean many other kinds of portable phones, including briefcase phones, pocketbook phones, and even wristwatch phones.
- The use of satellites will greatly expand the volume of communications traffic among nations; already, from 1965 to 1986, transmissions via the 112-nation INTELSAT satellite system have increased from eighty channel-hours to nearly 61,000.

Accompanying this vast expansion in the use of the century-old telephone is its much more recent use in conjunction with computers and television sets. Through the use of a modem (a device to which a telephone can be connected to convert its electrical analog signals into digitized signals readable by a computer, and vice versa) one computer can talk to others.

One important use of this interactive capability is the exchange of written messages, either displayed for immediate reading or stored for later retrieval. Thus is created a form of electronic mail which is gradually evolving in sophistication from Generation I (hard-copy messages converted for electronic transmission and then reconverted into hard copy at the point of receipt) to Generation II (electronically formatted messages transmitted electronically and then converted into hard copy—the stage originally marketed as E-COM by the U.S. Postal Service) to Generation III (fully electronic at all points). Another important use of the telephone-computer interactive capability is the querying of a central computer memory for specific information, such as the growing use by researchers, attorneys, and other professionals of data bases containing bibliographic and textual materials. In the same way a remote computer, using a modem, can make use of an operational program stored in a central computer to which it has access.

The interactive capability of the telephone can also be used in conjunction with television. It has long existed in the simple form of television commercials providing phone numbers a viewer can use to order products or services just shown on the screen, a service that has been greatly expanded by the proliferation of new cable TV retailers, such as Home Shopping Network, offering viewers a large variety of discounted products 24 hours a day. In somewhat more sophisticated systems, such as Cableshop, first introduced in Peabody, Massachusetts, a viewer can request by phone specific items of programming (commercial messages, in this case) from a list appearing on one channel of a cable system and then watch the selected material as it appears on another channel. The most sophisticated systems usually add a small computer to the telephone-television combination, producing a form of videotex, which allows viewers (depending on the capabilities of the system) to request specific items of information, make inputs, and interact with others similarly hooked up.

Although a variety of interactive systems do exist, employing different combinations of telephones, television sets, and computers, they have been slow to develop and most have not yet been commercially successful. The reason is that so far few services have been available to justify the purchase and installation of the necessary equipment, and since there is little equipment in place there has been little incentive to develop services for it. Like most log jams this one will break slowly at first, then suddenly become a noisy high-volume rush.

The break will occur—probably within this decade—when it is seen that the same relatively inexpensive equipment can simultaneously provide several high-value services. These will be grouped around certain core activities such as home and building security, environmental controls, banking and shopping, education, communications, employment at home, and entertainment. As they fall into place they will collectively constitute a major structural change in interactive communications, the first since the invention of the telephone itself over a century ago.

Changes in communications mean
changes in business and society.

Structural changes in communications are creating new ways of doing business and altering old ways, and in the process they are rearranging long-standing relationships. The net results for all who communicate are new problems and new opportunities. Understanding the changes will be essential to overcoming the former and taking advantage of the latter.

It is common wisdom that the vast increase in the number of people who can simultaneously receive the same message—because of the development and expansion of electronic media—is in effect making the world a "global village." Not only can news be immediately and widely shared, but so, too, can ideas and opinions. In both cases the widespread sharing creates the impression that a particular piece of information is "well known," and thus it acquires both an enhanced credibility and a staying power that for a time is self-reinforcing.

This growing universality of communications, and the greater force messages acquire by being widely shared, is creating a wholly new environment for businesses and other organizations. It is enhancing the development of national attitudes and consciousness, and it is also—and increasingly—contributing to the growth of global attitudes, and even to a global consciousness. News of the fatal gas leak at the

Union Carbide plant in Bhopal, India, in December, 1984, was so quickly and vividly transmitted around the world that all other chemical plants of the company (and those of other companies, too) immediately felt the impact, and one community (Livingston, Scotland) that earlier had vigorously lobbied for a Union Carbide plant did an immediate about-face and rejected it. Fifty years ago, even twenty-five years ago, such a reaction would have been unlikely. Structural change in communications has made the difference.

Less commonly understood, but equally important, is that structural changes in communications are also making it economically possible to direct an increasing and varied flow of specific information to specific individuals, whether grouped in a certain geographic area or widely separated but sharing similar concerns. Advances in the technology of communications media, by reducing their cost, have made possible a proliferation of publications, broadcast channels, and transmitting stations, facilitating the reaching of particular groups with particular messages. Advertisers understand that residents of the Sixteenth Arrondissement in Paris have much in common with those of Manhattan's Upper East Side, for example, and developments in communications media are making it increasingly possible to target similarly ranked consumers. Structural change increases our ability to share *and* to separate; it is making possible to communicate both to the masses and to discrete segments.

Still another factor which must be taken into account is that the structure of communication systems and the pattern and timing of the traffic that flows through them will itself influence the operation and output of organizations.

- A system structured to handle messages with reference to their geographic or institutional origins will cause the opportunities and problems of an organization to be viewed in geographic or institutional categories.
- A pattern of traffic flow that routes messages to recipients serially rather than simultaneously will reduce the number of copies but at the cost of retarding response time.
- A schedule that sets precise times for transmitting communications (quarterly reports, weekly briefings, daily summaries, etc.) will give the timing of actions a

very high priority, possibly far higher than other more substantive considerations.

It is startling to hear Lloyd Cutler, counsel to former President Jimmy Carter, refer to the imperative created on operations at the White House by the evening television news. It meant, for example, said Cutler, that if something significant happened during the day, more important matters had to be set aside to frame a response by air time—regardless of the inherent need or value of such a response—lest the President be seen as indecisive or his staff divided.

The structural change in communications from mechanical to electronic, and especially the more recent shift from single-sensory electronic (audio) to multisensory (audio and visual), has reduced the time it takes to receive a message and—more important—has affected the impact it has on the recipient. The electronic signal is received instantly; to get the news it is no longer necessary to take the time to go buy the paper (or even to pick it up at the doorstep), open its pages, and read through its columns. With the addition of the visual dimension, the impact is further heightened. It is not so much that, in Marshall McLuhan's famous phrase, "the medium is the message" (as NBC News executive Reuven Frank has wisely observed, "the medium is the medium. . . . What is put in at one end comes out at the other"); it is instead that the medium affects our perception of the message, whatever it is. Our reaction is instant, not measured or reflective (one cannot put down the TV, even for a moment, like a newspaper, and think about it; it goes on, relentlessly); and the visual image enhances the credibility of the message. "Seeing is believing" is an ancient and honored maxim, and since the late 1950s (the beginning of the widespread availability of television), public opinion polls in the United States consistently have shown credibility in television exceeding that in newspapers by twenty or more percentage points. Furthermore, according to a 1984 survey undertaken for the Radio-Television News Directors Association, 54 percent of the American public "claim to depend on television most to obtain news and information," and only 25 percent "rely on a daily newspaper."

In addition, the shift from audio to audio-plus-visual is creating a structural change in our "information habits," the way we acquire information. Television attracts us with what is visually exciting, and the two recent technological developments of cable—with its great increase in available channels and hand-held remote controls, which enable us to switch channels without leaving our chairs—have put a premium on constant visual excitement and decreased the need for order, sequence, and logically developed story lines. As we become accustomed to receiving information in this fashion we will come to expect it this way and will respond to it, and we will be less patient with the earlier sequential mode of the mechanical media. And so these media, too, to gain and retain our attention, will have to adjust their presentations to our changing "information habits," giving greater emphasis to color, layout, and other techniques that provide visual excitement. An early and increasingly successful example of a print medium now doing this can be seen in *USA Today*.

Structural change in communications has also altered the relationship between senders and receivers. When human media were predominant, communications were interactive and face-to-face. With mechanical media there was a great increase in noninteractive one-way communications. Electronic media have increased further the noninteractive component, but they have also made possible a new form of *non*-face-to-face interactive communications, through telephones, computers, two-way cable systems, and other links. This is a profound alteration, for its continued development means a major shift in the social conditions accompanying interactive communications. Throughout most of human history both sender and receiver were physically present during interactive communications. Electronic media, however, have successively reduced direct contact, altering the quality of the interaction. The telephone removes physical presence while maintaining direct aural contact, requiring callers to cooperatively engage in speaking and listening roles—lest there be no conversation—and probably causing them to restrain emotional outbursts. The computer goes a step further, entirely removing direct contact, and preliminary studies of participants using computers to communicate indicate more frequent resort to emotional language, longer time to reach agreement, and more extreme final decisions than occur among those meeting in person.

But while structural change in communications is increasing our ability to communicate while physically separated, it also is enabling us to learn more about each other and to discover and develop more shared interests. As a result, networks are being created that cross traditional boundaries of nationality, race, and creed; and along these networks are flowing messages creating institutions and activities whose continuation is itself a strong common interest of those exchanging the messages. Almost imperceptibly, then, structural change in communications is making us more interdependent, and because in many cases the new institutions and activities being created are to facilitate the exchange of goods and services, the major form of that interdependence is economic.

INDUSTRIALIZATION

More than fifty years ago—in the depths of the Great Depression—the renowned British economist John Maynard Keynes wrote an essay entitled "Economic Possibilities for Our Grandchildren." In it he reached the following startling conclusion:

> I draw the conclusion that, assuming no important wars and no important increase in population, the *economic problem* may be solved, or be at least within sight of solution, within a hundred years. This means that the economic problem is not—if we look into the future—*the permanent problem of the human race*. [Emphasis by Keynes]

Today, we are in the midst of a long-term structural change that seems likely to prove Keynes right. This change is the worldwide transition—on a country-by-country basis—from preindustrial to industrial status. Where it has occurred it has shifted the axis of economic activities from meeting basic "needs" to satisfying desired "wants," from providing subsistence to generating surplus. When finally completed it will mark the achievement of mankind's passage between what French historian Fernand Braudel has called "the two shores of human existence"—from the shore of poverty to the shore of prosperity.

Keynes's two caveats remain, but they have changed enormously in importance. The second, increase in population, is no longer a worldwide problem but may still be very important to certain countries in completing their own industrial transitions. The first, war, has become *the* overwhelming worldwide problem, and although we did survive a very "important war" (and resumed our path of industrialization) after Keynes wrote, should there be another "important war" its anticipated consequences raise far greater doubt about our ability again to survive and resume. Nevertheless, if the nuclear superpowers can continue their rivalry in tacit agreement that stability is the first and most important rule of its conduct, then we may be able to "hold the ring" to enable succeeding generations to make their transit between the shores of rich and poor; and we can hope that as more do, the conditions that might prompt an important war will be diminished.

Industrialization brings great improvement in the lives of those in the countries that achieve it. It makes possible a better diet, improved health care, and programs of public education. It means that indicators of human development which for years had been mostly stagnant—floating around the lowest common denominator of bare subsistence—begin to rise and finally reach new higher levels from which they do not retreat. The people of industrialized countries become better producers and bigger consumers; they make more things for themselves, and eventually for others, competing with earlier industrialized countries but also playing a larger role as their customers.

This is a structural change that affects everyone—those who have already achieved it, those who are going through it, and those who have not yet begun it. It is achieved for a country when its principal economic activities shift from extractive (agriculture, fishing, primitive mining), done principally with human labor on a small scale, to the production of goods, and contract construction, accomplished mainly with inanimate energy and on a much larger scale. Because the use of inanimate energy and the machinery powered by it increase the scale of production, outputs usually are greater in value than the inputs used to create them. It is this added value that causes rapid economic growth and a rise in per capita incomes, producing a better standard of living for all of the inhabitants of the country.

The industrial countries of today—led by England and the nations of Western Europe—were the first to begin the transition to industrial status. Several have already reached and passed the peak of their industrial stages and are now rapidly becoming postindustrial, with economies dependent principally on service activities. Not far behind them, and often only a few years into their industrial transitions, are most of the world's middle-income countries, led by a group known collectively as the NICs, or newly industrializing countries. Farther back, still in the early stages of development, though sometimes considerably advanced in one industry or in one geographic area, are the low-income countries of the world. Eventually all of these developing nations will make their own transitions from preindustrial to industrial, as the developed did before them. Their pace will vary, as will the composition of their economic activities, and on the other shore of human existence there still will be differences in endowment and wealth; but for these countries—like those that preceded them—the passage will result in a structural change that eventually will solve mankind's "economic problem."

> *The developed countries have completed*
> *the transition to industrial status.*

Each country's progress along its industrial transition can be gauged by the proportion of its workforce and product attributable to extractive, industrial, and service-type activities. It is the percentages of employment and output accounted for by these activities at any one time that largely determine the rate of growth of the country's gross product, and the per capita incomes and well-being of its people at that time; and it is change in these percentages that signals the country's movement from preindustrial to industrial, and eventually to postindustrial.

When a country is preindustrial the pattern is one of domination by the provision of goods of the extractive type, usually from agriculture. This is seen in the substantial portion of its total output attributable to farming and the very large percentage of its workforce involved in the growing of food. In such a country the provision of finished goods consists of the output of local cottage industries, supplying small quantities of clothing, footgear, and simple tools. Some producer services may exist, such as the facilities for permanent markets, means of transportation of goods along established routes, and even financial services for exchange purposes and the provision of credit. But these services, like those that might be available for consumers (inns, taverns, medical care, etc.), will be limited and simple. The only service likely to employ significant numbers—and only by the better-off classes of the society—is that of household domestics.

Until the middle of the eighteenth century this was the pattern exhibited by all countries. It has been estimated that two hundred years ago the annual gross product of the world (measured in 1975 U.S. dollars) was approximately $150 billion. For a population which was probably about 750 million this works out to about $200 per capita. Most of this product was obtained through the provision of extractive goods, primarily agricultural. But by this time forces already were at work that soon would transform this long-standing pattern, first in England, then in the other countries of Europe. These included:

- The voyages of discovery which led to a large influx of precious metals from the New World, raising prices, stimulating trade, and fostering a money economy
- The remarkable discovery, in the depths of rural Shropshire, of the coking process that made the production of iron easy and cheap
- The shift in society's transforming resource from human and animal power to the energy of steam, and the invention of machines to make use of this far more powerful resource

With these events the transition from preindustrial to industrial began. Factories were built, workers left the countryside, and small rural towns became large industrial cities. Eventually the production of both extractive and manufactured goods was made more efficient, but it was the latter that grew the fastest because their supply could be increased most quickly and because the very process of their production was creating the wealth with which they could be purchased. Thus, by adding value in the course of manufacture, industrialization ensured its own perpetuation and growth.

This transition is seen in the major shift that took place in shares of product and employment attributable to different economic sectors in England. At the beginning of the nineteenth century, the output of industry climbed rapidly, and by 1821 its share of national product exceeded for the first time that of agriculture. Throughout the nineteenth century, and halfway into the twentieth, this gap continued to widen. Finally, in 1951, industry's share peaked at 43 percent, and shortly afterward agriculture's reached its lowest and current level of 3 percent. A similar shift occurred in the distribution of the English labor force as the proportion in agriculture diminished and that in industry increased until the low for the former and the high for the latter were reached in the early 1950s.

England led the way. Its economy was the first to begin the transition that eventually saw its industrial sector outstrip its agricultural in shares of both product and employment. Following England, during the eighteenth and early nineteenth centuries, other nations of Europe underwent similar structural changes. In Germany the industrial sector exceeded the agricultural in 1889, in Sweden this occurred in 1897, in France it was 1909, and in Czechoslovakia 1919; and in each of these cases the distribution of the labor force underwent a similar shift a few years later.

In America the industrial transition began later than in England but occurred more rapidly. While the number of those involved in food growing did fall during the first half of the nineteenth century, by 1850, as shown in figure 3.2, almost 65 percent of America's workers were still on the farm, while less than 20 percent were in manufacturing and construction. Then, during the long period of reconstruction following the Civil War the number of workers in agriculture fell below 50 percent for the first time, and three decades later, early in the twentieth century, as indicated in figure 3.3, the percentage of national income accounted for by food growing began to decline while that for goods production continued to rise. In the following years, except during the downturn of the Depression of the 1930s, the share of manufacturing and contract construction rose steadily, reaching a peak of 39.1 percent of total national income during the mid 1950s, approximately the same period during which employment in these sectors also peaked, at 35.5 percent.

Accompanying the structural change from preindustrial to industrial in Great Britain, the United States, and other industrial countries was a sustained increase in total product and in product per capita, and with these increases came a better standard of living for the inhabitants of the countries achieving them. In every case, indicators of human development which had not changed at all during the years they had been recorded—and probably for centuries before—improved dramatically. In England, for example, crude death rates—after hovering in the twenties per thousand throughout the first eighty years of the nineteenth century—dropped below 20 in 1881 and thereafter fell steadily until they reached the low teens fifty years later. Deaths of infants under one year—which had shown no downward movement during the 1800s—also fell dramatically, from over 150 per thousand live births in the 1890s to less than 30 by the middle of the twentieth century. In the United States the development of industry was followed by the same declines, with death rates falling from approximately 20 per thousand (around which they had fluctuated throughout the nineteenth century) to less than 10 during the 1950s, while infant mortality during the same period dropped from over 100 per thousand live births to less than 30.

Overall, passage through the transition from preindustrial

FIG. 3.2. Distribution of U.S. Employment by Major Sector, 1850–1983 (in percent).

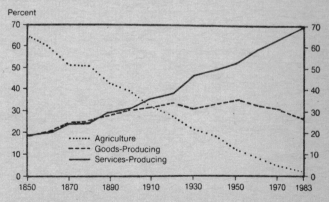

Sources: Michael Urquhart, "The Employment Shift to Services: Where Did It Come From?" *Monthly Labor Review,* Apr. 1984, p. 15; U.S. Bureau of the Census, *Statistical Abstract of the United States 1985* (Wash., DC, 1984), p. 404.

to industrial means impressive improvement in terms of human development for those who achieve it. By the middle of the twentieth century, for the countries which it defines as industrial, the World Bank reported gross national product per person of $4,130 (in 1980 dollars), life expectancy at birth of sixty-seven years, and 95 percent adult literacy. In simple human terms, the structural change from a preindustrial status has meant for most of the people of these countries lives that are richer, healthier, longer, and more satisfying.

The developing countries are in the midst of the transition to industrial status.

In their widely acclaimed book *Famine 1975!*, published in 1967, William and Paul Paddock recommended that India be placed in the "can't be saved" category of their triage classification for determining which nations in the world should receive U.S. food aid. In other words, India's situation was considered so hopeless that no amount of assistance could prevent inevitable catastrophe. So, no aid should

FIG. 3.3. Distribution of U.S. National Income by Industrial Origin, 1869–1983 (in percent).

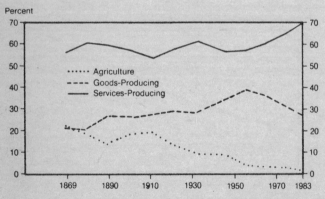

Sources: U.S. Bureau of the Census, *Historical Statistics of the United States, Colonial Times to 1970*, Vol. I (Wash., DC, 1976), p. 240 and *Statistical Abstract of the United States 1985* (Wash., DC, 1984), p. 437.

be given, for to provide it would be to waste it. "To send food to them," wrote the Paddocks, "is to throw sand in the ocean."

Today, millions of Indians have a problem that is the very opposite of the grim forecast made in *Famine 1975!*: they are getting fat because they are eating too much. Weight reduction centers, Jane Fonda exercise studios, and aerobics classes are proliferating in India, yet still not rapidly enough to meet the demand for them. Jogging and working out are fast-growing pastimes for the country's large and growing middle class, and in a nation long considered one of the world's basket cases, dieting is becoming the habit of many.

To be sure, nearly 50 percent of the country's 700 million people exist at or below the poverty line, and most of these are probably undernourished. But the remainder have diets that range from nutritionally adequate to lavish, and their number is increasing. In spite of a burgeoning population, bureaucratic mismanagement, and endemic corruption—all readily conceded by most Indians—wheat production has increased 300 percent in the past twenty years and the country is today essentially self-sufficient in food grains on a per capita basis. As Joan Holmes, executive director of the San Francisco–based Hunger Project, has written, "A bad agricultural year now means that some food must be imported rather than spelling disaster and death for millions as it always did in the past."

By the World Bank's reckoning, India—with a 1984 per capita gross national product (GNP) of 260 U.S. dollars—is still in the "low-income economy" category, the bank's lowest. Yet this huge and diverse nation—the world's second-largest in population—is rapidly emerging from preindustrial status, entering its own transition to industrialization; and it is this structural change that is improving the lives of its people. Although India's food production has increased, its industrial production has grown so much faster that agriculture as a percentage of gross domestic product has fallen from 50 in 1960 to 35 in 1984, while industry has grown from 20 to 27 during the same period. Accompanying this shift has been a slowly increasing growth in overall domestic production, from an annual average of 3.4 percent in the decade of the sixties to 4.1 percent from 1973 through 1984; and with this growth have come measurable improvements in human development factors in addition to a better diet:

- Crude death rates have fallen from 24 per thousand to 12 and infant mortality from 165 to 90.
- Life expectancy at birth has risen from forty-three to fifty-six years.
- School enrollment has increased in all categories, and with 85 percent of the eligible age group now in primary schools, adult literacy should quickly surpass the increase from 28 to 36 percent achieved from the 1960s to the 1970s.

In the "middle-income economy" category of the developing countries (defined by the World Bank as those with 1984 GNP per person of 400 U.S. dollars or more, and including sixty countries), the structural change from preindustrial is even further advanced. Leading this group are the newly industrializing countries, or NICs. With a large labor supply (expanding at a faster pace—because of higher birthrates—than that of the developed nations) employed at wage and benefit levels far below those in most industrial countries, and with the help of new technology and relatively unsophisticated but adequate transportation and financial infrastructures, they have carved out for themselves a large and steadily growing area of industrial production, one heretofore dominated by the already industrialized countries. This area includes steel and other basic metals; some chemicals; basic producer goods such as motors, engines, and simple office machines; a growing number of consumer goods, among them toys, cookware, household appliances, bicycles, motor scooters, and mass-market electronic items; textiles, clothing, and low-priced footwear; and the assembly of high-technology products from components produced elsewhere.

As a result of this productive activity, the percentage of the labor force of the middle-income countries in agriculture has fallen below 50 percent for the first time while that in industry has risen from 15 to 22 percent. Accompanying this has been a similar shift in the distribution of gross domestic product. In 1960 almost a quarter of the production of the middle-income countries was in agriculture; by 1984 it was down to 14 percent. At the same time the share of industry rose from 30 to 37 percent. And, as was the case with the developed nations which preceded them in the transition from preindustrial to industrial, this structural change has been accompanied by high rates of growth of production and GNP per capita.

Countries in the World Bank's "low-income economy" category (thirty-six in number) are mostly preindustrial, though several (like India) are involved in advanced industrial activities (steel mills, national airlines, research and development laboratories, etc.) characteristic of middle-income and highly developed nations. For the most part their economies are based on the development and production of particular commodities or raw materials (for example, jute for Bangladesh, bauxite for Guinea, copper for Zaire, etc.). Where there is manufacturing, it is far less sophisticated than in the higher-income nations and often solely for domestic consumption and not yet suitable for export.

Sectoral distribution of employment and product reflect this preindustrial state. The percentage of the labor force in agriculture in 1981 averaged 73 for these countries, and in all but four the proportion of production from agriculture was greater than that from industry. Growth rates, too, were lower than in the middle-income countries.

Yet even in this group of nations, where terms of trade (the amount earned for exports versus the amount paid for imports) are often adverse and the burden of worldwide economic downturns falls most heavily, structural change is underway. The percentage of those employed in agriculture was even higher (77 percent) two decades ago, while that for industry was lower (9 percent) than its level of 13 percent in 1981. In sixteen of the twenty-two countries for which data are available the distribution of product attributable to industry has risen while that for agriculture has fallen.

Most important to the people of these countries is the change in factors of human development that follow the transition from preindustrial to industrial. For both middle-income and low-income countries the data show steady improvement.

• By 1984, crude death rates had fallen below 10 per thousand, infant mortality had dropped to 72, and life expectancy had risen 20 percent since 1960 for the middle-income countries and an astonishing 44 percent for the low-income, due especially to the higher than average gains made by the two largest countries, China and India.

- From 1960 to 1980, the number of physicians as a percentage of total population tripled in the middle-income and more than doubled in the low-income countries.
- Daily per capita calorie supply for the middle-income countries in 1982 was 114 percent of what is needed to sustain a person at normal levels of activity and health, and in the low-income countries it was 105 percent.
- For both groups of countries, adult literacy has climbed past the 50 percent mark since 1980.

More immediate—though less comprehensive—than the hard data of human development indicators are the first-hand observations of those who have visited these countries. One of the best-qualified and most perceptive of such observers is Richard Critchfield, a journalist who has vividly recounted the microcosmic dimensions of structural change in his book *Villages*, a chronicle of personal visits over a period of nearly a dozen years to the rural areas of Africa, Asia, and Latin America. What Critchfield has seen in the longer perspective of his return trips is neither instant triumph nor sudden tragedy, but rather the slow steady increase of output through the application of technology and dedicated effort, and the use of the greater value of that output to apply still more technology and raise still higher the output. "It hasn't got much zing," he has written, "but the biggest story of the late twentieth century could well be the sum of countless small decisions and actions by little nobodies out there in their villages."

No country continually moves upward. All fall back at times, some stay back for a long time; and a few have yet to begin to move at all. For some years to come the gap in GNP per capita between the richest and the poorest will continue to widen, in part because the poorest grow most slowly, and in part because in the poorest population is still growing at high rates while in the richest it is slowing. But in all developing nations the structural change from preindustrial to industrial is underway. After years of being principally the suppliers of raw materials to the developed nations, the developing nations are increasingly becoming industrial producers for the markets of the developed, and for their own markets as well. In the process they are also becoming larger customers for the high-technology products and the services of the advanced industrial countries. Because of the economic growth inherent in this structural change, the gap between richest and poorest eventually will begin to close, and even the poorest will be en route to solving their economic problem, as Keynes prophesied.

The precursor to the eventual closing of the gap is already visible. In nineteen of the twenty years from 1965 to 1985, rates of growth of gross domestic product in the developing nations have exceeded those in the developed nations. This has occurred, as has been argued thus far, because the developing nations—advancing in their industrial transitions—are growing faster. But just as important, it also has occurred because the developed nations—now becoming postindustrial—are growing more slowly.

POSTINDUSTRIALIZATION

It is very difficult to increase the productivity of a string quartet in live performance. The number of performers cannot be reduced, they cannot play more than one piece at the same time, and while they conceivably could increase the speed of their performance, the result would hardly please their audience.

A string quartet playing for a live audience is a service-sector economic activity; in this case a service directly to consumers, the listeners. No lasting product is created, and when the performance ends the service is completed. While there may be other economic activities associated with the performance—such as transporting the audience to the hall and lighting the environs—these are of a one-time nature; no further ongoing economic activity is stimulated by the service.

In the United States and other advanced developed nations which have passed the peak of their industrial stages, services are the major economic activities and services directly to consumers are their fastest-growing component. Since productivity increases are smallest, frequently nonexistent, in many services directly to consumers, they exert a dampening effect on economic growth rates in the countries in which they are increasing. Combined with other growth-dampening factors that develop in such advanced economies this means that as a country becomes more postindustrial it experiences a long-term structural change toward progressively slower average annual rates of growth.

Nevertheless, a country at such an advanced level of development most likely will have highly sophisticated services for producers and an industrial sector involved in the production of high-technology and high-value-added goods. These will offer the opportunity for continued economic growth—albeit at a rate lower than when the country was at the peak of its industrial stage—because they will be in demand not only internally, but also, and increasingly, by other industrial, middle-income, and low-income countries at various stages of their own industrial transitions. The provision of goods and services to these countries will, in turn, enhance their economic growth, and with it the lives of their citizens. In the process still more threads will be sewn in the widening and strengthening fabric of worldwide economic interdependence, itself yet another long-term structural change of great importance for the future.

As economies develop, their service activities increase.
There is no precisely delineated boundary between a country's industrial and postindustrial stages, but as in the case of the transition from preindustrial to industrial, the movement into the postindustrial stage can be seen in the shifting percentages of employment and product attributable to different kinds of economic activities. The structural change from preindustrial to industrial is seen when the percentage of product and employment in manufacturing and construction exceeds that in agriculture and other extractive activities and the gap between the two continues to grow. In a similar way, the movement into postindustrial can be discerned when the percentages of production and workforce attributable to service activities grow, while those attributable to industrial activities decline, steadily widening the gap between the two.

Service activities are of several kinds:

- Services to producers to facilitate the manufacture of goods and the provision of other services, like public utilities, transportation, communications, wholesale and retail trade, financial services, legal services, engineering, management consulting, advertising, etc.

- Services directly to consumers, including many services to producers, such as public utilities, transportation, communications, etc., plus a number mostly meant for consumers, such as education, health, tourism, restaurants, recreation activities, entertainment, personal services, etc.
- Services to society at large, such as different levels of government and their various activities, including national defense, law enforcement, social services, etc.

The characteristic pattern of the evolution of these services is for their increase (especially in terms of numbers employed) to coincide in the beginning with the growth of goods production. In time, as a country's industrial transition matures, its service activities grow more rapidly, exceeding the pace of growth of manufacturing and construction. Eventually, the growth of these industrial activities as a percentage of the country's total economic activity stops altogether and begins a permanent decline, signifying the onset of its postindustrial stage. In the United States, as shown in figures 3.2 and 3.3, the percentage of goods production increased fairly steadily from the turn of the century, and for most of the time service activity increased with it. Then, following the mid-1950s, when manufacturing and contract construction peaked as a percentage of both employment and national income, services continued to climb. Today, in the mid-1980s, more than 70 percent of the American workforce is employed in service activities, accounting for a similar portion of U.S. national income.

Within this general evolution there is a further distinct pattern of development of the different kinds of service sector activities. During the period when a country's manufacturing and construction activities are growing rapidly, services to producers also grow rapidly. Then as industrial activity matures, services to consumers—both those which are also for producers and those mostly for consumers—grow more rapidly and become a larger portion of employment and product, as do services for society at large. Thus in the United States in the last quarter-century:

- Transportation as a percentage of gross national product and as an employer has actually fallen (at the same

time the percentage of pleasure versus business travel within this sector has risen).
- Wholesale and retail trade have increased only slightly.
- Financial services (especially those related to real estate) have grown somewhat faster.
- Direct consumer services (notably for health care, tourism, and entertainment) and government have grown fastest of all.

In fact, in economies rapidly becoming postindustrial, services of all kinds are playing such a large and growing role that the distinction between goods and services is becoming less clear. Computers are manufactured goods, but it is preeminently a service (information) they provide, and their most important component, which will grow more so in the future, is their software (good or service?). Likewise, a vending machine (a manufactured good) is designed exclusively to provide a service (retailing), and exercise studios (providing a service) usually require equipment and physical premises, often built exclusively for their purposes.

In time the service component (especially the use of information for design and fabrication) of all goods production will be so large and the use of manufactured goods as an adjunct to many services so pervasive that the distinction between the two will be both impossible and meaningless. In the future, as more of the world's economies become postindustrial, we can expect the classification of all economic activities to be—like services—increasingly according to the ends they serve: for producers, for consumers, and for society at large. In the meantime, however, the distinction between goods and services can still be seen, and it serves a useful purpose, for it helps us understand better the likely future growth rates of all nations—preindustrial, industrial, and postindustrial.

Services contribute less to economic growth than goods.
When men can be replaced by machines, output and productivity usually can be increased. Because of this the use of automation in both extractive and manufacturing industries results in faster and more efficient production. The same is true of service industries where machines can substitute for or supplement human labor. In transportation, communications, financial services, and many forms of

personal services (for example, laundry and dry cleaning), the use of new-technology machinery yields gains in productivity.

However, the limitations on such gains are greater in service sector activities than in goods producing. The provision of a service is more often an ongoing activity, while that of a product is usually one-time. Human intervention in the service activity is thus more frequent and for longer periods. Replacement of men by machines is therefore restricted, and because relations between persons can never be made as efficient as relations between machines, productivity is inherently limited. In addition, as students of productivity often point out, with services the knowledge and ability of the recipient are also factors in determining how effectively those services are provided (for instance, how well can the customer use the automatic teller machine or the patient describe his symptoms to the doctor?).

Furthermore, because most services are perishable and cannot be stored, their provision can never be made as efficient as that of goods. An empty seat on an airliner or in a restaurant during an off-peak period cannot be stored for later use during peak demand. If not used, its value is entirely lost. But with storable products those not sold remain available for disposal later, and if finally they must be sold at a discount—or even for scrap—some of their value will be recovered.

These limitations affect the provision of all services, but their influence is greater in services for consumers. Service to a consumer directly is the most labor-intensive and involves the greatest amount of human contact; hence it has the narrowest range of potential productivity increase. It is also a type of service that has less "ripple" effect in the economy. While services to producers enable them to perform better their producer functions and thus to stimulate further economic activity in a society, many services to consumers end with the consumers, producing little or no further economic effect. In addition, wages to those providing services to consumers are usually less than those doing the same for producers. Many women (who still earn less than men in most cases) and low-paid part-time workers are used, and many of the jobs are the poorest-paying in society, such as attendants in nursing homes, maids in hotels, and employees in fast-food restaurants. Thus they make much less contribution to a country's overall economic activity.

Other characteristics of postindustrial-type societies also contribute to slowing rates of economic growth. Many of these characteristics derive from the higher levels of prosperity and well-being achieved in the course of industrialization. Such higher levels encourage the preservation and protection of what one has earned and accumulated, and discourage bold ventures and risktaking. They also prompt regulatory activity to reduce hazards and ensure greater safety, spurred still further by the consequences of new technologies. In addition, affluence encourages current consumption, which means less willingness to sacrifice and save to improve future productive capacity. Accompanying this is a greater reluctance to be discomfited and uprooted and a larger preoccupation with self and direct satisfaction. Convenience becomes more important than growth, and increasing attention is paid not only to the quantity but also the quality of leisure activities.

Prosperity also means less need and less desire for children; and the improving technology of family planning and birth control provides the means to make such choices. The result is a lower birth rate, slower population growth, and eventually fewer net entrants into the labor market, reducing one of the two major components (the other being productivity) of long-run real economic growth. Higher wages in advanced industrial nations can also mean less manufacturing for them (unless they purposefully seek to raise productivity by replacing labor with machines) and more for less advanced middle-income countries; and less manufacturing becomes to some extent a self-reinforcing tendency, for as manufacturing grows more slowly it both absorbs and generates less new technology, thus slowing its growth still further. In addition, maturing industries—especially as they automate—tend to promote and retain more supervisory personnel, whose contribution to productivity is usually less than that of factory-floor personnel.

Finally, since prosperity means that there is more available for more to share, it frequently leads to public policy programs that seek to redistribute a portion of the society's greater wealth to its less fortunate. These programs can have two growth-slowing consequences: They can mean an increase in government personnel needed to carry out the redistribution, thus enlarging a service activity that contributes little to economic growth; and, designed with little attention to changing conditions, such programs can mean entitling growing numbers for lengthening periods to benefits whose costs may eventually undermine the economic growth that prompted their creation in the first place.

There is, therefore, a complex skein of factors at work in the passage from industrial to postindustrial that together amount to a long-term structural change constraining the future economic growth of nations making the passage. Yet in the course of their transition—from the emergence from preindustrial status to the movement into postindustrial—these nations have grown considerably, raising the incomes of most of their people and enabling them to enjoy levels of well-being never before achieved in human history. Their progress, measured to date in purely quantitative monetary terms of gross national product and income levels, has thus produced a change that is qualitative in nature; and this suggests the need for new measures of achievement appropriate to the structural change that has occurred.

Thus, while it is true that the 1969 Coal Mining Safety Act in the United States did contribute to a decline in mining productivity measured in purely monetary terms, it also improved the health of the miners, which in time can be expected to mean longer productive lives with less time lost to accidents and illness. Furthermore, it also represents a sharing by the miners in the greater attention to health, comfort, and safety that is one of the hallmarks of a society reaching its postindustrial plateau.

In the same way how might we measure the contribution to society of a modern pharmaceutical company? In commonplace terms of costs of materials, overhead, capital, and labor versus selling price of products, its revenues and earnings can be calculated and from this some quantitative indication of its contribution to the growth of the nation's economy can be made. But its drugs do more. If effective, they can cure disease, ease suffering, and lengthen lives—all obvious pluses to national well-being. Yet if in the course of making its sophisticated products the pharmaceutical company also dumps toxic wastes into local streams, it can destroy wildlife, reduce recreational opportunities, and even cause disease—all obvious minuses.

In a service-activity-dominated economy the problems of productivity measurement do become more complex. The contribution of many services to producers can be measured fairly easily in quantitative terms, as for example in transportation, communications, and financial services; but for others, like architecture, basic research, or advertising, for example, traditional quantitative measures seem less useful. For the growing area of services to consumers the problem is more difficult still. How do we measure the effectiveness of legal services? (No less an authority than the Chief Justice of the United States has asserted that much of their effect may indeed be negative.) To what extent is reduction of social unrest a benefit derived from the provision of welfare services? And how do we calculate the real productivity of entertainers?

As we become more postindustrial, secure in the acquisition of most of our "needs" and more in pursuit of our "wants," we use more services and pay increasing attention to the quality of the intangibles they provide; and so, to supplement the quantitative measures of productivity that sufficed for the earlier industrial era, we need to devise and use new measures to chart our progress in the new postindustrial era.

The United States is getting richer more slowly.
In a ranking of 143 countries of the world according to their average annual rates of economic growth for the period 1971 to 1980, published by the U.S. Department of State, the United States—with a rate of 2.9 percent—stands ninety-ninth. To many this statistic may seem startling, and to some, perhaps, it is an indication of poor and declining performance. Yet, although the U.S. growth rate has declined from its peak years in the two decades following World War II, it is still positive and growing—hardly a record of poor performance. It is closer to the truth to say that the United States is getting richer more slowly while two-thirds of the rest of the countries of the world are getting richer more rapidly.

This is a simple reflection of the fact that the United States is quickly becoming a postindustrial nation with an economy that is service-activity-dominated and thus growing less rapidly. This long-term structural change is reflected in the growth rates of the different sectors of the American economy during the past twenty years. These show that the shrinking industrial sector—as expected—was an important cause of the slowing of America's average annual rate of growth from the decade of the sixties to the decade of the seventies. For the first period the average annual rate of growth of production of the industrial sector was 4.6 percent; during the second period it fell to 1.9 percent. But the *enlarging* service sector also added less, declining from an annual average rate of growth of production of 4.4 percent to one of 3.2 percent from one period to the next.

But slow growth is not no growth. The structural change occurring in the American economy—and in other industrial market economies—means that in these countries growth in the future will come more from improved operations and other kinds of activities than from the basic manufacturing and construction industries that moved it along so rapidly in the peak years of their industrial eras.

Some of the activities of the future still will be manufacturing. Although the newly industrializing countries are moving quickly into the "smokestack" industries dominated in the past by the United States and other now-advanced industrial nations, there is still a role for the latter—if they know how to play it. Steel, for example, has been written off by many as a viable profit-making industry for the United States, and all of the major integrated companies have closed plants, reduced capacity, and laid off workers in recent years. But a combination of state-of-the-art equipment, new technology, and carefully selected product lines can mean a profitable operation, as mini-mills and specialty steelmakers such as Lunens, Allegheny Ludlum, and the Nucor Corporation are showing.

Other aspects of improved operations are just as vital. The most important probably involve the in-house service functions where productivity is hardest to measure and personnel often hardest to cut. These include such traditional management roles as control of finances, marketing, and personnel, areas often overlooked in the rush to modernize operations on the factory floor. That attention to all such aspects can prove profitable, even in an old-line industry inundated by imports, is illustrated by the success of the Brown Group, which is still earning money manufacturing Buster Brown shoes.

In addition to improving the operations of their traditional industries, the United States and other industrial nations are uniquely positioned to play the leadership role in a host of new industries. These include the large number that fall under the rubric of high-tech, such as data processing, communications, optics, biotechnology, and pharmaceuticals. But they also include a whole series of industries whose growth lies mainly in the future because they will serve needs and markets that are still to mature. Among these are recycling, pollution control, alternative energy sources, new types of materials, manufactured food, and the particular needs of certain groups—such as the elderly—whose presence will loom much larger in years to come, both in numbers and in buying power.

Finally, there is the whole sector of activity that is growing fastest in the United States and other advanced industrial countries—the services. Those that contribute most to growth are services to producers, and here the United States has a large and still growing advantage. Most important are the information and knowledge services, since these are essential to the development and appropriate use of technology that can increase productivity and contribute to growth. Particularly significant will be the large and still infant field of computer software. Throughout the development of information technology the capabilities of hardware have outstripped the means to utilize them fully. Closing that gap will be a growth industry for years to come.

In a society whose incomes are still growing and whose citizens are accumulating more and more assets, financial services of all kinds (accounting, investment, insurance, real estate financing) will continue to grow rapidly. So, too, will services relating to the increased priority being given to health, comfort, and safety, including especially those involved in regulatory activity (lawyers and technicians) and medical care (practitioners and institutional staff personnel), this last now accounting for over 10 percent of U.S. gross national product, double the percentage of twenty years ago. With more leisure time and more disposable income, consumers will also increase their demand for travel and entertainment services. Tourism, which grew steadily during both recent recessions (1974–75 and 1981–82), will continue to boom.

All of the above—traditional industries, new industries, and services—will contribute to further economic growth for the United States. But because of the structural change that is moving America into its postindustrial stage, that growth will be at slowing rather than rising average annual rates.

Part of the reason will be the slower growth of the nation's labor force. It is now increasing at an annual rate of slightly over 1 percent, and though that rate will fluctuate as a result of successive baby booms and subsequent "echoes" of these booms, it will continue to fall as the nation's population growth rate falls, reaching zero in the early decades of the twenty-first century.

Even more important to slowing economic growth will be the continuation of the trend to lower rates of productivity growth due to the structural change of the American economy to service-activity dominance, and especially to the increasing role of less growth-producing consumer services. Overall, in the decades to come, total productivity in the U.S. economy is likely to grow at an average annual rate that will be falling from slightly over 2 percent to slightly under 1 percent. This will mean the real rate of economic growth will be higher only by the also falling percent by which the labor force continues to grow, in other words a total average annual rate of economic growth declining from 3 percent. There will, of course, be fluctuations, and these will be important when they occur, as when productivity rises at the onset of a recovery and declines at the crest of the upturn. But overall the long-term change will continue to be one of gradually slowing economic growth.

However, in the structural change of this slower growth environment there will be some important new benefits:

- Information, the transforming resource of postindustrial economies, is not only steadily falling in cost but is also less subject to the price fluctuations and possible shortfalls of sources of energy, the transforming resource of the passing industrial era.
- The demand for services tends to be steadier than that for goods, hence service sector employment falls less during recessions (as seen during the recent 1981–82 downturn), and thus fluctuations in business cycles are likely to be less severe as the U.S. economy becomes more postindustrial.
- Because service sector employees usually work in facilities that are smaller and have lower concentrations of labor than those of manufacturing establishments, they are less able to press for higher wages. As a result, the pace of inflation should be slowed somewhat.

Services also constitute a major portion of U.S. exports, which are themselves a large and growing portion of total American production. In 1972, exports accounted for only 6.5 percent of U.S. gross national product. Ten years later the percentage had risen to 11.5, with total two-way trade constituting 20 percent of GNP. Services have been a steadily growing part of this trade, and by growing three times as fast as trade in goods in the 1970s they allowed the United States to maintain a surplus in its current account balance for most of the decade. While the cyclical climb of the dollar against foreign currencies during the mid-1980s increased imports and turned this surplus into a deficit, it still did not slow the growth of services which continued to rise as a percent of total U.S. exports.

But it is more than just a growing trade in services that is linking the future of the American economy with the economies of its neighbors. Among the nations of the world there is an increasing exchange of merchandise, credit, investment capital, and licensing and royalty arrangements which more and more is tying the growth of any one nation to the growth of all.

Most of the rest of the world is getting rich more rapidly.
For years, since the first voyages of the first traders, the common wisdom has been to think of the "international economy" as merely the cumulative sum of the individual actions and exchanges of the world's nations. But in our time a new wisdom is emerging, one that recognizes that a structural change is occurring, that the national economies are becoming the parts of a larger whole, a world economy which increasingly influences their decisions and affects their fates. "It simply has not sunk in how rapidly the world has changed," writes Albert Bressand, deputy director of the Institut Français des Relations Internationales. "We confuse stagnant growth with 'no change' scenarios," he continues, speaking especially of the slower-growth 1970s, "when in fact the level of interdependence between countries may never have increased faster and the underlying structure of power changed more deeply."

Like all emerging economies, the evolution of the international economy can be seen especially in the development of a division of labor among its component parts. Increasingly more and more countries are making deliberate choices to pursue activities most appropriate to their particular levels of development, physical endowments, and intellectual resources. The Japanese have shown the way. Having cornered a considerable segment of the world market for consumer electronics and small efficient automobiles, they are now focusing on communications gear, advanced computer technology, robotics, and biotechnology. Others are following suit. France is moving ahead in nuclear power, West Germany leads in chemicals, Israel is high in pharmaceuticals, and the Scandinavian nations offer the state-of-the-art in many types of high-technology machinery, telecommunications, and applied microbiology.

The developing nations are following the same course, moving into heavy manufacturing (South Korea, Brazil, India), and light manufacturing and financial services (Singapore, Hong Kong, Malaysia), making their choices on the basis of both capabilities and market opportunities. Evidence of their progress is seen in the fact that in 1981, for the first time, the value of the manufacturing exports of the developing countries exceeded that of their exports of primary products (excluding petroleum).

Further indication of the growing division of labor in the international economy is the recognition by manufacturers that parts of their products can be built and assembled more cheaply in other nations than at home. This has led to a dramatic increase in what Peter Drucker calls "production sharing," literally the farming out of different parts of a product for manufacture in other countries, usually to take advantage of more abundant—and therefore cheaper—sources of labor. Drucker cites examples, like leather goods, where the design of a product and the management of its manufacture originate in a developed country—with the requisite knowledge and skills—while its labor-intensive manufacture takes place in a developing country which has an abundant supply of workers but not yet the infrastructure to develop its own integrated industries.

Even more important in the future will be the production sharing that takes place because different countries have the technology, skills, materials, and available capital to most efficiently produce the best version of a particular part or whole product. This is dramatically seen today in the automobile industry. The Ford Motor Company has parts for its Escort model made in England, Northern Ireland, France,

Belgium, Spain, and West Germany, as well as in the United States; and General Motors and Chrysler, tacitly admitting they cannot at present profitably produce low-cost small cars, have created joint ventures with Japanese companies (Toyota and Mitsubishi) to use their technology, equipment, and management to produce Japanese-designed subcompacts in U.S. plants. Other examples abound, in the auto industry and elsewhere:

- American Motors—already in partnership with France's Renault—plans to produce jeeps in Peking.
- Boeing is having parts of the fuselage and wings of its new 767 jetliner manufactured by Japanese companies.
- Matsushita, the world's largest electronics producer, expects that by the end of 1987 25 percent of everything it sells worldwide will be made outside of Japan.
- In the harbor of New York, a French company from Reims, outside of Paris, had the contract to mold copper sheets for the torch and flame of the Statue of Liberty, refurbished for its centennial in 1986.

These and numerous other ventures are part of a rise in world trade that has been increasing faster than world output. In the thirty-five years from 1950 to 1985, trade among the world's nations grew nearly 50 percent more than their combined production. For most of this period, trade among the developed nations grew faster than trade between them and the developing nations and among the developing nations. But in the mid-1970s this pattern began to change. Since then—excepting for cyclical downturns—although trade among the developed has continued to grow, trade between them and the developing nations and among the developing nations has grown faster. This pattern can be expected to continue. As nations develop they are more able and more likely to engage in foreign trade. Furthermore, because the developing nations as a group will grow faster than the already developed industrial countries, then so, too, will their trade, steadily increasing the flow of goods and services among more and more nations.

Since development and trade require funds, along with this structural change in the amount and direction of trade there has been an equivalent structural change in the flow of credit and investment capital and the institutions providing both. The main feature of this change has been an enormous expansion of private lending, especially to middle-income nations (most loans to the low-income nations still come from official sources), a situation that not only has increased the dependency of borrowers on lenders but also has increased the dependency of lenders on the arrangements they have created and spurred their cooperative efforts to maintain them. The debt of all developing nations has risen from just under $100 billion in 1973 to just over $900 billion at the beginning of 1985, and even though very few new large loans have been made in the last several years, emergency credits and debt-restructuring plans alone will soon lift the total over $1 trillion—over 70 percent of it owed to private sources, twice the share they held in the early 1970s.

The increased flow of funds has also changed the roles of some players and brought new ones onto the stage. The United States, for the first time since 1914, has itself become a debtor nation, joining the ranks of the developing countries. With foreigners lending and investing more and more money in the United States—attracted by high interest rates and opportunities that look relatively secure—their holdings have exceeded those of Americans abroad. On the other hand, China has quite suddenly emerged as an important and sophisticated participant in international financial circles, using exports and its new industrialization policy to generate foreign exchange reserves growing at an annual rate of over $4 billion and at the beginning of 1985 totaling over $21 billion.

Throughout the world, new financial links are being created, often between unlikely partners, and far fewer are being broken.

- In December 1984 the European Economic Community floated a bond issue in the United States denominated in a mix of currencies called the European Currency Unit, the first public debt issue in America in a currency other than dollars.
- During all of 1984, American corporations raised over $180 billion in bonds in European markets while the Japanese invested nearly $50 billion in the United States, much of it in Treasury bonds.

- Net foreign purchases of U.S. Government bonds and notes are projected to rise from $7 billion in 1981 to $72 billion in 1987 while purchases of U.S. equities will increase from $5.8 billion to $30 billion in the same period.
- Middle Easterners are buying shares in American brokerage houses; U.S. mortgage securities are being marketed in Asia; and mutual funds that package foreign stocks and bonds are proliferating.

For centuries, production and consumption, two of mankind's three major economic activities, have occurred principally within the boundaries of individual nations. In our time, because of the rapid internationalization of the third major activity, the exchange function that links the other two, the locus of all economic activity is shifting—from within boundaries to across them.

This shift will accelerate the growth of the developing nations, and because it will also hasten the transition to postindustrial status of the advanced industrial nations, it will continue to slow their growth. To the end of the century the developing nations should continue to grow at an average annual rate of between 5 and 6 percent. The middle-income countries (especially those in Asia) will grow faster, while growth in the lower-income countries (principally those in Africa) will be slower; but in time (into the twenty-first century), growth in some of the middle-income countries will slow—as they begin to become postindustrial—while more of the low-income countries will grow more rapidly. The industrial countries as a group will grow more slowly—at an average annual rate of between 3 and 4 percent during the next decade and a half, and slower still in the twenty-first century—but though they will decline in economic strength relative to the developing nations, they still will be the dominant nations in a world steadily growing wealthier for all of its people.

Two further structural changes of great importance follow from this discussion of change in the rate and timing of the economic growth of the countries of the world.

One is simply that the era of the rise and fall of nations, empires, and civilizations has passed. It is now part of history. Growing economic interdependence—bound still tighter by new lines of communications and mutual obligations—means that in the future we will think and talk and act increasingly about the rising and falling of the whole world rather than its individual parts. It also means that it will be more and more difficult for nations to employ economic means in pursuit of political ends, for in so doing—as the United States discovered in attempting a grain embargo against the Soviet Union—they will damage what they too value and still will not be assured of achieving what they desire. It is a very long step from such economic self-restraint to similarly motivated military self-restraint; but the rationale is the same, and the realization of the former can be the most important lesson in teaching the latter.

The other structural change is that for some time to come economic growth worldwide will continue. There certainly will be spurts and relapses, economic upturns and downturns; but there seems no denying that, barring major nuclear war or ecological catastrophe (the only foreseeable events that really could imperil mankind's survival agenda), the total world product will grow larger. Since studies of economic development show that strongly correlated with it is better distribution of income, it can be assumed that a growing world will provide a larger pool of goods and services that more will share. With such a change it is likely that ideologies born in an era of less equitable distribution of a smaller total product—and thus calling for its allocation by central command—will appear more anachronistic and finally lose their appeal.

Thus, more interdependence and more product hold out more hope for the future. That hope grows even larger when we consider another complementary long-term structural change, probably the most important in the history of the planet—the slowing of the rate of worldwide population growth.

POPULATION

The population "bomb" has fizzled. Sometime in the early 1960s the world population growth rate—which had been steadily increasing since the mid-eighteenth century—reached its peak and began to slow. Since then the rate of growth has continued to decline. In about ten years the total number of people added to the world's population each year (about eighty million in 1985) will begin to decline. Eventually, in another hundred years, or even earlier, the population of the world is likely to stop increasing altogether, perhaps to stabilize and fluctuate around a total of approximately ten billion or, more likely, to decline in absolute numbers.

While the rate of population growth has been slowing, the length of human life has continued to increase. The average life expectancy worldwide of a person born in mid-1985 is calculated to be sixty-two years, a remarkable increase of seven years over what it was just a decade before. And with lengthened life—thanks to advances in public health and medicine—has come an increase in the number of years a person can expect to be a healthy, fully participating member of society.

Both the rate of population growth and the length of life expectancy vary greatly around the globe. In the advanced industrial countries the rate is very low and falling and life is long and its number of years is increasing, while in the poorest the rate is still very high and life expectancy is still very short. But in more and more countries growth rates are slowing and life expectancies are lengthening, improving the human condition for steadily increasing numbers. Taken together, these two measures of population constitute a structural change of immense importance. The turnover of the population growth rate from its previous exponential climb means that the answer to the question of whether the world will have sufficient resources for its future numbers can be changed from a certain "no" to a likely "yes"; the lengthening of life expectancy means that long-established patterns concerning the provision and consumption of society's goods and services will be fundamentally altered; and the future direction of both measures is likely to give new meaning to the two stages of life at which human existence has always seemed most fragile and most vulnerable—childhood and old age.

Rates of population growth are slowing.
As figure 3.4 shows, the birthrate per thousand American white women fifteen to forty-four years old (the category of women for which the longest U.S. time series exists) has fallen from nearly 280 in 1800 to less than 63 in 1983. This means that the number of children a woman in this category could expect to have during her lifetime has dropped from

around seven at the beginning of the nineteenth century to less than two today. Had some farseeing public servants back in 1800 viewed with alarm the continuation of the high fertility at that time and initiated a program to bring it down, their successors today could count it a job well done. But no such program was begun in 1800 or thereafter. In fact, only in recent times has there been a strong movement to deal with the population growth "problem" in the United States, ironically when it is no longer really a problem.

Economic development reduces death rates. This occurs because as countries develop they are able to improve food distribution, institute public health measures, and increase medical care. But in the early years of development, birthrates still remain fairly high, and with falling death rates this means population increases rapidly.

FIG. 3.4. Birth Rate for White U.S. Women, 15–44 Years Old, 1800–1983.

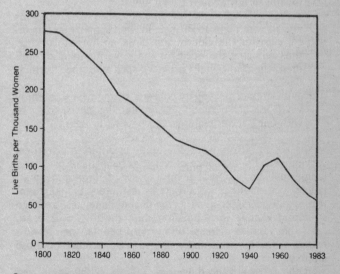

Sources: U.S. Bureau of the Census, *Historical Statistics of the United States, Colonial Times to 1970*, Vol. I (Wash., DC, 1976), p. 49 and *Statistical Abstract of the U.S.: 1986* (Wash., DC, 1985), p. 57.

However, economic development also inevitably brings a second result. In time, for a number of important irreversible reasons, birthrates also begin to slow:

- Families which had always had large numbers of children because so many perished at birth or during childhood see more surviving and thus the need for fewer to be born.
- Many people move from villages and small towns to cities where resources are limited and there is less space for large families.
- Access to education means that girls stay in school longer, enter the labor market, seek careers, stay single, or marry later—having fewer children or none at all.
- Literacy increases accessibility to information about family planning; and a more developed country has the means to disseminate both advice and equipment for practicing birth control.
- Advanced societies develop both public policy programs and private plans to provide income support and medical care for the elderly and those no longer working, thus reducing the need for the large numbers of children who traditionally provided such assistance for their parents.
- With greater prosperity comes a strong desire to enjoy what one has earned and an enlarging legacy to share with one's fewer children and pass on to them.

The above factors work differently in different countries, varying with the influence of religious beliefs and practices, long-established cultural habits, levels of development attained, and public policy programs instituted. But all countries experiencing economic growth simultaneously undergo structural change in population, first toward lower death rates that tend to increase numbers of people, then toward falling birthrates which slow the rate of increase of those numbers.

In the most advanced nations, falling fertility rates and birthrates appear to move steadily toward—and in some cases even below—replacement-level rates. If maintained at replacement level, such rates will mean stabilized populations for those nations; if they fall even further, the result will be an absolute decline in population.

In the industrial market economies the total fertility rate (the number of children each woman would have during her lifetime, if, at each year of age, she experienced the birth-rates occurring in the specific year) for 1983 was 1.7, and for Eastern European nonmarket economies it was 2.3. Since replacement-level fertility is usually calculated at between 2.1 and 2.5 (depending on mortality rates, which are higher in Eastern European countries than in other industrial nations), it is clear that the continuation of these rates or their further lowering—which appears likely—will mean that the populations of these countries will soon stop growing and, unless successful *pro*-natality programs are adopted, will actually decline.

Every Eastern and Western European country (except Albania and Ireland), according to the World Fertility Survey (a multinational endeavor begun in 1972 and recognized as the largest social science research project ever launched), is below, at, or close to replacement-level fertility. In fact, several—Denmark, Sweden, Belgium, Italy, and Hungary—have zero annual rates of natural increase (i.e., crude birth-rates equal crude death rates), and one—West Germany—has a negative rate. Projecting this continuing structural change, *Euroforum*, the journal of the Commission of the European Communities, calculated in 1980 that by the year 2050 the number of inhabitants in the nine European Community Countries will have fallen from 260 to 243 million, with the most notable drop in West Germany, from 61 to 38 million.

In the United States, where women are marrying later, working more, and planning and having fewer children, the total fertility rate has also fallen below the replacement level. For 1984 the figure was 1.8. If total fertility per woman were to continue at this rate and net migration to be maintained at its current pace of approximately half a million a year, the natural increase in U.S. population would cease in about fifty years at a figure close to 310 million, 72 million more than the 1985 total of 238 million. If fertility were to continue to fall—consistent with recently expressed views of American women—then the natural increase would cease much sooner and at a lower figure.

But even if fertility were to rise, as it has done recently in a faint echo of the postwar baby boom, it is unlikely ever again to reach the 3.5 rate achieved during the decade 1954 to 1964, much less the far higher rates of earlier years in American history. The factors discussed above (economic development, urbanization, education, increased female employment, public policy programs, new attitudes and priorities, etc.) are all structural changes. Together and cumulatively they mean a slower U.S. population growth rate. There will be fluctuations, and these will affect when the peak total is reached; but it will be reached, and more than likely within the lifetimes of at least half of those Americans alive today.

In the developing nations the same factors are at work that have led to lower fertility and slowing population growth rates in the developed industrial nations. Because these factors are less advanced and because many of the developing countries have been able to move quickly to introduce programs and technologies to reduce mortality rates, the gap between these and their higher birthrates has remained wide, meaning a net growth in population that will continue for some time to come. Nonetheless, a combination of economic development and public programs, in different mixtures in different countries, is having an effect on their population growth rates.

The kind of progress associated with higher income and the public policy programs it can make possible in developing countries can be seen even in those long regarded as having the most severe population growth problems. One such country is Mexico—predominantly Catholic, long culturally biased toward big families, and with a major metropolitan center (Mexico City) literally choking on an ever growing stream of migrants from the countryside. Yet, since the institution of an intensive family-planning program in 1972 there has been considerable progress. Mexico's crude birthrate, which stood at forty-five per thousand in 1960, had fallen to thirty-three by 1984, lowering its population growth rate from 3.3 percent in the 1960s to 2.9 in the period 1973–84, a figure that by the last year of this period had fallen to 2.6 percent. Obviously, there is still much to be done (Mexico City is projected to be the most populous urban area in the world—nearly thirty million—by the year 2000), but the direction of its growth rate is down, not up—the result of economic growth and policy-making.

There also has been progress in the low-income developing countries, although this is largely due to the efforts being made in the two largest, China and India. The case of China is the most dramatic. With over a billion people, 80 percent of whom are rural and with traditional values that favor children, China has instituted a program to limit married couples to one child. Its stated objective is zero population growth, with a specific target of a peak population of 1.2 billion people. The inducements are bonuses and preferential treatment in housing, medical care, and education for the child; the penalties for exceeding the limit are docked salaries and slower promotions. Although the program is meeting some resistance, especially in rural areas, it is evidently working. In 1965 China's growth rate—the number of births minus the number of deaths—was 28.5 per thousand; by 1984, according to family planning minister Wang Wei, it had fallen to 10.8 per thousand.

In India, ever since the first administration of Prime Minister Indira Gandhi was toppled—principally over the issue of forced sterilizations—the family-planning effort has been through voluntary cooperation rather than political directive. Using education and government-provided services, India is currently aiming at the more modest goal of a two-child family. With 35 percent of its married women of childbearing age using contraception, the Indian total fertility rate for 1984 was still 4.6, reflecting an average annual population growth rate that is falling much more slowly than China's. The lower goals and slower pace of the Indian program—if maintained—will have an important result: Sometime in the twenty-first century India will replace China as the world's most populous country.

In the other low-income countries (with a total 585 million people in 1985) the population growth rate is declining more slowly, from an average annual rate of 2.7 percent during 1965–73 to 2.6 percent during 1973–84; and in one area (sub-Saharan Africa) it is still increasing, from 2.7 to 2.9 percent during the same two periods. But even here the crude birth rate is no longer rising, having leveled off at 47 per thousand from 1965–73 to 1973–84. With economic development, education, and greater female participation in the labor force, too, these nations will join the industrial and middle-income nations that have already slowed their growth rates. Even more important for many will be the introduction and wide utilization of programs for family planning, programs that will increase in impact and effectiveness as a new generation of birth control technology comes on line, including male and injected contraceptives, the replacement of steroid drugs by synthesized hormones, and sterilization without surgery.

The net result of what is occurring in both developed and developing countries is a long-term irreversible structural change that is slowing the worldwide rate of population growth. In effect mankind has turned a great corner, and it will not turn back. We must, therefore, reorient our view of the future of world population. For several decades we have been brought up to see it as the steeply rising exponential curve depicted in figure 3.5. The more realistic view is the longer-term perspective of growth rate displayed in figure 3.6. Although the second figure was first published over ten years ago, it is the exponential view that has persisted in most minds—a clear indication of the power of the familiar and the difficulty of acknowledging change.

Life expectancy is lengthening.

More readily apparent, though still not well understood, has been the increase in life expectancy. In 1850 in Massachusetts a male at age seventy could expect to live 10.2 years longer; one hundred years later a seventy-year-old male in the same state could look forward to only 9.9 more years of life, *less* life expectancy than a century earlier! Yet during the same period life expectancy at birth for a male rose from 38.3 to 66.7 years, and for a female from 40.5 to 72.1 years.

This surprising lack of increase in life expectancy at age seventy, and yet its dramatic increase at birth, can be explained by the fact that the extension of the latter from 1850 to 1950 was mostly due to reductions in infant mortality and childhood diseases in conjunction with improved environmental sanitation and better food distribution and nutrition. In the United States and other developed countries, further increases in life expectancy have come—and will continue to come—from reducing and delaying deaths from diseases that occur more commonly in the later years of life. However, in the developing countries, all of the means for lengthening life can be expected to be working concurrently—those that save the young and those that give more years to the elderly—thus accelerating the increase in life expectancy in these countries.

FIG. 3.5.   Usual View of World Population Growth.

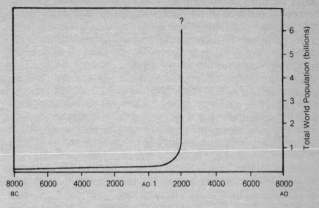

Source: Adapted from *The New York Times*. Oct. 6, 1981, sec. C, p. 1.

FIG. 3.6.   Realistic View of World Population Growth

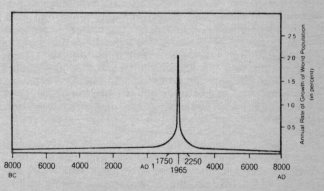

Source: Adapted from Ronald Freeman and Bernard Berelson, "The
Human Population," *Scientific American,* Sep. 1974, pp. 36–37.

An American born in 1984 can expect to live 76 years (approximately four more years for females and four less for males), a record high for the United States. What has lengthened life expectancy in the United States in recent times, and where are further increases likely to come from in the future? To answer these questions we need to look at the changing contributions of the causes of death to the total death rate. Since 1900 the U.S. death rate has fallen about 50 percent, from 1,622 per 100,000 to 863 in 1984. Most of the reduction has come from the virtual elimination of diseases that can strike at any age, not necessarily in the later years. Tuberculosis, for example, at 194 deaths per 100,000 population, was the third leading cause of death in 1900; in 1984 it accounted for less than one death per 100,000. Likewise, "enteritis and other diarrheal diseases," the fourth-highest killers in 1900, accounted for so few deaths in 1984 that they no longer appeared on the National Center for Health Statistics list of seventy-two selected causes.

What remain today as leading causes are two that occur principally in the later years of life, major cardiovascular diseases and cancer (which accounted for 48 and 22 percent of all deaths in the United States in 1984), and accidents (which accounted for 5 percent). Clearly, then, further increases in longevity in the United States and in most other developed nations will have to come from the reduction of deaths due to these three causes. What are the prospects?

Although cardiovascular diseases remain the leading cause of death in the United States, mortality rates from them have fallen dramatically during the last decade, dropping from an age-adjusted rate of 340.1 per 100,000 of population in 1970 to 23.3 in 1982. While these diseases are unlikely ever to be completely eliminated in the United States—in the same sense that typhoid fever has been and cancer may be—there are a number of reasons to expect continued progress in reducing their mortality rates. These include:

- Earlier and more accurate diagnosis using genetic, ultrasonic, magnetic, and other new technologies
- Improvements in prevention through better diet and more precisely prescribed physical regimens
- New therapies that lower blood pressure, stabilize abnormal heart rhythms, and clear clotted arteries

- Sophisticated surgical techniques, such as the use of ultrathin catheters and laser beams to unclog blocked arteries
- The use of human—and, increasingly, artificial—transplants to replace diseased organs and body parts, both partially and fully

Cancer as a cause of death is still increasing (it has risen from an age-adjusted rate of 129.9 per 100,000 of population in 1970 to 132.5 in 1982) largely because it is usually a disease of older people, and people are living longer. At the same time there is rapidly growing optimism that cancer finally will be conquered. Dr. Lewis Thomas, chancellor of the Memorial Sloan-Kettering Cancer Center in New York City and a prize-winning author on biological topics, has gone so far as to foresee "the end of cancer before this century is over." Recently he wrote: "I now believe it could begin to fall into place at almost any time, starting next year or even next week, depending on the intensity, quality and luck of basic research."

The reasons for this rising tide of optimism are an increasing number of developments—evolving from research spurred by the discovery of the structure of gene-bearing DNA thirty years ago—that have identified genes that appear to be involved in producing cancer and suggested the mechanisms by which they operate. It is still a long way from this basic research to effective techniques for halting or preventing the growth of cancer cells; but understanding how they are produced is a major step forward, one hardly imagined just a decade ago.

In the meantime, diagnosis and treatment of cancer are also going forward, increasing survival rates and lengthening the lives of those afflicted with the disease. For some types of cancer the turnaround has been dramatic. For example, ten years ago 80 percent of young adults with bone cancer died within three years; today 90 percent are free of the disease three years after diagnosis. For other types, such as lung cancer, the survival rates have improved only marginally. But overall, according to the American Cancer Society, three out of eight cancer patients are surviving at least five years after their cancers are diagnosed, resulting in declines in death rates in the past decade of 30 percent for patients under thirty, and 15 percent for those under fifty.

As for accidents, the third leading cause of death in the United States and the number-one cause among people from one to thirty-eight years, there is no solid evidence that their number per capita has significantly increased or decreased over time, only that they have changed in kind and may occur more often in areas of higher density; but it appears clear that *deaths* from accidents of all kinds have been reduced. At the turn of the century the death rate from accidents was 79.2 per 100,000 of population; by 1982 it had fallen to an age-adjusted rate of 36.6, over half of which were attributable to motor vehicles. Better emergency care, new surgical techniques, and faster-acting drugs have undoubtedly saved lives that would have been lost earlier, a trend that is likely to continue, though at a diminishing rate as it approaches the limit set by the numbers who succumb instantly.

Death rates from other causes will also be lowered by advances in biogenetics, which will improve preventive measures, diagnosis, and therapy, and by further progress in surgery and nongenetic therapies. Together these developments will continue to add more years to the lifespans of

FIG. 3.7.   Increasing Life Expectancy in More Developed and Less Developed Regions, Actual and Projected, 1950–2020.

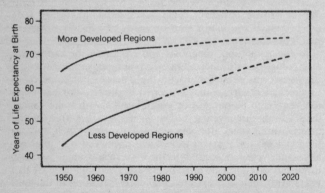

Source: United Nations, "World Population Prospects as Assessed in 1980," *Population Studies*, no. 78, 1981, pp. 82–83.

inhabitants of the United States and other developed nations. In fact, it is quite likely that an American born in the first year of the twenty-first century will be able to look forward to a life expectancy that will last to within twenty years of its end.

In developing nations, where the causes and technologies for life extension have been collapsed into a far shorter span of time than they required in the developed, progress has been more rapid and, for a time, will continue to be. From 1960 to 1983, male life expectancy in the middle-income countries increased ten years, from forty-nine to fifty-nine, and in the low-income countries it rose sixteen years, principally because of a twenty-four-year increase reported for China. In the industrial market economy countries during the same period the increase was only four years (from sixty-eight to seventy-two), and in the Eastern European nonmarket economy countries it was one year (from sixty-five to sixty-six).

Since most of the increase in the middle-income and low-income countries during these decades is attributable to dramatic reductions in infant mortality and child death rates—in conjunction with more regular food distribution and improved public health measures—further lengthening will come from reduction in mortality rates for diseases of the later years of life, as has been happening in the developed nations. As progress continues in the developing at a faster rate than the developed, the difference in life expectancy between the two will narrow, as shown in figure 3.7, until both slowly will approach together the natural limit of human life—which specialists in geriatric medicine believe to be between the tenth and eleventh decades of life—most likely by the middle of the twenty-first century.

Just as important as the lengthening of life will be the quality of the additional years added. In many of the more affluent developed nations a good deal of life extension has been little more than the prolongation of infirmity, often in long-term-care facilities designed specifically for that purpose (20 percent of Americans over sixty-five spend some part of their lives in nursing homes). However, recent research on aging has tended to deny the widely held view that certain crucial areas of human intelligence decline with advancing age, while other studies have raised the possibility of retarding the incidence of senility and even reversing it when it does occur. These reports, as well as increasing anecdotal evidence of vigorous healthy lives of people in their seventies, eighties, and even nineties, suggest that the additional years added by lengthening life will be more active for more people; and since life expectancy itself will be a less important measure as it finally begins to level off near its outside limit, we should begin to think about supplementing it with a new, more useful measure, namely "active life" expectancy.

> *Slowing population growth and longer lives indicate dramatic changes ahead in numbers of people, dependency ratios, and family relationships.*

It is ironic, but true, that Europe—which inaugurated the Industrial Revolution and with it higher per capita income, lower mortality rates, and lengthening life expectancy—likely will have as its ultimate reward the diminution, perhaps even the disappearance, of its numbers. Yet this is perfectly possible if the current low fertility rates in most European countries continue. According to one United Nations projection, a fertility rate of 1.5 in Europe (approximately 25 percent below the replacement-level rate) would mean that by the year 2000 the population of the continent (including the entire USSR) would begin to decline, dropping below its present numbers in the second decade of the twenty-first century and continuing to fall.

The converse of Europe's (and North America's) likely eventual population decline is the continued increase in numbers in most of the world's developing nations, where fertility rates are still high and average age is low (meaning a larger number of future births). According to the Population Reference Bureau, in mid-1985, 24 percent of the world's then 4.8 billion people were inhabitants of more developed countries and 76 percent were in the less developed. The bureau projects that because of lower fertility in the more developed and higher in the less developed these percentages will change to 21 and 79 in 2000 and 17 and 83 by 2020.

Such an increase in the developing countries will at first constitute a large burden for many of them, straining their capacity to meet both the basic needs and the increasing expectations of their enlarging populations. This will be especially true if, as the World Bank's figures show, urban

populations continue to increase in the lowest-income nations, those least able to bear the pressure of their growth.

Eventually, however—and at different rates and not necessarily everywhere—the burden is likely to become a bless-
ing, for people are, finally, a country's most valuable resource.
The change will occur because of the slowing of urban
growth that comes with higher income and the shift in
dependency ratios that occurs when fertility rates (at whatever level) begin to fall. Data on development do suggest
that with higher income there is a slowing in the rate of
growth of urban populations. While urban populations in
the low-income nations did grow at higher rates from the
1960s to the period 1970–82, rates of growth fell in the
middle-income nations and still more in those middle-income
nations that were considered *upper*-middle-income.

Changes in dependency ratios (the combined population
under fifteen and over sixty-four as a percentage of the
population between those ages) will also help. Less developed nations typically have very high dependency ratios
because of the large number of people under fifteen in their
populations. As their fertility rates fall the first effect will be
in the youngest ages, whose numbers will increase more
slowly. By then the earlier larger youthful generations will
be at nondependent producing ages, but not yet in their
older and again dependent years. Thus, for a time—a time
when it will prove most useful—many developing countries
will be able to benefit from uncharacteristically low dependency ratios before further falling mortality rates cause them
to rise again, bringing them closer to those of developed
countries. Evidence of this can be seen in past and projected
average annual growth rates of labor forces in developing
nations.

As more countries transit the stages of the passage from
preindustrial to industrial to postindustrial and experience
the lowering effect this transition has on their population
growth rates, the earth's population will continue to grow
more slowly until eventually it stops growing. In this regard,
the annual projections of the United Nations Fund for Population Activities make interesting—if sometimes curious—
reading. In 1981, for example, the fund projected that world
population would "stabilize" at 10.5 billion in 2110; two
years later it lowered the stabilization figure to 10.2 billion
and gave the date as "the end of the twenty-first century"

(presumably a decade or so earlier than its 1981 projections), and by early 1987 it was using 10.1 billion as an unpublished "working figure."

These forecasts reflect the slowing population growth that is occurring—even faster than many, including those on the fund's staff, suspect—for all of the reasons discussed above. But why will population "stabilize"? What is so magic about replacement levels of fertility that once countries reach them they will stop there? In fact, once they reach them they may find it very difficult to stop, for when fertility rates drop below replacement levels their further fall becomes self-reinforcing. If, for instance, a country's total fertility rate falls to 1.5 (as some in Europe have), this means that each woman can expect to have 1.5 births during her childbearing years. But because this rate is below the replacement level the next generation of women will be smaller, and so on, until conceivably the population of the country disappears.

It is strange indeed, at a time in history when the world's population is still rising—and when many regard its increase as the world's most serious problem—to contemplate its ultimate fall. But it may well turn out that preventing the downward spiral of population will require far more sophisticated and comprehensive public policies than slowing its upward rise. Future generations could in fact find themselves resorting to some form of the artificial parthenogenesis described by Aldous Huxley in *Brave New World*, not because they want to, but because they have to.

The composition of the population within nations also will be changed by different rates of fertility and growth. In the United States the fertility rate of minority groups (blacks, Hispanics, and Asians) is above the replacement level, while that of the majority white group is below it. The difference means that minority groups will constitute a steadily growing portion of the total population, reaching levels that could only be reversed in the very unlikely event that the majority white group moves well above its replacement-level fertility rate. Thus blacks, who constituted 11.7 percent of the population in 1980, are expected to make up 12.4 percent in 2000, while Hispanics will increase from 6.4 to 8.6 percent during the same period and, because of their faster growth rate, will overtake blacks as the largest minority group by the end of the first quarter of the next century.

Such irreversible structural changes raise important questions about the nature and distribution of public services, such as education and medical care, and influence the future course of demand for goods and services in the marketplace. This is already occurring in areas of high Hispanic immigration, such as Florida and the Southwestern United States. It will increase in these areas because Hispanics will go where others are already located, meaning that in the future parts of America will be largely minority-inhabited and growing rapidly while the rest of the country will be largely of the white majority and growing much more slowly.

In the Soviet Union a different version of this same phenomenon is occurring. There the fertility rate of the non-Russian nationalities (especially those in Central Asia) is rising so much more rapidly than that of the Great Russian that the former will soon overcome the latter in total numbers. Because this development is due entirely to fertility rates and not at all to immigration, its growth is liable to be steadier and stronger over time. It is too much to expect that anytime soon the increasing non-Russian majority could generate centrifugal forces that would weaken the hold of the Russian-dominated leadership over the USSR's various nationalities. Nevertheless, this structural change in population will require the diversion of more economic and management resources, will make it more difficult for the Soviet Union to recruit and train its large conscript army, and will require greater attention to be paid by the leadership at the center to a variety of divergent and growing interests on the periphery. The demonstrations and near riots in late 1986 in Alma Ata, the capital of Kazakhstan, are indicative of the problems likely to arise.

Even more important than ethnic composition is the combined effect of slowing population growth and lengthening life expectancy on the age composition of populations. As the population "pyramids" of figure 3.8 show, the age compositions of the more developed and less developed regions vary considerably. The pyramid for the more developed—with their longer life expectancies—has more the shape of an obelisk, its steep sides enclosing a far larger proportion of under-sixty-five adults than the less developed—with their shorter life expectancies—and its larger cap almost three times the number of those aged sixty-five and over. The wide base of the pyramid of the less developed—with their higher fertility rates—means a much larger number under

FIG. 3.8.   Approximate Age Composition of Populations of More
Developed and Less Developed Regions, 1982.

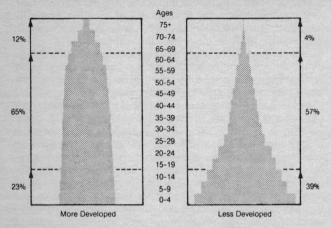

Source: Adapted from data in Population Reference Bureau, *1985
World Population Data Sheet* (Wash., DC: April, 1985.)

fifteen in these countries than in the more developed—with
their lower fertility rates.

Because population growth rates are slowing and life
expectancies are lengthening in almost all countries, there is
a long-term structural change which is making the upper
dimensions broader and the lower ones narrower in both
pyramids. Thus, in 1970 the percentages for the three age
groups (children, adult, and post-sixty-four) for the more
developed countries were 27, 63, and 10, while for the less
developed they were 42, 55, and 3. In both cases the percentages in the two older age groups had increased by 1982,
while those in the youngest had decreased. This means,
first, a steadily increasing number of persons in the age
group that contains the countries' most active and most
productive members. It also means a slow but steady shift
in dependency burdens, away from youthful members and
toward the elderly; and with this shift clearly must come new
public policies and different allocations of resources, public
and private.

Within this long-term structural change in the age composition of the human population, there are also shorter-term cyclical changes due to temporary surges in fertility rates (baby booms and their "echoes"). The effect of these surges is to create bulges in the population pyramids of the countries where they occur which, over time, pass up the pyramids, diminishing in size as they reach their apexes.

This is what is happening now in the United States and in a number of other developed nations. As the population pyramid for the United States in figure 3.9 illustrates, there was at the time it was constructed (1982) a bulge at the 15-to-29-year-old levels. This bulge represents the children born during the seven years preceding and the seven years following 1957, the peak year of the postwar baby boom. During the next decade this group will be establishing households, starting families, gaining work experience, and moving up career ladders. Its earnings and purchasing power, which will be steadily increasing during this period, will peak during the first decade of the twenty-first century. In 2016 the oldest members of this group will reach the traditional retirement age of sixty-five, and the numbers of those subsequently doing so will increase until 2023, when the total turning 65 will peak and begin to decline.

Behind this group, as figure 3.9 shows, is a trough of 14-year-olds and under, the children of the "baby bust," starting with those born in 1970 (the year the U.S. birthrate was back to its 1945 level) and centered around those born in 1976, the year of the American bicentennial and, ironically, the lowest birth rate to date in U.S. history (14 percent below the previous low of 1936, in the depths of the Great Depression). This is the group that is currently responsible for declining school enrollment rates, and also—because fewer of them will be in their teens and early twenties—a continuing decline in crime rates. As they enter the labor force, from about 1990 onward, they should also find—barring cyclical economic factors—a favorable labor market and relatively low levels of unemployment. Following them are the children of the baby boom generation, born later and fewer in number than their parents but still enough to raise enrollments in schools and colleges and to increase the demand for products ranging from toys (already occurring) to housing and furnishings (to begin a new rise twenty to twenty-five years from now).

Unknown levels of immigration will shape further this

FIG. 3.9. Percent Distribution of U.S. Population, by Age and Sex, 1982.

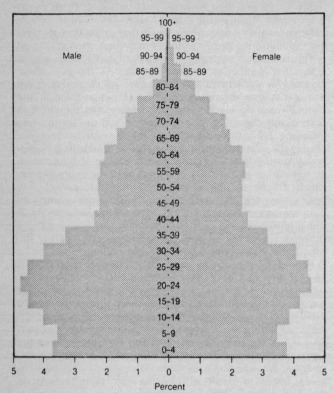

Source: U.S. Bureau of the Census, "Projections of the Population of the United States by Age, Sex and Race: 1983–2080," *Current Population Reports*, Series P-20, no. 952, 1984, p. 9.

pattern of changing age composition in the U.S. population, which also could be significantly altered by a great economic upheaval or a long costly war. But barring these events, the factors discussed earlier (more women working, later marriages, more disposable income, a desire for fewer children, and more reliable and widely available means for birth control) portend a dampening of future fluctuations in age composition in a context of steadily declining fertility rates and slowing population growth.

The consequences of these combined structural and cyclical demographic changes are clearly predictable: a larger number and proportion of Americans in the upper age groups.

- The number sixty-five and older growing only slowly until 2011 when the first "baby boomers" reach that age, will then accelerate, doubling by 2020 and nearing more than sixty-four million (over one-fifth of the total U.S. population) by 2030.
- The number eighty-five and older will grow even faster, reaching sixteen million (more than 5 percent of the population, versus 1 percent in 1982) by 2050.

But this acceleration of the growth of the elderly will *not* continue indefinitely. As population growth rates decline, bringing stable or still falling numbers of people (depending on public policy measures and other factors), and the extension of life expectancy slows as natural limits are reached, the increase of the elderly will also slow, probably eventually to fluctuate narrowly around a fairly stable percent of the total population. In anticipation of the attainment of this plateau, we should be better able to evaluate the demand and the resources required for entitlement programs for income maintenance and medical care for the elderly in the future. Thus, understanding these future changes could go a long way toward calming the fears and restraining the rhetoric of both those who claim these programs are certain to bankrupt us and those who argue they are certain to be inadequate, and instead should prompt them to adopt—well in advance—public and private programs consistent with the better-understood changes.

Fewer births (with universally low infant mortality and low childhood death rates) and longer lives (with more active years) will mean different age compositions than exist today, and with these new age compositions are likely to come new attitudes toward the family, especially toward its children and its elderly. The axis of the new "extended family" —with its fewer children and longer-living members—will shift from being mainly horizontal to being increasingly vertical, encompassing four and even five generations with fewer members in each.

In what most likely will become a nearly "perfect" contraceptive society, there will be virtually no unwanted births, and children will be born not, as in the past, because they are needed, but because they are wanted. Recognizing that they are indeed an economic drain, no longer an economic gain, will change the "value" a family seeks in having them; and one cannot help but think that such children will live happier, more satisfying adult lives if raised in an environment where they are viewed as the potential recipients of their family's welfare rather than as its future source.

Grandparents will be joined by great-grandparents and even great-great-grandparents; and longer lifespans will give generational change a larger context in which to be understood. It is possible, too, that longer life may close generation gaps as people living more years begin to see as contemporaries all of those who are one, two, and three generations beyond the formation of their own families. With so many elderly alive, the veneration some societies accord them is likely to diminish, but in its place is liable to come more participation, and this should be reason enough to look forward to the later years of life.

The implications of slower population growth and longer life expectancy also indicate an increasing opportunity and an increasing desire to exercise more control over our lives and to participate more actively and more fully in the decisions that affect them. This, too, is a long-term structural change, and it is seen especially with regard to the activity that occupies the longest and most active part of our lives— our work.

WORK

"In the sweat of thy face shalt thou eat bread, till thou return unto the ground." With these words in the Book of Genesis God expelled Adam from the Garden of Eden and condemned him to a life of labor. Throughout history, work has been regarded as man's central activity. Variously described as a punishment, a burden, an obligation, and an ennobling activity, it has been the means by which we have traditionally identified ourselves, even to our very names— Farmer, Smith, Cooper. Always work came first. It was the time away from it, our "spare time," that was left for leisure pursuits, but even the very nature and quality of these were determined by the kind of work we did and the compensation we received for it. Today, however, we are in the midst of a structural change that is altering the role of work as the central activity of our lives, a change that is affecting all who work and all who employ people, in both developed and developing nations.

This change is occurring as societies evolve through the phases of their industrial transitions. In the early part of the transition from preindustrial to industrial, work times become regularized. In manufacturing and construction activities, periods of work are scheduled and fixed, not flexible and varying as they were on the farm. Then later, as labor becomes organized and social reforms are instituted, work days and work weeks are shortened and vacations and paid holidays are increased. At the same time, wages rise above subsistence levels and reflect more closely the value added by workers' skills. Finally, as industrial development proceeds further, more economic growth occurs, per capita incomes rise, and workers themselves begin to acquire property.

The combination of more free time away from work and rising above-subsistence wages allows workers to develop new skills and acquire other interests. It also gives them the means to relocate and pursue other opportunities. Thus, increasingly, workers gain control over their work rather than have their work controlling them. But at the same time the compensation for work undergoes a further change. Other factors help to determine it, including the power of workers' organizations, the progress of the industries in which it is done, and government fiat. Less and less is it a measure of skills attained and value added. Pay no longer measures only individual performance.

In the second part of the industrial transition, from industrial to postindustrial activities, several additional developments modify still further the structural change occurring in work:

- Service sector activities increase, and because performance is harder to measure in these activities, the relationship between work and pay is further blurred.

- In the postindustrial world of advanced developed nations, where there is relative abundance, work loses some of the esteem in which it was held in an earlier time of relative scarcity when it alone created value.
- In the most advanced nations, the work of a single breadwinner is no longer the sole source of a household's income; it is supplemented with grants, entitlements, transfer payments, pensions, asset-based income, and the income of other members of the household.

The net result of this change toward greater control and reduced status is that work has become merely one of a number of elements in our lives, and no longer necessarily the one that determines the others. This does not mean that one's job is unimportant. It is still very important. But now it has to be a certain kind of job, one where there is action, where success is rewarded, where the opportunity exists to move up and to move out, to do something more interesting with more opportunity. In this sense work has become less an end and more a means. This structural change is reflected in alterations in the composition of the workforce, in the kind of activity involved in work, and in the conditions under which it is done—changes which are underway now and will develop still further in the future.

The composition of workforces is changing.
The labor forces of all the nations of the world are undergoing a complex structural change in their composition, but because the factors driving this change are all inherently limited it will be a one-time event, moving workers from a relatively stable status through a period of considerable alteration to arrive finally at another relatively stable status. The factors are:

- Slowing population growth rates
- More years in school
- Lengthening life expectancy
- Increasing female participation
- The transition from preindustrial to postindustrial

When all of the above have run their course—populations have peaked, education has been attained by most, limits of longevity and female participation have been approached, and industrial transitions have been completed—it is likely that a new workforce composition, fluctuating only narrowly around fairly stable parameters, will be attained, first in the advanced industrial countries and then finally in the world as a whole.

For the next generation at least—and possibly for the next two—it seems clear that the labor force of the world as a whole (the percentage of the population aged fifteen to sixty-four years) will grow more rapidly than the total population. This will be true for several reasons. One is simply that even though birthrates are slowing, more people still are being born, and most will live to join the labor force. But because the rate at which they are born is falling, the number of those under fifteen will increase more slowly and will be fewer than those fifteen to sixty-four. At the same time, lengthening life expectancy means more will live to the end of their normal working years (age sixty-four), though not yet so much longer as to offset the growth in numbers aged fifteen to sixty-four.

Even more important than the increase in numbers will be the growing contribution to these numbers of women as active members of the whole workforce. This phenomenon, seen now in the more industrialized countries and certain to be repeated, at varying rates of growth, in the developing nations, is the single most important structural change ever to occur in the composition of the labor force. For the industrial nations it represents what Peter Drucker has called "Unmaking the Nineteenth Century," the undoing of what one hundred years ago was one of the greatest goals and proudest achievements of social reformers: to release women from the burden of work so that they would be free to stay at home to devote themselves to family and children. Until the beginning of this century, Drucker points out, this was what was meant by "female emancipation."

The widespread employment of women—out of necessity—during World War II, and then following the rapid increase in their participation in higher education in the decades after the war (from 32 percent of all those in colleges and universities in the United States in 1950 to over 50 percent by 1980), has swiftly and permanently increased their participation in the labor force. As figure 3.10 shows, in forty-two years the percentage of women in the U.S. labor force nearly doubled, from 27.9 in 1940 to 52.9 in 1983, while for men it has actually decreased. Several factors indicate that this change in female participation is not likely to be reversed. One is that rearing children is not seen as incompatible with working; in fact, the percentage of married women in the workforce with children under eighteen (estimated to be 60 percent in 1985, up from 40 percent just fifteen years before) is higher than that for all women. Another is consistent poll data showing that women value jobs as much as family life. A third is the steady increase of women in fields traditionally dominated by men and their rise to positions of authority and leadership.

FIG. 3.10.   Labor Force Participation Rate, U.S. Men and Women 16 Years Old and Over (Except Prior to 1947, 14 and Over), 1940–1983.

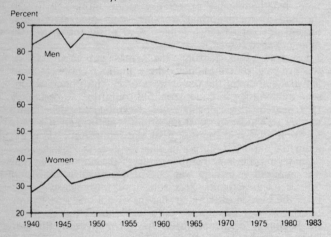

Sources: U.S. Bureau of the Census, *Historical Statistics of the United States, Colonial Times to 1970,* Vol. I (Wash., DC, 1976), pp. 131–32 and U.S. Bureau of Labor Statistics "Handbook of Labor Statistics," Bulletin 2217, Jun. 1985, pp. 18–19.

The implications of this change beyond the labor force itself are even more profound. Not only does the participation of women in work contribute importantly to lowering fertility rates (currently below replacement levels in almost all industrialized nations), but it also necessitates very important alterations in social services, including medical care, education, and child-care facilities. Equally important are the economic implications (still not well understood) of a whole new group of wage earners exhibiting new patterns of demands for goods and services. Finally, there are political implications (only beginning to develop) which will affect voter participation (in 1980, for the first time in U.S. history, the percentage of eligible women who voted exceeded that of eligible men), office-holding (women were mayors—a traditional first step to higher political office—in eighty-seven cities with populations over 25,000 in the United States in 1984), and eventually more legislative and executive policymaking (women are more likely than men, for example, to favor public policies for wider income distribution and to oppose those relaxing environmental-protection laws).

The rate of increase of women in the labor force will vary considerably from nation to nation, and so too will changes in fertility rates, increases in lifespans, and numbers of in and out migrants. All of these factors will in turn mean important variations in the overall forecast of labor force growth. Generally speaking, growth will be slower in the advanced developed nations where birthrates are falling and most members of the postwar baby-boom generation have already entered the workforce. In the developing nations, where birthrates are higher and postwar baby booms are less a factor, labor force growth will be more rapid in the decades immediately ahead.

In the United States the labor force grew at an accelerating rate from the late 1950s through 1979, faster in fact than the population growth rate, because of the entrance of the postwar baby-boom generation and of more women. Since 1979 the growth rate has been decelerating because of the peaking of baby-boom entrants at about that time and the slowing of the rate of growth of female participation.

This trend—a U.S. labor force now growing more slowly than its total population—will probably continue through the decade of the eighties and into the early nineties. Already in 1983 the labor force grew only 1.2 percent, less than most economists expected and far less than the average annual growth of 2.7 percent during the decade of the seventies. Not only will the number of teenage entrants continue to fall, but also the number of female entrants will not rise as rapidly as it did from 1960 to 1980. In part this is because the female participation rate is getting close to its upper limit (likely to be somewhere between 15 and 20 percent below the male rate, given projected female fertility), and in part it is because some baby-boom women are beginning to absent themselves periodically from the labor force to have children. Eventually, as more women enter and return to the labor force and their grown children become workers, the rate of growth of the labor force will approach and again—for a time—exceed that of the population, though probably at rates that will steadily decline as total population growth continues to slow.

Several important benefits will accrue to the United States and other developed countries because of the near-term slowing of the growth of their labor forces:

- Fewer untrained young entrants to the labor force will mean generally lower rates of unemployment.
- The fewer new workers who enter the labor force—including especially minorities in the United States, whose percentage of the total will increase—will benefit from the greater availability of training.
- As the current large cohort of baby-boom workers continues to age and to gain in skills and experience, the ratio of experienced to unexperienced workers will grow, undoubtedly contributing to higher productivity.
- Employers, faced with a scarcer labor supply and rising wages, will be encouraged to modernize plants and invest more in labor-saving equipment.

Structural changes underway in the composition of the labor force of the United States will also be of considerable help in easing major changes in employment patterns occurring as the country continues its transition from industrial to postindustrial. Accompanying this transition is a rapid shift of jobs from industrial to service sector activities. In the United States the average annual rate of growth of employment in manufacturing has been steadily falling during the past two decades. From 1959 to 1969 the rate was 1.9 percent; from 1969 to 1979 it dropped to .4 percent; and from 1979 through 1982, instead of growth there was an absolute decline of 3.5 percent. That much of this drop is indeed structural and not cyclical (due to the recession of the early 1980s) is seen by the fact that during the same period employment in service-producing industries *rose* 5.1 percent, while in the period of economic recovery that followed, factory employment continued to decline.

Automation in U.S. factories, replacing workers with machines, has been blamed for much of the drop in employment in manufacturing, and its further growth is stirring fears of widespread future unemployment. While it is true that automation has reduced factory production personnel and resulted in selective layoffs in certain industries, it does not appear to have contributed significantly to unemployment, nor is it likely to in the future. Since 1960 the U.S. employment/population ratio (civilian employment as a percent of the noninstitutional population) has been remarkably stable, fluctuating from a low of 56.5 percent in 1975 to a high of 60.1 percent in June 1985 (latest date of available data), a ratio exceeded only by Japan among industrial nations.

In the future, although new jobs in manufacturing in the United States will continue to fall, so too will the numbers seeking them, both because there will be fewer entrants in the labor market and because a rising proportion of those looking for work will be coming with educations and expectations for which traditional factory jobs will not be suitable. In addition, the very activity of automation—including the design, manufacture, operation, and maintenance of both its hardware and software—will itself continue to create new jobs and require new skills; and since industries that do not automate will find it increasingly difficult to survive, there should be a continuing demand for automation-related products and services. Finally, the vast majority of those displaced have been—and will continue to be—transferred or retrained for other jobs, usually within the same companies. The specter of large-scale unemployment due to automation is just that—a specter. It will not materialize. More disruptive, and potentially more difficult to handle, will be the effect of long-term structural change occurring in the kind of work available.

The nature of work is changing.
Silicon Valley, south of San Francisco, has quickly come

to symbolize the work of the future: high-technology electronics produced in environmentally clean fast-growing companies staffed by well-educated upwardly mobile young men and women with rising salaries that enable them to partake fully of California's abundant recreational activities—outdoors and indoors.

It is true that in the United States and other industrial nations jobs in high-technology fields will grow rapidly. Purchases of high-technology equipment—especially computers and their peripherals—by more businesses (extractive, manufacturing, and service) alone will guarantee increased employment in the future for the scientists and the engineers who design and build the equipment and the software to go with it. Still more will be employed in wholly new or fast-changing industries, such as biotechnology, plastics, ceramics, digital communications, optics, scientific instruments, alternative energy sources, and environmental protection. Many service industries, like health care, will require increasing numbers of highly trained personnel. Also growing will be jobs in a number of occupations (private and public) that are necessary adjuncts to high-technology fields, such as lawyers, administrators, technicians, inspectors, and regulators. And particularly in demand will be people with training and expertise in more than one field: for example, lawyers who understand biotechnology, engineers with marketing experience, and information specialists with training in finance.

But even though the number of "high-tech" jobs will grow, their total still will be relatively small. In the United States the Bureau of Labor Statistics projects that the vast majority of new jobs in the future—as in the past—will be those that require little education and modest skills. They will be "low-tech" and "no-tech." The bureau's list of occupations, with projected new openings through 1995, starts with the following ten jobs:

Building custodians	779,000
Cashiers	744,000
Secretaries	719,000
General clerks	695,000
Sales clerks	685,000
Registered nurses	642,000
Waiters and waitresses	562,000

Teachers	511,000
(kindergarten and elementary)	
Truck drivers	425,000
Nurse's aides and orderlies	423,000

None of these are high-tech jobs. In fact, not a single one of the top twenty occupations expected to produce the most jobs (a total of 9.2 million) during the next decade can be considered high-tech. All are decidedly low-tech and, except for nursing and teaching, require only limited training and expertise; and all but three (supervisors of blue-collar workers, carpenters, and electrical and electronic technicians—numbers 14, 19, and 20 on the list) are service sector jobs. Even in high-tech industries it has been estimated that only 15 percent of new positions are technically oriented, down to the associate engineering degree level. Most of the rest are clerical and assembly-line jobs.

This major structural change in the kind of work available in evolving postindustrial societies has many important implications. One concerns the length of time workers will remain at a particular job and the frequency with which they will switch jobs. Although low-tech jobs will grow rapidly, and as a form of employment are likely to be more resilient to fluctuations in the business cycle (especially in service activities), the minimal training required for most of them means that no one job will be permanent, nor will many employees fill them for long periods. Unlike the skilled and semi-skilled jobs in many manufacturing plants (for example, machine tool operators), these will not be lifetime jobs. Instead, workers will enter and leave them frequently, either to seek new opportunities or in pursuit of higher-priority non-employment objectives in their personal lives.

This means that many of these jobs will be particularly suited to women—who do move in and out of the labor force more often than men and are often "supplemental" wage earners in a family—and for part-time workers, especially teenagers and other people in schools and the elderly. The fact that most of these new jobs will be in service sector activities (not making special demands for physical strength or exposing employees to unusual hazards) will reinforce their suitability to women. Partly as a result of these factors, participation by women in the labor force will continue at the high rates attained in recent years in the United States and other developed nations, and at the same time their unemployment rate is likely to fall even farther below that for men, a circumstance that in the United States has already produced a statistical landmark: For the first time white males no longer constitute the majority of the nation's workforce; their share dropped below 50 percent in mid-1983 and has continued to fall.

Another important implication of the kind of work available in postindustrial societies derives from the relationship employees have to the technology that drives their industries. Those who can exercise control over the technology (or, in other words, are essential to its functioning) have considerable leverage in matters of job security and compensation. Those who do not exercise control (are not essential to the functioning of the technology) have far less leverage. Two recent labor strikes in the United States illustrate this growing dichotomy.

National Football League players, in their strike against team owners in the fall of 1982, were able to effectively stop the high flow of income from conventional and cable TV broadcasts that makes the operation of a team profitable. Without their very specialized talents, no money could be made; the efforts to provide surrogates (elaborately rigged all-star games) were abysmal failures. From their strong position the players were able to make extraordinary demands and achieve a very generous settlement, including substantially higher minimum salaries and a lucrative severance program. Employees in other industries, similarly placed by virtue of their expertise and their control over the technology essential to the industry's revenue, will be able to exert similar pressure.

The opposite case was dramatically illustrated in the strike by 675,000 telephone workers against American Telephone and Telegraph and the Bell System in the summer of 1983. Because telephone communications are extensively automated, most of the system was able to continue functioning without the workers; and since their work stoppage had only a small effect on the company's operations and its income, their demands could be more strongly resisted. This is true for an increasing number of industries—like utilities, oil refining, chemicals, telecommunications, publishing, and highly automated manufacturing—where many workers are merely adjuncts to key technologies, not essential to their functioning. Because they are easily replaceable and unable to affect operations significantly, their leverage in job security and pay issues has been greatly reduced.

While some labor unions (like the one representing the NFL players) stand to gain from high-technology developments in postindustrial societies, most will lose influence and leverage. In the future most new jobs will be formed in service sector activities (nine out of ten in the United States in the 1980s, an even higher ratio later), and most of these will be in small businesses. In both categories unions traditionally have found it hard to organize. The increasing importance of service activities and small businesses in job formation will thus further reduce what has been a declining union share of the U.S. workforce, from over 35 percent at the end of World War II to less than 20 percent in the mid-1980s.

The combined effect of all of the above (more low-tech and service sector jobs, more women and part-timers in the labor force, a smaller percentage of workers in unions) will be to slow the trend toward wider income distribution that developed during the industrial era. In its place a new trend is likely to arise, one that sees a diminishing share of income going to the middle ranks of society while the share to the lowest stays the same or decreases and that to the highest increases. While it is too early to say for certain that this is definitely happening, the change thus far in family income distribution is in this direction. In the United States from 1974 to 1984, according to the Census Bureau, the income share of the middle three-fifths of families declined from 53.5 to 52.4 and that of the lowest fifth dropped from 5.5 to 4.7, while the income share of the highest fifth increased from 41 to 42.9.

Such a change in income distribution, should it continue to develop, will be increasingly out of phase with a workforce entering the labor market with steadily growing educational credentials and commensurate economic expectations. It will mean a shrinking of the middle-income ranks whose earnings have been a major spur to the consumer-led economies of most industrial nations, and it will reflect continuing difficulty by women (heavily employed in low-tech service sector jobs) in achieving pay equal to that given men for work of comparable worth in non-service-sector jobs. It will also mean that programs to retrain workers laid off from manufacturing jobs will either have to equip the workers with far higher skills to achieve equivalent pay in high-tech industries or prepare them to accept the lower pay of low-tech jobs for skills at a level comparable to those in the jobs they lost. Finally, there are likely to be noticeable changes in attitudes and self-esteem as the traditional division of labor between white collar and blue collar gives way to the new categories of information-rich and information-poor, something already being seen in cities like Pittsburgh, Pennsylvania, and Akron, Ohio, now fast changing from centers of heavy industry.

Even more subtle, but no less important, will be the change in the nature of work itself brought by the shift from preindustrial and industrial to postindustrial. Throughout history most work has involved the manipulation of physical things—soil, wood, ores, chemicals, animals, etc. and the products derived from them. These are tangible, their properties are known, and their responses under different conditions are generally predictable. The labor that is applied alters them and combines them; and the result is a finished product, or the completion of a step toward a finished product.

The work of the service sector activities that will dominate the postindustrial era is very different. It deals with information that is representational and intangible, and with people who are varying and usually not predictable. To give a tangible quality to service sector work we use the vocabulary of the industrial era and often call what we create a "product," as for example in "insurance product"; but in fact it is not a product in the industrial sense at all. In industrial work we construct, in service work we connect—information to information, people with people, funds with more funds, and each of these with the others. Often the result is not clearly visible, and it is frequently understood differently by different people. It is sometimes incomplete, and what is done can become undone; and it may never be finished, left always to be reordered and rearranged by others and in ways bearing little resemblance to the intentions of those whose work it once was.

This will be the nature of most of the work of the future. It thus will require a different kind of training, one that concentrates more on information and people, less on physical things and finished products; one that deals with probabilities and contingencies, not certainties; one that seeks to understand irrationality, not just order and logic. Above all, since it is connection, not construction, that characterizes the work of service activities, process will be more important than outcome; and so in the future it may well be that those who do good unfinished work will be more highly paid and praised than those who do good finished work.

The conditions of work are changing.

Two trends, seemingly divergent but actually part of a larger pattern, characterize the structural change occurring in conditions of work. In one trend, employees are playing a greater role in determining and shaping the conditions of their work; in the other, they are viewing their job as less central to the lives they are living. Both of these trends are seen in changes in conditions concerning the location, hours, and compensation for work.

In the preindustrial era most work was done at home or close to home—on the farm, in the barn, in a workshop adjoining the home. By contrast, the work of industrial societies is concentrated around major sources of energy and around the equipment run by it, and in the manufacturing process itself many discrete steps are done by large numbers of workers. For these reasons industrial work is done in mills and factories that draw people from their homes. However, the work of the postindustrial era will less and less require large concentrations of people in central locations. More of it will be distributable to remote locations, and so more of it—though not all of it—may again be done close to home, or even at home.

The Association of Electronic Cottagers was formed in November 1984, and though its membership is still small its very establishment is indicative of the increasing attention being given to the movement of work back toward the home. Employment at home—made possible especially by the growth in service activity work and the increasing use of computers—has given new opportunities to the severely handicapped, and it has increased the potential participation in the workforce of the elderly and of mothers with small children. And, in addition to various side benefits—less time and money spent in commuting, reduced rush-hour traffic, and increased energy conservation—there is the central one of productivity. Control Data Corporation, which has eighty of its employees working at home, claims that the shift has resulted in productivity gains of up to 40 percent. Noting all these factors, a number of forecasters have labeled work at home a "wave of the future." Marvin Cetron of Forecasting International has even predicted that "twenty-two percent of our population will work at home [on computers] by the year 2000." Assuming a U.S. population of 265 million at that time, an astonishing 58.3 million, or nearly half the nation's workforce, will be employed in their homes in just thirteen years!

But because work in the industrial era mainly has taken place in a central location, it has developed characteristics and procedures which will continue to mandate such a location for most jobs well into the postindustrial era. Companies need physical premises for employees to meet, know each other, and interact in ways not constrained by seriatim exchanges on a computer terminal; they need a place for entry-level workers to learn their businesses and for all employees to develop a sense of organizational loyalty. Many workers—accustomed by cultural upbringing, at least, to regard work as done with others outside the home—will still want and need the camaraderie of their fellow workers; and they also will sense that advancement rests partly on visibility. Finally, one of the most important tasks of any job—making decisions—often needs more than remote communication can provide. Decisions are not made solely on the basis of data presented. Frequently just as important are expressions of qualification, confidence, certainty, and uncertainty—conveyed best in person.

Yet, while only a limited amount of specially suited work will move back to the home, it is clear that the location of much of the work of the postindustrial era will be less and less dictated by criteria of the past, such as supplies of energy and raw materials, accessibility to transportation arteries, and available labor pools. Citibank of North America has established its credit card operations center in Sioux Falls, South Dakota, far from its New York City headquarters; Satellite Data Corporation of New York offers its customers word-processing and data-entry services based on the Caribbean island of Barbados; and one Swedish fire department even uses a computer located in Ohio! The nature of many service-sector activities is such that they can either be centralized and done at literally any location or they can be decentralized at the physical location of the client or customer.

It is this quality of mobility of much postindustrial era work that is providing new options for those who perform it. As workers come to realize that employment opportunities in a number of fields exist in a variety of areas, choice of location will become as important as choice of company or even field of work. And once located, they may decide to stay (a decision reinforced by other structural changes such as working spouse, a compatible life-style, and lower mortgage rates in one's current dwelling) even when staying means switching companies, and careers too. Where the rule was once fixed jobs and mobile people, it is rapidly becoming fixed people and mobile jobs; in the postindustrial era it will be the employee more than the employer who will decide the work location.

FIG. 3.11.   Average Annual Hours Worked per Person, United Kingdom, United States, and Japan: Selected Years, 1870 to 1981.

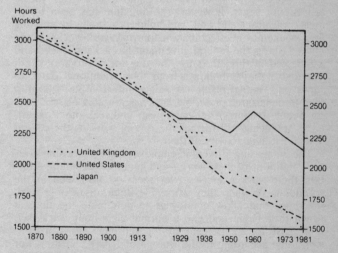

Sources: Angus Maddison, "Long Run Dynamics of Productivity Growth," *Banco Nazionale del Lavoro Quarterly Review*, Mar. 1979, p. 42; American Productivity Center, *Productivity Perspectives 1982*, Dec. 1982, p. 20.

Hours of work are also becoming increasingly flexible and increasingly the choice of workers. This is possible first because they are shorter. They no longer occupy the major part of a worker's time, closing out almost all other activities.

As figure 3.11 shows, the average annual number of hours worked per person in three selected industrial countries has fallen dramatically during the last one hundred years. In 1870 it was over three thousand hours a year in all three countries. Expressed as ten-hour working days this meant a year of six-day work weeks with only 13 nonworking days other than Sundays; in other words, little time for anything else. By 1981 the figure had fallen to 2,140 hours for Japan and to the low 1500s for the United States and England. In the latter two countries this meant 188 eight-hour working days, leaving almost half of the days of the year to pursue other activities.

Furthermore, the means of reducing work time has also changed. In the beginning it was done principally by reducing the work day (from ten to nine to eight hours) and the work week (from six to five-and-a-half to five days). In the last twenty years, however, the direction has been to increase vacations and add paid holidays, usually by creating long weekends, in effect making four-day work weeks. In the United States the federal goverment has acknowledged and acquiesced in this effort by changing the observance of all but four national holidays from their traditional dates to Mondays. The net result has been a shift from short-term to long-term leisure, providing larger aggregates of free time for people to pursue other interests and seek other experiences, reducing still further the role of work as the central and controlling activity of their lives.

The increasing direction employees are exercising over the conditions of their work—and hence the lessening direction their work exercises over them—is also seen in the scheduling of when they work. Flexitime, or flexible work schedules that allow employees to determine the time at which they begin and end a normal eight-hour work day, now exist for 12 percent of the full-time nonfarm U.S. workforce according to the Bureau of Labor Statistics. For many, even more varied options are available, such as "flexitour," in which employees set daily hours for themselves, "gliding time," which permits altering starting and quitting times, and various ways of configuring monthly and

yearly schedules (as is done by firefighters and flight attendants) to cluster work time so as to have longer periods free
for other purposes.

Part-time work is also rapidly increasing in popularity,
especially for the elderly and second wage earners in a
family. In the United States the percent of the nonfarm
workforce in part-time employment (less than thirty-five
hours a week) has risen to over 20 percent from less than 15
percent in 1974. Other variations on part-time work include
job sharing, in which one full-time job is shared by two
workers, and work-sharing, a reduction of work time (usually temporary) that can be used to reduce layoffs or create
unpaid free time.

It is in the area of compensation, however, that the most
important changes arising from greater employee involvement in shaping the conditions of work are occurring.
Throughout the era of industrialization the main issues at
stake between labor and management have been wages and
hours, and the main thrust of labor's efforts has been to
increase the former while decreasing the latter. Today, in
the rapidly arriving postindustrial era, it is not so much
more employer dollars that are demanded, but rather their
reallocation.

Benefits of various kinds have become adjuncts to salaries
and wages. The first of these were confined to such matters
as sick leave, pensions, and different kinds of medical plans.
Later they became more extensive, including life insurance,
dental care and eyeglasses, maternity leave, physical exami-
nations, memberships in health clubs, matching savings plans,
and—for executives—even personal financial counseling. More
recently the trend has been toward "flexible" or "cafeteria"
benefit plans, allowing employees themselves to "spend" or
allot a fixed dollar amount of benefit value among different
alternatives. For example, an employee of the American
Can Company (one of the first to establish a flexible benefit
program) with a working spouse already covered by a medical plan under another employer might opt for a longer
vacation and reduced medical benefits.

To motivate workers and maintain—and presumably
increase—profits, some firms have tied benefits directly to
company performance. Lincoln Electric Company of Cleve-
land, Ohio, has done this since 1907 through an incentive
pay system which essentially pays bonuses to workers for

higher rates of production. Other companies tie benefits to overall performance by providing shares of stock or actually dividing a portion of their profits among their employees. Electro Scientific Industries of Portland, Oregon, pays its employees 25 percent of its pretax profits each quarter, a fourth in cash and the rest into retirement or stock ownership accounts.

But when employee compensation increasingly is being tied to overall company performance, employees can be expected to seek and be given greater roles in determining company policies; and this, too, is occurring in more and more firms. At lower levels, in what has become known as the work reform movement or, more popularly, "quality circles" (following the Japanese model), selected self-managing work teams make many production decisions previously made without their input. At higher levels—and in fewer companies so far—employees participate in more important decisions, such as product choice, work scheduling, and quality standards. At the highest levels—notably at the Chrysler Corporation, starting in 1980, and more recently in a sweeping new agreement at Eastern Airlines—representatives of labor sit on corporate boards with full access to confidential company information.

This growing employee role in determining and shaping more of the conditions of work (location, hours, and compensation) indicates a slowly evolving structural change in the relationship between employers and employees. In the industrial era, dominated by the manufacture of specific products, the nature of each employee's task could be precisely defined and the result accurately measured and evaluated: So many pieces were completed and they were either acceptable or they were not. Under such conditions employees were clearly obligated to employers and the relationship between them was essentially an adversarial one: Employers provided the work and employees—organized with others—extracted as much money as they could for their labor.

In postindustrial work, dominated by the provision of services and heavily dependent on the creation and distribution of information and knowledge, quality replaces quantity as the main measure of an employee's contribution. But quality is a matter of range—from very good to not good at all—not a question of either/or, and since it is in employers' interest to have work at the higher end of the range, what they must do is enlist the cooperation of employees. At the same time, postindustrial employees no longer see themselves subordinated to their work roles. Work is but one facet of their lives, and not necessarily the most important one. Thus, they want to be recognized for who they are, and they want to play a role in determining what they do.

Under these circumstances, employers become more obligated to employees, and what was once primarily an adversarial relationship becomes more a cooperative one. In this new relationship, employees play a larger role in the design of their jobs and in decisions concerning the conditions under which they work. But for this they pay a price. No longer are they adversaries, standing apart from management; now they are a part of it, and thus less free to withhold their labor to demand higher wages. In fact, in this new situation their compensation will reflect more how their company does altogether than how they do individually. This in turn reflects yet another structural change underway as countries become more postindustrial, one that sees personal income less the result of what one earns for the work done in one's sole job and more the outcome of a far larger number of private and public activities.

INCOME

Changes in income mean changes in what we buy, in kind and quantity. They affect our standard of living as well as the activity and income of those who provide our goods and services, those who support them, and those who create and maintain the links between primary producers and ultimate consumers.

For these reasons, changes in income are extremely important to the course of a nation's economy, to the vitality of its businesses and professions, and to the well-being of its people. If we can understand them we will have a better idea of what will be purchased, how much should be produced, and to whom it can be marketed. Examining the incomes of those in advanced developed nations rapidly becoming postindustrial—like the United States—we can see that they are undergoing three important structural changes:

- They are growing more slowly.
- They are changing in composition.
- They are rising in buying power.

Incomes are growing, but more slowly.

As a country develops and its gross product increases, the share received by its people increases; and if the rates of increase of gross product and population are the same, then so, too, will be rates of growth of gross product per capita and income derived from it. But this rarely happens. Usually product and population grow at different rates, and these create characteristic patterns of per capita growth which vary with a country's development status.

Generally speaking, low-income countries with low rates of gross product growth and high rates of population growth have low—sometimes even negative—rates of growth of product per capita. Zaire, for example, from 1965 to 1984 had a low and falling rate of growth of gross product and a rising rate of population growth, resulting in an average annual rate of growth of gross national product (GNP) per capita of minus 1.6 percent. On the other hand, rising rates of product growth and slowing rates of population growth, a pattern found in many upper-middle-income countries, usually bring high per capita growth rates. The Republic of Korea, for instance, had high rising rates of product growth and low falling rates of population growth from 1965 to 1984, yielding an impressive average annual rate of growth of GNP per capita of 6.6 percent during that period.

In advanced industrial countries the pattern is more complicated, because there the growth of both product and population are slowing, but at rates that while falling are usually positive, meaning GNP per capita continues to rise. In the United States the rate of growth of both gross product and population fell from 1965 to 1983, yet because both rates were still positive, GNP per capita during the period grew at an average annual rate of 1.7 percent.

A similar pattern can be seen in the growth of personal income in the United States. Here it is most useful to refer to the figure for real disposable personal income. This is personal income expressed in constant dollars of a specified year (and hence adjusted for inflation) and reduced by personal tax and nontax payments. It thus provides the best measure of actual income available for consumer purchases and the best means to compare changes from year to year.

Aside from cyclical downturns during recessionary periods, total real disposable personal income has risen steadily throughout America's industrial period. But in the last two decades, as the United States economy has become increasingly postindustrial and as the growth rate of its gross product has slowed, so, too, has the rate of growth of personal income. In the 1960s the average annual rate of growth of total real disposable income was 4.4 percent; a decade later that rate had fallen to 3.1 percent. However, because the decline in the rate of growth of population from decade to decade was not as great, the fall in the average annual rate of growth of per capita real disposable income was somewhat steeper. In other words, relatively less income was being divided among relatively more people.

The important point in this structural change—of vital interest to the future planning and operations of all producers and purveyors of goods and services—is that although the growth of disposable personal income is slowing, both overall and per capita, it is still positive, not negative. More is available—in real inflation-adjusted terms—to spend each year. But this significant fact has been obscured—in fact, seemingly denied—by regular news reports to the effect that throughout most of the 1970s and into the early 1980s real family and household incomes in the United States have declined, not growing at all. While this trend in family and household incomes is true, it is not an accurate representation of what is happening to real disposable personal income, which is continuing to rise. The explanation for these opposed conclusions concerning the growth of income is found in structural and cyclical changes occurring in families and households.

With regard to families, the most important change has been the entry of more women (especially mothers) into the labor force. On the one hand, as supplemental income earners their wages and salaries have tended to increase the total income of many families; but because they are heavily employed in service activities, earn less than men, and in growing numbers (especially among blacks in the United States) head families, as a whole they have tended to depress median (the midpoint of all figures arranged from highest to lowest) family income. More cyclical is the fact that in recent years large numbers of the baby-boom generation have been forming families and joining the workforce in lower-paying entry-level jobs, also tending to depress median family income.

Median income for households, a larger category including nonrelated persons as well as families, has been affected by both of these changes plus the increase of the number of the elderly living alone. More men and women remaining single longer, more nonrelated younger people living together, and more older people living longer have swelled the number of nonfamily households (in the 1970s they increased from 19.2 to 27.3 percent of all households); but because many of these new households, too, tend to be headed by lower-level wage earners, median household income has also fallen.

It is these changes in the structure of families and households, not economic performance, that explain the difference between gloomy reports of steadily falling incomes and the more accurate—and more hopeful—reality of steadily, though slowly, rising real disposable personal income. In time this difference will narrow as the growth of female participation in the labor force slows, life expectancy increases less rapidly, and cyclical population change moves the baby-boomers to their higher-income middle years and follows them with a smaller generation of lower-income entry-level workers. Then median household and family incomes will track real disposable personal income more closely. Until then the two are likely to diverge, as different measures in a larger pattern of slower growing income. A further explanation for this pattern, and an indication of its likely future development, is found in the changing composition of income.

Incomes are changing in composition.
Wages and salaries are accounting for less of our personal income; nonwage components for more. In the United States this important shift is relatively recent, less than fifteen years old. During the quarter century after World War II there was little change in the wage and salary share of personal income. In 1970 it stood at 67.7 percent, 1 percent less than it was in 1945. But fourteen years later it had fallen to less than 60 percent. During the same period, as figure 3.12 shows, the share of nonwage components of personal income rose rapidly: transfer payments (principally from government agencies) from 9.9 to over 14 percent, personal interest income from 8.5 to 14.5 percent, and other labor income (benefits provided by employers) from 4 to 6.5 percent.

FIG. 3.12.   Distribution of Personal Income by Selected Categories, United States, 1960–1984.

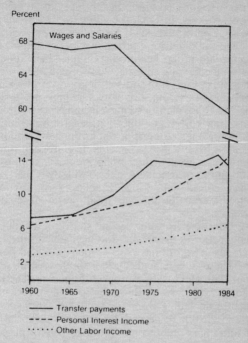

Source: U.S. Bureau of the Census, *Statistical Abstract of the U.S.: 1986* (Wash., DC, 1985). p. 438.

What this indicates is a structural change in the composition of personal income in the transition to postindustrial status. In this change the role of salaries and wages grows smaller while that of "supplements" to salaries and wages becomes more important. These growing supplements come principally from three sources: benefits provided by employers, transfer payments from various government sources, and income from personal assets, both financial and property.

Employer benefits include, first, contributions to social insurance, which in the United States have risen from slightly over 5 percent of total private salaries and wages in 1960 to

9.6 percent in 1984. In addition, employers, and unions in conjunction with employers, provide a large and growing number of pension and group health plans to an increasing number of workers. In 1983, according to the Bureau of the Census, 43.4 percent of all U.S. civilian employees fifteen years of age and older were provided with pension plans and 61 percent with group health plans. Other benefits to employees supplementing income include paid time off (rest time, holidays, vacation, and sick leave), various kinds of insurance plans (accident, disability, and life), profit-sharing and stock purchase plans, and miscellaneous programs covering loans, transportation, education, legal services, and recreation. Altogether, American employers pay an additional 38 percent of basic wages in benefits. In European countries the figures are even higher: 80 percent by employers in Germany and France, and 94 percent in Italy. Clearly, what were once considered "fringe benefits" have become an indispensable portion of the total fabric of employee compensation.

In 1929, income from the second source of supplements, government transfer payments, was negligible in the United States; today it constitutes over 14 percent of all personal income. These supplements include both federal government and state and local government programs. The largest of the former, by far, are those that provide direct income maintenance, including OASDHI (Old-Age, Survivors, Disability, and Health Insurance, which provides Social Security for retirement and income for the disabled), public and railroad employee retirement, veterans' pensions, unemployment benefits, workers' compensation, public assistance, and—since 1974—supplemental security income. The percent of personal income provided by these supplements alone rose from 6.4 in 1960 to 10.4 in 1982. Also important as contributors of supplements are the large number of federal programs providing noncash benefits, including medical care, food assistance (food stamps and school lunches), jobs and training, housing, and education aid. Their impact is large and growing. In 1983 they provided 24.5 percent of all households with medicare aid, 9.5 percent with medicaid, 8.4 percent with food stamps, and 21.5 percent with school lunches. Altogether, according to a new statistical series begun by the U.S. Census Bureau in September 1984, three out of every ten Americans and 47 percent of all households currently receive direct federal government benefits.

State and local governments add their own supplements to income, principally in the area of education, but also for social insurance programs, public aid, and health and medical programs. Altogether they accounted for 37.9 percent of government supplements to U.S. personal income in 1983, a share that has been steadily shrinking as that of the federal government (62.1 percent) has grown larger. In 1976 the split was 47.7 percent federal, 52.3 percent state. Because the largest federal programs (income maintenance and medical care) are non-means-tested and because the U.S. population is growing more slowly and older, this shift in burden will continue; and for the same reasons the percentage of all personal income provided by the federal government also will continue to grow.

The third source of supplements, income from personal assets, is the least well known and most difficult to document; but it is also increasing the fastest and has the most potential for future growth. In terms of sources of income, personal assets can be considered in two general categories, financial and property (principally real estate).

In the United States in 1984, households held financial assets of over $6.6 trillion, consisting principally of deposit and market instruments (including checkable deposits and currency, time and savings deposits, money market fund shares, and various credit market instruments), corporate equities and life insurance, and pension fund reserves. Of these, the fastest-growing over the past 13 years have been the pension fund reserves, increasing from 12.4 percent of financial assets in 1970 to 21.7 in 1984. Because their status has been strengthened by the Employee Retirement Income Security Act (ERISA) and they have been augmented by new Individual Retirement Accounts (IRAs), their proportion of total assets and their role as a supplement to wage and salary income will continue to grow. In addition, since they are heavily invested in credit instruments, the continuation of interest rates at relatively high levels will mean that they—along with other interest-bearing financial assets—will make still larger contributions to personal income.

Property assets of Americans have been increasing at an even faster pace. In fact, between 1962 and 1976 (the last date for which complete data are available), real estate displaced financial assets as the principal source of personal wealth in the United States. In 1962 the proportions were 37 percent of wealth in real estate and 46 percent in financial assets; by 1976 the shares were 43 and 40 percent (in both years the remaining 17 percent was accounted for by the category "miscellaneous"). Since inflation in the late 1970s significantly increased the value of real estate, the difference between these shares has undoubtedly increased still further, though less rapidly as lower inflation subsequently has slowed the pace. Because this growth in real estate assets has been principally for owner-occupied homes, it has not led to an increase in rental income (which has, in fact, declined). But it has created a large and growing asset for homeowners which can be used to fund many other kinds of consumption, from additional property to travel, recreation, and luxury goods; and almost every major bank in the United States—suddenly alert to this new supplement to income—has announced "equity" accounts or lines of credit to take advantage of it, creating a financial service that will get a further impetus from the 1986 Tax Act, which phases out the deduction on interest for most other types of loans.

All three of these supplements will continue to grow. Employers will continue to provide supplements of various kinds, in part because they will be demanded and in part because the relationship of wages to value added by individual employees—particularly in dominant and growing service sector activities—will be increasingly more difficult to measure and relatively less important. Government-provided supplements will also increase, especially as an older population receives more funds for income-maintenance; and income from personal assets will increase as these assets continue to grow.

In addition, there will be a shift of more income to those in their later years. Pensions and transfer payments to the retired will constitute an increasing share of total personal income, particularly as they continue to be indexed to cost of living increases—a policy that may be slowed or delayed from time to time, but that politically will be all but impossible to end. Appreciating assets of the elderly will also add income, especially as longer life allows them to be held for more years. This rising share of income to the elderly is already visible. From 1978 to 1982, median income for all age groups below sixty-five in the United States declined;

yet for those sixty-five and over it increased. Thus, not only is the American population growing older, but the income of its oldest group is increasing faster than that of all its younger ones and will continue to do so, a combination of structural changes of obvious importance to providers of goods and services.

The buying power of incomes is rising.

Because personal incomes are still growing—though at a slowing pace—in countries becoming postindustrial, people in these countries are enjoying increasing buying power. In addition, because these countries are at an advanced stage of industrial development, their production of goods and services has become very efficient and their per capita incomes stand at a relatively high level. Under these circumstances basic needs are produced at less cost and require a smaller portion of each person's income.

In the United States the average farm worker, who in 1950 produced enough to feed fifteen people, in 1982 produced enough to feed seventy-eight. This helped reduce the share of food, the largest single item of personal consumption expenditure, as a portion of total consumption expenditures in the United States from nearly 25 percent in 1950 to less than 17 percent in 1984, notwithstanding the fact that an increasing amount of spending on food is going for more expensive meals away from home. In the same way, a general package of what roughly could be considered "needs" (food, clothing, housing, and household operation) required 65 percent of U.S. consumption expenditures in 1930, 59 percent in 1950, and 47 percent in 1984. In fact, the reduction over time has been even greater since the quality of the needs bought in successive years has steadily improved even as their share of expenditures has continued to fall.

Furthermore, changes in the composition of income have tended to regularize and widen the provision of needs. During periods of economic downturn not only do government transfer payments, certain employer benefits, and many forms of income from personal assets continue, but some also grow (for example, unemployment compensation), replacing lost wages and salaries and assuring the means to continue to purchase necessities, at least. Thus, as the role of supplements to traditional income increases they will tend to maintain buying power and smooth out its rises and falls.

What remains after needs have been met is discretionary income, the amount available to satisfy "wants," the goods and services people would like to have—for comfort and convenience, for self-identity, and to establish a certain style of life. It is the share of this kind of income, as a percent of total disposable income, that has steadily grown as the share required for needs has shrunk. This increasing ability to satisfy wants is reflected in the reduction of nondurables (food, fuel, clothing, etc.) as a percent of U.S. per capita personal consumption expenditures, from 46 percent in 1960 to slightly over 37 percent in 1984, and in the same period the rise in the share of durables (motor vehicles, furniture, household equipment, etc.) from 11 to 16.9 percent and services from 42 to 46.2 percent.

These wants are of many kinds. Some are simply the upgrading of needs, such as greater variety in diet and more meals eaten in restaurants, or more expensive clothing; some represent an improvement in the quality of wants already acquired, such as a better car or the replacement of a black-and-white television set by one with color; and some are new luxury goods and services, such as a video cassette recorder or a foreign vacation. But many expenditures for wants also lead to future increases in income, including money spent for specialized and higher education; and many others purchase income-generating assets, both financial and property. Thus, the additional buying power released for wants by the diminishing share required for needs itself helps to produce still more buying power. The end result, in all countries passing from their industrial to their postindustrial stages and experiencing these changes in the growth, composition, and buying power of income, is the acquisition by more and more people of measurable and enduring personal wealth and a status of relative affluence. This in turn generates structural changes in attitudes.

ATTITUDES

With a basic stream of income—from some combination of private and public sources—increasingly assured, we attain a measure of economic security. At the least, we know, we will not starve, we will not freeze, we will—somehow—get by; at the best—with minimum effort—we may even enjoy a modicum of comfort. In such circumstances, the traditional attitudes and priorities which once imposed on most of us a regimen of self-discipline, hard work, postponement of gratification, and obedience to rules and authority—lest we put at risk the very necessities of life— have become less important.

In place of such long-standing "societal levers," as the late Herman Kahn called them, we are developing new attitudes and new goals. These include:

- Tolerating and pursuing a variety of experiences and life-styles
- Giving higher priority to quality than quantity and seeking what is new and different, especially what provides self-identification
- Paying greater attention to preserving and protecting what we have acquired
- Putting more emphasis on the values of health, comfort, and safety
- Demanding, and playing, a larger role in the decisions that shape all of the facets of our lives

Lately, in the United States, many of these attitudes and priorities have been associated with a particular demographic group, the higher-educated children of the postwar baby boom, now a large cohort group aged twenty-three to forty-one and often referred to as "Yuppies" (for "young upwardly mobile professionals"). Born and reared in the high-growth years of the 1950s and 1960s, educated in a socially active environment of civil rights, feminist, and anti-war movements, they are affluent, aspiring, and confident of their ability to make things happen. But they are not a unique phenomenon, the product of a one-time demographic bulge. They are part of a long-term structural change occurring in all countries where development and growth have endowed succeeding generations with far more economic security than their parents and far less interest in the preferences and goals that motivated them.

The shift from traditional goals to new attitudes and priorities is already well developed in the advanced industrial countries of Europe and North America, many of them with programs that provide virtual cradle-to-grave economic security. It is coming rapidly in Japan, where long-standing values of conformity, commitment to the group, and self-sacrifice are steadily giving way to more individual choice, personal achievement, and self-gratification; and it is beginning in the NICs, the newly industrializing countries, like India, where a modern Western-style consumer culture is emerging in a land where many decisions are still made by referring to the movement and position of heavenly bodies.

These structural changes are altering demands for many goods, especially in the direction of greater variety and better quality; and they are requiring new kinds of services, both more flexible and more specifically tailored to particular needs. In the future these changes will continue to evolve. To meet them with products and services appropriate to their evolution requires that we understand them and make use of them.

Old ties are waning, new options are waxing.

The basic thrust of Western civilization—from the time of ancient Greece to the present day—can be summed up in a single phrase: the pursuit of individual freedom. In recent centuries the pace of that pursuit has quickened as successive discoveries, revolutions, and evolutions have "freed" individuals from the institutions that have guided and controlled them, leaving their destinies increasingly in their own hands. Copernicus and Galileo, by challenging the egocentric view of the earth as the center of the universe, and Darwin, by hypothesizing human evolution from lower species, provided viable alternatives to the teachings of the great religions, thus offering "freedom" from their hold. The Industrial Revolution, by creating an alternative to life in the village, "freed" people from the communities in which most had always spent their entire lives. And in this century the level of individual economic security attained in advanced industrial countries is "freeing" their inhabitants from the last social institution to which traditionally they have been tied, the family.

Throughout history, in most places at most times, families have been bound together by economic necessity, and household formation has been coterminous with family formation. This is no longer the case. Growing economic security has lowered the age at which households are being formed and dramatically increased the number of nonfamily and one-person households. In 1960, over 85 percent of the 53 million households in the United States were family households;

by 1985 the percentage had dropped to 72 percent of a total
of 86.8 million. During this period nonfamily households
more than tripled, from 7.7 million to over 24 million, with
the fastest growth occurring in households consisting of two
unrelated persons.

These figures indicate the acceptance and exercising of
options that only a few years ago would have been considered unusual, risky, and—in some cases—outside the realm
of socially acceptable behavior. These include single women
deciding to delay marriage or not marrying at all, setting up
their own households, and unrelated couples of the opposite
sex—or even the same—deciding to live together. Yet today, such practices are widely accepted.

Within the family, too, more new options are being exer-
cised. First, a greater number of marriages are ending and
more remarriages are occurring. While there probably has
been little change in the percent of unhappy marriages over
time, changes in divorce laws, and the economic security
that has prompted many of the changes, have greatly increased the opportunity to terminate such marriages and
enter new ones, something that until recently seemed possible only for movie stars and others of substantial means. In
the United States, census figures show that 50 percent of
marriages eventually end in divorce. But divorced persons
are also remarrying, and the number of "serial marriages,"
people divorcing and remarrying several times, is steadily
increasing, suggesting not the decline of marriages and families as institutions but rather the erosion of the attitude that
marriage is for life.

Another important new option within the family is work
for the wife, and in some cases even a switch in the traditional roles of principal and supplementary breadwinners. In
the United States more women than men are now attending
college (in 1984 51.3 percent of all enrollees were women
while only 48.7 percent were men), and in the past two
decades nearly 25 million women have joined the labor
force, compared with only thirteen million men. In a growing number of cases, in two-income families, women are
making more than men and becoming the major wage earners, a trend that will accelerate as the rapidly rising number
of women graduating from professional schools move up in
their fields. Children, too, have more money to spend, in
part from their own earnings but even more from allow-

ances from the rising percent of discretionary income available to many of their parents. With money they, too, have more options available than before. But since their needs are mostly taken care of, they will be choosing principally among leisure and recreation options, reinforcing an exposure to the unique life-styles and behavior patterns of many in the entertainment industry. One social critic, Allan Bloom of the University of Chicago, has even suggested that such expenditures—notably for rock music recordings—mean that children, during their most formative years, will be increasingly exposed to "leveling" rather than "elevating" experiences.

Finally, there is the increasing phenomenon of the one-parent family. To the ever-present possibility of such a situation being created by the death of one parent has been added a very large increase in other possibilities, including divorce, abandonment, mothers with unwanted children, and even mothers without partners by their own choice. Between 1960 and 1984 the percent of one-parent families with children in the United States increased from 8.5 to 25.7. During the past decade, the fastest-growing portion of this group has been never-married mothers. Most of them—for a variety of reasons—had no other choice; but a growing number of unmarried women, with the economic security of a career or profession, are choosing to bear children for the experience of having them, usually through the rapidly improving technology of artificial insemination. While it is probably true that a happy single-parent family is better for a child than an unhappy dual-parent one, single-parenting creates its own problems for both parent and child, and—in the case of deliberate choice to be a single parent—creates a new option where future consequences (particularly to the child) are completely unknown.

Traditional nuclear families—mother, father, and children, all in one home—will, of course, continue, and the numbers of them will grow; but so, too, will new options and alternatives, most of them not long ago regarded as odd, tragic, or simply beyond the pale. Economic security has made the exercise of many of these options possible, and modern communications—especially television—has made them known, brought them into our daily sight, and given them respectability. Television situation comedies like *The Odd Couple* and *Kate and Allie* depict household types most people do not experience; but by presenting them regularly—and humorously—television has not only made them acceptable but also by implication suggested that nontraditional life-styles *in general* are acceptable.

For the citizens of most democratic Western nations, toleration of optional behavior patterns—short of the point where they do visible harm to others—is further reinforced by ideology and law. Very few may desire to pursue a nonheterosexual life-style, but so strong and pervasive is the notion of free choice in Western democratic ideology that very many will stoutly support the right of others to do so. Thus, rules designed originally to prevent restrictions on political expression and religious belief are by extension being used to protect new forms of social behavior. Only by stepping back, and viewing with a much longer perspective, can one see the extent of the structural change created by the inexorable movement of economic and political progress: Individuals, once firmly tethered to the familiar norms of church, community, and family, are now free to roam, seeking their own norms down unfamiliar paths.

The danger in the creation and tolerance of new options—and of the complementary ethic that proclaims "anything goes" and counsels "hang loose"—is that there will be an erosion of commitment, the critical means by which people dedicate themselves to the building of relationships and the completion of projects, small and large. Furthermore, with this erosion comes its corollary, a sense of loneliness and alienation from both society and nature. It is no surprise, therefore, that social critics warn of excessive concentration on self and that expressions of alienation have been major themes of modern Western literature. Even hit movies, like *E.T.* and *Greystoke*, have struck a respondent chord in audiences by focusing on aliens and depicting their ultimate rejection by society's authorities.

It is true that the pursuit—and achievement—of greater individual freedom has exacted a price, the price of being more alone. But this, too, has its corollary: It forces self-examination and encourages self-actualization. Commitment does not disappear; instead it shifts, from old emphases to new. With greater economic security our priorities change. Instead of seeking what others have, we look for what will be ours alone; instead of trying to keep up with the Joneses, we attempt to distinguish ourselves from them.

Variety, self-identity, and quality are becoming more important.

Beverly Hills Kitty Litter, with each package consisting of $10,000 in shredded U.S. currency, was one of 143 new products that entered the American marketplace in December 1982, as reported in the monthly Dancer Fitzgerald Sample *New Product News*. That month's total of new products was the largest of any month in 1982, which in turn was the biggest year since the newsletter began nineteen years earlier, even though for the U.S. economy it was a year mainly of recession.

New products are increasing because even during economic downturns people have the economic security and discretionary income that provide a growing market for them. Not only are such people pursuing a greater variety of options in the households and families they are forming, but they are also seeking and purchasing a greater variety of products and services. Even though they may be satisfied with a particular product they have been using for years, their increasing incomes are giving them the means and in a sense, even the obligation, to try a new item or a new brand, from necessities to luxuries.

Food is a good example. Although total food consumption per capita appears to peak at a certain level of economic growth and income (as has happened in the United States), the variety of food available for purchase continues to increase. In 1930 the average American grocery store offered less than nine hundred food items; by 1985 the total was nearly eleven thousand. Where only a few varieties of a product once existed—in condiments or cheeses or coffees, for instance—whole sections of stores are now devoted to them. Faster transportation, better refrigeration, and longer shelf life have made it possible for items to be sold far distant from where they were produced, and the combination of advances in food chemistry with the fertile imaginations of scientists schooled in it are creating endless new mixes of old and new substances, from Bacon and Cheddar Hot Dogs to Hedgehog-Flavored Potato Chips.

Eating out is highly correlated with increasing income—and also with greater education—and as both rise, so, too, do desires for greater variety and improved ambiance, which usually translates to foreign or more exotic types of food offered in fancier locations. Thus, in the fast food business, hamburger shops are adding new menu items, and specialty and ethnic food chains—like Long John Silver's Seafood Shoppes, Bojangles (chicken), Taco Bell, and the felicitously named Wok Inn—are proliferating. Further upscale, table service restaurants (including more with tablecloths) are springing up in greater numbers of shopping centers and village malls, and columns regularly reviewing them are becoming standard fare in most newspapers.

In the leisure and entertainment areas, both at home and away from it, the same pattern of activity is seen. Even during the recession years of the early 1980s, leisure spending—for foreign travel, recreational activities, and home entertainment—continued to grow. In the United States today leisure activities constitute a $300-billion-a-year business, ranking second only to food. The majority of this spending (approximately 60 percent) is still on travel, testifying to the continuing pull of what is different, unfamiliar, and exotic. But this percentage has fallen from the 70 percent it was twenty years before, indicating the growing importance of at-home entertainment. Evidence of this is seen in the purchase of new varieties of electronic devices for our increasingly "wired" homes, such as additional and improved television receivers, cable installations, and video cassette recorders. It is seen also in the increase in pool installations, motor and water sports equipment, and other domestic recreational gear. While Americans are getting richer, they are also getting older and finding more to buy that provides leisure at home rather than away.

A second goal that motivates us in the spending of our rising discretionary income is an interest in the "experience" that is provided by the purchase. Is it an experience that is fun, lively, worth doing again? Does it appeal to our senses in a direct and immediate way? Thus shopping for food is enhanced not only by having a wide variety of products available, but also by the environment in which it is done, including the extent to which it engages and involves the shopper, such as the opportunity to compare, smell, taste, or to buy in bulk, or from bins and barrels (hence, the growing fascination in the United States—particularly on the part of city dwellers—of farmers' markets and even warehouses). Increasingly, in postindustrial countries where service sector activities dominate and process becomes as important as product, consumers will be evaluating their activities—from the simplest to the most elaborate—more and more in terms of the total sensory experience they provide.

In addition, there is a growing desire for convenience, and for satisfaction and gratification to occur now rather than later. Since the dual wages earned by many households will provide more income but less time in which to enjoy it, convenience (being able to acquire something or do something or prepare something with a minimum of fuss and discomfort) will be increasingly important. Higher income also will make near-term satisfactions more possible, thus reinforcing decisions not to postpone them. Furthermore, the desire for now rather than later will be strengthened both by the increase in number and kinds of activities to be experienced and by the growing exposure to media—especially television—whose mode of presentation is temporary rather than permanent, and whose dominant format for transmitting information is short bursts of news rather than longer essays of analysis.

Beyond variety, having a good "experience," and doing so now, there comes a desire for activities that are unique, that provide a measure of self-identification. Once we are readily able to acquire what others have, we show a growing interest in doing and having what is special, what will distinguish us from others. During much of the industrial era, where the achievement of economic security was still an unmet goal for most, mass production—in creating "economies of scale"—enabled a person to have exactly what everyone else was having. In the rapidly arriving postindustrial era, where economic security is increasingly being achieved, segmented production, by creating "economies of scope," is making it possible for more people to have what is unique or what only a few others have.

The recent success of "Cabbage Patch Kids" dolls is a good illustration of this desire for the unique. The dolls are mass-produced, but through a process that randomly selects different combinations of skin, eye, and hair coloring and clothing, thus ensuring that no two are alike. Their one-of-a-kind character is then attested to by an "adoption certificate" which accompanies each doll. The same desire for products that are unique, that respond to the wish to set oneself apart, to make a "statement" about oneself, has been recognized also by the automobile industry. The 1984 Ford Thunderbird, with different combinations of engines, transmissions, and optional accessories, was available in more than 69,000 varieties; the Chevrolet Citation in more than 32,000. In a very real sense, the economic and technological progress that has made variety and segmentation possible has at the same time fueled the demand for it.

Finally, from a desire for what is unique it is only a short step to a strong preference for quality and value. Much has been heard of late, particularly in the United States, about the need to improve quality in goods and services. In particular, there has been an effort on the part of manufacturers to match the perceived cost efficiency and high quality of Japanese production by instituting Japanese practices such as "just-in-time" inventory systems and "quality circles." This is in part a recognition that many foreign-made goods are superior in quality to their American counterparts. But it is attributable even more—as numerous polls and research studies testify—to a growing emphasis on quality once a certain level of sufficiency, or quantity, has been achieved.

This growing emphasis on quality has two facets. One stresses products that are the very best in their class and that have a recognized reputation for superior workmanship and high performance; the other looks for good value, to get the most for one's money, especially for low-cost utilitarian products. Hence, there is a tendency for the purchasing patterns of consumers in advanced industrial countries to show a "dumbbell" or "inverse bell curve" effect, increasingly clustering at the higher and lower ends of the price spectrum. At the upper end of the scale there is a large and—even during periods of recession—growing demand for expensive products of recognized high quality, such as foreign luxury cars, designer clothes, and gourmet foods. At the lower end there are many consumers—both well-to-do and less-well-off—looking for bargains, especially in basic standard items. These are the consumers who are buying no-brand "generics" and patronizing off-price and warehouse stores.

Many merchants, seeing this bifurcation in buying patterns, are catering to both ends of the scale.

- Howard Johnson's motel chain, long targeted on a broad family-oriented middle-class market, is planning to acquire twenty-five to thirty full-service hotels in choice

metropolitan locations, appealing to a different higher-class clientele.
- The Marriott chain, on the other hand, noted for its resorts and more upscale properties, is taking aim at the other end of the market with a new group of hotels called "courtyards," designed for travelers of more modest means.

Caught in the middle are companies like Revlon, many of whose cosmetics are positioned in what formerly had been the broad area between upscale and downscale. That area is now steadily being abandoned as more and more consumers with higher discretionary incomes, better educations, and access to more information are sensing that the middle is ordinary, distinguished neither by high quality nor by high value. No longer driven principally by the desire for "more than," they are shifting their priorities to "better than"—at both ends of the scale.

There is an increasing emphasis on preservation and protection.
As we acquire more things of quality our interest in protecting them, and in maintaining our environs, grows. With more potentially at risk, there is less willingness to take risk and a greater desire to play it safe. In the United States this shift in priorities manifests itself in a number of ways, including increasing expenditures on rehabilitation and remodeling, greater attention to physical security and home protection, and regular immersion in ever larger waves of nostalgia for artifacts of the past. But most important are the dual and complementary tendencies of more people to stay put when once finally settled and to limit the entrance of others to their areas of settlement.

During the 1960s, 20 percent of the U.S. population moved each year; by the mid-1980s the figure was 16 percent and falling. While many Americans once moved to obtain better jobs in other companies or to enhance their promotion potential in their own, fewer are doing so today. Some are even opting to forgo opportunities or turning down promotions in order to stay put. For most the main reason is the large stake they have in where they are—in home and property, community ties, friends, and, above all, a life-style that has become comfortable and satisfying—and their reluctance to abandon it.

Other equally enduring reasons serve to reinforce decisions against moving on. These include the income of a well-established working spouse, increasing home ownership versus renting and the attendant difficulties of selling and buying properties in an ongoing climate of uncertain inflation and interest rates, and—for some—the opportuntity to pursue an information-based service type of occupation that can go where they are located. Together these reasons buttress a structural change that is slowly giving more long-term importance to the assets and life-styles people acquire than the means—the work—used to obtain them.

Once settled, people strive to preserve and protect their nest and its location. In the United States, exclusionary zoning, to control the type of development that occurs in a town by specifying kinds of construction and sizes of lots, has long been practiced and has been specifically upheld by the Supreme Court. But in the late 1960s and early 1970s a new trend began. The preceding decades had brought rapid growth to a number of areas, improving the lot (and lots!) of many and at the same time threatening that improvement with the consequences of further uncontrolled growth. The response was to slow, even to halt, any growth at all, of any type.

It began in areas that were considered particularly desirable, and thus particularly vulnerable to further growth.

- In 1972, Petaluma, California, just north of San Francisco, adopted an ordinance limiting the number of building permits that could be issued in any one year. Other cities and counties in the state followed suit with similar programs to curtail and control growth, including Santa Barbara, San Diego, San Jose, and, most recently, Contra Costa and Orange counties.
- In Boulder, Colorado, in the foothills of the Rocky Mountains, a citywide vote approved regulations to limit population increases to no more than 2 percent a year, a sharp drop from annual rates that had run as high as 8 percent in the 1950s and 1960s.
- Farther into the Rockies, the residents of the picturesque village of Crested Butte waged a pitched battle to keep the giant Amax mining corporation from developing a molybdenum mine in nearby Mount Emmons,

a project that would employ more people than were in the town, but at the cost of threatening its Victorian serenity.

Entire states also have sought to hold off activities that raised the possibility of disturbing an environment and a life-style that they wished to preserve. Colorado voters in a move apparently designed to both deny and protect their superb endowment and facilities for winter sports, rejected the state's bid for the 1976 Winter Olympics. The more or less official slogan of Oregon is "Come and see us—but don't stay too long"; and in Wyoming, a popular bumper sticker urges, "Preserve Wyoming's wildlife, shoot an out-of-state hunter."

In the future more such actions will be regularized and legitimized, in tacit recognition of a steadily growing preference to preserve and protect what has been attained through greater economic security and increased discretionary income. Closely linked to this preference is another which seeks to extend the same protection to life itself.

> *Health, comfort, and safety are rising higher on our list of priorities.*

There is good news and there is bad news in the industrial transition. On the one hand, it steadily reduces the number of dangerous, dirty, physically unpleasant jobs and increases the knowledge and facilities that help reduce pain, cure illnesses, and make life longer and more comfortable. On the other hand, in the very process of advancement it pollutes the air, fouls water supplies, accumulates dangerous wastes, and breeds technologies which can maim and kill large numbers of people a few at a time (like automobiles) or all at once (like weapons of mass destruction).

It is the achievement of the first that has made even more imperative the mitigation of the results of the second, because as we live longer, better, more comfortable lives we become even more concerned with the dangers that threaten them. Thus, health, comfort, and safety have steadily risen to a high place on our list of priorities. This is seen especially in our concerns about the environment in which our bodies exist and the food that we take into them.

In *The Greening of America,* published in the fall of 1970 at the height of the antiwar movement in the United States,

Yale University law professor Charles Reich proclaimed the coming of a "revolution by consciousness." This revolution, he argued, would in time replace the impersonal system of the "Corporate State" with one based on a renewal of self-knowledge, seeking individual fulfillment and brotherly love. Reich's impassioned utopian essay captured the mood of many young people at the time, but in retrospect its only enduring contribution has been the goal suggested by its title. America and most of the world's developed countries, and even some of its developing ones, are indeed being "greened"; that is, through various combinations of public policy and private effort they have embarked on a lasting commitment to improve and protect their physical environments.

In reviewing the results of opinion polls over the years it is impressive to see the continuing strong support for environmental protection, despite energy problems, bouts of inflation, and increasing trade deficits. In mid-1978, in the wake of quadrupled oil prices and long lines at gasoline pumps, more Americans (47 percent) still favored protecting the environment over producing energy (31 percent). Similarly, 50 percent were unwilling to cut back on pollution and safety regulations even though they raised the cost of products. Five years later, 58 percent agreed that "protecting the environment is so important that requirements and standards cannot be too high and continuing environmental improvements must be made regardless of cost."

Support for environmental issues like clean air and water and disposal of wastes is fairly well correlated with the perceived dangers of not dealing with them when those dangers are often readily visible, in the form of pollution and rotting dumps. In the same way, the results of policies made and resources applied are often also visible, from the clearer water of the Willamette River in Oregon to the cleaner air over downtown Pittsburgh, Pennsylvania.

More complex, and more difficult to deal with, are dangers to the environment whose consequences usually must be anticipated rather than cleaned up after or as they happen, because should they occur their damage would be done all at once. Yet such dangers are the very ones that are likely to increase as our societies become technologically more sophisticated. The prototypical illustration today is the nuclear power plant.

A typical survey of voters and experts asked to rank the

risk of dying in the United States from thirty activities and technologies saw the voters ranking nuclear power first while the experts ranked it twentieth. Since the desire for greater health, comfort, and safety is a long-term structural change, likely to grow stronger and unlikely ever to be reversed, this skewing of opinion portends great difficulties in allocating funds (a political decision in most democratic nations) where they will be most effective. As our technology produces more potential dangers for our environment of the anticipated rather than the developing kind, then a corollary obligation (not yet attended to) arises on the part of science, industry, and the government to educate people about the changing character of the risks they face in everyday life. This does not mean curbing technology (impossible to do in any event) or making it a scapegoat, but rather understanding that we cannot be passive in the face of its development. It mandates our response, continuously.

A similar challenge arises with regard to the food we ingest. As countries experience economic growth, the incomes of their inhabitants rise and their attitudes toward food change. When a country is poor, in a preindustrial status, the main priority of most of its people with regard to food is simply to get enough of it and to do so regularly. As the country develops, becoming industrialized, and its people have more income with which to purchase food, they seek larger quantities and greater variety, altering their diets and eating different kinds of food, even eventually taking some meals outside the home. Finally, as the country matures economically, becoming postindustrial, a further shift in attitudes occurs. There is increasing interest in the quality and content of food; attention turns to the likely effects it will have on the body, both harmful and helpful.

Low-cal and no-cal, de-caf and low-salt are the results of this structural change in attitudes as more products are appearing without substances that allegedly are harmful to health, or to persons with health problems. Eating habits are changing, too. In the United States, per capita consumption of eggs—which contribute to cholesterol buildup, increasing the risk of heart attack—has dropped nearly 20 percent since 1963; milk consumption is down more than 22 percent and coffee nearly a third. On the other hand, the quantity of vegetables, fruits, fish, and poultry in the American diet has risen during the same period, with that of poultry nearly doubling. Alcohol consumption also is being affected. The increase in the drinking of wine has slowed since the early 1980s, and for liquor and beer there has been an absolute decline.

Slowing alcohol consumption is also attributable to another trend that accompanies rising incomes and a better standard of living: a high priority to controlling weight, both for health reasons and to make a better appearance. It is this priority that has been responsible for the success of "light" beers, for the proliferation and rising popularity of diet and no-cal soft drinks, for the introduction of more products—like Stouffer's "Lean Cuisine" and Swanson's "Le Menu" frozen dinners—that emphasize their fewer calories, and even for the tentative (but not yet successful) entry into the marketplace of low-cal wine. Hand-in-glove with attention to diet has been the rising interest in exercising and physical fitness programs and the proliferation of health clubs, television shows, and do-it-yourself books that provide instruction in them.

Slower to develop has been the realization that if we can be harmed (or made less attractive) by what we eat we can also be helped by it. According to a study by the Wheat Industry Council, a group of food providers and manufacturers, among the Americans they surveyed there was a well-founded desire to cut down on salt and sugar, but only 39 percent were concerned with eating a balanced diet. But here, too, a change in attitude is occurring, with a big assist from those who market food and prepare it.

- ITT Continental Baking has produced a series of TV commercials touting the nutritional value of Wonder Bread.
- The National Pork Producers Council has run full-page newspaper advertisements across the United States, headlining pork as "right for the shape you want to be in."
- The Paperboard Packaging Council—with an ad with two graphs, lots of copy, and a pigtailed moppet clutching a glass of milk—has proclaimed: "University studies show paper milk cartons give you more vitamins to the gallon."

There was a time not long ago when the search for meals prepared with fresh natural ingredients—and presumably with considerable attention to nutritional value—would lead one principally to health food restaurants, peopled with earnest abstemious folk wearing beards and blue jeans. For those who sought other company, different surroundings, and perhaps a drink with dinner, there was nothing available with similar fare. This is changing. Now even well-known temples of haute cuisine, like New York City's Four Seasons Restaurant, are nightly offering "spa cuisine," a selection of appetizers and entrees low in calories, sodium, and fat, high in nutritional value, and equal in standards of taste to the menu's more calorific alternatives.

All of these structural changes—in attitudes, preferences, and priorities—are reflections of a still larger structural change, a change toward greater participation and control in all of the decisions affecting one's life and greater attention to creating and maintaining one's own life-style.

> *There is an increasing desire to play*
> *a greater role in the major decisions of life.*

In the late fourteenth and early fifteenth centuries, in the city-states of northern Italy, the Renaissance celebrated the rebirth of man, alive again, after the long dark gestation of the Middle Ages. Giotto's bell tower, erected at the beginning of that period beside the Duomo, the great cathedral of Florence, stands in vivid contrast to the Romanesque Baptistery—built three centuries earlier—that it faces across the square. The latter—low, squat, admitting little light—humbles man, lowers his eyes, makes him supplicant to the incomprehensible purposes of an all-powerful deity. Giotto's tower—tall, graceful, growing seemingly lighter as it rises, its widening arches opening to more and more sky—lifts man, draws his eyes upward, proclaims his new life, a life to be lived, now, on this earth.

Six hundred years later the steady attainment of economic security by more of the world's people heralds another rebirth, this time from centuries of dependency on the plans of others and only occasional fleeting control over one's own destiny. In this new renaissance, people are demanding and playing a larger role in decisions affecting all aspects of their lives, including the content and timing of their education; the nature of their work, the compensation they receive for it, and the conditions under which it is done; their family or nonfamily status and the numbers, timing, and place of birth of their children, if they decide to have any; their leisure and recreational activities and how and when and where they will pursue them; and the care of their illnesses, and even the places and circumstances of their dying. This is happening regardless of sex or race, and it is occurring in both the young and the old.

With less constraint in their choices, with more choices available, and with greater means to pursue them, people are determined to control their own lives and establish their own life-styles. This is seen especially in one of life's most important decisions—where to live. In the past the choice was often foreordained by place of birth or upbringing, and if a move was made it was almost always done for the economic opportunity it promised.

Today the reason of rising importance for where to live—in many cases of dominant importance—is the style of life a person wishes to lead. It is for this reason, more and more, that people are moving or staying put. It is not a matter only of North versus South or Sunbelt versus Snowbelt, but of the kind of life to be led.

Contrary to popular opinion, most people who move in search of a favorable life-style are young—single or just starting families—not retirees seeking a place in the sun for their years of declining activity. Arizona, for example, has long been considered a haven for retirees, but statistics show that they constitute only 15 percent of total migration to that state. Young Americans move to Arizona, and to other Sunbelt states, because they like the better climate, the abundant out-of-doors activities, and perhaps the more innovational and less rigid social and economic structures they find there. For most, jobs come later. Even more significant are the many—again mostly young—who are leaving the central cities for the suburbs and especially for the rural areas beyond, reversing what had been considered virtually a permanent trend toward urbanization. In the United States this is happening in the North and South and in the East and West, and it will happen in other countries as they achieve mature economic development and their citizens—with more means at their disposal—seek space and facilities commensurate with the style of life they wish to lead.

The elderly, increasingly, are staying where they are. Studies by the American Association of Retired Persons indicate that 70 percent of those sixty-five and over will probably occupy for the rest of their lives the dwellings in which they are now living, and that only 4 percent are migrating to other states. The reason, again, is principally the style of life they wish to lead—near family and friends and in areas whose facilities and attractions they know; and when they do move, within or outside their states, they are moving in the same direction more younger Americans are going, away from cities and into rural areas.

What all of this indicates is a long-term structural change—accompanying, complementing, or made possible by the others discussed in this chapter—in which more people are now saying, and more will be saying: This is my life, I want to live it in accordance with my preferences, and I am determined—and increasingly able—to play a greater role in seeing that I do.

CHAPTER 4

CYCLICAL CHANGES

SHORTLY AFTER THE TURN of the century, J.P. Morgan, the famous American financier, then in his later years, made one of his rare public appearances in order to testify before a committee of the U.S. Congress. Toward the end of his testimony a young congressman, evidently unable to resist what he thought was a unique opportunity to get an inside tip, blurted out, "Mr. Morgan, what will the stock market do?" Morgan paused for a moment, then answered solemnly, "It will fluctuate."

Morgan's laconic reply is true not only for the stock market, but also for many other activities. They change, often fluctuating in cycles that repeat patterns of previous occurrences. The most familiar cycles—and the most regular—are those that occur in nature, like the cycles of the earth's rotation and its revolution about the sun, producing night and day and the temperature changes and weather phenomena of the seasons, or the cyclic beat of the human heart, sustaining life by regularly pumping blood to carry oxygen to the brain and other parts of the body.

Less regular and uniform, but still exhibiting cyclical patterns, are many changes resulting from human behavior. The characteristic that makes most of these changes cyclical is their recurrence over fairly narrow ranges within self-limiting boundaries. What happens is that when the level of an activity approaches a boundary (established by previous experience), information to that effect causes an alteration in the amount or pace or direction of the activity, returning it to a previous state.

This adaptive behavior—better known by the term cybernetics, coined by its most famous investigator, Norbert Wiener—also occurs in nature, as in the means by which information coming from the surface of the human body causes it to take steps to keep its heat loss and heat production in balance at a constant temperature of 98.6 degrees. The well-known mechanical analog to this is the thermostat. If the temperature in its vicinity falls below a preset figure—when set to keep an area warm—it closes a circuit which activates a mechanism to deliver heat until the desired temperature is reached, at which point the circuit opens and the mechanism is shut off. In the same manner, stocks of goods in a grocery store are replenished in accordance with information collected about what has been sold. Much of this activity is also cyclical, in patterns that could be daily (bread and baked goods), weekly (certain dairy products), and seasonal (soups in the winter, paper plates and cups in the summer).

These changes are very different from the structural changes already discussed. They are not evolutionary and irreversible; they do not result in fundamental alterations of the institutions associated with them or in wholly new patterns of activities; and they do not usually require responses that are new and different. They are most often changes of quantity rather than quality; they occur within the parameters of longer-term changes; and they require adjustments that are usually temporary and often similar to those made before. Yet, mastering change requires that they, too, be understood and be used. Failing to do so will cause costly errors and mean missed opportunities.

Many activities display cyclical changes. Four important categories are:

- Business cycles
- Demand-supply cycles
- Cycles of organizational behavior
- Cycles of social behavior

BUSINESS CYCLES

Like the weather, the economies of free-market countries are inherently unstable; and like the weather, their instability occurs within relatively narrow boundaries. Reaching the limits of these boundaries, as in times of extreme inflation or extreme depression, can be very painful—just as can be the extremes of floods or droughts on the weather scale—but this occurs infrequently and it is seldom fatal to the country afflicted. Most of the time these economies fluctuate more narrowly, in relatively small cycles of movement. Among the measures of economic activity which exhibit cyclical patterns of change are the rate of growth of total product (accounting for recessions and recoveries), prices and wages, interest rates, and the behavior of various kinds of markets.

> *There has never been a recession*
> *without a recovery, and vice versa.*

"Business history repeats itself, but always with a difference," wrote Wesley C. Mitchell, the founder of the National Bureau of Economic Research and one of the great scholars of business cycles. In the business history of the United States, repetition is clearly seen in the forty-three cycles of recessions and recoveries in the rate of growth of gross national product that have occurred since 1790, averaging out to one complete evolution approximately every four and one-half years. But while their repetition has been unceasing over the entire period, each cycle has had its own particular dimensions.

Many theories have been offered to account for these repeated risings and fallings of the rate of growth of total product, and many policies have been proposed to reduce, if not eliminate altogether, its fluctuations. But in fact these cycles are rooted in the nature of the free market system itself, for they represent the sum total of countless individual decisions to buy and sell, invest time and money, hire and fire, and expand and contract economic activities. Public policy can indeed influence these decisions, as when governments reallocate income, increase their own purchases, and expand or contract supplies of credit and money. However, just like individuals and businesses, governments, too, are making decisions—based on information available—with a view toward maximizing particular objectives. Since the information available to both private and public participants is necessarily incomplete (no one can know what every other player will do) and since each is seeking to maximize different—and often conflicting—objectives, results will never precisely match intentions; and so, still more decisions will be made ensuring that the system will be constantly in flux, never coming to rest.

Yet, awareness on the part of the participants (both private and public) of the overall state of the system will cause

them to make decisions over time that will tend to keep its
oscillations from becoming too great. Thus, when in the
course of a recovery capacity becomes more fully utilized,
demand (still being fueled by the recovery) will press against
supply, and producers seeking to respond will compete even
more vigorously (and since they are doing fairly well, with
somewhat less care about costs) for available resources and
capital to expand production still further. Their combined
efforts eventually will create supply in excess of demand,
leading to a slowing of the recovery as inventories build up,
production is cut back, and workers are laid off.

On the downside, when the growth of total product is
falling, producers will do everything possible to reduce costs
to remain in business. While this process will often mean
laying off workers and thus dampening potential demand, it
eventually will attract the nascent demand that does exist,
even though it may be brought forward in very different ways
(through deep discounts, innovative credit arrangements,
even some forms of barter). In modern practice, in most
advanced industrial countries, this demand usually will have
a strong public foundation, built on institutionalized income-
transfer plans, like social security and unemployment insurance, and supplemented with ad hoc fiscal policies such as
tax cuts and job creation programs. As consumers return to
the market—both attracted by lower costs and funded with
government-created demand—inventories will be drawn down,
eventually stimulating production (and with it employment
to build demand still further), starting the whole cycle all
over again.

In addition to these three-to-five-year cycles of economic
growth—spurred by adaptive changes in demand, production, and inventory—there are longer cycles created by similar cybernetic-like responses to other factors. Kuznets cycles,
named after Harvard University economist Simon Kuznets,
depict fifteen-to-twenty-five-year periods based on rises and
falls in capital investment, a process which necessarily extends beyond the shorter time span of the traditional business cycle. Of even longer duration are the better-known
Kondratiev waves, named for Nikolai Kondratiev, a Russian
economist of the 1920s and 1930s who was sent by Stalin to
a Siberian labor camp where, according to Alexander Solzhen-
itsyn's *Gulag Archipelago*, he finally perished. Kondratiev's
"crime," in Stalin's eyes, was evidently his suggestion that

capitalist economies recover from their crises in regular fifty-year cycles. He described three of these cycles, each having a peak shortly after a major war (1815, after the Napoleonic Wars; 1870, after the American Civil War; and 1920, after World War I), to be followed by a deep depression reaching a trough fifteen to twenty years later.

Kondratiev never offered a theoretical explanation of what caused these regular waves, but other economists, noting the cycles of economic activity he described, have supplied several.

- Joseph Schumpeter, who is responsible for attaching Kondratiev's name to the fluctuations he described, thought they were caused by the successive accumulation and application of innovations in the productive process.
- Walt W. Rostow of the University of Texas believes their explanation lies in the rise and fall of commodity prices.
- Jay W. Forrester of MIT sees them created by the interaction of internal economic processes, particularly those involving the consumer-goods and capital-producing sectors.

Whichever explanation of these (or combination of explanations, or still others) is valid, they all indicate adaptive actions on the part of participants, the sum total of which results in regular cyclical patterns of change. Furthermore, Kondratiev's waves today have special interest because now—in the mid-1980s, fifteen years after the end of the Vietnam War—a further repetition of his cycle would seem to put us on the brink of another great depression.

As long as economies exist that respond to the many decisions of imperfectly informed participants with varying objectives, the rate of growth of their total products and the economic activity associated with it will continue to rise and fall in these cyclical patterns—short, medium, and long. But what it is important to know—especially for future planning by all businesses—is how the dimensions of these cycles are being altered by the effect of structural changes, particularly the transition to postindustrial status through which most developed nations are passing today. Although the evidence to date covers only a short historical period, two distinct changes in business cycle dimensions appear to be emerging.

First, swings in traditional short-term business cyles in the United States—from troughs of recession to peaks of recovery and back—appear on the average to be becoming less wide. In particular, it is the depth of the downside swings below zero that have been reduced. As figure 4.1 shows, oscillations in the rate of growth of U.S. real gross national product (GNP) generally have been dampening since the early 1950s, the approximate date when industrial sector activity peaked in the United States. The most recent swing in this sequence, from a trough of -2.1 percent in 1982 to a peak of 6.4 percent in 1984—if finally confirmed—would be the largest since the late 1940s and could be interpreted as a reversal of the moderating of cyclical amplitudes of the past thirty years. More than likely, however, when averaged with the data of the years before and after, it will appear as a single large swing in a sequence of others of narrower range. This conclusion is supported by data showing similar smaller average swings in percent changes in industrial production, total employment, and business investment for the period since 1950 compared with the years before.

Second, examination of the duration of U.S. business cycles since the mid-nineteenth century shows them to be slowly getting longer, with the greatest lengthening occurring since the end of World War II. Through 1919 their average trough-to-trough length was about forty-eight months; from 1919 to 1945 the average was fifty-three months; and for the period through November 1982 it was fifty-nine. If, however, the brief recovery from mid-1979 to mid-1980 is considered part of the longer recession that ended in November 1982—as many economists believe it should be— then the postwar average goes even higher, to sixty-seven months.

These two changes, toward narrower average swings between the troughs and peaks of U.S. business cycles and toward their lengthening, are accounted for in part by new government income transfer programs, such as social security and unemployment insurance, and by increased fiscal and monetary policy activity by the federal government. But even more, they are due to the shift taking place in the American economy from industrial activity dominance to service activity dominance, a shift that means slower overall

FIG. 4.1   Annual Percent Change in U.S. Gross National Product, 1910–1986.

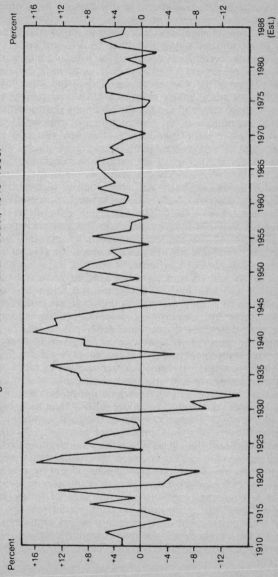

Sources: U.S. Bureau of the Census, *Historical Statistics of the United States, Colonial Times to 1970*, Vol. I (Wash., DC, 1976) pp. 226–27 and U.S. Bureau of Economic Analysis, *Survey of Current Business*, Oct. 1986, p. 20.

growth and smaller variations in the demand for employment and other factors of production.

These same changes are also likely to affect the dimensions of Kondratiev waves and other longer-term cycles. In the past these cycles have described the rises and falls of the economies of major countries which were independently passing through the various phases of their industrial eras. But most of these major countries have now passed the peaks of these eras and are rapidly becoming postindustrial; and the economies of all the countries of the world are becoming more interdependent. In this new situation the factors that served as explanations for many longer-wave cycles are themselves being altered by other changes. Capital is flowing more quickly and more widely in ever larger amounts, the development and absorption of innovation is rapid and widespread, and both production and markets are becoming more integrated. These developments will tend to change the shape of longer-wave cycles, varying their peaks and troughs and making their durations less regular. As a result, they will be weaker as descriptions of the present and poorer as forecasts of the future.

Yet cycles will continue, and we need to know not only how wide and how long their upturns and downturns will be, but also how they will affect other business conditions. Among these are employment, buying patterns, and the fortunes of different industries and geographic areas.

Employment regularly changes with recessions and recoveries. Generally speaking, during recessions fewer are hired and more are laid off, while during recoveries more are hired and fewer are laid off. But this generalization masks important variations. In an economic downturn those who provide products can cut back more quickly than those who provide services (especially those that are essential or government-related); thus employment in industrial activities will fall faster than in service activities, indicating that as economies become more service-sector-dominated they might not suffer as wide variations in total employment from peaks to troughs of business cycles, a development already seen in the U.S. economy. Furthermore, the pace of hiring and firing varies. Once a downturn is clearly underway, layoffs come fairly quickly; but when an upturn begins, employers—eager to keep costs down—resume hiring more slowly.

Buying patterns are affected too. There is, above all, a

distinct difference in the mood of consumers during periods of upturns and downturns. When the economy is up, expectations are that it will keep going up, and so consumers respond not only by spending more freely but even more important, by *planning* to spend more freely in the future. During downturns the mood is very different. Consumers are cautious and, if they are suddenly out of work, frustrated. Many assume things will get worse, and they hold back on new initiatives and new purchases, concentrating instead on security and protection. These different moods result in very different buying patterns. "Big ticket" items, especially those that are bought on credit and that, like homes and cars, regularly will require future expenditures, sell poorly during recessions but do better in recoveries, particularly at their outset. Other items, though, like women's clothing and costume jewelry, games, snack and gourmet foods, and meals eaten out, hold their own during downturns or even do better as consumers conclude that though they must postpone big purchases they can still afford more modest but satisfying ways to treat themselves.

Industries feel the impact of these buying patterns as well as other consequences of cyclical changes in the rate of economic growth. In general, during recessionary periods consumer nondurables do better than consumer durables; then, in the early months of recoveries, durables begin to pick up followed eventually by capital goods, commodities, and raw materials. Thus, in a recovery retailers will improve before manufacturers, who in turn will pick up before machine tool and heavy construction companies.

But even this typical recovery pattern will be breached with important exceptions, some produced by just-ending recessions and others by longer-term structural changes.

- Some manufacturers who lose market share during downturns—especially to importers—may never regain it; others will close lines or send work elsewhere.
- Industries structurally able to concentrate capital outlays on sophisticated new productivity-enhancing equipment will emerge stronger than those simply adding new plant through basic construction.
- Service sector activities—not burdened by problems of sudden inventory disposal and buildup or high capital costs for plant improvement—will resume their growth

more quickly, further adding to their dominant position in advanced industrial countries.

Finally, cyclical changes will also influence the growth of different geographical areas, already being altered by the impact of longer-term structural changes. In the United States it has been common in recent years to speak of a growing Sunbelt and a slowing Snowbelt. In fact, the pattern is much more complex than such a simple dichotomy suggests.

Rapid growth has been associated with high technology, particularly electronics; and much of it has occurred in Sunbelt areas, including California, Texas, and Florida. But high tech requires special resources—large universities, laboratories, highly skilled personnel—and these are also found in the North, around Boston, New York, Chicago, and other major population centers. In fact, it is from the North, by far, that the largest number of high-technology factory shipments have come, indicating continuing opportunity and growth in many sections of the Snowbelt.

At the same time, many of the slower-growing basic manufacturing industries—considered the low-growth albatrosses about the neck of the North—are also located in the South, in Alabama, Mississippi, Louisiana, and parts of Texas. When these industries suffer, these areas suffer, too. But not as well understood is that during upturns they may not do as well as many northern areas. This is because more younger workers, with higher birthrates than older ones who stayed behind, have migrated to the South, an area already heavily populated with Hispanic and ethnic minority groups who also have relatively high birthrates. This means large and growing labor pools in these areas; and when basic industries introduce labor-saving equipment, as many do during recoveries, there will be fewer jobs and more people looking for them, slowing economic upturns. In many parts of the North, on the other hand, labor pools will be relatively smaller, meaning greater opportunity and growth.

Thus, the popular view of an expanding and ever brightening Sunbelt and a shrinking and ever darkening Snowbelt is a misleading one. It ignores not only the structural changes that are giving these areas new form, but also the cyclical changes—produced by the adaptive behavior of many companies and individuals—that are regularly shaping that form.

Prices and wages: Disinflation is not deflation.
The classic explanation of inflation (rising prices and wages) is too much money chasing too few goods. The converse, deflation (falling prices and wages) or disinflation (a falling rate of increase in prices and wages), is usually explained as the opposite: too little money and too many goods. These conditions arise because in free market economies, demand (expressed as available money and credit) is never precisely in balance with supply (goods in inventory and currently being produced).

When an economy is just emerging from the trough of a cyclical downturn, it has idle production lines, workers seeking jobs, and unsold inventory. In such a situation, demand is relatively low and supply relatively high, resulting in little or no upward pressure on prices and wages. Eventually—as utilization of plant capacity attains optimum levels—fewer workers will be available for hire, inventories will have been drawn down, and demand will press on supply, moving up prices and wages.

However, as demand exceeds supply, the economy works less efficiently and becomes distorted. With greater demand and rising prices there is less need for strict discipline in production; tendencies toward greater "tightness"—born during austerity—give way to increasing sloppiness. In addition, not all prices and wages rise at the same rate, and some do not rise at all. This leads to various destabilizing consequences. In some industries, higher prices encourage increases in production which turn out to be too large for available demand; in others, stickier prices rising slower than costs mean lines have to be shut down and workforces cut back. Higher interest rates, which accompany rising prices and wages, reward some, penalize others, and make planning more difficult for all. As a result, both future demand and future production become less certain. In these circumstances, economic activity begins to decline, recession sets in, and the rate of increase of prices and wages slows and, in some cases, even falls.

It is this cybernetic adaptive behavior—the product of countless decisions by producers, consumers, and those who bring the two together—that causes cyclical variations in prices and wages, variations that generally follow the same pattern as rises and falls in economic growth rates, though usually lagging them by as much as a year or more. But prices and wages also change in longer cyclical patterns, each one covering a number of evolutions of the traditional business cycle. These longer cycles are explained by several factors, and their continuation is at this time—in the closing decades of the twentieth century—a matter of considerable interest and conjecture.

Since inflation occurs when too much money chases too few goods, a sudden influx of money can be expected to raise prices and wages. This is exactly what happened between 1550 and 1680 when large quantities of precious metals—notably silver from the New World—flooded the markets of Europe. During that period there was a sustained inflation which brought prices and wages to new higher levels. Since that time there has been a series of longer-term cycles due to another money-increasing cause— war. When governments go to war, they need not only funds to fight their battles but also supportive populations. Fearful of undermining this support by excessive taxation and limited in their ability to borrow, they often resort to the printing presses to increase supplies of money.

As figure 4.2 shows, sharp increases in the level of consumer prices in the United States have occurred in conjunction with the War of 1812, the Civil War, and the First and Second World Wars. In each of the first three cycles there has also been deflation, an absolute drop in the price level to values near those that prevailed before inflation began. However, in the period since World War II, as the figure illustrates, the decline of past cycles has not recurred. Instead, there has been a sustained *increase* in the level of prices, interrupted thus far only by shorter periods of disinflation. What has caused this long rise? Is it likely to continue upward? Or will it level off, establishing a new plateau like that following the increases of the late 1500s and early 1600s? Or will there be a deflationary plunge, back to a previous level?

The answer can be found by looking at the forces stimulating demand (by increasing money and credit) and those stimulating supply (through the production of goods and services). Since the late 1940s, for two major reasons the former have been stronger than the latter in the United States and other developed countries; and though these reasons are now slowly losing force they will be strong

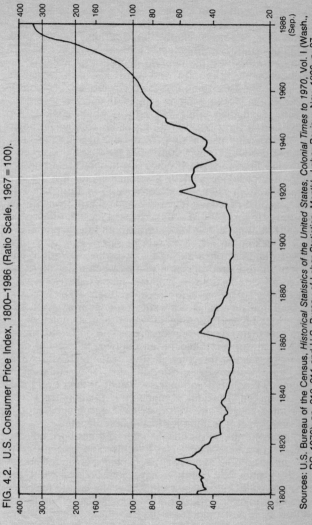

FIG. 4.2. U.S. Consumer Price Index, 1800–1986 (Ratio Scale, 1967 = 100).

Sources: U.S. Bureau of the Census, *Historical Statistics of the United States, Colonial Times to 1970*, Vol. I (Wash., DC, 1976), pp. 210–211 and U.S. Bureau of Labor Statistics, *Monthly Labor Review*, Nov. 1986, p. 87.

enough to maintain inflation at rates above zero well into the twenty-first century.

The first reason is simply the coinciding of the peak period of worldwide industrialization—and with it, high economic growth—with the pent-up demand and need for reconstruction that followed World War II, the most destructive war in history. This situation created powerful expectations—expressed and spread more rapidly than ever before by modern communications—that growth would continue on an ever-upward curve, and with it steadily enlarging production and steadily increasing personal incomes. In this environment producers saw a constantly growing market where more and more upscale products, with increasing margins for profit, could be sold to more and more higher-wage-earning consumers; and the consumers, in turn, came to regard annual raises in their wages and salaries (constituting two-thirds to three-fourths of the costs of most businesses) as virtually automatic. During upturns, both sides scrambled—always seeking an added margin of safety—to "catch up" for what had been lost during the preceding downturn, and even in those extraordinary instances when a downturn required price reductions to maintain market shares or wage concessions to preserve job security, there were few who doubted that such measures were only temporary setbacks.

Workers regularly got higher wages (and abundant credit to go with them), and producers created products with higher prices to absorb that income, encouraging workers to seek still more. One of the consequences of the high wages paid U.S. auto workers was, after all, that they could more frequently buy better and bigger versions of their own products. In this environment, demand-push inflation begot cost-push inflation and vice versa; demand encouraged supply, and supply met it, calling forth still more demand.

The second major stimulant to demand has been government. With a nearly universal franchise and access to government institutions at many different points, organized groups in most democratic countries have both political clout and means to make known their objectives and ensure that they are met. Governments of the postwar advanced industrial nations have not only responded to these groups (whose representatives they, of course, are), but also have sensed that because of the economic growth they have achieved they could and should do more for more of their people.

From these complementary external and internal pressures have come two kinds of stimulants:

- A number of programs—some of which are means-tested, most of which are not—have been created that provide recipients with income or supplements to income, such as social security, medical care, and different forms of welfare. Since these are virtually permanent and many will have increasing numbers of recipients for some time, they can be said to have institutionalized a certain level of demand, regardless of what economic conditions may ensue.
- Various institutions, laws, or regulations exist which from time to time can influence demand. For the United States these include:
  - —The Federal Reserve Board, which can loosen or tighten the supply of money
  - —Fiscal policies controlling both government expenditures and revenue collection
  - —Minimum wage laws, and statutes which provide cost-of-living adjustments to income-maintenance programs and government pensions
  - —Subsidies to farmers and, occasionally, other industry groups
  - —Environmental and other types of health and safety regulations which mandate expenditures
  - —Various ad-hoc programs to create jobs, provide or guarantee credit for different purposes, and support certain industries or, at times, even companies.

Both kinds of government activities mean, therefore, that there is a powerful, continuing built-in stimulus to demand which most of the time grows more rapidly than the growth of total product to meet it and fund it. Because the governments of most advanced industrial countries have created many such stimulants, and because their economies have become increasingly interdependent, they have made a major contribution to over thirty years of sustained worldwide inflation in prices and wages, an inflation whose very endurance contributes to its continuation by encouraging actions in expectation of that continuation.

Yet there is growing understanding of all of this in both public and private circles, and it is certainly true that what has been done *can* be undone—however difficult the task may be. There are also signs that help may be coming from the productive side. It seems increasingly clear that what many once took—in the late 1960s and early 1970s—as a sign of the arrival of the era of scarcity was in fact the last loud gasp of the passing of the age of limited resources. In the future, as technology continues to rapidly improve our ability to produce food and commodities, and to find and recycle natural resources and to create new artificial ones, the potential supply of what a slower-growing eventually peaking world population needs will increase. In such a situation, scarcity may become less a function of supply and more a function of demand (the availability of money and credit to buy what is needed); and with such a change— from a virtually built-in stimulus to demand to a virtually permanent state of sufficient supply—the long postwar cyclical phase of sustained inflation may finally top out.

> *Interest rates: What goes up does not necessarily*
> *come all the way back down.*

During a downturn in economic growth, consumers make fewer purchases, and because of the increased pessimism and uncertainty engendered by the downturn they especially make fewer of the large purchases that must be paid for in installments over long periods of time. In other words, they borrow less; but at the same time and for the same reasons— pessimism and uncertainty—they save more. Since consumers buy less, producers produce less. They do not grow, do not expand, do not add new lines, and hence they, too, borrow less. With less borrowing and more saving there is more money available, and since in many ways money behaves like a commodity, its greater supply and lesser demand means that its price—the interest rate—tends to fall.

When an upturn in economic growth begins, and for some time into it, borrowing is still fairly low. Uncertainty wears off only slowly; consumers remain wary, and businesses still have a lot of idle capacity to put back to work before they have to borrow to expand. Thus, for a time, interest rates remain at prerecovery levels, and in so doing serve to stimulate the still-growing upturn. By the second year of a recovery, when it is evident that it is lasting, optimism about the future is strengthened. People buy more and more (and save less), spurring cyclical upturns that have already begun in major industries, like housing and automobiles, with effects that reverberate throughout the economy. With demand for money growing rapidly and the supply available for borrowing not growing as fast—as people withdraw funds from savings—interest rates begin to rise.

At this point, government borrowing would normally tend to drop as rising economic growth adds to tax revenues and reduces expenditures for income support programs like unemployment compensation. But most modern nations have very large debts that constantly have to be refinanced and annual expenditures that regularly run ahead of revenues, even in the very best of times. Thus governments continue to be large and important borrowers, competing with growing numbers of consumers and businesses for available funds at rising interest rates. However, since governments must be served they will pay whatever price is demanded in the credit markets for the funds they need. This is not so for consumers with fixed incomes or for businesses which must attend to profit and loss sheets and report to shareholders; and so as rates continue their rise more and more borrowers are forced to drop out, slowing the upturn, bringing lower rates, and starting the cycle again.

In addition to tracking cyclical changes in economic growth, interest rates also reflect longer cycles of change in prices and wages. Since rising prices really mean that the value of money is falling, lenders demand higher interest rates from borrowers in order to replace the value of the capital they are lending that is lost to inflation. This means that in addition to the cost they charge for letting their money be used (traditionally 2 to 3 percent) and the risk premium they add, based on their evaluation of the borrower and his projected use of the funds, lenders also demand an inflation premium to protect the value of their capital. Thus, at a time of 10 percent inflation, a lender might ask a 15 percent interest rate consisting of 3 percent for the use of the money, 2 percent as a risk premium, and 10 percent as an inflation premium.

If inflation continues at high rates over a long period, this will strengthen expectations of its continuation, and lenders will demand that inflation premiums be high and rise with the length of the term of loans. Ten years ago, an investor who had never seen yields on high-grade corporate bonds climb over 10 percent certainly would have snapped up a long-term issue offered at that rate as an unusual opportunity to make a good investment; today the same investor, having seen interest rates rise much higher during the interim period, would evaluate such bonds more carefully, factoring in estimates of likely future inflation and considering possible returns on alternative investments. It is just such reactions that contributed to the sustained rise in long-term interest rates depicted in figure 4.3. The pernicious consequence of this process is that it locks in an element of inflation for periods far longer than normal cycles of price changes, and in so doing helps give an upward bias to these cycles.

FIG. 4.3.   Yield on New Issues of High-Grade U.S. Corporate Bonds, 1947–1986.

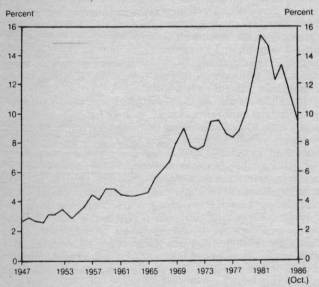

Sources: U.S. Bureau of Economic Analysis, *Handbook of Cyclical Indicators* (Wash., DC, 1984), p. 101 and *Business Conditions Digest*, Oct. 1986, p. 73.

One final factor—an outcome of the long postwar inflationary trend—is serving to sustain and reinforce the ever higher rise in the last three decades' interest rate cycles. While money does behave like a commodity in many ways—responding to changes in supply and demand—it is also unique and in other ways behaves and is treated quite differently. Because it plays such a central role in society, especially in modern economies heavily dependent on credit for acquiring public buildings, factories, inventories, houses, and many kinds of consumer goods, money tends to be closely regulated. But regulations designed to meet one particular set of conditions often become ineffective and obsolete when those conditions change. In economic matters their continuation can have even worse consequences, distorting operations and fostering the very inequities and excesses they were designed to prevent in the first place.

In the United States this has been especially true with regard to the regulation of financial services, particularly banking. With rising inflation and accompanying higher interest rates, banks found themselves increasingly handicapped by restrictions on the operations they could conduct and by limits on the interest rates they could pay to lenders and charge to borrowers. As a result, since the mid-1970s, and now more or less completed, there has been a widespread deregulation in the U.S. banking industry accompanied by a veritable explosion of new products and services, all designed to allow banks to operate more competitively.

This sweeping deregulation has had several important effects. One is that the freeing of interest rates has virtually institutionalized them at higher levels than in the past, thus further strengthening expectations that they will remain there for the foreseeable future. This, of course, attracts investors and savers (though less so during periods of economic recovery when more is spent and less is saved), and, in the early and middle 1980s, higher interest rates in the United States especially have attracted very large amounts of foreign money. This has helped fund the U.S. federal deficit and probably also has helped keep interest rates from rising higher; but at the same time it has driven America's current account deeper into deficit each year since 1981, finally making the U.S. a debtor nation.

The effect on savers, who have benefited from high interest rates comfortably above inflation levels (meaning, in effect, that they earn a higher "real" rate of interest), is to make paying such rates appear to be less of a burden than it previously was; hence houses do continue to sell, even when mortgages are at higher than traditional rates. But the increased spread between actual interest rates and the rate of inflation has had a different effect on producers. Paying a "real" interest rate at times as high as twice the traditional amount has increased the cost of capital spending for them, thus raising the rate of return they have to show in order to attract outside investment or effectively use their own internal resources. Over the long term this can only mean less expansion and weaker companies, dampening economic growth.

In sum, cyclical changes in interest rates will continue, but for well into the future they will fluctuate around higher levels than in the past, especially for long-term borrowing. Born of inflation, they will in their maturity contribute to further supporting their own higher levels.

Markets: Bulls and bears chase each other.
There are two kinds of markets in the world: those where tangible items of value (hard assets) are traded, and those which trade intangible promises of value (financial assets). Both markets are used for investment purposes, and both fluctuate in cyclical patterns which reflect other business cycle changes. But because each responds to different changes they seldom display the same patterns.

Cyclical changes in markets for hard assets reflect periods of tension and crises in international affairs which in turn increase uncertainty about the future. Such periods raise the possibility of sudden large expenditures by governments, and even their collapse, threatening the value of the financial assets they issue and control. Under these circumstances, investors shift funds to the more certain value of hard assets, driving up their price. It was, for example, in the aftermath of the Soviet invasion of Afghanistan that the price of gold soared to its record height of $875 an ounce in January 1980.

Inflation also causes a rise in hard assets' markets. When the value of money falls, confidence in all financial assets falls with it and investors turn to tangibles to preserve their wealth. During disinflation and deflation the cycle reverses. Prices increase more slowly, or fall, and the value of money rises; capital flows back to financial assets and the value of tangibles drops. Thus, whenever the rate of inflation is low, the market for hard assets will be weak.

Because markets for tangibles respond to changes in inflation, wide swings in prices make these markets especially volatile. This is exactly what happened from the mid-1970s to the early 1980s when the U.S. consumer price index twice swung through cycles that ranged almost 10 percent between their highs and lows, and the hard asset markets followed suit. Such volatility makes these markets extremely susceptible to speculation, where prices reflect less the real underlying value of assets and more what traders expect others will be willing to pay at some future date. Diamonds, for instance, became highly speculative from 1977 to 1980, increasing over 300 percent in price, far more than almost all other tangibles during this period. Such speculation not only roils markets and sends misleading signals to investors, but also draws funds away from productive investments.

In hard asset markets, precious metals play a special role because of their universal recognition as stores of value. The most important of these is gold, historically recognized as a monetary metal, but with strengths and weaknesses whose importance varies depending on the economic environment in which it is traded.

- With less industrial use than other precious metals such as silver or platinum, gold will be more subject to speculative trading.
- Since it is a hard asset, gold's price will respond to outside factors, rising in times of crises and prolonged periods of high inflation and falling during periods of relative stability and lower inflation.
- However, gold will always have some minimum irreducible value; unlike financial assets it can never become worthless.
- But during good times gold's weaknesses weigh heavily: Its price is vulnerable to changes in supply and demand and the efforts of producers to manipulate the market; it pays no income and no dividends yet at the same time can have costs for assaying, holding, and insuring; and it issues no annual reports and has no officers to hold accountable for its cyclical fluctuations.

As an ultimate safe haven, gold will always have a role as

insurance, but those who want opportunities for regular return on their money still will turn more frequently to the intangibles of financial markets.

Stocks, bonds, government and commercial debt instruments, mortgages and mortgage-backed securities, foreign currencies, and various options on many of these and their indexes are all intangible financial assets that offer different opportunities to invest for growth and income. All of these financial assets are traded in markets which exhibit regular patterns of rises and falls in cycles of varying lengths. Several of these cycles can be seen in the largest and most closely watched financial market in the world, the New York Stock Exchange (NYSE).

In its longest pattern, as represented by the Standard and Poor's Index of prices of 500 common stocks, the NYSE has had two large upturns and two large downturns in this century.* In the first of these cycles, stocks rose rapidly in value in the great post–World War I boom of the 1920s, crashed abruptly in October 1929, and then descended through the Depression years of the 1930s. The second great cycle, depicted in inflation-adjusted values in figure 4.4, began its upward rise a few years after World War II, peaked in the mid-1960s, and declined irregularly until finally reaching a new trough in early August 1982. Since then, as the figures' plot shows, inflation-adjusted stock values have been moving upward in what is evidently the ascending phase of a third great cycle.

Within these longer cycles, stocks also move in the more familiar shorter patterns of "bull" (rising) and "bear" (falling) markets. Since 1949 there have been eleven of these cycles. As figure 4.5 shows, their troughs usually fall during periods of economic recession while their peaks rise during recoveries, although it is possible for whole market cycles of this kind to occur between recessions, as happened notably in the 1960s.

Bull markets in stocks occur for a number of reasons, but simply stated they represent the accumulated responses of many institutions and individuals to a growing realization

---

*Since 1976 the Standard and Poor's Index of 500 stocks has included some issues traded outside the NYSE, but the total market value of the index still represents approximately 80 percent of the aggregate market value of common stocks traded on the NYSE.

that the stock market—relative to other markets for investment—has become a good buy. This usually occurs when both interest rates and stock prices have fallen, thus improving the environment for business in the future and making equity positions in corporations appear to be very good values. In this way, bull markets often signal—some months in advance—the beginning of economic recoveries, as they have done without fail for every one since World War II; and the optimism, and even euphoria, that they generate itself contributes to the coming upturn.

Bear markets are created when something similar occurs in reverse. At advanced stages of recoveries (which could be intermediate points in especially long upturns), interest rates and stock prices both rise and stocks become less attractive relative to what is available in other markets, such as Treasury bills, certificates of deposit, and other money market

FIG. 4.4. Inflation-Adjusted Values of Index of Prices of 500 Common Stocks, United States, 1947–1986.

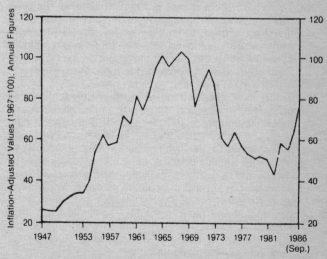

Sources: Calculated from U.S. Bureau of Economic Analysis, *Handbook of Cyclical Indication* (Wash., DC, 1984), pp. 103, 131 and *Business Conditions Digest,* Oct. 1986, pp. 84, 96.

instruments which benefit from the higher interest rates. Declines in the stock market thus foretell downturns in the economy, but with greater ambiguity than rises indicate upturns. Although the market has never failed to signal a downturn since 1929, it has foreseen some that never occurred, leading to the famous observation of economist Paul A. Samuelson of MIT, back in 1962, that the stock market "had forecast nine out of the last five recessions."

Finally, the stock market also fluctuates in even briefer cycles, lasting days (and occasionally whole weeks) rather than months and years. These cycles reflect the responses of traders to both news and rumors—concerning international events, economic data, particular industries or companies, and pronouncements by decision-makers and opinion molders—followed by their subsequent efforts to make profits on the changes caused by the responses they originally made. In recent years, however, several structural changes in the stock market—which are continuing—have accelerated these cycles and widened their swings between highs and lows.

- There has been a change in who is trading. In the early 1960s, individuals did approximately half the trading in the stock market; today they do less than 10 percent, while institutional investors—who trade in large blocks of shares which can quickly move market averages over large point spreads—account for more than 70 percent of the market's volume.
- Trades now can be handled much more rapidly using fast large-capacity electronic data processing equipment; this same equipment has been used to create the phenomenon of "program trading" in which computers are programmed to alert traders almost instantaneously to profitable spreads between stock index futures and the current prices of stocks making up the indexes.
- News that might affect trading is instantly available to all participants in the market. Where once news traveled slowly and for a time could be in the hands of a select few, today video terminals on traders' desks everywhere ensure that everyone can have access to the same news at the same time.

These changes have increased volume on the NYSE from an average of less than ten million shares daily twenty years

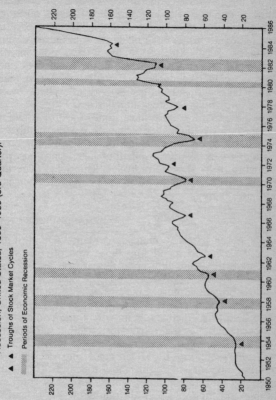

FIG. 4.5. Stock Market Cycles (In Index of Prices of 500 Common Stocks) and Periods of Economic Recession, United States, 1950–1986 (3rd Quarter).

▲ ▲ Troughs of Stock Market Cycles

░░░ Periods of Economic Recession

Sources: U.S. Bureau of Economic Analysis, *Handbook of Cyclical Indicators* (Wash., DC, 1984)., p. 75 and *Business Conditions Digest*, Oct. 1986, p. 69.

ago to nearly one hundred fifty million during 1986. They also frequently have produced daily swings in excess of 10 points in the Dow Jones industrial average, an event that not long ago happened only rarely. To many observers, including Nobel economist James Tobin, the new ease and volume of stock trading have made the market increasingly an arena of speculation, where prices bear no consistent relationship to the underlying value of the companies whose shares are being traded—a trend reinforced by increased corporate takeover and merger activity as well as by low margin requirements for stock purchases.

What these changes also have done is cause traders to ever more quickly adapt their behavior to large numbers of signals from both the external environment and immediately prior states of the market itself, thus increasing the cybernetic quality of its short-term cycles. This same cybernetic quality is also seen in the short-term cyclical changes of demand and supply.

DEMAND-SUPPLY CYCLES

Supply never precisely matches demand. Either it falls short or it exceeds demand. But those who provide supply are attentive to signals indicating the size of demand, and when those signals show more supply is wanted they will respond by providing more. Likewise, when signals indicate demand is low they will cut back. Through this cybernetic adaptive behavior, fluctuations in supply and demand constantly occur in cycles that move mostly within fairly narrow boundaries. Thus, though supply never does precisely match demand, they are never too far apart and decisions are constantly being made to bring them together. This is true for products and commodities whose supply is constantly renewable and for those that are nonrenewable because of physical and economic limits; and it is also true for the demand and supply of persons in various occupations and professions.

The demand for renewables is inherently unstable.
Renewables are manufactured goods and commodities, and services, too, whose production is not normally limited by a fixed supply or, more accurately, by economic costs that would be required to significantly enlarge the supply.

For example, in a factory with an annual production run of a million can openers, or on a large farm with an annual output of a million bushels of grain, the cost of the millionth can opener or bushel will be the same as the first. However, in a mine producing copper, a *non*renewable commodity, the cost per ton of extracting ore far below the ground will be much higher than that of extracting ore at or near the surface, thus effectively limiting the total supply.

For producers of renewables, signals indicating rising demand prompt increased output to meet it. But typically the signals that do so are the appearance of orders, not intentions to buy. So, during a period of rising demand there will be a lag between signals and completed responses to them; and demand will exceed supply. However, production will not drop until orders fall or disappear, meaning supply will continue growing after demand has slowed or even stopped. Furthermore, rising demand will encourage additional producers to enter the market. Since there will be some delay between their decisions to do so and the availability of their finished products or competitive services, the demand situation when they are finally in the marketplace will be different than when they made their decisions. If that difference is a slowing or absolute decline then the result will be greater supply than demand. In such circumstances competition will be stronger, price cutting is likely to result, and weak and less efficient producers will be driven out. These sequences of demand-supply changes occur frequently, but especially when demand rises very rapidly, as did the early demand for home computers, a brand-new market which was misread by most manufacturers, who failed to understand that following the initial burst of demand—fueled mainly by hobbyists—there would have to be a pause while the preconditions of a mass market—education, services, software—developed more slowly.

Other short-term cyclical changes also affect demand-supply cycles for renewables. In the 1970s and early 1980s, demand for jeans boomed, causing traditional manufacturers—like Levi Strauss—to greatly increase their production and other clothing companies, many of which had never made jeans, to add them to their lines. But fashion in clothing is also highly cyclical, and in time interest in jeans began to slow. This, in turn, coincided with the aging of the largest market group for them—teenagers in the United States and other

Western industrial nations—as the postwar baby boom gave way to the baby bust. Finally, all of these changes occurred in the midst of a worldwide economic recession, dampening demand still further. Thus, several short-term cyclical changes reinforced each other, accelerating the downturn in the demand-supply cycle for jeans.

Longer-term changes also influence the duration and dimensions of demand-supply cycles. Deregulation of the commercial airline industry in the United States in 1978 encouraged the growth of new carriers, spurred the creation of new routes, and brought aggressive price competition. This in turn increased passenger traffic demand, encouraging still further growth—and competition—by carriers to meet it. On an even longer term, new technology can mean structural changes which improve products, increase variety, lower prices, and even create obsolescence. In response, demand-cycle changes will boost some products and weaken, even eliminate, others.

- Color television, in a few short years, caused a transformation as great as that which occurred in the motion picture industry when it moved out of the black-and-white era.
- Digital readouts have changed the clock and watch industry and created a whole new demand for the display of measurements, from radio dials to thermometers.
- Automatic teller machines (ATMs) have so revolutionized the delivery of banking services that every bank of any size—including all those slow to understand the change made by ATMs—eventually will have to install them.

Foodstuffs, agricultural crops, and commodities grown from the soil constitute a special class of renewables. In the first place, a farmer, unlike a manufacturer, cannot easily "modernize" his product, nor can he switch to a new model or an entirely new product. He has either only one crop for his particular soil, acreage, and environmental conditions (an apple grower cannot switch to oranges if the apple market is glutted) or perhaps a few limited choices (for some plains farmers, variation among wheat, corn, and soybeans may be possible, though only over relatively long periods of time). In addition, while manufacturers can with great certainty count on their products having a particular size, shape, and quality, based on the inputs used to produce them, farmers regularly face a risk that can drastically alter their output regardless of how precisely they have measured the inputs. That risk is, of course, the weather, which can even destroy their output.

This means that farmers and other crop producers have far less control over demand-supply cycles, and for this reason these cycles oscillate more widely than do those of most manufactured products. Typically, farmers or other food producers plan to obtain the largest possible yield they can through the best use of the land or livestock available to them. Not only is this the optimum strategy for dealing with the uncertainties of weather, but it is also necessary to repay large loans needed for seed, machinery, and other inputs and still net a profit that makes the whole enterprise worthwhile. Yet the cumulative effect of each producer's doing this, in a free market environment during a year with good weather, will be to increase supply far above demand, thus depressing prices and income. In a bad weather year prices may rise but output will drop, still causing a fall in income.

The ironic outcome is that the efficiency and hard work of agricultural producers may actually bring them less rather than more return, a situation that has caused the governments of most high-income industrial countries to create programs to buy and stockpile crops, subsidize food producers, and even pay farmers to keep land out of production. These programs have helped to smooth out excessive swings to the supply side in demand-supply agricultural cycles, but because these cycles are also being affected by structural changes, the programs are only stopgap measures which constantly must be revised.

The most important of these structural changes is the steady increase in production—using technologies developed in the United States and other advanced countries—by more and more agricultural producers in both developed and developing lands. This increase, which has finally created a permanent food surplus in the world, has already begun to affect U.S. agricultural exports, which, after rising steadily for over thirty years, have fallen since 1981, their peak year. Although conditions in other countries may cause American exports to rise again for brief periods, they are unlikely ever again to resume the steady growth they experienced in the

1970s. The same is also likely to be true of other exporting countries as more lands reach self-sufficiency and even become food exporters themselves.

There are also structural changes in demand in advanced industrial countries—due to their increasing prosperity—that are affecting demand-supply cycles for certain foods. These can be seen by comparing the consumption of two prestige food items in the United States.

On the one hand, changing attitudes toward health and appearance have caused a decline in the growth of demand for beef. As figure 4.6 shows, there have been regular short-term cyclical changes in the "cows per 100 people" ratio from 1949 through 1985 as herds are liquidated and rebuilt. But a trend line through these changes also shows a long-term structural decline in the ratio.

On the other hand, higher discretionary incomes and improved technology in refrigeration and transportation have increased the demand for other kinds of foods, particularly some not quickly or easily produced and hence rising in price under conditions of greater demand. In the eighteenth century, lobsters were considered a "trash" food in Massa-

FIG. 4.6. Cows per 100 People Ratio, United States, 1949–1985.

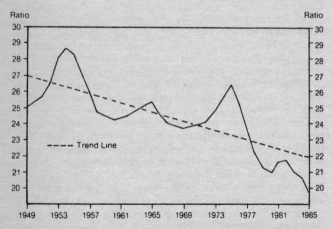

Sources: *Commodities*, Jun. 1979, p. 27 and U.S. Dept. of Agriculture, *Agricultural Statistics 1985*, p. 256.

chusetts and fed to prisoners in jails (it is not recorded what effect, if any, this had on the crime rate in the Bay State!). Today, live lobsters are shipped from New England all over the United States and even to places beyond its borders. They are appearing as a prestige item on menus in more restaurants; and with an increasing number of affluent diners able to afford them, demand for them regularly exceeds their supply, driving up prices still further.

Cycles for nonrenewables are self-limiting.

Although lobsters are renewable commodities, the renewing process is slow, and until they can be successfully farmed on a large scale, demand-supply cycles for them will behave more like those of more traditional nonrenewables. In general, nonrenewable commodities are either mineral deposits found in the earth's crust or fuels derived from long-since-fossilized plants once growing on the planet's surface. Although minerals can in many cases be recycled and reused, both their supply and that of the fossil fuels is ultimately fixed; and it is this characteristic that makes their demand-supply cycles unique.

Because many nonfuel mineral resources can be reused, their demand-supply cycles behave somewhat differently from those of fuel resources. Typically, rising demand—for metals, for example—will encourage increased production from existing mines and the exploration for and development of new sources. From these efforts will come more supply to meet the rising demand.

This process is not smooth, however. Exploration and development take time, and when new supply finally comes on line, demand no longer may be rising. Furthermore, high-grade ores usually are mined first and usually are the most readily available. Extracting the same amount of metal from lower-grade ores will in the beginning, at least, cost more, raising prices to consumers, some of whom may then drop out of the market. If demand falls enough, producers will try to hold market share by cutting costs and operating more efficiently, and steadily improving technology for ore extraction will almost always give them the potential to do so. Prices will then stop rising, or perhaps even fall, bringing back demand.

Greater disruptions to mineral demand-supply cycles are caused by the perturbations of business cycles. During economic downturns demand for commodities falls. But producers still have costs to meet, often including regular principal and interest payments on loans taken out during prior cyclic upturns to boost capacity. Thus, they must continue to sell products and—in a market with weak demand—can do so usually only by lowering prices or selling at a discount. It is this situation, in the extreme, that has become the fate of many third-world commodity producers. Countries like Chile, for instance, can earn foreign exchange to make payments on their very large international debts, and to buy goods abroad, only by selling more of their principal exports—in Chile's case, copper. But selling copper in a glutted market only boosts supply still further above demand, driving down prices paid to all producers, including Chile. It is this that has contributed importantly to a decade-long crisis in the copper industry.

In addition to the influence of business cycle changes on mineral demand-supply cycles, there is the even greater effect of structural changes. The most important of these is simply the increase in the number of producers. During upturns in demand, new production capacity is added and new producers enter the market. During downturns the new capacity and new producers do not disappear; there may be cutbacks, but they are still there, adding to total supply. Furthermore, since many of the new mineral producers are in developing countries, they have the advantage of low labor costs, and because they are often government-owned or government-subsidized enterprises, no need to regularly show a profit. Under these circumstances the efforts of some advanced industrial countries to encourage the construction of new facilities to maintain mineral production, even from low-grade sources (as the United States did in the case of iron ore), makes little economic sense. The increase of supply from cheaper producers turns such facilities into expensive relics, and advancing technology ensures they will be obsolete by the time they are needed, if ever.

Another important, and usually overlooked, structural change is increasing efficiency in the use of raw materials over time. It was the failure to understand this that led to wide margins of error in the Paley Commission report of 1952, the most famous and most ambitious effort in recent times to forecast long-term demand for minerals. In retrospect, what the Paley report did was to *under*estimate economic growth and *over*estimate mineral demand. This seemingly inexplicable outcome can be explained by understanding that the larger economic growth it failed to forecast made possible technological progress that, by increasing efficiency in the utilization of minerals, meant less would be used than it predicted.

Especially important in influencing demand-supply cycles for many nonrenewable minerals is the structural change toward increased recycling and reuse. Today in the United States, half of the copper used in new production of the metal is scrap copper. Recycled aluminum, with over two million tons being recovered each year (boosted in part by many new state "bottle laws" mandating deposits on beverage containers), has recently replaced copper as the number-one recycled metal and accounts for 40 percent of the domestic aluminum market. This structural change will continue. Recycling technology will go on improving, further reducing production costs from scrap relative to extraction from ore (already savings of nearly 100 percent on energy costs are possible using scrap rather than primary bauxite to produce aluminum); and, of course, the amount of scrap will continue to grow.

But in time the most important structural change affecting these demand-supply cycles will be the substitution of new laboratory-created materials for traditional minerals. In many cases these new materials can be constituted from virtually inexhaustible sources and have properties far greater than those of the materials they are replacing. Fiber optic cables, for example, are fabricated out of glass (made from abundant silicates) and have far greater capacity and far better communications characteristics than copper wires. It is the increasing development and use of such new materials that has led to the *falling* per capita consumption of many basic minerals in advanced industrial countries; and it is their growing utilization in the future that will continue to affect the characteristics of demand-supply cycles for basic minerals.

Cycles of nonrenewable fuels display many characteristics similar to those of minerals; but because these fuels are used up and can never be recycled, short-term changes in their demand and supply also display their own unique qualities.

Energy, like food, is a daily necessity. If the source of energy is constantly renewable, or eternal, like the sun, wind, falling water, or the heat of the earth itself, then its provision is principally a matter of appropriate distribution—in the quantities, to the places, and at the times needed. But most of the energy sources of both developed and developing countries today are nonrenewable, mainly the fossil fuels of coal, oil, and natural gas.

As long as quantities of these nonrenewable fossil fuels are abundant they can be treated almost as if they were renewable and eternal. Until the early 1970s this was largely true, especially for what was then the cheapest fossil fuel for the amount of energy it delivered—oil. By 1970, the world price of oil was slowly falling toward $1 a barrel, and so great was the supply and so eager were some of its largest producers to pump it out of the ground that the greatest fear of many in the oil business was that the price might fall still further. (After all, the true cost of production of the largest potential producer, Saudi Arabia, was then about ten cents a barrel.)

That such fears were indeed misplaced and misinformed is now clear in the light of the enormous problems and opportunities created by the events of the decade that followed. The preconditions for these momentous events were laid in 1970 when crude oil output peaked in the lower forty-eight states of the United States, while at the same time, demand—stimulated by the war in Vietnam and almost ten years of uninterrupted economic growth—continued to rise strongly. Although discoveries in Alaska (the giant field at Prudhoe Bay) would eventually cause U.S. production to again rise, in the early 1970s it was falling, necessitating a steady increase in imports, principally from the great oil fields of the Middle East. Because the largely American-owned companies who pumped oil from these fields were able to determine its price, there seemed to be nothing immediate to fear in the growing U.S. dependence on imports. But this condition soon changed when Colonel Muammar al-Qaddafi, the leader of Libya, succeeded in obtaining major concessions from the American firm of Occidental Petroleum. Other Arab and Middle Eastern regimes followed suit, and in a few years the balance of power in the oil fields had shifted away from the companies.

It was this combination of circumstances—lower U.S. production, rising demand and imports, and loss of control by the companies—that set the stage for what followed in the aftermath of the Arab-Israeli War of October 1973.

Displeased by American support for Israel, the Arab leaders of the Organization of Petroleum Exporting Countries (OPEC) declared an embargo on sales of oil to the United States and, over the next nine months, quadrupled its price. After a brief few years in the late 1970s during which the price gradually fell in real terms, panic buying in the wake of the Iranian revolution caused it to double in late 1978 and finally reach a peak of $40 a barrel in the spot market the following year.

This unprecedented price increase within such a short span in a widely used commodity that many felt was vital to the survival of both industrial and industrializing countries was a great shock, and perhaps this explains the nearly total failure of most observers and government leaders to foresee the demand-supply cyclical change through which it would evolve. Instead, the perception was that demand would continue to rise virtually unaffected by price, which, therefore, also would continue to rise. On this basis a number of ill-considered decisions were made, the consequences of which are still unfolding.

Oil companies rushed to increase their exploratory activity, paying premium prices to buy and rent drilling equipment and setting it up in any areas that looked promising, no matter how remote, believing that rising prices would cover the increased costs they were paying. The Canadian government, for instance, projected that oil would rise to $70 a barrel by 1986, and with such a forecast felt justified in supporting the efforts of thirty companies, including giant Dome Petroleum, to drill below the Arctic ice for crude that could be extracted and shipped only at prices far above those then being paid. On the same expectations, banks hastened to loan money to fledgling companies long on plans but short on collateral, and still other banks eagerly bought these loans. Old tankers were outfitted to carry oil and construction was hastily begun on new ones; American automobile manufacturers moved quickly to produce smaller vehicles, all but abandoning larger ones; and "oil patch" cities, like Houston and Calgary, raised skyscrapers of office space to accommodate the managers of the apparently endless boom.

But oil and natural gas, although essential and nonrenewable, are not immune from demand-supply cycles. Demand for energy is indeed continuous, but it is not without elasticity. Faced with skyrocketing prices, consumers did everything possible to conserve, and with a resource whose costs had been so low as to be almost negligible for many, there was a great deal of room for conservation.

- In the beginning, equipment was simply turned off when it was not needed and windows were closed to save heat or opened to cut down on air conditioning.
- In time, more permanent measures were taken, such as installing insulation, retiring energy-wasteful machinery, and rearranging work processes and schedules with the specific goal of saving energy.
- Finally, buildings and equipment not yet begun were designed anew to reuse heat, control temperature, and operate with greater energy efficiency.

Transportation—especially automobiles—was a major user of oil-derived fuels, and so it became a prime target for conservation. In the United States, by act of Congress, newly manufactured cars were required to meet gradually rising fuel efficiency ratings. As a result, between 1973 and 1985 the fuel efficiency of the average American automobile on the road rose from 13.1 to 17.9 miles per gallon. Translated into gasoline consumption, this means that a peak of 112.2 billion gallons consumed was reached in 1978, an amount that may never be surpassed by the more fuel-efficient cars of today and tomorrow, even though they continue to increase in number and miles driven.

Higher prices for oil and natural gas also encouraged the development and use of alternative energy sources. Coal became the fuel of choice in many areas where supplies were readily available and equipment could be converted or built to use it, and though the burning of some types of coal meant increased pollution, the savings from using it made possible the investment to reduce the pollution. In other areas, particularly outside the United States where supplies of fossil fuels were not readily available, nuclear fission was chosen for power plants generating electricity. Also encouraged by the rise in oil and gas prices were research and development in eternal, renewable alternatives, such as solar and geothermal energy and nuclear fusion.

But not only do higher prices prompt adaptive behavior on the part of consumers to reduce demand and search for alternatives; they also encourage adaptive behavior by producers to increase supplies. Because fossil fuels are nonrenewable, hidden in different places in the earth, the cost of extracting them varies greatly. In the oil-rich desert of Saudi Arabia, petroleum literally pops out of the ground, at a recovery cost that is today somewhere near fifty cents a barrel. In the Alaskan oil fields the cost is closer to $5 a barrel; much farther north, above the Arctic Circle, it may be nearly $50; and, obviously, the cost of the last barrel on earth—dispersed and inaccessible—is so great that it will never be extracted. In other words, raising the price increases the supply. A lot more oil is available when the selling price is $30 a barrel than when it is $3.

It is because of this adaptive behavior on the part of both consumers and producers that higher prices produce falling demand and rising supply, resulting in surpluses, not shortages. How little this was understood in the turmoil of the 1970s can be seen in the very wide margins of error in projections of petroleum consumption made even *after* the OPEC embargo. One of these, an authoritative and frequently quoted forecast made by the Bureau of Mines of the U.S. Department of the Interior in December 1975, is depicted in figure 4.7. How costly was this failure of understanding is evident in the consequences that have followed from it: debt-plagued countries, bankrupt businesses, laid-off workers, idled tankers, vacant office space, failed (and some barely rescued) banks, and lower morale and reduced confidence in the future.

As figure 4.7 illustrates, the next cycle in American consumption—bringing rising demand and higher prices—is already underway, and U.S. dependency on imported oil very quickly has risen halfway back to its 1977 peak of 46.5 percent from the low of 22.5 percent in early 1985. However, the combination of circumstances that created the sharp price run-up in the most recent cycle was extremely unusual, and the probability of another such unusual combination occurring in the near-term future is still fairly low, in part because in response to what has happened major alterations are now in place (built-in conservation, increased capacity, different expectations) that will help prevent the conditions for such an occurrence from developing. Thus, the upward phase of this next cycle is likely to rise more slowly, lengthening the availability of nonrenewable petro-

FIG. 4.7. Projected and Actual Consumption of Petroleum, United States, 1974–1986.

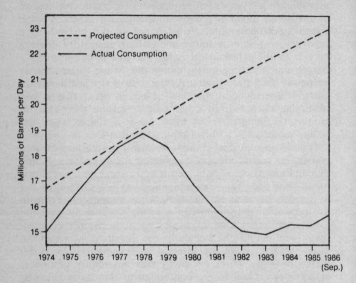

Sources: Dupree, Walter C. and John S. Corsentino, *United States Energy Through the Year 2000*, revised (Wash., DC: U.S. Department of the Interior, Bureau of Mines, Dec. 1975), p. 29 and Energy Information Administration, *Monthly Energy Review*, Sep. 1986, p. 11.

leum and providing more time to develop alternative fossil fuels as well as eternal renewable sources of energy—if we choose to do so.

Applicants for occupations and professions are either too many or too few.

Enrollment in law schools in the United States increased over 150 percent from 1963 to 1982, doubling the total number of lawyers in the country. But in 1983, after twenty years of steady increases, applications to law schools began declining. They were down 1.6 percent that year, 10.6 percent in 1984, and over 16 percent halfway through 1986. Even the prestigious law schools have been affected: In two years applications to Columbia University's School of Law have fallen more than 18 percent.

What has happened? Why are students suddenly losing interest in a profession in which top firms have been paying entry-level salaries of up to $50,000 a year? The answer is the steadily growing awareness of the existence of a glut of lawyers, a phenomenon that periodically affects all occupations and professions, especially those that experience sudden spurts of growth. During periods of growth, applicants to professional schools and to programs offering appropriate training increase rapidly. In time, the schools and programs fill up, more applicants are trained and graduated, and the number of qualified people exceeds the number of opportunities available. When information about the excess of supply over demand becomes widely available, the number of applicants falls and the cycle begins again.

In reality, such demand-supply cycles vary greatly, depending on the kind of occupation, its size, the extent of the training required for it, and the availability of information concerning employment opportunities. These cycles are also affected by other cyclical changes and by structural changes. Business cycles have the most apparent and most regular influence on employment cycles. Generally speaking, during recoveries employment is up and during recessions it is down. But here, too, there are important variations, such as the tendency during economic downturns for less decline in employment in service activities than in industrial.

In many fields, cyclical demographic changes have a very important effect. One example is teachers. The large number of children born in the United States during the postwar baby boom led to an increase in both schools and teachers to staff them. The baby bust that followed left a glut of both, a clear signal to potential applicants to teachers' colleges that prospects for jobs in the profession were poor; and so the number of college graduates in education plummeted, from 317,000 in 1972 to 146,000 in 1984. Now, in the mid-1980s, as the first children of those born during the baby boom are beginning to enter school, there is a shortage of teachers and demand for them is again growing.

Other cyclical changes that occur less regularly can significantly shape employment cycles in certain fields. The crisis caused by the run-up of oil prices in the 1970s resulted in a sudden large increase in demand for every category of energy specialist, from petroleum engineer to solar consultant. In the aftermath of slowing energy demand and falling oil prices, hiring virtually stopped and many energy specialists were on the street looking for other work. Too little supply also prompts short-term responses, as when the U.S. Congress responded to an apparent lack of dentists in the early 1970s by subsidizing dental education. However, as often happens in efforts to smooth cycles of short-term change, the net effect was to vastly increase supply over demand, eventually creating an even larger glut of dentists. When cyclical change is not understood, priming the pump can turn the next natural surge of supply into a flood.

The great increase of women in the workforce is one of the most important structural changes affecting demand-supply employment cycles, especially the entry of women into fields long dominated by men. This can be seen by examining changes in the number of science and engineering bachelor's and first professional degrees per thousand twenty-

FIG. 4.8. Physicians per 100,000 Population, United States, 1870–1981.

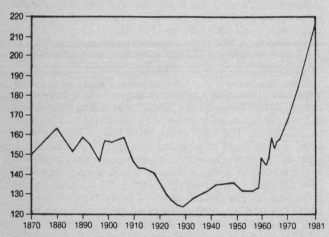

Sources: U.S. Bureau of the Census, *Historical Statistics of the United States, Colonial Times to 1870*, Vol. I (Wash., DC, 1976) pp. 75–76 and *Statistical Abstract of the United States 1985* (Wash., DC, 1984), p. 102.

two-year-olds in the U.S. population from 1950 to 1980. During this period the normal cyclical pattern for men saw the number fall from a peak of 119 per thousand in 1950 to a trough of 64 in 1954 followed by a rise to 115–16 from 1968 to 1973 and thence a steady fall to 89 in 1980. For women, however, during the same period there has been an almost unbroken rise, from 13 per thousand during 1953–55 to 51 in 1980. As a result of the increasing number of women, the cycle for *total* degrees per thousand twenty-two-year-olds for the late 1970s does not show the cyclical fall indicated for men alone. Instead the curve is fairly flat, and even indicates a rise from 1979 to 1980.

Structural changes can also result in a longer-term rise or fall—in what is still a cyclical pattern—of those in a particular occupation or profession. This is seen, for example, in the change in the number of doctors over time in the United States. Figure 4.8, charting physicians per 100,000 population, shows that for nearly a century the number fluctuated up and down, dipping to a low point halfway through the period and then—in the early 1960s—rising back up to the level of the 1870s. In the late 1960s, however, the cumulative effect of a number of longer-term structural changes (increased knowledge and specialization in medicine, more graduates accredited from offshore medical schools, a longer-living population, prepaid health plans, government-supported medical care, larger discretionary incomes, and attitudes favoring a higher priority to health) began to influence the demand for and supply of physicians, steadily raising the number per 100,000 well above past historical rates to a level which most now acknowledge represents an excess of supply over demand, presaging a new downward phase in the current cycle, though not to the lows of the last hundred years.

Changes in demand and supply for positions in different occupations and professions will vary from region to region and country to country, depending on rates of population growth, levels of development, opportunities available, and styles of life to be lived. But because these changes are the products of innumerable individual and corporate decisions responding to a combination of information about the present and expectations for the future, they will continue to occur in cyclical patterns alternately producing shortages and surpluses.

All of the above cyclical changes of demand and supply, like those of business cycles described before, will continue in the future, in patterns very similar to those that have occurred in the past. Because these changes are indeed cyclical, the general dimensions of their patterns can be examined and known. Doing so in advance of their future evolution can enable us to manage them better—that is, to take steps to avoid or mitigate their undesirable consequences as well as to exploit fully the new opportunities they present. Similar patterns requiring similar responses are seen in the behavior of organizations.

ORGANIZATIONAL BEHAVIOR

Just as nature abhors a vacuum, organizations abhor the status quo. While stability may be the state in which most organizations objectively would prefer to operate, the status quo is not the status most of them want. They want a better status—one that enables them to earn more, to acquire more of a market, to operate more efficiently, to increase satisfaction and security for themselves and their members. Thus, their actions tend regularly to upset the status quo.

The sum total of these actions, usually taken by an organization's leaders, carries it in a particular direction beyond the status quo. At a certain point, further movement in that direction no longer yields increases in the values sought in moving that way and may even bring negative consequences. So, the leaders—or perhaps new leaders who have replaced them—begin a countermovement, leading the organization in an opposite direction, until in time the gains in doing so are no longer being realized and the cycle begins again.

This adaptive behavior on the part of organizations means that many of their activities take them in swings between polar positions. Among the cyclical swings that occur are those between centralization and decentralization, liberalism and conservatism, and war and peace.

> *Organizations swing between the poles of*
> *centralization and decentralization.*

In the Bolshevik Revolution of November 1917, when Lenin and his supporters seized power from the disintegrating and floundering Russian Provisional Government of Alexander Kerensky and established the first Soviet regime, one of their major tasks was to extend the power of the Bolsheviks beyond their two main operating areas, Petrograd (then the capital of Russia) and Moscow. This Lenin did by giving considerable autonomy and individual responsibility to the few Bolsheviks and their close allies who were scattered across the vast reaches of the country, large portions of which were in the hands of counterrevolutionary and even foreign elements. Five years later the anti-Bolshevik opposition was largely crushed, all foreign forces had left the Russian mainland, and Lenin, having suffered the first of the three strokes that would eventually kill him, was no longer able to command the party and the country. For Stalin, the party General Secretary who aspired to succeed Lenin, these circumstances called for greater control over the party, and so the Bolsheviks were duly reorganized under the strong central direction of the Party Secretariat.

By 1930, Lenin was gone and Stalin had routed both the "right" and "left" opposition to his rule. He now wanted to ensure party control over every facet of Russian society—schools, factories, farms, the military, the administrative apparatus, even cultural organizations. To do so he proceeded to decentralize the Bolshevik Party (now formally called the Communist Party of the Soviet Union—CPSU), installing units throughout the countryside, each with considerable local power. In time, however, this began to reduce unified party control from above over the main sectors of Russian society. To restore it the party was again reorganized in 1934, this time under strong central direction. A new decentralization then followed in 1939, and since then, to varying degrees and over differing periods of time, further similar reorganizations have regularly occurred; and undoubtedly they will continue to occur.

While the example of the CPSU is probably extreme in that it concerns an organization involved in every aspect of a very large society, it is not atypical. Every large organization seeking to advance its goals is continually in movement, attracted alternately by the magnetlike poles of centralization and decentralization. Centralization has undoubted advantages:

- It maximizes control.
- It brings broad expertise to bear on decision-making.

- It enables resources to be allocated most efficiently among subordinate units.
- It reduces waste caused by the duplication of staff and their activities at lower levels.

But centralization also inhibits innovation and the development of experience farther down the organization, reducing the morale of personnel there; and it can lead to the creation of excessive staff at the center.

Decentralization responds to these problems and offers advantages of its own:

- It relegates more decision-making to the levels that have the most information and the most direct experience.
- By not requiring recourse to the center it speeds up and reduces the cost of the decision process.
- It fosters enterpreneurial spirit and helps develop management skills.

But decentralization has its disadvantages, too, the most important being the reduction of control and coordination by the center and the loss of the synergism that is gained through the simultaneous consideration of a number of different matters by centralized management.

Because business firms want the advantages of both centralization and decentralization, and because the advantages of one tendency are often the disadvantages of the other (more control at the center, for example, means less opportunity for innovation on the periphery), companies are in constant movement between the two. However, the extent of this movement and its frequency vary considerably depending on the company and its industry.

- General Electric, a multiproduct firm, has tended strongly toward decentralization in its reorganizations in order to give maximum autonomy to each of its major lines of business; yet care has also been taken to preserve a clear chain of command to the top and to centralize major financial activities.
- USX, formerly U.S. Steel and for most of its history a single-product company, has experimented with decentralization, but in each of its successive reorganiza-

tions it has tended to move more in the direction of centralization.

- Sears Roebuck, a market-oriented firm, has undertaken several wide reorganizational swings between centralization and decentralization as the company has moved from an exclusively mail order firm to a company retailing clothing and dry goods to one vertically integrated for obtaining and marketing a great variety of products to—most recently—diversification into insurance, brokerage, and other financial service activities.

Other changes also affect cycles of corporate centralization and decentralization. During downturns in business cycles, companies may tend to move in the direction of centralization to conserve and better control resources and to reduce personnel; during upturns, they may go in the opposite direction to encourage innovation on the periphery and reduce the time required to take advantage of local opportunities that may arise quickly. Structural changes are influential, too. Greater product diversity and increasing interdependence and corporate development across national boundaries require more centralized control over many activities, yet at the same time they emphasize the importance of decentralization in many functional areas such as marketing. The increased availability and speed of handling information also contribute to both tendencies. On the one hand, they greatly enlarge the amount of, and reduce the cost and time of acquisition of, information at the center, thus enhancing centralized control. On the other hand, especially through the growing use of large-capacity distributed information systems, they give local units a much wider perspective in which to evaluate and execute their own decisions.

These changes, and others whose effects are yet to be felt, will continue to shape short-term cycles of centralization and decentralization, but they are unlikely ever to terminate them. Beatrice Foods provides a good example of a company regularly moving between the poles of centralization and decentralization in response to both internal organizational dynamics and external changes. For nearly a quarter of a century, under the leadership of its former chairman, William G. Karnes, Beatrice used its stock to buy other companies at bargain prices, leaving their management largely in the hands of the entrepreneurs from whom they had been bought. This practice of decentralized management worked so well that by the early 1970s Beatrice had earned a reputation as one of America's best-run companies. But changes were occurring in the food industry environment, and Beatrice was not changing with them. Its competitors—household names like Procter & Gamble and General Mills, with consolidated rather than decentralized businesses—were using research and development and advertising to create new products and increase market share in lines where Beatrice traditionally had been dominant. Beatrice, however, continued as before, increasingly weakened by carrying the burden of longtime but ever more superfluous employees at the center who further distanced themselves from the changing decentralized businesses on the periphery. Another cyclical change became the final straw in this burden when in the midst of the 1981–82 national recession Beatrice posted its first quarterly earnings decline in thirty years.

James L. Dutt, Beatrice's chairman since 1979, then set about to reverse the company's sagging sales with a major reorganization that had consolidation and centralization as its principal themes. Sick and cyclical businesses were divested and others were regrouped in larger units, advertising and purchasing operations were centralized, research and development was made into a business unit, and atrophied management was pruned. The initial results have been gratifying; net earnings for the year ending February 1984 were ten times what they had been the year before, and for the following year they were up another 10.6 percent. But the company still has a long way to go to achieve the status of its big rivals who changed while it slumbered; and with its recent major acquisition of giant Esmark, Beatrice finds that once again the pole of decentralization is beckoning, attracting it back from the long swing so recently taken in the direction of centralization.

> *Democratic governments are alternately attracted to liberalism and conservatism.*

The American essayist Henry David Thoreau heartily accepted the motto "That government is best which governs least," and in his journal he gave witty testimony to his distrust of government:

I went to the store the other day to buy a bolt for our

front door, for, as I told the storekeeper, the Governor was coming here. "Aye," said he, "and the legislature too." "Then I will take two bolts," said I.

His contemporary, the English philosopher John Stuart Mill, had a far higher trust in government, and saw for it a far larger role in society. In *Principles of Political Economy* he wrote:

> The ends of government are as comprehensive as those of the social union. They consist of all the good, and all the immunity from evil, which the existence of government can be made either directly or indirectly to bestow.

In actual practice, modern democratic governments have found a middle ground between doing nothing and doing everything. But on that middle ground there is room for considerable movement, and governments characteristically have moved back and forth in cycles of greater and lesser involvement in the affairs of those they govern. Current parlance loosely labels the periods of these cycles of increasing and decreasing government activity as liberalism and conservatism, and in the United States they have recurred regularly since the founding of the Republic.

Arthur M. Schlesinger, Sr., in a fascinating essay first published in 1939 and later updated for inclusion in a book in 1949, identified eleven such periods of cyclical behavior in American political history, covering the years 1765 to 1947. The first two encompassed the founding years of the country and included the broad-based activism that led to the War for Independence followed by the creation of the Constitution that limited government and preserved dominance for the conservative commercial classes. During the next three periods the country swung from the active pursuit of popular rights during Thomas Jefferson's presidency to the renewal of conservative principles from 1816 through the 1820s to the inauguration of Andrew Jackson at the end of that decade and the ascendancy of liberal democratic ideals.

The next phase of these cyclical changes, starting in 1841 under President John Tyler, saw a return to conservatism and measures to strengthen the institution of slavery, until finally that episode was terminated by the short violent period of the Civil War and the activist presidency of Abraham Lincoln that preserved the Union. Because the wounds of war were so deep, the period of conservatism that followed—to repair and reconstruct—was very long, lasting until the end of the century. Finally it gave way to the presidency of Teddy Roosevelt and an era that culminated in the liberalism and global activism of Woodrow Wilson, who led the country into the World War and spearheaded the postwar effort to build an institution to prevent its recurrence.

Conservatism followed under Harding, Coolidge, and Hoover until the Great Depression ushered in the liberal presidency of Franklin Roosevelt that saw both a vast extension of government activity at home and a new wider role on the global stage during World War II and the period that followed. FDR's successor, Harry Truman, carried on his work, but by 1947, with Republicans controlling both houses of Congress, the tide of liberalism was receding and conservatism was again sweeping in. Writing in 1949, this was as far as Schlesinger could carry the story; but based on his calculation of the average length of the phases of liberalism and conservatism in the cycles he had examined, he went on to make the following remarkable forecast:

> Assuming that no such catastrophe [totalitarianism displacing the democratic system] impends, we may expect the recession from liberalism which began in 1947 to last till 1962, with a possible margin of a year or two in one direction or the other. The next conservative epoch will then be due around 1978.

Schlesinger was right on target. The accuracy of his forecast and the validity of the cyclical nature of the organizational behavior he described are seen in the political history of the years that followed. The "recession from liberalism" persisted through the Eisenhower years, until 1961 and the liberal presidency of John Kennedy, which then began a period of activist rule at home and abroad carried on by his successors until the late 1970s, when the tide again began to recede, to be overtaken finally by the strongly conservative regime of Ronald Reagan in the 1980s. To now carry Schlesinger's periodicity one swing further would produce a forecast of a return to liberalism around 1994–96.

Schlesinger considered a number of explanations to account for this cyclical behavior and finally concluded that "something basic in human nature" propels the electorate and its representatives in a particular direction until "the quality of their performance tends to deteriorate" and additional efforts no longer yield proportionate results. "Holding office as a means," he wrote, "tapers off into holding office as an end," until finally a new group with a new direction comes to hold office and a new phase in the cycle begins.

This is simply another way of observing that governments, like many other organizations, exhibit adaptive cybernetic behavior, planning new actions in response to signals indicating the outcome of previous actions taken. In *The Nerves of Government,* political scientist Karl Deutsch—borrowing imaginatively from communications theory—has made a more formal explanation of this behavior. Noting that the word "government" comes from a Greek root that refers to the art of the steersman, he shows that the "governing" of human organizations is indeed similar to the steering of a ship. Both use feedback in the form of information about past performance and present position to make adjustments for the future, and it is this use that keeps behavior bounded and causes it to fluctuate in fairly regular short-term cycles.

But Deutsch also goes further and adds that it is possible for the goal of an organization to change, that over time the cyclical movements back and forth may themselves cumulatively and gradually indicate a new direction. And so it is worth inquiring whether the relatively short-term cycles of greater and lesser government activity in the United States and in other modern democratic countries exhibit any longer-term cyclical changes. The answer is that indeed they do. Through successive administrations of both liberal and conservative stripe there has been a change in the direction of bringing more and more activities within the ambit of government, a change evidenced by increased numbers of public employees and a growing share of gross national products attributable to government activity. New conservative administrations do regularly pledge to reduce their governments' roles; but in practice disassembly is very difficult, and often the best that can be done is to slow the pace of future construction, raising the specter of an infinitely encroaching public authority as endlessly fecund as Li'l Abner's famous Shmoos.

However, further reflection indicates that even such a longer-term change operates within limits—the ultimate limit of doing everything. Clearly, long before this upper limit is reached (unless a different nondemocratic type of government is installed) the pace of increasing government activity will slow. At what level of activity this will occur will depend on the structure of the government and the history and political tradition of the country. In the United States it already may be starting to occur, and here the operative principle is not the idea that government activity per se should be reduced, but instead the notion that structural changes indicate both new areas for government involvement and old areas where involvement is no longer necessary.

Examples of new areas are those activities in which the unhindered allocation of resources in the open market—normally the optimum means for allocating most resources—might deprive or burden future generations not yet here to participate in the market. However, these activities are not those usually mentioned involving some finite store of raw materials that theoretically can be used up (advancing technology makes the better argument that an eventually peaking world population can have everything it needs as long as earth itself exists), but instead those that involve a troublesome legacy that will have to be dealt with or avoided or undone. Areas of likely increasing government involvement of this kind include:

- Controlling technology with extremely harmful consequences and/or potentially enduring effects
- Regulating the building of long-lasting facilities that are likely to present an increasing burden to future generations or fairly soon become obsolete and require large expenditures for dismantling
- Ensuring security for, and access to, information about individuals which could affect their future employment, welfare, and even health care

But there are also structural changes that indicate activities where government involvement selectively can be reduced. Because of technological developments, for example, the government's role as an author and administrator of regulations can be eliminated or considerably reduced in certain activities.

- The Federal Communications Commission has decided that the market for commercial satellite operations is now sufficiently competitive to justify an end to reviews of customer rates.
- The development of new financial instruments and services—made possible in many cases by the use of high-volume, high-speed electronic equipment—has prompted the alteration and removal of a number of federal regulations affecting the financial services industry.

For businesses and professions, and for individuals in general, mastering change means understanding that modern democratic governments will continue to swing back and forth in cycles of greater and lesser activity, of liberalism and conservatism; and that over still longer periods of time the nature of their activities will alter, too, influenced by various structural changes. Translated into daily practice this means giving more time and resources to being able to respond flexibly to them.

> *Nations periodically choose war when peace does not give them what they want.*

In the celebrated passage in the third chapter of the Book of Ecclesiastes the Preacher counsels, "To everything there is a season, and a time to every purpose under the heaven," and he concludes his lyrical enumeration of times and purposes with "a time to love, and a time to hate; a time of war, and a time of peace."

There have in fact been many "times of war." In his famous study of war, Quincy Wright listed 278 "wars of modern civilization" begun between 1482 and 1940, each involving over fifty thousand troops. Using more elaborate criteria, two other scholars, J. David Singer and Melvin Small, have listed ninety-three "international" wars begun after January 1, 1816, and ended before December 31, 1965. So frequently and regularly have these wars occurred that there have been far fewer "times of peace," actually only twenty-four years from 1816 to 1965 during which there was no war underway at all, even though two-thirds of that period was taken up by the years 1815 to 1914, an era often referred to by scholars of the period as "the ninety-nine-year peace."

An examination of these wars reveals that in their evolution—from onset through duration to termination—they too illustrate cyclical organizational behavior. When in time of war a country achieves the goals for which it went into combat, or fails to achieve them and realizes that the cost in lives and resources of continuing to try to do so is too great, it finds a way to terminate its participation. In other cases, when neither side can prevail and a stalemate results, a truce or armistice occurs which eventually becomes a settlement, either de jure or de facto.

But if during the ensuing peace the issue which prompted the resort to arms in the first place persists, or a new one arises from the settlement, then a desire for restitution may develop and grow. In due course, as the country's economy recovers and the memory of the horror of the last war fades, a new generation may arise dedicated to recovering what was lost and unafraid of threatening military action as a means of doing so. If other countries in the area or beyond—alarmed by the course of developments—decide either to isolate themselves or intervene, then the security arrangement which had helped maintain the peace will collapse, helping to hasten the next phase of war and perhaps even making it more general.

It is this adaptive organizational behavior that has created distinct cyclical patterns in the almost continuous warfare that has occurred on earth during the past five centuries. One study, subjecting Quincy Wright's data to statistical analysis, has charted an upswing in the level of violence about every twenty-five years, or approximately every one to one and a half generations, and another longer-term series of 80-to-120-year cycles of rising and falling violence. Singer and Small, having computed the number of "nation months of international war underway" during the 1816–1965 period, have also found a strong periodicity, with dominant peaks of warfare about twenty years apart.

Cyclical patterns of war and peace are also seen more narrowly in the behavior over time of the world's great powers and of different pairs of nation-states. George Modelski of the University of Washington has described a "long cycle" of global politics covering five distinct periods of international relations from 1494 through 1945. He found each of these periods dominated by a particular world power— Portugal, the Netherlands, Great Britain (twice), and the United States—which attained its position through a formative global conflict followed by a legitimizing settlement or treaty. The first part of the period, which Modelski labels the "ascending phase," originates in the common goals and coalition building of the global war and then carries through the settlement and for a generation or so beyond it. Eventually exhaustion sets in, problems arise that are not attended to, and the "descending phase" begins, leading finally to a new global conflict. Since each period lasts about a hundred years, the continuation of Modelski's long cycle would mean that the present period (legitimized by the post–World War II international meetings at Yalta, San Francisco, and Potsdam) is now in the early years of its descending phase.

Periods of war and peace between pairs of nation-states have also followed general cyclical patterns. In two historic rivalries long periods of enmity eventually gave way to periods of partnership and cooperation. France and England opposed each other regularly—and frequently on the battlefield—from the beginning of the Hundred Years War in the first half of the fourteenth century to the end of the Napoleonic wars early in the nineteenth. Then, as their interests shifted, cooperation in their pursuit became more efficacious than conflict, and during the rest of the century the two were more frequently on the same side, including episodes as allies in arms in such distant places as the Crimea and China. But the rivalry between the empires still endured, almost burst into flame when their forces crossed in the remote African outpost of Fashoda in 1898, and was finally snuffed out in the formation of the Triple Entente in 1904, ushering in a cycle of friendly relations that has seen them become close military partners in World Wars I and II and the Suez crisis of 1956. Similarly, France and Prussia-Germany, bitter enemies in three major wars, each about a generation apart, now see their interests better served as partners in the economic, political, and military institutions created in Europe since World War II.

Today, other pairs of nation-states with historic rivalries remain more or less locked in cyclical patterns of belligerency.

- Greece and Turkey have fought each other five times since 1816.
- Israel and its Arab neighbors have been at war four times (five, if the 1982 invasion into Lebanon is counted) since they first fought in Israel's war for independence in 1948.
- China and Japan, who fought each other four times in less than half a century, today stand poised between phases of enmity and possible growing cooperation.

It seems evident, therefore, that in the world at large, among its great powers, and between pairs of nation-states, periods of war and peace have alternated in cyclical patterns of various magnitudes and durations. Yet there are also longer-term changes that encompass shorter-term cycles: Areas of the world become more belligerent or more quiescent, membership in the ranks of the great powers shifts, and rivalries between countries begin and end.

So, to understand the possibilities of war in our time and to aid the prospects for peace, it is necessary to ask why these longer-term changes occur and how they influence the phases of the cycles they bound.

The explanation for the longer-term changes is found in the reason why nations fight. They do so simply because they rank other values higher than peace. If they did not, if peace were ranked highest, nations would simply refuse to fight. It is in pursuit of the values they rank higher that they go to war. But if through war they find they cannot further their values, or if new values arise more important than those for which they are fighting, or if war is incompatible with the values they are pursuing, then they cease fighting. Over time it is just such longer-term changes that have altered cyclical patterns of warfare, ending some and beginning others.

For over five hundred years, from the eighth to the thirteenth centuries, Muslims and Christians engaged in sporadic warfare interrupted by periods of peace of varied lengths in different places, from the shores of the Atlantic to the eastern Mediterranean. The first two centuries were marked by the conquest and spread of Islam throughout North Africa and into southern Europe; the last three by the sporadic efforts of Christian-led and -supported armies to regain lost territories and—through the Crusades—to recapture the holy places of the birth of Christianity. In the end the long warfare between the two sides ended, not because either had achieved its goals, but because it had become clear that neither could.

Three centuries later, in the year 1517, Martin Luther nailed his ninety-five theses to the door of the court church at Wittenberg, and the Christians were soon at war with each other. On one side were the princes and potentates who supported the Protestant reformers inspired by Luther and later John Calvin; on the other were the Catholics loyal to the Pope in Rome, supported by their newly formed intellectual strike force, the Society of Jesus. For nearly a century the two sides skirmished across Europe, finally culminating their battles in a lengthy four-act drama that has become known to history as the Thirty Years War (1618–48). When at last they stopped fighting and signed the Treaties of Westphalia, it was not because one had scored a decisive victory over the other, but because both realized they had better things to do. Other values—in the form of burgeoning commerce and a new world to explore—beckoned, and to give full pursuit to these they decided to live and let live.

In our time have there been similar major changes underway that might also influence the cyclical pattern of war and peace that in this century has twice peaked in global conflict? The obvious one that suggests itself is the development of nuclear weapons. Presumably such weapons would be employed in the pursuit of values ranked higher than peace by those using them. But if they are used on a very large scale it may not be possible—because of widespread and lasting destruction—to secure the higher values for which they are employed. In other words, their use in large numbers would be incompatible with the goals sought in employing them.

Here then is a change that holds the possibility of altering the current historical cycle of war and peace. But as in the past, recognition of the change that has occurred is required, and so, too, is a willingness to behave accordingly. Since historical examples of similar recognition and behavior do exist, such an expectation is not an impossible dream. It can begin with the general acknowledgment that to initiate the use of nuclear weapons—*no matter how serious the provocation*—is an intolerable threat to humanity and the universal commitment (by prior agreement) to make any country or group doing so an international pariah, cut off from all intercourse with other nations and subject to their sanctions.

To successfully take such a large step there must first be small steps. The most helpful would involve agreement regarding analogous behavior at a lower level of activity. One example could be in the treatment of commercial airline hijackers. It should be universally agreed that since all hijackers pose an intolerable threat to the passengers on the plane they seize, they must be prosecuted by the nation capturing them *no matter what motive they had in taking the aircraft* (including, for example, "flying to freedom").

Even if such a policy of "pariah" treatment of those initiating the use of nuclear weapons can be agreed to, no one should overestimate its immediate effects. In the beginning it simply will not be feasible to think of it as principally directed against the two nuclear superpowers, the United States and the Soviet Union. While in good faith they must accept it as extending to themselves, in reality it is their self-restraint that will have to be counted on for some time to come as the main hope in preventing their use of nuclear weapons. Yet such a policy still would be very helpful.

- Initially directed against new nuclear nations—those with small forces or those contemplating such forces—it would serve to deter their development and use of nuclear weapons.
- It would help reduce the possibility of one important nuclear war scenario, the triggering of a larger conflict by a third-power use.
- Agreement to such a policy would represent a significant extension of superpower cooperation in a vital but essentially nonideological area (the USSR has regularly espoused a no-first-use declaratory policy, and in the United States a similar policy has been urged by responsible spokesmen across the political spectrum).
- Most important, it would formally establish the idea that exploding nuclear weapons (like hijacking airplanes or poisoning wells in desert oases) constitutes an intolerable threat to society and is incompatible with the values for whose pursuit other means—including non-nuclear war—are normally used.

An agreement of this kind would, of course, require changing many assumptions and much thinking that underlie current deterrence theory. A preliminary step, therefore, would be to think through such changes under various scenario conditions.

Organizational behavior which results in the cyclical occurrence of periods of war and peace is the most important such behavior, because it has the most serious consequences. Yet nations rarely seek war or peace as values in themselves; they seek other values, and war and peace are conditions which result from their efforts. Other changes help shape these values, and they affect the costs of obtaining them. Understanding these longer-term changes, and making use of them, can enable us to influence the evolution of cyclical changes of war and peace.

SOCIAL BEHAVIOR

In the Olympic Games at Helsinki in 1952, American prestige was heavily engaged. The exploits of Mal Whitfield, Bob Richards, Harrison Dillard, Bob Mathias, and the entire eight-oared Navy crew—among others—made headlines in the United States and swelled national pride. Points for medals were carefully tabulated, and almost every news story began with a comparison of the running totals for the United States and the Soviet Union. After the games the American athletes, returning from Europe in five chartered planeloads, received a triumphant homecoming from a nation that seemed eager to celebrate not just their individual achievements but even more the fact that in the final days of competition they had overtaken the Russians in total points.

Sixteen years later, in 1968, the Games at Mexico City evoked a different response. Instead of an outpouring of nationalist sentiment in the United States there was ambivalence and uncertainty. Shame alternated with pride, and it was the former that got the headlines when Tommie Smith and John Carlos, medal winners in the 200-meter dash, hung their heads on the victory stand and raised gloved fists in the black power salute during the traditional flag-raising and playing of the national anthem. George Foreman's parade about the boxing ring, clutching a tiny American flag following his heavyweight victory, was notable because it was such a singular event—a brief flash of patriotic pride on a darker canvas of doubt and self-abnegation. Except for a few local celebrations there were no triumphant homecomings, and in that season of national discontent America's athletes slipped back almost unnoticed into a land too troubled to cheer their exploits.

By 1984 and the Olympic Games at Los Angeles, the tide had turned again and was running high on the shores of American nationalism. The chant of "U.S.A., U.S.A.," first heard for the victorious American hockey team four years earlier at the Winter Games at Lake Placid, became a full-throated roar accompanying the efforts of almost every U.S. athlete on the field. Winners in previously unheralded events like Greco-Roman wrestling and the triple jump became overnight heroes, and pictures of medal winners made the covers of mass circulation magazines across the country, almost always bathed in red, white, and blue and with an American flag close at hand. Immediately after the games the athletes dined with the President and then began a triumphal tour of major U.S. cities including a ticker tape parade in New York reckoned the most enthusiastic since the one almost sixty years earlier that had celebrated another event suffused with fervid patriotism—Lindbergh's solo flight across the Atlantic.

These shifts in patriotic behavior from 1952 to 1968 to 1984 can be accounted for by many specific factors. The year 1952 was one of the coldest of the Cold War, and American achievement in competition with the USSR—in any arena—was eagerly desired and widely praised. It was also the year of the nomination and landslide election of Dwight D. Eisenhower, symbol of an era when the nation's goals had been simple, direct, and universally accepted. But in the fall of 1968, sixteen years later, the early 1950s were a distant memory and national unity was a tattered remnant, soiled by riot and assassination at home and rent by a foreign war that seemed without purpose or end. Then, in the summer of 1984, the nation was buoyant again. Economic recession had given way to rapid recovery, hope was in the air, and as the Olympic torch coursed the land, it lit national pride anew.

But in larger perspective these rises and falls of patriotism are merely the most recent episodes in a much longer cyclical pattern that has seen the United States throughout its history swing between the poles of national fervor and national indifference. These swings are like many kinds of social behavior which exhibit patterns of cyclical change. Such behavior, which is the cumulative total of many unco-ordinated individual acts, reflects other changes—economic, political, social, demographic, international—that are occur-ring. Once underway it tends to be self-reinforcing, adding to its magnitude and increasing its pace in the direction in which it is moving. In time, however, the changes spurring such behavior lose their momentum and the gains achieved in pursuing it diminish or, alternatively, reactions against it develop. Then a period without any clear direction sets in, until finally a new impetus spurs movement in the opposite direction and the cycle is underway again. Illustrations of such social behavior are seen in cycles of fads and fashions, marriage and divorce, and crime.

Fads and fashions come and go.
In décolletage in women's dress fashions, the extreme of high ruffled collars at the beginning of the 1600s gradually opened to the bared necks and shoulders of the 1670s, which were then closed again by the tight neckerchiefs of the middle and late eighteenth century. But by the end of that century, necks and shoulders were once more being bared, only to be covered again in the mid-1800s. Yet this was but a prelude to their opening to new dimensions of exposure by the time of the gay nineties and to their closing again by the 1930s, the era of worldwide depression.

This cyclical alternation in covering and uncovering is one of several changes in women's wardrobes over three centu-ries examined in a detailed 1940 quantitative study by two University of California anthropologists. In their investiga-tions they also found similar changes in skirt length and width and in the positioning and diameter of the waist, with each dimension alternating "with fair regularity between maxima and minima which in most cases average about fifty years apart, so that the full-wave length of their periodicity is around a century."

The interesting conclusion of these researchers is that changes in this cycle apparently run from periods of "strain" (in which dimensions go to extremes, tending to exaggerate certain anatomical features) back to the "ideal" (which is characterized by "a skirt that is both full and long, a waist that is abnormally constricted but in nearly proper anatomical position and a décolletage that is ample both vertically and horizontally"). They also note that the periods of strain have coincided with major social and political upheavals (the early 1600s, the revolutionary period of the late eighteenth and early nineteenth centuries, and the first half of the twentieth century), and while they reject the notion that these upheavals actually produced exaggerated dimensions in women's clothing, they do offer the plausible conclusion that they disrupted established dress style and tended "to its overthrow or inversion."

This same cyclical behavior in women's—and in men's—fashions, reflective of other changes in the political and economic environment, has continued to this day, though in the second half of the twentieth century its pace has accelerated and its manifestations have been influenced more strongly by structural changes. Generally speaking, poorer economic times have coincided with somber colors and less flashy styles, and for women in particular, longer skirts and longer hair. During economic upturns the pendulum has swung the other way, toward brighter colors and more flamboyance and toward shorter skirts, shorter hair, and greater frivolity in dress. But total war (as in World War II) imposed its own restrictions, mandating utilitarian styles and freezing them in place. Later, postwar prosperity and the greater freedom from conventional ways provided by increasing economic independence combined to make more options available and encourage more people to pursue them resulting in greater varieties in fashion at any one time. More recently the great increase of women in the workforce, and particularly their entry into executive and business positions traditionally held by men, has caused unique excursions from normal cyclical fashion patterns. At first, women were emulating men (dark suits and white blouses); then, as more have gained confidence in their roles, they have returned to more distinctively feminine modes of dress.

The foregoing fashion dimensions—including colors, length of skirts and hair, width of ties and lapels—all move within clearly bounded limits: There are only so many colors, skirt lengths can range only from ankle to upper thigh, hair can be grown only so long, ties and lapels can be only so wide or so narrow. For these fad and fashion changes, magnitudes of cyclical changes are fairly predictable; only their timing and pace will vary.

Of a different type are fads and fashions driven by new products. These are generally of two kinds. One kind consists of new products, often the result of technological development, which either replace other useful products or provide a new service which becomes a permanent activity for society. When the first automobiles appeared early in this century they were greeted—skeptically by many—as simply a new fad. However, when they soon proved to be a more rapid and more efficient means of transporting people and goods than the buggies and carts they were replacing, their fad quality passed and they became an essential part of contemporary society. Since then their principal changes have been fashion changes of design and styling; the technology of their power source, the internal combustion engine, although greatly improved, has remained essentially unchanged for almost a hundred years.

The first phonographs—like the first radios and the first television sets—were a fad, too; but they provided an entirely new service. Unlike the automobile they made no prior technology obsolete. They were *sui generis,* and in time what was originally a fad became a permanent industry. However, the evolution of the industry so greatly improved the product that—unlike the automobile—it spawned two further generations and is now launching a fourth. The second was the long-playing record, a fad that rapidly became a permanent replacement for its faster-spinning, shorter-playing predecessor. The third was—briefly—wire, then magnetic tape, later made much more convenient by being packaged in a cassette. The fourth generation of recorded music and speech is digital sound, now commercially available on laser-read compact disks (CDs) and soon to be heard on small digital audio tapes (DATs). Both technologies are so superior in their operating characteristics and in accurately rendering distortion-free sound that they are certain to soon supersede second-generation vinyl discs. In fact, our descendants are certain to regard the reproduction of sound by scraping a spinning surface with a needle as downright primitive—a curious item for the science and technology museums of the future.

While automobiles, phonographs, and other technological innovations have successfully made the leap from temporary fad to permanent product, this is not true of the other kind of fad and fashion product. These are generally consumables. Most have short lives and usually no resale value. Many are new versions of well-known products designed principally to acquire market share for the companies producing them.

Food is a unique fashion product, though it is a daily necessity, the ultimate daily necessity. To survive we need new supplies of food every day. Yet an infinite variety of foods can satisfy our needs; no one kind, certainly no one brand, is a necessity. This provides a very wide potential market for food companies, and to attract it a major element of their strategy requires appearing with products that are new and different, that excite food purchasers to try them.

Part of that strategy is to appeal to structural changes in attitudes, such as the greater interest in nutrition and weight control of those who are increasingly better off in industrial and industrializing countries. It is this change that has fueled the boom in health foods during the past two decades. But attention also has to be paid to the shorter interest spans preoccupied with texture, color, shape, and various kinds of taste appeal. It is these considerations that have led to a proliferation of different kinds of snacks and sweets as well as the re-forming and repackaging of more traditional foods like soups and breads. In 1986 an average of ten new products a day were thrust before consumers, compared with just three a day in 1980.

The result has been to reinforce the fashion aspect of food, to push what is novel and different. But a product that stands principally on its novelty will not stand long; when the novelty wears off, sales will fall. And so food manufacturers, attentive to the fashion aspect of their products, are assuring the growing importance of that aspect—and with it higher costs (94 percent of new food products eventually fail)—by responding to it so vigorously.

Other consumables, akin to food but not daily necessities for survival, are also subject to the cyclical changes of fads and fashions:

- Toothpaste makers, between technological leaps like fluoride and tartar control, mainly compete with colors and flavors in different combinations of gel and paste packaged in a variety of dispensers.

- Cigarette manufacturers, prey to tax increases and required to advertise their product as hazardous to health, woo the fickle public by changing length and width, by using chic names and striking packages, and by injecting flavoring to make "cool" what is actually on fire.
- Less quickly consumed, but still fad- and fashion-oriented, are toys. Hula Hoops, Rubik's Cubes, and Cabbage Patch Dolls all burst upon the scene, soar in popularity, and finally fade, their only hope for rebirth perhaps as collectors' trophies during some distant future bout of nostalgia.

Style and fashion move in curious counterpoint. Style is what distinguishes each person individually; fashion is what everyone is doing. But it is the search for style that creates fashion, for in pursuing it each person seeks what is new, what is unique; and when everyone has it, it is no longer unique and no longer wanted. Thus fads and fashions, like enthusiasm for flag and country, come and go in cyclical patterns. Is this also true for more serious forms of social behavior?

Marriage and divorce rates both rise and fall.
The nuclear family is alive and well, and it always will be. The common wisdom, however, has been a much darker diagnosis and an even gloomier prognosis. "The American family is in severe crisis," wrote a columnist in the *Wall Street Journal* in April 1984, and a few months later a comprehensive scholarly report entitled "The State of Families," issued by Family Service America, forecast continuing erosion of the traditional nuclear family and continuing divorce "at its current high level."

This purported decline of society's most basic institution is often depicted as part of a long-term moral deterioration of society in general, and the evidence offered to support such a severe indictment usually is a combination of decreasing marriage rates and increasing divorce rates. In fact, careful examination of both rates shows that they are cyclical, neither constantly decreasing nor constantly increasing.

It is true that as more women in advanced industrial countries have entered the workforce and deferred—or decided against—marrying, there has been a long-term structural change in these countries toward fewer marriages. It is

also the case that increasing economic security and liberalized divorce laws—again principally in advanced industrial
countries—have resulted in a larger number of divorces.
However, in historical perspective these changes in marriage
and divorce rates have not been extraordinarily large, and,
over time, like other forms of social behavior they have
risen and fallen in cyclical patterns, never continually moving in only one direction.

Finland and Sweden are among the few countries where
marriage statistics exist in continuous series for long periods
of time. These do show a very gradual decline over time in
marriage rates. For Finland, for example, the average annual rate for the years 1751 to 1799 was 17.2 per thousand
population; for 1800 to 1899 it dropped to 16.3, and for the
first seventy-five years of this century it declined a little
further to 15.7. In addition, as might be expected, marriage
rates fall very sharply during periods of wartime and rise
very sharply immediately following such periods. Thus, in
1791 and 1792, following three years of war with Russia,
marriage rates in Finland and Sweden soared to the low
twenties per thousand from the mid-teens to which they had
fallen during the conflict, a pattern which was repeated for
Sweden following its 1809 revolution and for Finland following World Wars I and II. However, for most of the 225-year
period the marriage rates in both countries fluctuated rather
narrowly from the low to the upper teens in cyclical swings
of ten to thirty years.

For France and the United Kingdom (England and Wales
only), where comparable statistics are available for a somewhat shorter period (1801 to 1975 for France, 1838 to 1975
for the U.K.), the pattern is quite similar. Both countries
have had very slowly falling marriage rates over the entire
time, sharp declines during periods of war and quick rises
afterward, and overall a cyclical pattern of fluctuating rates
like that of the Scandinavian nations. The main difference is
that France, whose land—unlike England's—was physically
invaded during the two world wars, had a far greater drop in
marriage rates during those conflicts and a far higher rise
afterward.

In the United States, cumulative data on marriage rates
for all states are available only from 1910, but as figure 4.9
indicates, these also show a cyclical pattern, from a peak of
12 per thousand in 1920 to a low of 7.9 in 1932 at the time of

the Great Depression, way up to 16.4 in 1946 immediately following World War II, down to the 8.4–8.5 range from 1958 to 1962, and to a new recent high of 10.8 in 1982.

Since birthrates determine future age compositions of the population and influence marriage rates for any particular year, a hypothesis of severe family decline would be expected to show far steeper drops and far shorter rises in marriage rates than occurred twenty to twenty-five years earlier in birthrates. However, this has not been the case. From 1975 to 1982 the marriage rate in the United States increased at an average annual rate of 1.1 percent. During the seven-year period 1950–57 (the years of birth of those ranging in age from eighteen to thirty-two during the period 1975 to 1982), the birthrate increased at a *lower* average annual rate of .7 percent. While the two statistics are not meant to indicate a cause-and-effect relationship (people younger than eighteen and older than thirty-two also married during 1975–82), they do support the view that the marriage rate, instead of steadily declining, has actually continued to follow historical short-term cyclical patterns and in recent years has risen.

For the divorce rate in the United States a somewhat similar pattern can be seen. As figure 4.10 shows, after cyclically rising and falling from 1910 through the late 1950s, it rose to a new high of 5.3 per thousand in 1979 and 1981. This sustained increase was due to a number of structural changes including:

- The great increase in the number of women in the workforce, providing careers that not only are alternatives to marriages but also sources of livelihood after terminating them
- Improved and more widely available birth control technology resulting in fewer or even no children in many marriages, thus easing the way to divorce when that is desired
- Increased economic security, including public policy programs like Aid to Families with Dependent Children, which makes divorce more feasible for those who might otherwise not be able to manage it financially
- Liberalized divorce laws in most states
- Changing attitudes which no longer stigmatize those whose marriages have ended in divorce

FIG. 4.9. Marriage Rate per 1,000 Population, United States, 1910–1986.

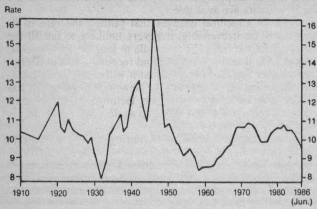

FIG. 4.10. Divorce Rate per 1,000 Population United States, 1910–1986.

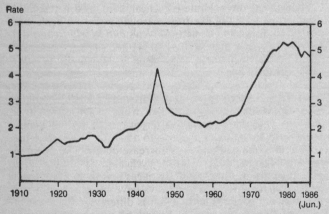

Sources for both figures: U.S. Bureau of the Census, *Historical Statistics of the United States, Colonial Times to 1970*, Vol. I (Wash., DC, 1976), p. 64 and *Statistical Abstract of the United States 1986* (Wash., DC, 1985), p. 56; U.S. National Center for Health Statistics, *Monthly Vital Statistics Report*, Sep. 15, 1986, p. 1.

But having reached this new level, the divorce rate has since been falling, dropping to 4.9 by mid-1986, the latest period for which data are available.

Since the structural changes that pushed the rate to its new highs are irreversible, it is very unlikely to fall all the way back to the level of the middle to late 1950s. However, the fact that it has now peaked and receded, and not continued steadily upward, suggests that it will continue to fluctuate cyclically, this time from the new higher plateau it has reached. At this level the same factors that in the past caused it to rise and fall will do so again. These include:

- Wars and their aftermaths (during the latter the rate rises)
- Economic upturns (during these the rate usually rises) and downturns (during these it usually falls)
- Changes in birthrates (more children do tend to inhibit divorces, but when children born in years of high birthrates reach their twenties, both marriage and divorce rates will rise)

Because the divorce rate is cyclical, care must be taken in interpreting it. If the rise from a trough year to a peak year is used to show change, as *U.S. News and World Report* did in choosing the very low rate in 1941 and the very high rate in 1981 for a "pictogram" in an issue at the end of the latter year, then the conclusion will be misleading and alarming. Using these two years gives a 141 percent increase in the divorce rate over the selected forty-year period. On the other hand, charting an increase from a peak year to a nonpeak year reveals a very different picture. For example, using 1946 to 1984, dates close to 1941 and 1981 covering nearly the same span, gives an increase of only 14 percent in the rate! The better view, as the cyclical pattern suggests, is that there always have been marriages and there always will be, and that some of them always have been unhappy and that this will continue, too. What is different—the result of structural changes—is that instead of unhappy marriages enduring or ending through desertion, divorce has become a more feasible and accepted means of terminating them.

Crime rates go down as well as up.
Crime is not out of control. In the early 1960s in the

United States the rate of occurrence per 100,000 inhabitants of both violent and property crimes did begin to rise steeply. At the time many cited this increase as yet another example of the moral deterioration of American society; and when the rise continued unabated into the 1970s what had been warnings became shrill prophecies of a continuing and permanent crisis. But in the last few years evidence has accumulated indicating first the slowing, then the absolute decline of both rates. To be sure, neither has fallen near the levels from which they began rising two decades ago, but the downward turn has been too strong and too sustained to mark it as merely a one- or two-year aberration in a continuing upward trend of lawlessness.

This increase and decrease of rates has occurred because crime, like many other forms of social behavior, rises and falls in cyclical patterns. In the United States, because law enforcement for most kinds of criminal activity is the responsibility of the individual states, the compilation of truly national crime statistics and the calculation of rates from them has been underway for only about fifty years, from

FIG. 4.11.   Murder Rate per 100,000 Inhabitants, United States, 1910–1984.

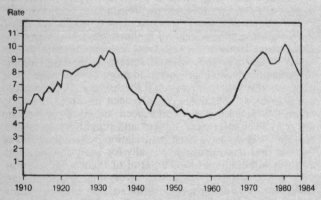

Sources: U.S. Bureau of the Census, *Historical Statistics of the United States, Colonial Times to 1870*, Vol. I (Wash., DC, 1976), p. 414 and *Statistical Abstract of the United States 1986* (Wash., DC, 1985), p. 166.

about the time Congress enlarged the investigative and co-ordinating roles of the Federal Bureau of Investigation. Nonetheless, the Bureau of the Census—using data from a representative and increasing number of states—has compiled a continuous annual series from 1910 of rates of homicide, the most serious and most reliably reported of all violent crimes. As figure 4.11 indicates, these rates display a cyclical pattern, rising from a low of 4.6 murders per 100,000 resident population in 1910 to a high of 9.7 in 1933, through a new low of 4.5 from 1955 to 1958, back up to 10.2 in 1980, and down—most recently—to 7.9 in 1984.

In an effort to identify earlier trends in American history, Northwestern University political scientist Ted Robert Gurr has examined studies of homicides in major U.S. cities covering various periods of the second half of the nineteenth century. From these he has concluded that an earlier strong upsurge in homicides began shortly before the Civil War and persisted into the 1870s before finally subsiding toward the end of the century, a finding that extends fifty years back the cyclical pattern revealed by the Bureau of the Census's twentieth-century data.

The available U.S. statistical series for rates of property crime, the other major crime category, begins only with 1957 and thus covers a much briefer period. But even this shorter series, supplemented with recently available data, reveals a rise and decline consistent with the homicide rate for the same period, suggesting that property crimes occur in cyclical patterns similar to those for violent crimes. From 1957 the rate per 100,000 inhabitants for total property crime (burglary, larceny-theft, and motor vehicle theft) rose annually through 1976, dropped the following year, rose to a new peak in 1980, and has since been falling.

A number of reasons have been suggested to explain these cyclical patterns of violent and property crime rates. Gurr, noting the very strong correlation between periods of warfare and rising crime, especially for violent crime, both in the United States and in several of the European countries whose data he examined, favors the view that wars contribute to rising crime. They do so, he argues, by legitimizing violence both directly (for those in the military service habituated to it) and indirectly (for those on the home front who see in war a license to act out their own feelings of anger). However, the correlations he points to vary greatly in their timing and magnitude. For example, crime rose *during* the American Civil War but only *after* World War II and then far *less* than in the periods after World War I and during the Vietnam War.

A second reason, also with compelling correlations, arises from the universally acknowledged fact that males in their teens and early twenties commit a disproportionately large share of all crimes. Thus, fifteen to twenty-five years after high birthrates, crime rates should be expected to increase. This undoubtedly was an important factor in the higher crime rate in the United States during the 1960s and 1970s and it also likely explains much of the decline since 1980 as the baby boom has been followed by the baby bust. However, since the fertility rate in the United States fell steadily in the final decades of the 1800s—running up only briefly at the turn of the century—no similar correlation can account for the strong rise in crime rates from 1910 through the early 1930s.

A third explanation for cyclical change that also seems compelling, though apparently it has received little systematic attention, lies in changing patterns of migration from country to city and back again. Statistics show very clearly that for every category of crime except homicide, rates are highest in urban areas, lower in small cities and towns, and lowest in rural areas. In America, as long as the migration to major cities continued at a faster rate than the growth of the total population, there was thereafter a built-in impetus toward higher crime rates. But when that migration finally shifted away from cities (in part *because* of their higher crime rates)—as it did in the middle to late 1970s—so too did the impetus, aiding the slowing and eventual falling of crime rates overall.

Finally, some effect on cyclical patterns is undoubtedly made by public policy measures and the selective use of resources targeted for law enforcement purposes. However, these are also slow to take effect and hard to measure. Thus, in the light of all the nonpolicy-related cyclical factors tending to bring down crime rates in the United States in the early 1980s it was somewhat disingenuous of former U.S. Attorney General William French Smith to take major credit for the Reagan administration as he did when he greeted the April 1984 Uniform Crime Report of declining rates with the comment "This marvelous news proves we are beginning to win the battle against crime with some of the most significant initiatives and results in years."

The seemingly inexorable cyclical rise and fall of crime rates for all of the above reasons—working both independently and cumulatively in different places at different times—will be disappointing news to both doomsayers with apocalyptic views of the future and reformers with pious hopes to remake man. Crime, it seems, always will be with us, though it appears unlikely ever to overwhelm us. Are there then any long-term structural changes acting to pull—in one direction or the other—these endless cycles of criminal behavior?

There are several that do seem to be giving them an upward push:

- Higher incomes and increasing prosperity heighten the expectations of those who have not attained similar levels of well-being, and when their expectations are not met some will turn to crime.
- As more high-value durable goods become small, lightweight, and portable (like compact stereo and TV sets), targets for theft increase.
- Other opportunities are provided by the larger number of residences that stand empty for extended periods because of the increase of families in which both spouses are away working.
- Whole new categories of crime exist. The growing number of managers and office personnel in mature industrial societies has given rise to "white-collar" crime; electronic information systems are now spawning the first generation of "computer criminals," a species whose offspring are certain to multiply.

New information and communication systems have also improved the reporting and recording of crimes committed. While this improvement does not change the numbers that actually occur, it certainly suggests that they are rising and thus increases the fear of crime in the public mind, an attitude which clever criminals can and do make use of (fearful citizens are more likely to be mute witnesses to criminals lest they become their next victims). Television also contributes to this fear, as well as to a distorted image of criminal activity. According to sociologists Linda and

Robert Lichter of George Washington University, while violent crime accounted for only 10 percent of the offenses reported to the FBI (in 1981), it constituted 88 percent of those shown on television.

Yet there are also several structural changes that are asserting downward pressure on cycles of criminal behavior. One is simply that with the advance of civilization, over time people are socialized to control and displace their anger, and thus they develop greater restraint and behave more humanely in their interpersonal relationships. Gurr's research in rates of violent crime in medieval and early modern England indicates that they were "probably ten and possibly twenty or more times higher" than in the twentieth century. When the ghost of Hamlet's father, at the outset of the play, speaks first of "the foul crimes done in my days of nature" for which he is "for the day confined to fast in fires," it is his own crimes he is speaking of, testifying to the normalcy of such behavior, an obvious reflection of Shakespeare's own time.

In addition, economic development and growth not only cause expectations to rise, they also cause them to be met, and as they are met for more people the numbers who might be inclined to turn to illegal activity are reduced and the numbers for whom the promise of the future holds too much to risk such activity are increased. Structural changes in education and population also tend to lower crime rates over the long term. In the case of the former, years of education correlate with less criminal activity, raising the prospect of lower crime rates as more people in more areas continue to receive more years of schooling. With regard to the latter, since both crime and victimization rates fall with age (past the teens and early twenties), the structural changes underway in most countries toward slower-growing, longer-living populations should exert a downward bias on criminal activity in those countries.

Finally, since there is an inverse relationship between criminals and crimes (a relatively small number of criminals are responsible for a large volume of all crimes), identifying, convicting, and incarcerating habitual criminals should bring down crime rates. With ever improving capabilities for compiling, storing, and disseminating information, this hope should be increasingly realized.

Like other forms of social behavior, crime will continue to

rise and fall in cyclical patterns. Yet the above review of long-term structural changes affecting criminal activity shows that over time they do affect the shape and magnitude of these patterns. Many of these structural changes, as well as many cyclical changes, result from the cumulative efforts of so many individual acts that their courses only can be observed and plotted; rarely, if ever, can they be altered. But many are also susceptible to efforts that seek to shape, divert, and even reverse them. Mastering change requires that both the inevitable and the alterable be understood and used.

CHAPTER 5

THE STRATEGY FOR MASTERING CHANGE

WHEN PETROLEUM REPLACED whale oil as the principal fuel for lamps in the second half of the nineteenth century, whalebone—used to stiffen and give structure to corsets and elaborate ball gowns—became less readily available. But an enterprising Michigan merchant named Edward R. Warren, noticing that turkey quills were discarded when their feathers were made into dusters, saw a replacement for whalebone. Wrapping the quills in cotton binding, he created a new, lightweight, low-cost stay material which he named featherbone; and thus was born the Warren Featherbone Company. Fifty years later, however, simpler dress styles were emerging, and so, too, were plastics, far more versatile and flexible than turkey quills. Undaunted by these threats to their main product, Mr. Warren's heirs and successors instead embraced them and created the first plastic baby pants, which quickly replaced the heavier and hotter latex rubber product then in wide use. Today, over a century after its founding, the Warren Featherbone Company (now located in Georgia) is a prospering concern, still innovating and growing.

This successful switch in both basic material and main product is an outstanding example of mastering change. But it is also an exception. Most of us, when we make plans for the future—for our businesses, professional practices, or even personal lives—rest them on the continuation of conditions we have experienced in the past or see occurring in the present. Such assumptions of continuity occur naturally because they are rooted in what we know, what we have seen happen, and, especially, what we have seen work. It is experience that gives us confidence in our plans and makes us comfortable with them. To assume discontinuity and project alterations from recent and current conditions is to venture into the unknown. It means selecting among a number of other possibilities, no one of which is as certain as what is currently happening. In such a strategy there is obviously more risk and less confidence, and so we tend to avoid it.

Yet, as the previous two chapters have shown, it is the alteration of present conditions, not their continuation, that we must expect in the future—in more areas and, in most cases, at a faster pace. Assumptions based on continuity will provide increasingly poor guidance on which to make plans because they will be positing conditions unlikely to exist. Thus, we need a new strategy for planning for the future, a strategy that assumes that change is more likely than continuity and that enables us to understand the changes that are coming and to make use of them. Furthermore, we would like this strategy to be sufficiently comprehensive so that in using it to make our plans we will feel as confident and comfortable as we do when we base them on the continuation of present conditions.

The purpose of this chapter is to describe such a strategy. Five steps are involved, each of which will be described in detail. In the order in which they should be taken these steps are:

- Recognize that change is occurring.
- Identify the changes likely to affect one's particular business, profession, or personal plans.
- Determine the type and probable pattern of each identified change.
- Rank the changes by the importance of their effect and the likelihood of their occurrence.
- Make use of the changes.

RECOGNIZING THAT CHANGE IS OCCURRING

E. B. White, America's gentle man of letters, once wrote, "The only sense that is common in the long run is the sense of change . . . and we all instinctively avoid it." History offers numerous illustrations in support of White's observation.

- When Robert Fulton presented his proposal for a steam-powered vessel to Napoleon, the French emperor replied: "What, sir, you would make a ship sail against the wind and currents by lighting a bonfire under her decks? I pray you excuse me. I have no time to listen to such nonsense."

- On December 10, 1903, seven days before the Wright brothers made their historic flight at Kitty Hawk, the *New York Times* editorialized, "There are more useful employments with fewer disappointments and mortifications than have been the portion of aerial navigators since the days of Icarus."

- In 1967, the final report on a study of life in 2067, commissioned by Keuffel and Esser, a well-known scientific instrument manufacturer, predicted numerous dramatic changes for a century hence, including domed cities, computerized traffic lanes, and three-dimensional television. It did *not* predict, however, that within five years cheap pocket calculators would entirely replace Keuffel and Esser's most famous product, the slide rule.

All of us readily acknowledge in the abstract that change occurs, and when asked we can readily give many examples to support our belief. Yet it is much more difficult to accept and operate on the notion that a particular situation or condition—especially one that is very familiar—is likely to be different in the future from what it is at present. When a business is doing well and sales of its products or services are strong there is a natural tendency to regard this as the normal situation, likely to continue and thus not to be tampered with. In the words of the old aphorism, "If it ain't broke, don't fix it." On the other hand, when circumstances are not good and the economy is down, and sales with it, there is often an inclination to view what are likely to be short-term phenomena as indicative of a long-term, even permanent, trend.

It is this natural bias in favor of continuity that must be overcome, to be replaced by the more accurate view that continuity is rare and, when it does occur, usually short-lived; it is change that is the more common experience. It may be wise not to fix something that is running well, but it is foolish to expect it to run well indefinitely and not to plan for the time when it is no longer doing so. In the same manner, expecting bad news to continue not only means ignoring change for the better but also probably helping to postpone it.

The expectation of continuity has a further, even more stultifying, consequence. It breeds inactivity. The response to good news is often "We should not do anything to interfere," while to bad news frequently it is "There is nothing we can do." In the inactivity of both responses there is stagnation, decline, and—ultimately—failure. Expectation of change, on the other hand, breeds activity. It means adjustments must be made, dangers have to be avoided; and opportunitities need to be seized. Responding to change keeps an organization and its personnel alive and alert. It ensures survival and is the necessary precondition for success.

We need, therefore, a new outlook for the future, one attuned to the reality of change and not the unreality of continuity, and thus more useful to us in making our plans for the future. To create such an outlook we need to reject the continuation of present trends and avoid projections based on business as usual.

Rejecting the continuation of present trends

The notion that what is happening now is the best guide to what will or can happen in the future is deeply embedded in our thinking and acting:

- On the second page of the recent best-seller *Megatrends*, John Naisbitt writes: "The most reliable way to anticipate the future is by understanding the present. That is the premise of this book."
- The opening sentence of the widely publicized and acclaimed *Global 2000 Report to the President of the U.S.* reads: "If present trends continue, the world in 2000 will be more crowded, more polluted, less stable ecologically, and more vulnerable to disruption than the world we live in now."
- Supply-side economists in the United States have regularly argued during the mid-1980s that all that is required to eliminate the large annual U.S. federal deficit is for the American economy to grow at its recent prevailing high rates for approximately the next decade.
- Banks and investors, during 1980 and 1981, believing that energy prices would continue to rise at their then

high rates of increase, supplied energy-related companies with over $500 billion of development capital.

Rarely, however, do present trends continue, and then
only very briefly. While much can be learned from the
present, to rely on it to anticipate the future is to miss the
changes that are essential to understanding what is to come.
To issue a warning based on a forecast of the continuation
of present trends is to ignore both changes that will invali-
date the forecast and actions to mitigate the consequences
of undesirable results as they develop. To argue that high
rates of economic growth will close the U.S. deficit is to
overlook the structural changes that are slowing American
growth and the business cycles that regularly create recessions and recoveries. To have invested so heavily in energy
on the basis of prices continuing to rise at prevailing rates
will mean—when the dust finally has settled—the costliest
single-industry debacle in the history of the world.

Not only are forecasts of the continuation of present
trends usually wrong and thus useless for future planning,
but they are also pernicious in that they give support to
several misleading attitudes about the evolution of future
activities and their influence on each other.

One of these attitudes can be called the "continuation
syndrome." This refers to the view that if a little of something is conceded or allowed to happen, then a lot is sure to
follow later, as expressed in the axiom "Give them an inch
and they'll take a mile." Such a categorical assertion of
inevitable continuation denies the possibility of change that
slows, alters, or even reverses a flow of activities. At one
level it may deter developments that entail short-term costs
to achieve much larger long-term gains (for example, it may
prevent replacing a worker by a machine, even though the
replacement eventually will mean improved productivity and
higher economic growth to the potential benefit of all); at
another level, it may discourage or even defeat attempts to
create new initiatives in response to new situations (for
instance, to place credence in the proposition "All arms races
have ended in war, and therefore the nuclear arms race is
bound to, also," rather than to understand why the nuclear
arms race is different and to try to proceed accordingly).

Another misleading attitude can be labeled the "infallibil-
ity of logic." Forecasts of the continuation-of-present-trends

type are frequently expressed as "if-then" propositions or imply such propositions. This is true especially of many doomsday forecasts concerning population, resources, and pollution. In each case, certain consequences flow from the forecast of further continuation. The problem is that when placed in the format of a rigorous logical if-then proposition these forecasts acquire an aura of credibility and certainty far greater than if they stood alone. What happens is that in such a format the seriousness of the consequences, and the fact that they flow so surely from the preconditions, ironically give unwarranted credibility to the likelihood of those preconditions occurring.

Finally, forecasts of the continuation of present trends give support to attitudes of "argument by analogy." The forecast that in one area present trends will continue and lead to certain consequences gives rise and acceptance to similar forecasts in other areas. Thus, when the OPEC nations in 1973–74 managed simultaneously to quadruple the price of oil and to cut back its production, many analysts, instead of seeing this as the singular and unique act that it was, were ready with forecasts of similar cartels springing up to choke off other resources. One distinguished commentator, who later served in a senior position in the Carter administration, wrote at the time that "oil is just the beginning." Cartels already had been formed for several other commodities, he pointed out; and he listed several, starting with copper, that could follow the path of OPEC. To cap his argument he noted that the price of copper for nearby delivery had reached an all-time high of nearly $1 a pound and quoted the prediction of the Shah of Iran (!) that "copper is next." Ten years later the price of copper was still less than $1, there was a glut of it in the world, and the cartel of copper-producing nations was as impotent as ever.

Adhering to any one of these attitudes will give a distorted view of the future. If plans are then made and resources are allocated in accordance with such views, governments, businesses, and individuals are likely to miss opportunities and incur losses. Assuming the continuation of present trends thus provides the poorest possible guidance for policy-planning purposes. Since it is the alteration of present trends that is most likely to occur, it is change that must be assumed, not continuity.

Avoiding projections based on business as usual

"You can never plan the future by the past," wrote Edmund Burke, the British parliamentarian and conservative political thinker. Nevertheless, this is what most firms do when they make their plans using "business as usual" as a baseline projection. Typically such plans then go on to project excursions from the baseline case by varying different factors such as costs and availability of materials, labor, and capital, changes in demand, effects of competition, alternative prices, and so forth. The net result is a projection resting almost entirely on past experience and biased toward perpetuating that experience.

But business as usual is unusual. It almost never happens. Structural changes create new technologies and materials, introduce new competitors, influence workforces, and alter attitudes in the marketplace. Cyclical changes mean variations in the cost of labor and materials, fluctuating interest rates, rises and falls in demand, and shifting preferences of clients and consumers. By not taking such changes into consideration a forecast developed from a business-as-usual base deliberately introduces error, and the further it is extended the greater the error.

In 1979 and 1980 the Pacific Northwest timber industry forecast for the 1980s a continuation of the high-growth, high-inflation business it was enjoying at the time, and on the basis of this business-as-usual projection signed long-term contracts with the U.S. Forest Service to buy approximately thirteen billion board feet of Douglas fir and other softwood lumber growing in national forests in the region. In fact, so confident were several companies of their forecast that at auctions they bid up to four or five times the original advertised price for some of the contracts offered. Within a year, however, recession and soaring interest rates collapsed the housing industry, leaving the Northwest timber companies with an obligation to buy large quantities of lumber at a price far higher than that to which it had dropped in a market barren of buyers. Across the border, the Canadian forest products industry fell into a similar bind when its business-as-usual projection indicated a steady U.S. demand for newsprint, which instead fell flat as electronic media grew faster than print media. The plaintive admission of a MacMillan Bloedel Company vice-president says it all:

"We gave into a mood of thinking that there would always be a shortage."

The same kind of business-as-usual forecasting has caused the American steel industry to overproduce iron ore, underrate technological change, overestimate demand, and largely ignore the growth of foreign competitiors. As a result, U.S. steelmakers have an iron ore industry far larger than they can use, obsolete and often inefficient equipment, and foreign competitors who can deliver slab steel at prices—including transportation—lower than they can offer. The same myopia regarding the combination of new technology and economic development abroad has afflicted U.S. farmers and those who ship their products. The growth of food production in other countries has sent many American farmers, including those of the nation's most productive agricultural state, California, into a downward spiral that will drive many out of business and mean lower earnings for those who do manage to survive. And companies in the business of providing the means to transport American produce to what seemed to be an export market that could only grow— like Scullin Steel, which makes railroad freight car castings— now face dwindling, perhaps even disappearing, sales. In the words of the chairman of Scullin's parent company: "Every forecast from every source had predicted demand would be strong for five, ten years, out."

Even high-growth, high-tech industries have come afoul of business-as-usual forecasts. Atari responded to the videogame boom as if it were the impossible dream of the toy industry incarnate, a fad that would never end; and while its executives and those of its boss, Warner Communications, blissfully slept on, competition and the ever-fickle tastes of the public turned their dream into a nightmare, colored with red ink. The Tandy Corporation had a similar jolt. When it discovered in 1977 that it could sell desktop computers to hobbyists and machine buffs in its Radio Shack stores, business-as-usual projections dictated it should continue doing so. But business-as-usual projections did not take account of the limited dimensions of the hobbyist market and the far larger dimensions of a growing market composed of potential purchasers who were not tinkerers and thus needed something more than friendly Radio Shack salespeople who could rap with them in the latest computer jargon. As a former Tandy manager put it, "We rode the tide of the computer business, and when it came around, we didn't"; and so, in August 1984, Tandy announced its first quarterly earnings decline in six years.

In all of these cases, projections of business as usual have been upset by change. The results have been wasted expenditures, declining sales, and lost opportunities. To avoid such consequences it is necessary to make projections that are based on the more likely assumption of change, not the far less likely one of business as usual. The next step, therefore, is to identify the relevant changes.

IDENTIFYING CHANGES LIKELY TO AFFECT ONE'S BUSINESS, PROFESSION, PERSONAL PLANS

All industries, professions, and businesses—and all individuals, too—need to identify the changes likely to affect what they are doing now and what they are planning to do in the future. Since at any time there are many changes occurring, such an identification would appear to be a formidable task. It can be managed, however, by understanding that only a limited number of changes principally affect any endeavor or individual and by employing a scheme of categorization that promises to identify most of those that are relevant. For this second step a simple scheme will be explained, and, using several different examples, its application will be shown.

Scheme

The basic scheme consists of two broad categories used to identify and organize the changes likely to affect one's business, profession, or personal plans. In one category are enumerated those changes affecting what a business (or organization or individual) requires in order to do what it does or wants to do. This category, which includes what must be used and acquired to accomplish tasks like producing goods or delivering services, can be called the "upstream" category. Some of the areas of changes in this category might be:

- Sources and kinds of information, and the equipment for processing it
- New technology and the maturing of current technology

- Changes in workforce composition, habits, and income expectations
- Changes in the cost of materials, labor, and capital
- Economic development in other nations and increasing competition
- Legislation and regulatory activity affecting such matters as environmental protection, product safety, and foreign trade

In the other category are enumerated those changes affecting the environment or target for which a business's (or an organization's or individual's) goods or services are being created. This category, which concerns the status, income, and desires of market middlemen, customers, and clients, and the factors which influence them, can be labeled the "downstream" category. Some of its areas of change might be:

- New and expanded means of communication
- Changes in content and levels of public and private education
- Changes in population age composition and life expectancy
- Changes in attitudes, preferences, and priorities
- The anticipated evolution of the business cycle in the short term, including employment levels, disposable personal income, credit availability, and interest rates

It is very important that attention be paid to *both* the upstream and the downstream categories of change. A company carefully attuned to advances in productive technology, foreign competition, materials availability and price, and workforce, legislative, and other changes may still not succeed if it pays little attention to restructuring occurring among its distributors or new developments in advertising media or changes in the needs or preferences of its customers. Conversely, a company with a flexible and innovative marketing organization and a good grasp of changing public tastes and buying power may fail unless it can provide products or services that are up-to-date, well engineered, and appropriate to its customers' needs. Mastering change requires being attentive to changes affecting both the product and the people who use it.

Using the scheme of categorization described here cannot guarantee that every relevant change will be identified. Some will be missed, perhaps because they are barely visible, or perhaps because the observer's focus is blurred or too narrow; and therefore the possibility of missed changes—albeit their content cannot be known—properly belongs with the enumeration of those identified. The fact that surprises occur should not be surprising.

The important point, however, is that this scheme provides a means of systematically seeking to identify the changes likely to be important to a particular business or profession. Its categories provide a search strategy and a framework for examining what is found, and their use increases confidence that no important changes will be missed.

This scheme can be used by those situated at any point in the process of creating and delivering goods and services. A company at one end of the productive spectrum, mining a raw material for example, still has many changes to identify in the upstream category, including developments in the technology it uses, changes in the availability and grade of the ore it is extracting, new union demands, evolving environmental legislation, and so forth, as well as all the changes downstream from it; and a business at the other end of the spectrum, like a retail store selling finished products, in addition to all its upstream changes still has many downstream changes to consider, such as changes in its neighborhood and in the age distribution, income, and preferences of its customers.

This scheme also can be of use to those in different departments and positions within a larger organization. Directors of research and development, financial managers, and heads of human resources departments—among others—all have upstream and downstream changes to identify and consider. And for an individual as well, this scheme can be useful. In contemplating a career, for instance, one can look upstream to one's own resources of education and experience and their likely and necessary evolution for achieving success in a particular field, and downstream to changes in opportunities, income, and other satisfactions that might occur in the field.

Application

Three examples can illustrate the application of the above

scheme for identifying changes. The first, for the automobile industry, shows the identification of selected changes likely to affect a manufacturing company and the functional areas within it, and is the most fully spelled out. The second, identifying changes affecting the profession of dentistry, is discussed in less detail; and the third, concerning changes facing individuals, is only briefly summarized. In each example the enumeration of changes is not meant to be inclusive of all those that are relevant, but rather to be suggestive of the kinds that should be considered.

An automobile manufacturer could begin its identification of "upstream" category changes by looking first at technological changes likely to affect the design and operation of cars. Today, this would mean variations in the internal combustion engine, new types of fuels, and totally new kinds of power plants as well as hybrid designs of old and new. It would also include improvements in traditional materials, such as the development of electrogalvanized steel, and the use of brand-new materials, like the some two dozen panels in the new Pontiac Fiero to replace the steel shell which forms the body in most modern cars. Among other changes would be the use of microprocessors to monitor and regulate more of the car's systems and radical new exterior design such as that used by Ford in the early 1980s in switching from a rather formal square style to one that is more rounded and more aerodynamically efficient.

Another area of technological change concerns the way in which automobiles are produced. It was the Japanese who first understood that the cost of manufacturing cars could be greatly reduced by replacing human labor with computer-controlled machinery, thereby creating what the report of MIT's International Automobile Program called the "third transformation" of the automobile industry (the first being Henry Ford's introduction of the Model T and the assembly line, and the second the coming of the Common Market and the lower tariffs that made possible large-volume European sales). Now, the same report points out, a "fourth transformation" is occurring involving "flexible" automation and the steady increase in cooperative ventures among automakers. Exemplifying this is General Motors' effort to upgrade its technology base by acquiring the Electronic Data Systems Corporation and the Hughes Aircraft Company as well as the increased foreign merger activity of all three major U.S. car manufacturers.

The upstream category for automobile manufacturers includes in addition changes in the availability, work habits, goals, and compensation of employees. A shrinking birthrate and the outflow of population that has occurred from traditional manufacturing areas in the North Central United States will mean a smaller older pool of workers in those areas, while increasing numbers pursuing higher education will mean that more of those remaining will have been to college and will be looking for employment opportunities commensurate with their educational attainments. Furthermore, the challenge of matching the quality of foreign-produced cars in the United States has coincided with a growing desire on the part of employees to have both a greater say and a greater stake in the fortunes of their companies, resulting in worker involvement in more areas of company policymaking and pay increases in bonuses tied to profits rather than in automatic wage hikes. An important outcome of this development—especially because of the steady growth of job-reducing automation in manufacturing plants—has been the shift in labor's emphasis from seeking more money to saving jobs, as exemplified in the fall 1984 agreements between the United Auto Workers and General Motors and Ford.

Also in the upstream category will be other changes, such as in the cost of finance capital and in the means of obtaining it, the development of federal and state regulations affecting foreign trade, engine efficiency, car safety, pollution control, and protection against defective products, and the ever growing and evolving role of foreign competition.

In the "downstream" category an automaker might look first to shifts in the distribution of population which will affect the distances automobiles must be shipped from assembly plants, and to changes in fuel costs and government regulations affecting transportation. Next it might be concerned with changes in the organization and attitudes of dealers, such as the growing interest in "dualing," whereby a dealer can carry two distinctly different cars of the same manufacturer (for example, larger Oldsmobiles and smaller Chevrolets) and thus appeal to a broader customer base, or the development of "automobile supermarkets," displaying many makes and models under one roof. At the same time, manufacturers have to be attentive to changes affecting the fleets, those who purchase cars in quantity. The Japanese, aware of such changes, made a strategic decision around 1979 to target fleet buyers with their smaller, more gas-stingy cars. They were startlingly successful. In 1972, 95 percent of the cars in the huge Hertz fleet were big eight-cylinder models; ten years later big cars accounted for only 5 percent of the total.

Another downstream area involves economic changes. There are, first, structural changes in economic development and growth—especially in developing nations—which influence per capita income and steadily increase the numbers who can afford to own and operate automobiles, thereby creating and enlarging export markets. Second, there are changes in the business cycle, creating upturns and downturns in national economies as well as rises and falls in numbers employed and in interest rates, all of which influence sales of new cars in any given year. And third, there are changes in the cost of buying and operating a car relative to other big-ticket-item costs, especially purchasing and maintaining a home. Because important parts of the costs of owning automobiles and homes are similar (interest rates and fuel), their rise can make it increasingly difficult to do both simultaneously; and since house payments must be met and new car purchases can be postponed, it is sales of the latter that will be most affected. This partly accounts for the decreasing frequency of new-car purchases in the early 1980s and helps explain why in the most recent U.S. economic recovery car sales were still appreciably below those of the record years of the 1970s. It also explains why car sales are stimulated during periods of sharply discounted financing terms.

The changing composition, education, and experiences of populations are also components of the downstream category. An aging population is likely to favor more conservatively styled cars, designed for both ease of access and operation. However, the younger elements of populations, particularly in advanced industrial countries, with more years of education per capita than their elders and especially with hands-on experience with computers during their schooling, will take more readily to digital readouts and computerlike controls and dashboard displays.

Preferences of customers also change, both cyclically and

structurally. Higher gasoline prices did slow the demand for large cars, but as prices stabilized, and especially as mandated fuel efficiency standards increased miles per gallon, the demand returned, surprising many automakers who not only should have understood the consequences of the changes that were occurring, but even more should have realized that an American population—more dispersed than ever as it began for the first time to leave cities in larger numbers than it entered them—needed and wanted the roominess Detroit had worked so long to convince them they should want. The poor sales of General Motors' downsized Cadillacs, Buicks, and Oldsmobiles illustrate its failure to understand the dynamics of this particular "downstream" change.

Other preference changes, more structural than cyclical, also have to be taken into account. People have always identified in some way with their automobile. This is why certain vehicles, makes, and models sell better in some regions of the United States than in others (for instance, Fords are strong on the West Coast of the United States, Buicks sell best in Chicago, and in sixteen Midwestern and South Central states the most popular vehicle on the road is a pickup truck); and it is why as self-identity changes so, too, will car preferences. Among young professionals in urban areas—the so-called Yuppies—the preference is for cars that reflect their values: recognizable quality and high performance, but in a socially responsible way. Thus a well-built foreign car with a small fuel-efficient engine assisted by a turbocharger allows them to experience the occasional thrill of fast acceleration in a vehicle that is normally conserving of nonrenewable petroleum. Likewise, a working woman—even though she also may be a young mother—will eschew a station wagon because it symbolizes the traditional life-style from which she feels she has liberated herself. However, a minivan—in effect a repackaged station wagon with a front-wheel drive—carries no negative connotations and has become a hot-selling item, filling the station wagon's still needed role.

All of these downstream changes can in turn be addressed by marketing strategies which themselves must be attentive to changes in communications media and advertising formats. Thus, within larger organizations, individual departments—like marketing, finance, human resources, production, research and development, and others—will have their own categories of upstream and downstream changes that must be identified. A human resources manager, for example, must be aware of changes in the education, experiences, backgrounds, and attitudes of the pool of personnel from which new employees can be drawn; and that same manager must be attentive to downstream changes in the positions to be filled and in the qualifications required and compensation available for those positions. In the same manner, financial officers need to consider upstream changes in the cost and availability of funds and downstream changes in the purposes for which they will be put to use. And so, throughout any organization, from the chief executive officer to the most junior employee, there is a need to identify the changes likely to influence one's activities.

This same need to identify changes also exists for those in professions. A dentist, for example, must identify a number of "upstream" changes likely to affect his practice. One area of change is the rapid development of dental research that is providing new means of diagnosis and new procedures for the treatment of dental diseases, new equipment using advanced sound, light and chemical technologies for preventive and restorative work, and new resins, ceramics, and other materials for coating and bonding teeth. Related and supplementary to this research are developments in the use of information technology for storing and retrieving diagnostic data as well as for handling traditional office tasks such as accounting, record-keeping, and tracking insurance claims. Also in the upstream category are changes in the cost of dental education and necessary retraining, as well as changes in the cost of setting up a practice and modernizing and replacing equipment. In addition, a dentist needs to consider changes affecting his competition, both with regard to the rise and fall of numbers of new graduates from dental schools and where they choose to locate and with regard to the development of auxiliary practices like dental hygiene and denturism.

In the "downstream" category, changes in the composition and condition of the population will be very important to the practice of dentistry. A slower-growing older population will require different dental services than a faster-growing younger one. And the increased use of fluorides—in drinking water and dentifrices—will reduce the incidence of dental caries, meaning less filling of cavities but more maintenance and preservative dentistry as a longer-living population retains their teeth for more years. Changes in education and income also will be important, since visits to dentists are strongly correlated with both. And higher per capita incomes and more widespread affluence—in the advanced developed nations and in more of the developing nations—will mean greater attention to oral hygiene and physical appearance, increasing the demand for orthodontic and prosthodontic dentistry. Further, the delivery of dental service is being rapidly and radically altered by changes in its setting and its payment. In the case of the former, the traditional single-chair private practice is increasingly being supplemented with corporate dentistry, franchise dentistry, and the delivery of services in department stores, hospitals, and health maintenance organizations; in the latter, prepaid dental plans and other forms of third-party payment are altering the traditional fee-for-service relationship between dentist and patient and changing the role of the dentist as an individual entrepreneur.

Finally, an individual facing an important decision in life, such as starting a family, changing jobs, or making a major purchase like a home, will want to identify changes likely to concern his or her choice. In the "upstream" category will be possible changes affecting what the individual is bringing to the matter of the decision, including resources, experience, attitudes, and goals. In the "downstream" category will be changes in the environment in which the prospective activity will occur, including what others are doing or might do that will affect a particular choice. Among such changes might be those involving economic prospects, the demand for certain goods or services, the evolution of an industry or a profession, the development of a geographic area or neighborhood, opportunities likely to be available, and problems that might arise.

As the above examples illustrate, the scheme of categorization described here provides a framework for identifying the changes likely to affect a particular business or activity. Since the scheme consciously encompasses the entire spectrum of possible changes and divides it into two logically distinct groupings, its use will also increase confidence that most relevant changes will be identified. The list of those that result will form the basis for the next step in the strategy of mastering change.

DETERMINING TYPE AND
PROBABLE PATTERN OF EACH CHANGE

Some changes that are likely to affect one's business, profession, or personal plans will be structural and will require responses that are new, different, and enduring; others will be cyclical and will need responses that are similar to ones made before and that usually will be temporary. In addition, each change will have its own pattern, with its own direction, magnitude, pace, and duration; and these dimensions will also affect the nature of the response made to the change. Therefore, to understand the changes that have been identified in the second step of the strategy and to know how and when to respond to them, it is necessary next to determine their type (structural or cyclical) and probable patterns.

Type of change

Structural changes are fundamental transformations in the makeup or operation of some activity or institution from a previous state. Cyclical changes, on the other hand, are temporary alterations, often following a pattern exhibited before and frequently returning to a prior state or condition.

In order to determine whether a particular change is structural or cyclical it is necessary to look at what is causing it and what results flow from it. In most cases, structural changes are caused by the appearance of something new that has not existed before. This is almost always the case with structural changes caused by new knowledge or new technology. New knowledge of the working of the human body and the causes of its diseases, for example, has made possible structural changes in life expectancy. In the same manner, new technology leading to the development of steam- and gasoline-powered engines caused structural changes in transportation.

Cyclical changes, however, usually have causes that have occurred before. Rises and falls in the rate of economic growth during business cycle changes, for instance, are the results of numerous decisions made by consumers, investors, and producers, all very similar in kind to decisions made many times before. Likewise, cyclical changes in the demand and supply for goods and services reflect responses by consumers and producers to information available to them about prices and quantities that are very much like responses they have made before to similar information. In such cases not only is the kind of response the same but often even its exact level.

Even more distinctive are differences in the results of structural and cyclical changes. Usually a structural change embodies a qualitative result, even though it may have been produced by activities measured in quantitative terms. For example, as increasing numbers of workers in a country move from extractive to fabricative activities and the latter account for a rising share of total product, the country undergoes a qualitative structural change from preindustrial to industrial status. In the same manner, as individuals and households accumulate increasing quantities of wealth and assets, they undergo qualitative changes in attitudes and preferences. In addition, the results of structural changes often permanently increase capabilities to achieve desired goals. For an individual, the structural change of the completion of higher education increases that individual's capability to enter a profession or hold a more responsible or better-paying job. Similarly, for a country the achievement of widespread adult literacy is a structural change that can assist the goal of modernization. For an industry or a particular company, the acquisition of a new technology represents a structural change that can result in an improved product, greater efficiency, and an increased ability to compete in the marketplace.

Cyclical changes, on the other hand, do not usually have qualitative results and do not permanently endow individuals or countries or organizations with enhanced capabilities to achieve goals. Cyclical changes, by their nature, are usually measured in quantitative terms, and at any particular moment they indicate an alteration of more or less of something, but not a change in basic quality. A shift by the electorate in favor of liberal or conservative candidates in a representative government, for instance, does not indicate a change in the basic quality of the government. It is merely a quantitative cyclical change that temporarily alters the numbers of representatives of different political persuasions. Likewise, the result of a fall in interest rates in a particular area may be to temporarily increase the number of people in the area who can purchase homes and the activity of mortgage lenders and home builders, but it does not represent a permanent change in capabilities either to buy or to build homes.

Finally, the most important distinction in the results of structural and cyclical changes concerns their permanence. Structural changes are almost always irreversible. They indicate the attainment of a new status or a new level from which there will be no return to a prior status or level. The advance of knowledge or the development of a new technology, for example, represents a wider understanding of some phenomenon or a better way of accomplishing some task. Old knowledge is not lost, but rather it is supplemented or replaced by the new; and while there occasionally may be special circumstances that call for the use of a superseded technology, it is the current technology that offers optimum performance and serves as the point of departure for the next stage of development.

Cyclical changes, however, have results that are temporary. They do not indicate the attainment of a new and different status not achieved before. Instead, they represent an incremental measure on a scale usually traversed earlier and likely to be crossed again. Like a football on the yard lines between opposed goals, they mark movement backward and forward over ground covered many times before. Rates of economic growth rise and fall; so do levels of demand and supply and numbers of staff at the center and periphery of organizations, as also do percentages of those who marry, commit crimes, and favor the fads and fashions of the time. In almost every case they return to some level of activity achieved earlier, settling but for a measured moment and then moving on to other points on cycles endlessly tracked.

To determine, therefore, the type of change (structural or cyclical) facing an individual, organization, or country, it is necessary to examine what is causing it and what results are flowing from it. If the cause is something new and the resulting change is qualitative, or permanently increases capabilities to achieve certain goals, and especially if the result means the attainment of a new level or status from which there will be no retreat, then the change is almost surely structural. On the other hand, if the cause of the change has occurred before and its result is quantitative, with no permanent increase of capabilities, and with the likelihood that the same result will be attained again, then the change is almost certain to be cyclical.

Pattern of change

Understanding the patterns of future changes means trying to know what has not yet occurred, and for this reason the usual view is that more change means less certainty and that, therefore, as the pace of change accelerates less and less can be known of the future. But such a view assumes that change is pure chance and that future occurrences are totally random, as completely unrelated to each other as the rolls of a pair of dice. In fact, very little change is random; most change is movement from related point to related point. Because it is movement it creates a pattern, and because the points are related, much change—as Charles Lyell, the founder of scientific geology, taught—is implicit in what has happened. Thus for some changes, the faster they occur the more visible their patterns will be. For these the "age of discontinuity," to use Peter Drucker's evocative label for our present times, is more accurately described as the era of continuous change.

Clearly, the patterns of some changes are more visible than those of others; but since few are completely invisible, at least something can be seen of the future of almost every change that is underway. Because each change contains—in varying portions—both the inevitable and the unexpected, by understanding its pattern we can increase our knowledge of the former and reduce the area of the latter.

When we look at the present we see only a fragment, a moment, of a much larger continuum. If we broaden our gaze, taking a longer-term perspective, we can see the pattern of many fragments over many moments. With that long-term perspective we can make out the dimensions of each change: its direction, its magnitude, its pace, and its duration.

The *direction* of structural change is usually constant. It is almost always measured as a continuous increase or a continuous decrease, either indefinitely or through to its completion. For example, the accumulation of information and the growth of its role as the transforming resource of postindustrial societies are obviously in continuous increase, as are the storage capacities of information-processing equipment and the complexity of the operations such equipment can handle. On the other hand, the direction of the structural change in employment in manufacturing is steadily downward, as automated machinery continues to replace human workers.

The direction of cyclical change, however, is not constant. In business cycles, rates of economic growth rise, then fall; and so, too, do prices and wages, interest rates and levels of unemployment. The direction of change also varies in cycles of organizational behavior such as shifts from centralization to decentralization and back, and in cycles of social behavior like rising and falling divorce and crime rates.

The *magnitude* of structural change can be either unbounded or bounded by certain obvious limits depending on the nature of the change. In the case of the structural changes of increasing information and knowledge, and of the growth of technology in general, clearly there are no bounds. The magnitude of these changes has no known limit. Other structural changes are bounded by physical limits of population or nature itself. The boundary of the magnitude of the structural change of increasing literacy is obviously all people of all nations at or above school age, just as the upper limit of those who can simultaneously receive communications is the total population of the world. In reality these limits will be only approached, never reached. Thus, the boundaries become guides against which to measure likely actual magnitudes of the changes. Nature also provides boundaries. The automobile has created a structural change in personal transportation. But the efficiency of its power plant—based on an internal combustion engine with reciprocating pistons—is definitely limited. Only by abandoning the present engine in favor of a new technology can the efficiency of the automobile's power plant be significantly increased.

The magnitude of cyclical change, on the other hand, is always bounded. Rates of different economic measures vary considerably during business cycles, but usually within fairly narrow boundaries; and even on the rare occasions when they go outside these boundaries, they are never in any sense completely unbounded. The same is true for the rise and fall of demand and supplies of commodities, products, and those who provide services. Over time their total may increase or decrease considerably, but the magnitudes of the cyclical changes they undergo are always limited.

The *pace* of a change is at once its most important dimension and the most difficult one to discern. Unbounded structural changes, such as the increase of information and technology, appear to be characterized by an ever-accelerating pace, at least over the long term. But in the short term the pace often varies. During wars, technologies serving military purposes may speed up while others (related to nonmilitary domestic activities) may slow. After the war the reverse is often true, though it may be that some technologies originally developed principally for military purposes (for example, the treatment of wounds on the battlefield) will subsequently have important nonmilitary benefits. The pace of technological change is also sensitive to major scientific breakthroughs. In the years following a new discovery the pace is very rapid, as was the case with radio and television in the 1920s and 1930s following the successful demonstration of wireless transmission a short time before. Then the pace slows as the new technology is "worked out" and perfected.

Bounded structural changes are usually characterized by a pace that is slow at first, accelerates, and then slows again. The long-term structural transition of a country from preindustrial to industrial to postindustrial status exhibits just such a pace, as does the corresponding demographic transition from slow population growth to rapid to slowing again.

The pace of cyclical changes, however, is often very rapid at the outset followed by a gradual slowing. Thus, in the recovery phase of a business cycle, growth usually rises quickly in the early months, literally fueling itself as consumer purchases stimulate production, which in turn generates increased employment and additional purchasing power. Then the pace slows and stutters as the recovery peaks, poised for the downturn to follow. In the same way a new fad or fashion spreads rapidly, then dies out more slowly.

Finally, the last dimension, the *duration* of change, is a function of its limits (unbounded or bounded) and its manner of evolution. The duration of unbounded structural changes, such as increasing information and knowledge, is obviously continuous. Bounded structural changes, on the other hand, continue only until their practical limits are reached. In most countries, the duration of the structural change of increasing literacy, for example, will be until some 98 or 99 percent of all the population of school age and above is literate. For a number of reasons (persons mentally handicapped or for some reason isolated from the mainstream of society) the figure will never be 100; yet clearly once it reaches the upper nineties the country's structural change to full literacy will have been completed. In the same way, the development of a particular technology continues until increasing efforts to improve it encounter physical limits that slow results to levels less than the cost of making the efforts.

The duration of the phases of all cyclical changes is, by the nature of such changes, limited. However, durations vary considerably, depending on the kind of change and the conditions affecting any particular iteration of it. In addition, many changes have several different cyclical patterns, each with its own distinctive range of duration. In the stock market, for instance, a rally may be measured in days, a bull or bear market in months, and a change in the real value of shares traded in years. Each of these cycles will in turn be affected by a number of other factors—many of them also cyclical—such as rates of economic growth, levels of interest rates, reports of corporate profits, etc.

Although these durations—and those of other cyclical changes—are all limited, determining them in many cases can be quite difficult. There are, however, several considerations that can help. One is to understand the nature of the change. Fads, for example, like bull and bear markets, have relatively short durations. Cycles of changes in commodity prices—because it takes time to extract, process, and market commodities—are usually longer; and cycles of social behavior, reflecting demographic changes that may be a generation in length, continue far longer. Second, since most cyclical changes are driven by other cyclical changes, examining these can often give indications of durations, as is commonly done with "leading indicators" in economic forecasting. Finally, when typical or average patterns of cyclical changes are examined, these can provide general guidelines for estimating future durations. Thus, the closer an ongoing phase of a cyclical change comes to its average duration—barring any extraordinary influence peculiar to the instance at hand—then the higher and higher the probability that it will soon complete its course. While this does not give a precise forecast of its duration, it still should alert an individual or organization that the end is near, not still distant, and—combined with the other considerations above—prompt responses appropriate to, and in advance of, the next phase of the cycle.

The following examples of changes—one structural, one with both structural and cyclical aspects, and one purely cyclical—show how the dimensions of direction, magnitude, pace, and duration can be used to describe their probable patterns.

One example of structural change is female participation in the labor force in the United States:

- The *direction* of this change has been upward, toward increasing numbers.
- Its *magnitude* is large. In 1940 slightly over a quarter of all women sixteen years old and over were in the labor force; by 1980 the proportion had risen to over 50 percent. At its peak the percentage likely will be nearly 60.
- Its *pace* was rapid in the 1940s because of the increase of women workers during World War II and the continued employment of many in the economic recovery that followed the war; then it slowed as more women stayed home to bear and care for children. In the early 1960s the pace again picked up, and in the 1970s it accelerated further; but in the 1980s it has been slowing, and it will continue to do so as the upper limit of female participation is approached and the number of those who are older and no longer working increases.
- The *duration* of this structural change will be about forty years, from the mid-1950s to the mid-1990s. After its completion, further changes will be cyclical as the percent of female participation rises and falls in small increments, reflecting cyclical demographic changes and alterations in business-cycle-influenced demand.

Population provides an example of change with both structural and cyclical aspects:

- The *direction* of its structural aspects (slowing rates of growth and lengthening life expectancy) is constant, with the former continually slowing and the latter continually rising for the world as a whole. In its cyclical aspect the direction of population change varies, reflecting short-term rises and falls in birthrates.

- The *magnitude* and *pace* of the structural aspects of slower growth rates and longer life vary considerably from country to country depending on levels of development. In most of the developed nations the fall in growth rates has been large and rapid and the lengthening of life expectancy has been small and slowing as natural limits of life are approached. In most of the developing nations the situation has been quite different: more slowly falling growth rates, except in China and India, and larger and more rapid increases in life expectancy. In the magnitude and pace of the cyclical aspect of population change there is greater similarity, with both dimensions growing smaller and slowing over time for most nations except for catastrophic events—like war—which introduce upward biases which reverberate through succeeding cycles.

- The *duration* of the structural aspects will be influenced by their magnitude and pace. In the developed nations the duration of the change to longer life will continue for some time, though at a slowing pace, while the duration of slowing growth to declining actual numbers will be much shorter; in the developing nations the duration of both aspects will be much longer, especially that of slowing population growth to an eventual peak and then decline in numbers. For the cyclical aspect, duration is usually a generation in length as children of high-birthrate phases begin producing their own children about twenty years later.

The rise and fall of interest rates provide an example of purely cyclical change:

- The *direction* of change in interest rates varies, rising and falling in reflection of other business cycle changes such as rates of economic growth and inflation. In the United States, since the late 1950s, the overall direction of cyclical interest rate variations has been upward, due principally to rising inflation rates.

- The *magnitude* of this cyclical change, from trough to peak, has increased as the overall direction has moved steadily upward. In the late 1950s it was around 4 percent; by the early 1970s and 1980s it had reached nearly 10 percent for some rates.

- The *pace* of interest rate change tends to be very rapid once a business cycle recession is underway and rates are falling. It then slows as the follow-on recovery commences, as interest rates tend to track more closely the inflation rate. As this rate steadies, the pace of interest rate change slows, to speed up again with either the onset of a new economic downturn or rapid change in the inflation rate.

- The *duration* of interest rate cycles, from peak to peak, tends to be approximately the same length as business cycles of recovery and recession. In the United States these historically have averaged four and a half years, though service sector dominance of the economy may now be lengthening them, as discussed earlier.

Having determined the type and probable pattern of the changes likely to affect one's business, profession, or personal plans, it is necessary next to rank these changes by the importance of their effect and the likelihood of their occurrence.

RANKING CHANGES BY IMPORTANCE OF EFFECT AND LIKELIHOOD OF OCCURRENCE

There was a time when the most important changes a farmer had to worry about were those that occurred in the weather. No longer. Today's modern large-scale farmer (increasingly the only kind that will be viable for growing basic crops) must pay attention to many other changes important to the success of his business, including such varied developments as scientific advances in crop breeding, new efficiency-enhancing equipment, current legislative and regulatory activity, and the latest data on the worldwide supply, demand, and prices for the crops he is producing. In his work he is likely to make use of aerial photographs of his own and surrounding fields, laser-guided equipment to level his land, and computers for such different functions as planting times, herbicide sprayer control, and the latest quotations from commodity exchanges. The same increase in the number and variety of changes important to their work is also affecting all of the organizations and institutions which support farmers, including equipment makers, seed suppliers, rural banks, regional cooperatives, grain elevators, transportation systems, and wholesalers and retailers of final products.

In farming, and in virtually every other business, profession, and personal occupation, there are more changes affecting more activities coming at a faster pace than ever before. Yet the time available to deal with such changes has not increased—in fact, in many cases, because they are occurring faster, it has become shorter—and the resources available to handle them remain limited. Thus, in order to use fixed time and limited resources where they will be most effective it is necessary to rank the changes that have been identified in the second step of the strategy and whose type and probable pattern have been determined in the third step.

Ranking changes

Appropriate responses to changes to come require that they be ranked not only by the importance of their effect but also by the likelihood of their occurrence. The reasoning for such dual consideration was aptly stated in another context by the great American jurist Learned Hand when he wrote that "courts must ask whether the gravity of an 'evil,' *discounted by its improbability*, justifies such invasion of free speech as is necessary to avoid the danger" (emphasis added). With regard to changes to come, this means that a change that would have a very important effect, but that in fact has a very low probability of occurring, might be less deserving of attention than one with lesser effect that is virtually certain to occur.

It is neither possible nor necessary to rank changes by precise orders of importance or exact probabilities of occurrence; but the use of general categories is feasible, and they can serve the purpose of giving guidance for the allocation of time and resources. For both importance of effect and likelihood of occurrence, three categories should be sufficient in most cases. For importance, the following can be used:

1. Most important (would have a major effect)
2. Moderately important (would have a significant effect)
3. Less important (would have a measurable effect, i.e., not vital but should not be ignored)

For likelihood, a similar sequence would be:

   a. Most likely (virtually certain to occur)
   b. Highly likely (more than 50 percent probability of occurrence)
   c. Less likely (less than 50 percent probability of occurrence)

FIG. 5.1. Matrix to Determine Amount of Attention to be Given to Changes According to Their Relative Importance and Likelihood.

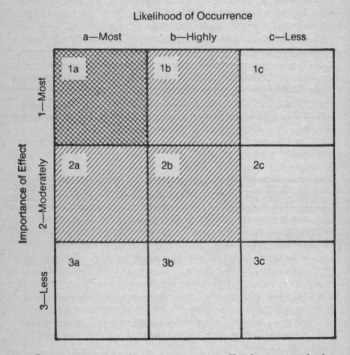

Likelihood of Occurrence

	a—Most	b—Highly	c—Less
1—Most	1a	1b	1c
2—Moderately	2a	2b	2c
3—Less	3a	3b	3c

Importance of Effect

In most cases, changes to come affecting a particular business, profession, or individual can be arranged in the above categories of importance and likelihood. Using numbers and letters for the rankings of importance and likelihood will then give an indication of the changes to which time and resources most effectively could be directed. Thus, changes ranked in both the "1" and "a" categories (most important and most likely) would deserve considerable attention; those in both the "3" and "c" categories (less important and less likely) would deserve far less.

To facilitate the inspection and comparison of a large number of changes, a simple matrix can be used. As figure 5.1 illustrates, a three-by-three nine-cell matrix will display all the possible combinations of the scheme of categories presented above. With such a display it is possible to quickly estimate the amount of attention that should be given to the arrayed changes. Thus, those in cell 1a (cross-hatched) should receive the greatest attention; those in cells 1b, 2a, and 2b (shaded) less attention, and those in cells 1c, 2c, 3a, 3b, and 3c (blank) the least.

Finally, since over time there will be alterations in the ranking of changes, both by their importance of effect and their likelihood of occurrence—as well as the addition of wholly new changes—it is necessary that rankings regularly be reviewed and adjusted after they are first made. In this way ongoing guidance can be obtained for reallocations of time and resources as changes move from category to category.

Applying the rankings

The use of the above scheme for ranking change can be illustrated by considering the rankings of selected changes for various kinds of business, professional, and other groupings.

For companies involved in basic extractive industries, like metals, rubber, petroleum, forest products, commodities, and different kinds of agricultural products, selected changes could be ranked as follows:

- Changes that might receive the greatest attention (those ranked 1a):
  —Changes in the amount of available supply of a given resource (actual and potential) and its quality and accessibility
  —Changes in the number of other suppliers, their output, and their likely future development and growth
  —New developments in production technology, including automation and cost-reducing equipment and processes

    —Alterations in demand due to changes in numbers of customers in different markets, changes in economic development and growth in other countries, and technology-induced changes in requirements for particular materials

- Changes that might receive less attention (those ranked 1b, 2a, and 2b):
    —Changes in wages and other forms of compensation, depending on the labor intensiveness of the industry or the size of a particular company's labor force
    —Changes in price levels and interest rates, depending on capital investment requirements
    —Changes in currency values, depending on the extent to which the industry or particular company depends on exports or competes with imports
- Changes that might receive the least attention (those ranked 1c, 2c, 3a, 3b, and 3c):
    —Changes in the security of sources of supply (this will vary from industry to industry, but even when the likelihood of loss is reckoned low, its effect—should it occur—would be so great that some attention must be given to it)
    —Changes in the availability, training, and compensation of workers—to which highly automated businesses can pay less attention, though not entirely ignore

Producers and distributors of higher-value-added and specialized durable and nondurable goods face a different set of changes that must be ranked according to importance of effect and likelihood of occurrence, including:

- Changes that might receive the greatest attention (ranked 1a):
    —New technologies (certain to occur and virtually certain to have an important effect) which will mean new products with new capabilities and will affect the life and limits of existing products
    —New methods of design and manufacture (such as CAD/CAM) which can reduce costs and mean efficient production in greater variety and diversity
    —The development of product demand, especially when it will develop and what its pattern (magnitude, pace, and duration) will be

—Changes in discretionary income, including changes in the growth (and limits to growth) of two-income families, asset-based income, and income of the elderly, as well as changes in the portion of income required to meet basic needs

- Changes that might receive less attention (ranked 1b, 2a, and 2b):
  —Production in other countries, depending on the product and level of sophistication of its manufacture
  —Changes in laws and regulations—domestic and foreign—concerning quotas, tariffs, and subsidies
  —Alterations in the availability of labor, the composition of the workforce (for example, the increase of women), and levels of compensation
  —Business cycle changes affecting pricing, interest rates, and currency values
  —Changes in fads and fashions, depending on the product
- Changes that might receive the least attention (ranked 1c, 2c, 3a, 3b, and 3c):
  —Demographic changes which, though highly likely, may be more or less important depending on the industry or company product
  —Changes not yet important but likely to be in the future (for example, more shopping at home via computer by a population with a higher percentage of elderly)
  —Discovery of danger or toxicity in a major product which, though of low probability, would have such an important effect that some attention must be given to it

The traditional professions, as well as newer providers of services, also need to rank coming changes by their importance and likelihood, especially as the societies in which they operate become more technologically advanced and more service-activity-dominated.

For the health care field, increases in information and technology are certain and must be ranked very high in importance. Not only will they extend knowledge of the human body and provide new means for the care of its illnesses and injuries, but eventually they will revolutionize health care by making it possible to provide preventive measures tailored to the particular genetic and biochemical makeup of each individual. Demographic changes are also important because they indicate a slower-growing older population, meaning more societies with larger percentages of people at ages where greater medical care will be required. This change, however, has built-in limits, and while a significant lengthening of life expectancy beyond natural ranges would have to be ranked as a development of enormous importance for health services (as well as for other services, like insurance), the low likelihood of its occurrence within any meaningful planning horizon means that little attention needs to be paid to it. Another set of changes, those due to business cycles, are far more likely to occur, but for most health services—except those practices like plastic surgery and dentistry where treatment usually is more elective—the importance of their effect can be ranked lower.

For financial services, however, business cycle changes will be ranked very high. Because they directly affect the amount and kind of business that is done, the value of assets held and how they are managed, and the advice that is given to clients, business cycle changes must be given maximum attention. Also to be ranked very high for financial services, though less certain as to their occurrence, are cyclical changes in laws and regulations, particularly their lifting or relaxation. Such changes can result in new competitors and new partners, the creation and growth of new services, and the radical restructuring of old ones. In the United States, in the last decade, deregulation and sweeping changes in current regulations have turned many financial services—especially banking—from steady, conservative businesses to volatile risk-laden ones. (In 1984, a recovery year, more banks failed than in any other year since the depression of the 1930s.) Other changes, with various probabilities of occurrence, also will be of importance to financial services. These include further changes in technology, the development of new financial products, and continued increases in per capita income and two-income families.

For entertainment and leisure services, changes in levels of income will be among those ranked highest in importance of effect. Higher per capita income and more two-income families, complemented by a slowing birth rate, mean more meals eaten out, more theater and sporting-event tickets sold, and more vacations involving travel to relatively distant locations. While the rate of increase of two-income families will slow, the rise in discretionary income—though varying at times—is likely to continue. Increasing longevity and the continued indexation of many sources of retirement income will also sustain purchases for entertainment services by another group, the elderly. Older people—with more active years to enjoy—are also likely to be a growing market for outdoor leisure equipment and activities, though for their needs redesign and restructuring will be required. This in turn should extend the demand for physical fitness services of various kinds, which have boomed with increased economic security and the concomitant growing interest in health and appearance—changes in attitudes which are likely to continue, though at slowing rates of increase. Other changes will be ranked differently by those providing entertainment and leisure services. An energy crisis, for example, would have a very important effect, but since its near-term likelihood is low, proportionally less attention can be given to any contingency planning for it. Business cycle changes, on the other hand, are certain to occur, but their effect will vary depending on the type and price level of the entertainment service—those at the lower and upper ends of the scale generally surviving downturns better than those in the middle.

Finally, geographic entities, organizations, and individuals, too, can rank by importance and likelihood the changes ahead that will affect them.

A region or a state in the United States heavily dependent on basic resource or manufacturing industries, for example, must rank high in importance and likelihood the future decline of these industries and the loss of their jobs and contribution to local economies. (The current troubles of "oil patch" states like Texas, Oklahoma, and Louisiana provide good examples of what happens when they do not do so.) Other states and regions will need to consider likely future changes in school-age and working-age populations based on nearer-term changes in birthrates, racial and ethnic makeup, and in- and out-migration. Cities will consider both existing economic activities and population composition in ranking their vulnerability to business cycle changes. New York City, for example, with its high service sector component, may not suffer extreme business cycle changes in employment; but its large low-income minority populations will continue to be a drain on public social expenditures, especially during economic downturns.

Organizations such as labor unions must rank high in importance and likelihood increasing factory automation that will mean fewer jobs, fewer members, and a declining ability to press demands through job actions and strikes. Political groups, too, almost always working with limited resources, must rank changes in populations, occupations, and attitudes in order to decide where best to direct those resources to achieve their goals. And individuals, in considering important decisions from career choices to major purchases, will have to make their own rankings of the importance and likelihood of changes to come that will affect the alternatives available to them.

For all of the above—preparing for the future in their businesses, professions, and personal lives—ranking the changes they have identified is the necessary preparation for the fifth and final step in the strategy for mastering change: making use of it.

MAKING USE OF CHANGES

The Hershey Bar is as American as Mom and apple pie, and the town where it is made—Hershey, Pennsylvania—is literally a monument to the country's long-standing love affair with the rich dark brown candy. Its main street is named Chocolate Avenue, and the lamps lining it are in the shape of Hershey Kisses, alternately wrapped and unwrapped; there is a Chocolate World, a Hershey Zoo, and a Hershey Amusement Park, and the local professional hockey team is the Hershey Bears—usually pronounced without the "e."

But Hershey is no longer undisputed king of the candy bars. It now shares the top spot with Mars, and its revenues in candy and confectionary goods have dropped from 88 percent of total sales in 1978 to 67 percent in 1985. What has happened? Is Hershey giving up on the product that made it famous? No. What it is doing is responding to change. The management of the Hershey Foods Corporation knows that an aging health-conscious population has a declining appetite for candy (consumption in the United States is 20 percent below its peak of twenty pounds in the late 1960s). It has also seen the prices of cocoa beans and sugar fluctuate widely as third-world suppliers have erratically entered and left the market, moved by forces other than supply and demand; and it understands well the dangers of being a one-product company when that product is not only vulnerable to shifting fashion but also prey to unknown threats that overnight could flatten its sales. So, Hershey is diversifying, moving into pasta and retail food services, areas related to its main business and responsive to a public with widening tastes and increasing discretionary income.

Hershey sees changes ahead and is responding to them. To continue as before, relying almost exclusively on the single product with which Milton Hershey founded the company ninety years ago, probably would mean continued earnings a while longer; but eventually it also would mean growing dangers and missed opportunities. No company can remain unresponsive in the face of change; and this is especially true for one that is doing well, for such a company is growing at a pace that both becomes increasingly difficult to maintain and at the same time encourages the competition that can reduce its market.

To avoid dangers and respond to opportunities, every business and profession, as well as the individuals occupied in them, must make use of change. While the time and effort employed to do so for any particular change will be a function of the ranking given its importance and likelihood, the nature of the response that is made will depend on the type of the change.

Responding to structural change

"Pop-Ins" sounds like a new kind of muffin for heating in a toaster; in fact, it is an imaginative response to structural change. Founded by Carol Brothers, a former interior decorator, in Columbiana, Ohio, in 1977, Pop-Ins is a fast-growing franchised maid service already operating in twenty-two states. With more married women working, homes are getting dirtier; but at the same time, two-income families are making more money. The logical response is a service providing house cleaners who can "pop in" for a few hours to handle basic chores for couples who no longer have the time to spare but do have the income to hire others. It was in response to these structural changes that Pop-Ins and other similar services, like McMaid in Chicago, were started. For the franchisee it is also a unique business opportunity. Pop-

Ins offers a start-up package that includes equipment (vacuum cleaners, polishers, etc.), manuals covering basic business skills, and even a two-week training course at "Pop-Ins University" in Columbiana.

The essence of structural change is that it creates a new situation, fundamentally different from that which preceded it. Thus, to respond by continuing to behave as before will be at best insufficient and at worst counterproductive. It may indeed be possible to "ride out" certain cyclical changes, but not any structural changes. The response to these must be as new and different as the changes themselves. In most cases it must be a substantial commitment of resources to a major objective involving an alteration in structure, direction, or operations. In short, it must be a strategic response.

There are, of course, many possible strategic responses to the structural changes that have been discussed so far. The following illustrate possible responses to two of them, the structural changes of new technology and postindustrialization.

Because both information and knowledge are increasing, always widening the base from which still more will develop, technological change will increase continuously in magnitude and pace. This will affect both existing and emerging technologies, shortening the lifespans of the former and hastening the birth of the latter. Responding to structural change in technology therefore requires paying attention to both the old and the new.

For existing technologies, several rules can be suggested.

One is to use extreme caution in making large-scale commitments of resources to mature technologies. In 1971 the Ford Motor Company built a huge iron-casting plant in Flat Rock, Michigan, to build engine blocks. The idea behind this mammoth project (big enough to enclose seventy-two football fields) was to achieve an economy of scale through the manufacture in very large quantity of a single product, V-8 blocks for big cars. But less than a decade later, production was discontinued and the plant was shut down. The problem was that in the intervening years Ford turned to lighter, smaller, fuel-efficient cars whose four- and six-cylinder engine blocks could not be produced at Flat Rock without very expensive retooling. Today, with newer designs for still lighter engine blocks emerging, the plant is being demolished to make room—ironically—for a Japanese-owned and -operated Mazda assembly plant.

Another rule is not to continue to commit to a technology when a better competing one already exists. In 1984, after five years of production, RCA finally decided to phase out its videodisc player business—at least three years after it became clear that the rerecordable videocassette was the technology overwhelmingly preferred by the public. The loss to RCA has been estimated at half a billion dollars.

A third rule is to not attempt to further refine a current technology when a superior one—even though still not fully developed—is clearly on the horizon. NCR made this mistake when it continued with electromechanical cash registers even though solid-state electronic ones were ready for the market; and Vickers in England and Lockheed in the United States went on to develop turboprop aircraft when they were soon to be made obsolete by jets.

Several rules also can be suggested concerning newer emerging technologies.

The first and most important rule is to put the highest priority in discovering, creating, and exploiting new technologies. Yet for large companies, with long-standing, well-established commitments to certain products and activities, and with detailed procedures for approving new projects that frequently trail through several levels of bureaucracy, technological innovation is often very difficult. New ideas usually come from independent inventors and small firms, free to pursue their own lines of investigation unencumbered by constant scrutiny and the often stultifying pressure of regular accountability. Recognizing this, many firms have sought to create just such breeding grounds within the territory of their own organizations. Tektronix, the Oregon electronics company, is one of a number of companies which have recently created in-house venture capital units to support former employees who want to set out on their own to pursue independent research and develop new products. In the Tektronix arrangement the company in effect swaps technology developed in its laboratories for equity in the new company, thereby profiting from any success it has and maintaining contact with those on the frontiers of research and development. In an analogous arrangement in a service-type company, Security Pacific Corporation, the Los Angeles bank holding company, has created an investment unit to serve customers who seek more aggressive investments with greater degrees of risk than are permitted by the bank's normally more conservative management.

A second rule in making use of new technologies is to understand the many implications of the changes they create. New inventions often make it possible to do something better than, or different than, before. In pole vaulting, for example, the development of a fiberglass pole immediately resulted in a significant increase in the height that could be jumped, while in figure skating the invention of latex costumes made it possible to perform more difficult maneuvers than had been done before. Similarly, as Daniel Boorstin, the American historian and Librarian of Congress, has pointed out, the invention of the clock, requiring precisely tooled gears and screws, made it the "mother of machines," spawning the modern machine tool industry that eventually followed.

New technologies also simultaneously create both new opportunities and new problems. Cable television, for instance, is a new medium for advertisers, but its proliferation of new channels reduces the audiences of the established networks and thus their income from many of the same advertisers. Even less understood is that while new technologies often do replace old ones they also frequently supplement them, making possible a wider and richer variety of activity than before. Thus, teleconferencing may indeed eliminate some business travel, but more significantly it will provide a new medium of communications whose real effect will be not to replace travel but to supplement it and enrich it with new possibilities.

Finally, a third rule is that new technologies will be stillborn unless markets exist for the products and services they create. Just as needs are often in search of technologies that will make their satisfaction possible, so, too, are technologies often in search of needs to be satisfied. Satellite telecommunications technology, for instance, is capable of transmitting huge volumes of data at very high speeds; but only now, a decade after its development and with vigorous marketing efforts by its pioneer company, Satellite Business Systems, is it attracting the customers who finally will make it profitable.

As the pace of technological change quickens, all companies seeking to make use of it will have to be increasingly attentive to the need to match discoveries with markets. Managing future technological change wisely will require both investment in innovation and an equally well planned and well supported program to find ready uses for it.

The development and spread of technology is in turn accelerating both the transition to industrialization underway in many middle- and low-income countries and the further transition to postindustrial status being experienced by most of the upper-income countries. Since the thrust of these parallel movements is a structural change in economic activities—toward more manufacturing in the former and more service sector activities in the latter—a strategic response is required, especially by industries in upper-income countries facing increasing competition from low-cost foreign firms. This response can include one or more strategies, singly or combined, depending on the industries and companies involved.

One strategy is to become the lowest-cost producer. The principal method is to speed production and reduce costs through the use of computer-controlled labor-saving automated equipment.

- General Electric, in its newly automated Erie, Pennsylvania, locomotive plant, can now turn out a diesel or electric-motor frame in a single day, a task on which sixty-eight skilled machinists used to spend sixteen days.
- Black & Decker of Towson, Maryland, for years a highly successful manufacturer of power tools, saw the competition coming from Japan and other potential producers, knew that it had to change its ways to maintain its position in the market, and launched an all-out program to reduce costs using robots in what it calls "flexible manufacturing," a procedure by which one robot can be programmed to perform different functions as needed.
- In textile making, America's oldest manufacturing industry, automated controls are displacing mechanical ones and conventional looms using wooden shuttles—a century-old technology —are finally being replaced with new imported looms which weave three or four times faster using jets of air.
- Just as important as improving process design, product design is also being altered to take greatest advantage of more efficient means of production, as General Motors is doing in creating its first entirely new automobile

trademark since Chevrolet in 1918 in order to produce an all-new, competitive small car, the Saturn, to be on the market early in the 1990s.

Another strategic response, especially for a company in a mature industry or dependent principally on one product, is to diversify into other product lines or related industries.

- Newmont Mining, understanding the structural changes affecting the production and demand for copper, has been phasing out its copper operations and getting into other metals, a strategic move that has kept it profitable in the declining hard-rock mining industry.
- Peter Kiewit Sons, a major Midwest player in the construction business and also involved in mining, has begun to move away from these mature industries by acquiring the Continental Group of Stamford, Connecticut, a diversified packaging company.
- Singer, also of Stamford, and Brother Industries of Japan, two companies that made their reputations producing sewing machines, are now heavily involved in high-tech aerospace and office automation activities.

Some companies have gone even further afield of their single-product lines and maturing businesses, and with the greater risk involved in doing so the results have been mixed:

- Mead Corporation, principally a producer of paper and forest products, has become deeply involved in computer data base information services (Lexis and Nexis are the best known), and while its revenues from these have been small they have been growing rapidly.
- Schlumberger, however, universally recognized as a premier company in the petroleum services industry, has had great trouble digesting Fairchild, the once-great semiconductor maker it swallowed in a high-tech foray out of the oil patch.

Closely related to diversification is the strategy of concentrating on higher-value-added and specialty products. This strategy is especially evident in the maturing petrochemical industry, where more and more producers are moving from basic commodities to specialty products whose profit margins are higher and whose demand is less cyclical.

- Cities Service has moved out of petrochemicals entirely.
- Monsanto has decided to produce far fewer petrochemicals and has diversified into pharmaceuticals by acquiring G. D. Searle & Company.
- Dow Chemical has set an objective of generating "consistently 50 percent of the Company's earnings from value-added products and services by the late 1980s."

Dow Chemical's inclusion of services in its objective reflects another important strategy, one especially appropriate to companies in advanced industrial countries, and that is to emphasize the service aspects of one's business and even to enter entirely new service sector areas. For some, like the U.S. manufacturers of nuclear power reactors who have been years without a domestic order for a new plant, service and refueling are now almost the only ways to remain in the business. But others know, too, that a sale is a one-time event for earnings, while service can mean a continuous flow, albeit smaller, over a long period of time. They also have come to realize the many benefits of servicing the products they make and sell, including keeping track of customers, maintaining records of products, and improving design of future models. Computer companies like Data General have seen the success that attention to service has brought competitors like IBM and Wang Laboratories, and they have responded with a new emphasis on providing service to customers. Other companies are making strategic moves into service activities or are expanding positions that are already well established.

- Ogden Corporation, once principally a builder of ships and freight cars, has pared its smoke stack businesses and is aggressively repositioning itself as a purveyor and supplier of services, telling the world that its new role is "putting America's house in order."
- Sears Roebuck has used its huge base of retail outlets as a foundation on which to build a multifaceted financial services empire.
- American Car, soon to cap its effort with a name change that reflects its new corporate identity, is near-

ing the end of a dramatic five-year transition that has removed it entirely from the packaging industry and transformed it into a financial service and specialty retailing company.

Finally, many of the manufacturing companies in developed countries are responding to structural changes in their countries and industries with strategies that entail a variety of offshore arrangements in foreign countries, many of them innovative and complex. Each of the three major U.S. auto makers (General Motors, Ford, and Chrysler) is planning to buy more parts abroad; so, too, are a number of U.S. computer makers, seeking not only more cheaply made hardware parts, but also software being written by programmers in such countries as South Korea, India, and Pakistan. Others, like the Tandon Corporation of Los Angeles, the nation's largest maker of data storage and retrieval devices for personal computers, are buying or building whole plants overseas. And the reverse is happening, too. In 1981, a Japanese machine tool builder, Makino Milling Machine, bought a 51 percent stake in the century-old LeBlond Machine Tool Company of Cincinnati. The new company, now called LeBlond Makino, also has a plant in Singapore and sells highly automated lathes built by a West German firm. These arrangements have increased access to both markets and technology for all concerned, helping to rapidly erase national boundaries for the entire machine tool industry. Joint ventures are also throwing corporate lines across national borders.

- Allied has teamed up with Mitsui of Japan to sell special Allied-developed alloys in Asia and Australia.
- Olivetti of Italy has announced a far-reaching deal with American Telephone and Telegraph to jointly develop and market new office communications equipment.
- General Foods has created new joint ventures for production and distribution of its food products in India, China, Spain, and Brazil.

All of these strategic responses reflect growing internationalization in research, production, and distribution and are indicative of a still larger structural change, emerging fitfully and often painfully through tangled thickets of protectionist rules and currency fluctuations, but one which is steadily demanding new strategic responses everywhere—the development of a truly global market for the goods and services of all of the world's nations.

Responding to cyclical change

In 1981, when *The Official Preppy Handbook* listed the Izod shirt—with its little green gaping alligator—as the shirt of choice for the well-dressed preppy, the company could not keep up with the demand. By the time it finally did catch up, three years later, demand was falling fast as a veritable menagerie of horses, unicorns, foxes, dragons, and little pigs trampled the market, swamping the alligator and all but killing the notion of emblem dressing. General Mills, Izod's parent, after acknowledging earlier that the shirtmaker probably would do poorly, finally let the other shoe drop in November 1984 when it announced that "Izod's current-year sales prospects are down nearly 50 percent from the peak [1982]," a result that further depressed the senior company's standing and share price on Wall Street and undoubtedly prompted it to sell off its fashion business. What General Mills apparently failed to understand was that the Izod alligator was a fad, and like all fads certain to be initially the beneficiary and finally the victim of cyclical change in public taste.

The essence of cyclical change is that it is limited and temporary. It rises and falls, grows larger and smaller, and often returns to levels it has attained before. Responses to it, therefore, are limited and temporary, and often the same as those made before in similar circumstances. Since these seek a specific short-term objective—solving a problem or taking advantage of an opportunity—they are tactical responses.

Examples of tactical responses to cyclical changes abound. The following illustrate behavior appropriate for two of them: business cycle changes and demand-supply cycle changes.

Responding to business cycle changes means, in most cases, making use of the differences that occur when various rates change, such as rates of economic growth, rates of inflation, and interest rates. Usually efforts should be directed toward minimizing dangers when rates are moving against one's interests and maximizing opportunities when they are moving with them. The greatest difficulties occur during the periods of transition, from one phase of a cycle to another, and so the most useful responses are those made in anticipation of future phases, though many responses appropriate to a particular phase can be made even after it has begun.

During one phase of a business cycle it does make sense to plan for the one to follow, and transportation companies like the Ryder System of Miami and Northwest Airlines, facing not only business cycle change but also a cyclical shift toward government deregulation, made just such plans and successfully rode out the transition from recession to recovery in the early 1980s. Others, facing similar changes, have not fared as well. Merrill Lynch, simultaneously confronted with a booming stock market and widespread government deregulation in the financial services industry, hired six thousand new employees between September 1982 and September 1983; but during the first half of 1984, in an effort to cut costs that were rising faster than revenues, it had to announce layoffs of 2,500.

Even more useful, though, is the effort to prepare a full cycle ahead, especially from upturn to upturn. It is during recoveries that companies tend to add fat, taking the opportunity afforded by higher earnings and rosy forecasts of their continuation to hire new personnel and add frills shunned in leaner times. But it is precisely during upturns—when it can best be done—that management should be moving not only to survive the coming downturn, but even more important to be in a position to take greatest advantage of the upturn to follow. This means a combination of balanced responses including reducing debt and accumulating cash, modernizing facilities and reviewing procedures to lower costs and speed inventory buildup when eventually needed, and setting aside resources for a marketing effort during the recessionary period ahead—the best time to pick up market share (as competitors drop out) and one during which advertisers (traditionally hard hit in downturns) will be most eager for business.

Equally challenging is the response to cyclical changes in wages and prices. Inflation and disinflation (falling rates of price and wage increases) each exhibit distinctive characteristics, and each require a different set of responses. During inflation, prices rise and the value of money and other paper assets (unless indexed upward) goes down. Under these circumstances it makes sense for businesses and individuals to increase their holding of things and decrease their holding of paper. It also makes borrowing very attractive, since the borrower will be repaying in the future with even cheaper money, and if borrowing costs (interest) are tax-deductible—as they often are—this simply ices the cake. So, during inflation or when anticipating inflation, businesses and individuals should borrow and spend, trying to stretch out maturities for their purchases and shorten them for what they sell. All of this helps maintain sales, raises the value of inventories, and keeps balance sheets looking good, notwithstanding the fact that much of the profit is often illusory.

Disinflation, however, has different characteristics. Prices rise more slowly and cash is king, raising the value of paper financial instruments relative to things. During disinflation money becomes more "real" and it makes sense to be a saver and a lender, selling things and liquidating inventory to acquire money to buy paper that earns income. But this tends to depress sales and thus to increase competition. It penalizes the careless behavior excused by inflation and puts a premium on tightening management at all levels, including especially the activities of borrowing, hiring, production, and inventory control.

The need to respond to inflation or disinflation, as the case may be, has always existed, and those who have not done so appropriately have suffered. But in recent years the need has become more acute, and in the future it is likely to be even more so. This is because price movements have become more rapid and have been extending over wider ranges; and since prices rarely move together—some being stickier than others, for a number of reasons—even greater attention will have to be given to responses appropriate to their disparate changes.

Similar challenges arise in responding to cyclical changes in interest rates; and here too the pace of change has speeded up. Between 1935 and 1950 the prime rate changed only three times, but since 1970 it has changed over two hundred times. This enormous increase in the frequency of rate changes has obviously created an entirely new environment for financial planning, requiring far more care in debt management and leading to what one business journalist has called "the Reign of the Finance Men." Responding appropriately to this cyclical change involves a number of considerations, some new and others more traditional, but all needing greater attention than before. These include:

- More careful timing of borrowing—sooner if rates appear likely to rise, later if they look like they will be falling
- Awareness and use of newly developed credit instruments (variable rate loans, for example) and of the increased availability of older ones (like commercial paper)
- Adjusting to historically higher average rates, especially for long-term loans
- Being more sensitive to trade-offs between debt and equity financing

Marriott Corporation, the motel and hotel chain, offers a good example of a company with a very challenging financial task: borrowing today to build facilities that will be paid back over a number of years with earnings subject to unknown rates of inflation. It has been managing this task very well by borrowing when rates are down and financing internally when they are up. A different and equally successful example is DuPont, a company with a long tradition of abhorring debt which suddenly found itself awash in it when it acquired Conoco in 1981. With a thoroughgoing reorganization of its management structure to shorten reaction times and speed financial decision-making, plus careful timing, it has managed a refinancing program that has steadily reduced its debt-to-capital ratio.

In addition, since long-term interest rates are likely to be at higher than traditional levels for some time to come, while in the interim inflation rates fluctuate more widely, "real" rates of interest (the difference between nominal rates and the inflation rate) also will fluctuate, and at rates above their historical levels. This "uncoupling" of inflation and interest rates means that companies no longer can borrow with the expectation of being paid back with future income rising at the same rates as those they are paying on their loans. The result will be to require still greater attention by management not only to borrowing costs but also to future pricing policy for goods and services.

Finally, interest rates that change more frequently and

tend to higher levels will affect producers of goods and deliverers of services differently, creating both problems and opportunities, and each will have to make appropriate tactical responses. Producers of goods, especially major durables like housing and automobiles that are traditionally purchased with long-term financing, will have to recognize how higher rates are increasing the cost of their products and be prepared to redesign them, produce them more efficiently, and participate in innovative financial arrangements in order to continue to make them affordable to their customers. Deliverers of services, on the other hand, generally have lower capital expenses than goods producers and, unlike them, are usually paid as they incur their costs rather than after they have met them. As a result, debt service expenses will be much less of a burden, permitting most of them to have lower total costs relative to those of manufacturers. In addition, for many financial services—like banks, insurers, and stockbrokers—who traditionally have a considerable cash float and hold large sums in credit instruments, interest rate income will continue to be a much larger portion of total revenues.

The changes of demand-supply cycles also create both opportunities and problems. When the demand or price of some good or service is rising, suppliers of it see an opportunity in this change and attempt to seize it by raising their output. But the combined effect of their efforts is often to create a supply that is greater than the demand and growing at a faster rate, resulting in excess inventory accumulation and a likely drop in price. This comes from either a failure to understand the nature of the demand and why and how it is changing or too exaggerated a response to it or both.

It took Americans a number of years—during the period after World War II—to discover the pleasures of drinking wine with their meals, and even longer, it seemed, to discover that a number of varieties of very fine wines were produced domestically, especially in the valleys along the coast of California. When finally they did, beginning about 1970, wine sales soared, increasing at the rate of 12 percent annually for those from the Golden State alone. The reaction was predictable. Growers and entrepreneurs—some barely knowledgeable in viniculture, but all with time and money to spend—rushed to plant vines and press grapes. Vineyard acreage increased 56 percent in ten years in California, and ground was broken for new seedlings all the way from the state of Washington to tiny Rhode Island on the other side of the country. But no demand grows forever at the same rate, and that of wine drinkers was no exception. In 1982, the year in which the efforts of the previous decade produced the largest crop ever, the demand for California wine showed no increase at all. In part the recession of the early 1980s was to blame; another factor was the growing interest in health and safety and the consequent dampening of sales of alcoholic beverages. But even more important was the fact that all those who were interested in drinking wine with their dinners were probably already doing so. Without a massive effort to bring aboard beer drinkers and others still unconvinced there was little new demand to soak up the product of all the new grapes being grown and squeezed. Supply had simply outrun demand.

The high-tech computer industry has also been plagued by failure to respond appropriately to demand-supply cycles; but here the problem has been created as much by purchasers as by producers. On June 29, 1983, the headline in the business section of the *New York Times* read, "Shortages Growing in Semiconductors." Sixteen months later, under the headline "Semiconductor Stocks Drop Again," the *Times* wrote: "Analysts continued to reduce their earnings estimates because of a slowdown in orders." What happened was that early in the period when purchasers found themselves short in their inventories and facing delays of twenty weeks or more for delivery—in the midst of what they projected would be an ever-growing market for their products—they simply overordered, months in advance, to keep from being caught short again; and in response to signals given by their orders manufacturers overproduced. Then in the following months the personal computer market slowed, several makers dropped out, and new machines—notably IBM's new PC-AT—requiring new chip designs were released. As a result, the shortage of 1983 became the glut of 1984 and at year's end Honeywell and Texas Instruments, the latter the world's largest maker of semiconductors, announced layoffs of one thousand and two thousand employees respectively.

Services, too, are affected by cyclical demand-supply cycles, and because many service companies are small and what they sell is rarely patentable and easily replicable they suffer especially from the rapid entry into their markets of new competitors who can quickly reduce each other's share of the available business. This prompts competitive practices which harm all players and frequently terminate the weaker ones. Just this sort of activity periodically plagues the U.S. property-casualty insurance business. With a veritable glut of underwriting capacity, insurers and reinsurers regularly cut rates in order to attract business, and when interest rates are very high—as they were in the mid-1970s and again in the early 1980s—they are willing to sell policies at a loss because they can still show a net profit from the investments they make with the premiums they receive. But when interest rates fall, even just a few points, the gap between cash and costs narrows, and as claims are paid out there is then even less cash to invest. If, simultaneously, catastrophe losses happen to run high, then insurers fall even deeper into the red, as they did in 1984 when underwriting losses of casualty insurance companies exceeded investment income for the first time since the 1906 San Francisco earthquake and fire. Such an outcome means that a rate-cutting response to cyclical demand-supply changes can actually become a self-inflicted wound.

Even more wrenching are the problems created and the adjustments required when factors outside the normal forces of the marketplace influence demand and supply. The most spectacular example of this in recent years was the embargo and quadrupling of the price of oil by OPEC in 1973–74 and the further doubling of the price in the panic of the Iranian revolution at the end of the 1970s. In these instances the demand changes that flowed from disruption of traditional supplies and increases in price were profoundly misunderstood. The effects of this misunderstanding, and of the responses made consonant with it—still being felt—reverberated around the world, weakening oil companies, the financial backers of their operations, the suppliers of their equipment, and the manufacturers of products using their fuels, as well as the economies of states, regions, and whole nations.

While the difficulties that arise in responding to changes of demand-supply cycles can never be entirely eliminated, some steps can be suggested to reduce the problems they create and increase the opportunities they offer.

- One is to do everything possible to obtain better, more comprehensive information—on the one hand, about the structure of one's market and the status of recent and current demand and supply in it; on the other, about the status of one's own operation and inventory.
- A second is to examine past cycles of demand-supply change, noting especially the magnitude and duration of their up and down phases.
- A third is to calculate the likely effects of one's own actions, and of the actions of competitors, in making changes in price and quantity and the timing of both.
- A fourth is to develop the capability to respond to change as quickly as possible—to speed up, slow down, and fine-tune as necessary to avoid dangers and seize opportunities.
- A final and most important step is to understand the cyclical nature of demand-supply change. It does not continue indefinitely in one direction; instead, it rises, slows, and then falls. Making use of such change therefore requires tactical responses involving such decisions as: when to get in and at what level, how long to continue, and when to get out.

While the above suggestions for responding to selected structural and cyclical changes are especially appropriate to business organizations, similar uses must be made of changes by geographic entities, nonbusiness organizations, and individuals.

Countries, states, and cities need to respond to the problems and opportunities that arise as the dominant economic activities in their geographic areas change from preindustrial to industrial to postindustrial; they need to be aware of the coming changes in the numbers and age compositions of their populations and prepared to provide appropriate facilities and services; and they also have to be attentive to the changes in social behavior (crime rates, divorce rates, etc.) that accompany cyclical demographic and economic changes.

Educational institutions also will have to respond to population change, both structural and cyclical, to changing needs in curriculum and course content, and especially to the changing role and presentation of information and its implications for vocational and professional training.

Labor unions need to adapt quickly to major workforce

changes, including the rapid rise of female participation and the shift in employment from industrial to service sector activities.

Political organizations and their candidates will need to be attentive to population changes and how they correlate with voter participation and to structural and cyclical changes in the attitudes of the electorate.

Individuals will have to be aware of the new opportunities provided by structural changes, as well as the decline of those formerly available, in pursuing educational programs and making career choices; they will have to be more attentive than before in the way they choose and finance their major purchases; and they will have to respond to both the opportunities and the problems created by the still evolving structural change to longer life expectancy.

In managing change it is neither possible nor necessary to respond to every change pertinent to any particular endeavor. But it is possible and sufficient to identify the major changes likely to affect our businesses, professions, and personal plans, to determine their type and pattern, to rank them by importance of effect and likelihood of occurrence, and to make use of them. To do so in a regular and systematic fashion, and thus to greatly increase the chances of achieving our goals in a world of accelerating change, requires a new approach to the future.

CHAPTER 6

A NEW APPROACH
TO THE FUTURE

"WE DON'T THINK of TRW as a static sort of business," explains Ruben F. Mettler, chairman and chief executive officer of one of America's most imaginative and innovative companies, "we have to adapt and change." And TRW has done just that, transforming itself in less than two decades from an auto and aircraft parts company to a high-tech multinational conglomerate. Along the way it has made important responses to the changes it has seen and anticipated in its business environment, including a shift from basic products to high-value-added electronics and space components for both civilian and military use; a move beyond manufacturing into services, acquiring a credit data company and building it into the largest in the industry and the core of what it sees as a number of other service businesses centered on computer-based information systems; and an expansion beyond the United States to be a producer in more countries and a supplier to more markets throughout the world.

Not all companies can pattern themselves after TRW, nor do they need to. Each should, in fact, pursue its own goals, depending on the nature of its business and the resources it has available. But every company—and every organization and every individual—can learn from TRW's approach to the future: an unabashed commitment to understanding and making use of change.

Such an approach is appropriate for the future, for it views change as natural and to be expected, and continuity as unnatural and to be suspected. It questions the "tried and true" ways of the past and consciously looks for changes, monitoring them and anticipating their effects. It sees the future in terms of degrees of certainty and it expects surprises. It knows that knowledge of what is to come will never be complete but that some knowledge is possible and will be useful. This new approach requires taking a long-term perspective and adopting long-term strategies, yet at the same time having the ability to be flexible, to adapt quickly, and to make appropriate short-term tactical responses; and it requires making plans on the basis of change, not continuity, and creating the capabilities to carry them out.

For such an approach it is necessary to have a simple method of applying the five-step strategy discussed in the preceding chapter, to institutionalize its use, and to practice it regularly.

A checklist for change

Before a pilot of an aircraft of any size embarks on a flight, he or she has an obligatory duty: to review the preflight checklist (or lists, as the case may be). The pilot's checklist is a sequential enumeration of the equipment, controls, dials, and indicators that must be visibly or audibly checked before boarding the plane, starting the engines, beginning the takeoff run, and any major evolutions connected with the flight. Since failure to properly review any one item (the fuel gauge, for example) later could prove fatal, all pilots take checklists very seriously and will not commence a flight without methodically completing them.

The checklist is thus an ideal method for carrying out any program containing a number of steps to be taken in a given sequence. Its principal value is its comprehensiveness. It gives the user confidence that nothing has been skipped, nothing left out. But there are other values, too. Arraying all the steps in a task and considering them seriatim facilitates comparisons and often reveals connections and interactions that might not have been seen in a more random consideration. This in turn enhances the discovery of synergistic effects that can be investigated and used. Going through the steps of a checklist also provides an overall view of an entire operation or activity, and this can help shape decisions concerning the allocation of resources and guide their timing.

For the five-step strategy for mastering change, the following simple checklist can suffice:

Step 1: Recognize change is occurring.
Step 2: Identify changes.
       a: in "upstream" category
       b: in "downstream" category
Step 3: Determine type and pattern of each change.
       a: type: structural or cyclical
       b: pattern: direction
                    magnitude
                    pace
                    duration
Step 4: Rank by importance and likelihood.
       a: importance: most, moderately, or less
       b: likelihood: most, highly, or less
Step 5: Make use.
       a: Strategic responses for structural changes
       b: Tactical responses for cyclical changes

The amount of time and effort that any organization or individual devotes to such a list—or to any particular steps in it—will depend on the size and complexity of the operation or activity for which changes are being examined and put to use. For a large corporation, involved in a wide range of activities in many markets, each step in the list should be greatly expanded and the entire undertaking should be a major project requiring a number of people. The more thoroughly the method is employed the greater will be the gain in using it. For a small office, the effort can be considerably reduced; and for an individual facing one well-defined decision, it might be a matter of a few hours or less. But the important point is that to realize the benefits of using this method, some time and effort—however brief—should be spent on each step. No step should be skipped; the need to check each one should evoke the same sense of obligation that pilots feel toward their checklists before takeoff.

For the strategy for mastering change to be effective, its use must be institutionalized. This means, first and foremost, that the top person sanction it, give its use high priority, and assign responsibility for its implementation to someone reporting to the highest levels of the organization. There also has to be a visible center, permanently established, with the resources to examine and consider the changes likely to affect the organization, the authority to obtain both information and cooperation from all subordinate levels, and channels for directing recommendations both upward and downward.

Implementation of the strategy also must be recognized as an ongoing activity, as important as research and development, human resources management, budgeting, production, marketing, and the other traditional activities of the company or organization. Especially it must become an integral part of planning, both short-range and long-range. All plans should be made "change-conscious"; that is, they should state the changes being assumed for their successful completion, the impact of other changes should they occur, and, as appropriate, courses of action to be "triggered" by the occurrence of certain changes or the attainment of specified levels of change.

Implementation also should be made common practice throughout the organization. Educational programs should be instituted to instruct employees in the importance of change to the future success of both the organization and themselves, and training should be given in using the strategy in every department and position. Policy should be established that makes managing change the responsibility of each person in the organization, and procedures should exist for the regular review, evaluation, and—where needed—revision of the practice at all levels.

Finally, institutionalization requires that capabilities be created to make use of change. These include sufficient organizational flexibility to slow, speed, or alter direction; sufficient structural flexibility to retrofit, diminish, or enlarge programs; and sufficient resources to make replacements, substitutions, or new commitments. Also needed is adequate insurance in the event changes exceed specified boundaries as well as adequate reserves to survive the consequences of adverse changes or take advantage of the opportunities offered by favorable ones.

Just as change is continuous, so too must be its management. Understanding and making use of change is not a one-time event, not an activity to be done on an ad-hoc basis as the need arises. To be effective in forestalling the crises and seizing the opportunities created by change, implementation of the strategy of mastering it must occur before they arise; it must be regularly practiced. To do so it is necessary to think of mastering change as more of a process than a series of discrete decisions, as akin to what

Peter Drucker has called, in referring to productivity's main requirement, "continuous learning."

Because most structural changes evolve over long periods and most cyclical changes repeat in familiar patterns, developments in both can and should be anticipated.

- It is clear that one of the most important advantages of the development of electronics-based technology is the opportunity to shift from inherently less efficient mechanical devices which touch, scrape, and wear out, are limited in range and speed, are expensive to build and maintain, and often require significant inputs of human labor to operate. Yet even today many of our most sophisticated products still use relatively inefficient hybrid technologies combining mechanical and electronic elements, like control systems in aircraft and disk drives in computers.
- In the advanced industrial countries, life expectancy has increased dramatically during the last half century, reaching beyond the ages of normal retirement and providing extra years of activity to more and more people. Yet we have barely begun to think of how to deal with the problems and the opportunities this change presents.
- The cyclical shift to government deregulation of financial services, transportation, and telecommunications in the United States has been underway for several years. One important consequence is that strategic planning and marketing—never before very urgent activities in these industries—now demand the highest priority. Yet many firms have only just started to give them serious attention.

To anticipate these and other changes and their consequences it is necessary to regularly apply the five steps of the strategy for mastering change and to view this as an integral part of the activity of management itself. To do so will enable all organizations and firms to focus on the future and to plan better for it. And it will do more. It will force them to raise more often those two crucial questions so vital to the future well-being of any company, yet so seldom posed: What business are we in? What are our goals in this business? It will cause them to imagine wholly new conditions in the future and ask: Will there still be a need for what we are making, what we are doing now? And it will make them respond to a vital dual challenge: What do we want to be five, ten, and twenty years from now, and what do we have to do now to ensure that we will be?

The first efforts at implementing the strategy for mastering change may be difficult and time-consuming, and the self-examination they generate might prove awkward. But if the practice is made regular it will in time become easier, quicker, and more comfortable; the rewards will then come sooner, and they will be worth the effort.

The hope of change

"For the times they are a-changin'," sang folksinger Bob Dylan in the 1960s, echoing the ancient Latin proverb *Tempora mutantur, nos et mutamur in illis* (Times change, and we change with them). The times will continue to change, and at an ever-quickening pace, and we with them. The result will be greater uncertainty, creating anxiety and fear; and our response often will be to ignore change, to avoid it, even to resist it.

But if we adopt a new approach to the future, if we see change as natural and to be expected, and if we understand that much of it can be known and used to our advantage, then our anxiety will be lessened and we will look to the future with greater hope and less fear.

When we review the two kinds of change that have been discussed and the strategy for mastering them, we see that there is indeed every reason for such hope. It is in the structural changes that we see history's achievement and mankind's prospects for a continuously improving future:

- Information is providing society with a new transforming resource that is imperishable, ever-increasing, and ever less expensive.
- Education is steadily being acquired by more of the world's people.
- Growing networks of communications are linking all of us more closely every day.
- The transition from preindustrial to industrial to postindustrial holds the prospect of a world whose long economic problem finally will be solved.

- A slowing population growth rate means the number of the world's people eventually will peak at a level where all can exist comfortably; and lengthening life expectancy augurs longer, more active lives for that number.
- The changing nature of work means that for more and more people work will be part of the goals of their lives rather than just the means to sustain them.
- Rising per capita and discretionary incomes will enable more people to achieve economic security and enjoy more of the variety and comforts of life.
- Changing attitudes, preferences, and priorities signal a shift from concern only for subsistence and quantity to greater care for quality, and for health, comfort, and safety—in our personal lives and in the environment we inhabit.

All of these structural changes point in a positive direction, and because they are structural they are evolving, lasting, and irreversible.

It is in changes of the other kind, the cyclical changes, that the problems lie:

- The periods of recession and inflation of business cycles
- The shortages and often equally troublesome gluts of demand-supply cycles
- The conflict and destruction of wars that periodically punctuate cycles of organizational behavior
- The rises in rates of family breakup and crime seen in cycles of social behavior.

But these changes are cyclical, and because they are they do not last, are not irreversible, and as often as they are negative they are also positive, increasing economic growth, adequately supplying demand, bringing peace and falling divorce and crime rates.

Clearly then the task for the future is to accelerate the oncoming structural changes, and with the knowledge and resources obtained from their continuing evolution ameliorate the cyclical changes, mitigating their negative effects and dampening their downward phases. And it is through this new approach to the future, through mastering change, that we can best accomplish this task. "The whole human ambience—the human house—is of our own making," Peter

Medawar, the Nobel laureate in medicine, has written. Most changes are part of this making, the collective results of our many separate individual decisions; and while we can never unilaterally control all of these decisions—nor should we want to—we can work to see that they are better informed and made with a fuller view of their likely consequences, and this can be done by understanding and using change.

Mastering change will not solve all of our problems, nor can it ensure universal peace and prosperity in the world. But the combined efforts of more and more people to understand and use change can reinforce the instinct and desire for cooperation that are basic to the human condition, can help make more lives safer, more comfortable, and more satisfying, and can enable us to plan more surely our own futures.

Change should not bewilder us, it should challenge us. In mastering it we can reduce the fear it holds and increase the hope it brings; and while life for each of us is an ever-nearing sunset, by mastering change we can help ensure that for the world it will continue to be a never-ending dawn.

NOTES

CHAPTER 1

3 Financial figures for A&P and J. C. Penney from *Chain Store Age Executive*, Aug. 1982, p. 35, and *Forbes*, Jan. 3, 1983, p. 205, and Jan. 14, 1985, pp. 202 and 194; brief accounts of the histories of the two companies given in Joel E. Ross, *Corporate Management in Crisis* (Englewood Cliffs, N.J.: Prentice-Hall, 1973), chap. 8; the story of A&P's turnaround reported in *Progressive Grocer*, Oct. 1983, pp. 65 ff. and the *New York Times*, June 23, 1985.

6 Figures for registered black voters in Alabama from U.S. Bureau of the Census, *Statistical Abstract of the United States: 1984* (Washington, D.C., 1983), p. 261.

6–7 Sloan described his auto-manufacturing philosophy in Alfred P. Sloan, Jr., *My Years with General Motors* (Garden City, N.Y.: Doubleday, 1963); quotation from p. 158.

7 The "sailing ship phenomenon" and the case of RCA are discussed by Richard N. Foster in his perceptive essay "A Call for Vision in Managing Technology," *Business Week*, May 24, 1982, pp. 24ff. The *Forbes* characterization of Kodak's Disc camera appeared in the Nov. 5, 1984, issue, p. 185.

8 International Harvester and John Deere, and Eastern and Delta Airlines, compared by Leslie Wayne in the *New York Times*, Aug. 27, 1982.

9 Changes of work organization because of the introduction of new office equipment are the subject of "The Mechanization of Office Work" by Vincent E. Guillano in *Scientific American*, Sept. 1982, pp. 149ff.

9 U.S. Council on Environmental Quality, *The Global 2000 Report to the President of the U.S.* (Washington, D.C., 1980).

10 Exxon Corporation, "World Energy Outlook," 1977; OECD, "World Energy Outlook," Paris, 1977, p. 27; U.S. Dept. of the Interior, *Energy Perspectives, 2* (Washington, D.C., 1976), p. 42; Central Intelligence Agency, "The International Energy Situation: Outlook to 1985" and "Prospects for Soviet Oil Production," both Apr. 1977; Massachusetts Institute of

Technology. Workshop on Alternative Energy Strategies, *Energy: Global Prospects, 1985–2000* (New York: McGraw-Hill, 1977); quotation from p. xi.

11 Figures for oil demand through the end of 1984 given in the *Wall Street Journal*, Jan. 11, 1985.

12 Airline traffic forecast discussed by John Newhouse in *The Sporty Game* (New York: Knopf, 1982), chap. 6; Deak's expansion of its currency offices described in the *New York Times*, July 15, 1982; its bankruptcy petition reported in the *Wall Street Journal*, Dec. 7, 1984.

14 U.S. Department of Labor estimates for future computer-type occupations are given in U.S. Bureau of Labor Statistics, "Employment Trends in Computer Occupations," Bulletin 2101, Oct. 1981.

15 The evolution of the Head Ski Company described in Carl R. Christensen, *Business Policy: Text and Cases* (Homewood, Ill.: Irwin, 1978) pp. 23–54.

17 Backer and Spielvogel's winning of the Campbell Soup account reported in the *Wall Street Journal*, Sep. 24, 1981; Tic Tac's "turnaround" described in the *New York Times*, Apr. 19, 1982.

CHAPTER 2

19 The medieval historian Lynn T. White, Jr., cites the case of the Arabs and the technology of printing in *Medieval Religion and Technology: Collected Essays* (Berkeley: University of California, 1978), p. 276.

20 Robert Oppenheimer, *The Open Mind* (New York: Simon & Schuster, 1955), pp. 140–41.

21 The notion of approaching, and ultimately reaching, a natural limit set by earth's size was eloquently expressed a quarter of a century ago by the great mathematician John Von Neumann, in "Can We Survive Technology?" *Fortune*, June 1955, pp. 106–108.

21–22 The dramatic vision of a future of endless boundless development, where "existence is a perpetual dawn," is a constant theme of the extended work of Patrick Gunkel, who, from time to time, has been associated with the Hudson Institute. It is set forth in a number of his writings, especially "The Efflorescent World View," summarized in Hudson Institute Report HI-2638-RR, Oct. 30, 1977.

23 The key role of the development of factories to the Industrial Revolution described in Paul Mantoux, *The Industrial Revolution in the Eighteenth Century*, new rev. ed. (London: Jonathon Cape, 1961), Part II.

24–25 Imaginative scenarios of the future of medicine presented in American Council of Life Insurance, "Health Care: Three

Reports from 2030 A.D.," Trend Analysis Program, Report No. 19, Spring 1980.

25n   Harrison Brown, *The Challenge to Man's Future* (New York: Viking, 1954), chap. 7.

26   Leo Marx, *The Machine in the Garden* (New York: Oxford University Press, 1964).

29   For the classic explanation of the tendency of systems to adapt in response to feedback, see W. Ross Ashby, *Design for a Brain: The Origin of Adaptive Behavior*, 2nd ed., rev. (London: John Wiley & Sons, 1960), especially chaps. 1–7.

30–31   The pulls of centralization and decentralization and the movement between the two discussed in Herbert A. Simon, *Administrative Behavior*, second edition (New York: Macmillan, 1976), pp. 157, 234–240; and Barry A. Liebling, "Riding the Organizational Pendulum . . . Is It Time to (De)centralize?" *Management Review*, Sept. 1981, pp. 14–20.

32   The pattern of business activity in the United States since 1790 has been conveniently charted by the Conference Board in "Economic Change: A Bicentennial Perspective," Road Maps of Industry No. 1776, Jan. 1976.

CHAPTER 3

37–38   The concept of "transforming resource" is discussed in Daniel Bell, "Communications Technology—for Better or for Worse," *Harvard Business Review*, May-June 1979, pp. 20 ff. The role of different resources (or "technologies" as Bell first called them) in different stages of development is set forth in his article "The Post-Industrial Society: Evolution of an Idea," *Survey*, Spring 1971, pp. 102–68; Bell's complete discussion of the concept of postindustrial society is presented in his *The Coming of Post-Industrial Society: A Venture in Social Forecasting* (New York: Basic Books, 1976).

40   Internist I is described in *The New England Journal of Medicine*, Aug. 19, 1982, p. 468–76.

40–41   The suburban Toronto Public Transit experiment described by Thomas Ronald Ide in "The Technology," chap. 2 of Guenter Friedrichs and Adam Schaff, eds., *Microelectronics and Society* (New York: Mentor, 1983), pp. 82–83.

44   Sears Roebuck's information management discussed in *Business Week*, Aug. 22, 1983, p. 32.

44–45   Post–World War II computer forecasts cited by Richard A. Shaffer in the *Wall Street Journal*, Apr. 16, 1982; IBM's initial decision not to produce computers for the market discussed in Robert Sobel, *IBM, Colossus in Transition* (New York: Times Books, 1981), p. 106.

44–46   Computer marts described in *Fortune*, Feb. 4, 1985, p. 64.

46 Jastrow's estimate in his book *The Enchanted Loom.: Mind in the Universe* (New York: Simon & Schuster, 1981), p. 144.

47 A computer based on beams of light rather than electric currents described by Etian Abraham, Colin T. Seaton, and S. Desmond Smith in "The Optical Computer," *Scientific American*, Feb. 1983, pp. 85–93.

47–48 The Japanese fifth-generation computer project and U.S. responses to it discussed in the *Wall Street Journal*, Sept. 25, 1981, and *Newsweek*, July 4, 1983, pp. 58–64.

48 Various perspectives on the nature of thought and artificial intelligence are presented by Douglas R. Hofstadter in his fascinating book *Gödel, Escher, Bach: An Eternal Golden Braid* (New York: Basic Books, 1979), especially chaps. 11, 12, 18, and 19. A brief explanation of some of Hofstadter's ideas is given by James Gleick in "Exploring the Labyrinth of the Mind," *New York Times Magazine*, Aug. 21, 1983, pp. 23ff.

51 Estimates of the numbers enrolled in schools worldwide can be derived from chaps. 2 and 3 of United Nations Educational, Scientific and Cultural Organization, *Statistical Yearbook 1982* (Paris: UNESCO, 1982).

52–53 Estimates and projections of worldwide illiteracy from UNESCO, "Statistics of Educational Attainment and Illiteracy, 1945–1974," Publication No. 22, 1977, and "Estimates and Projections of Illiteracy," Publication CSR-E-29, 1978.

54 Examples of computer use in public and private schools discussed in "Spring Survey of Education," *New York Times*, Sec. 12, Apr. 25, 1982, and Sec. 12, Apr. 14, 1985.

57 The Johns Hopkins–Wharton School and Columbia Business School Programs described in the *New York Times*, Oct. 27, 1982, and Feb. 20, 1983.

60 The Downriver Community Conference discussed in the *Wall Street Journal*, Mar. 30, 1983; Statistics on job changing in the U.S. from the *New York Times*, Jan. 27, 1985.

61 Elderhostel Inc., a non-profit corporation located in Boston, described in the *Wall Street Journal*, Apr. 12, 1983.

61–62 Data on the amount allocated to education and training by business and industry from the American Society for Training and Development, as reported in the *New York Times*, Aug. 30, 1981.

65 Data for book titles published worldwide given in UNESCO, *Statistical Yearbook 1984*, Table 6-1, p. VI-11; data on circulation in U.S. public libraries reported in the *New York Times*, July 31, 1983.

66 Time, Inc.'s expansion in the video area reported in the *New York Times*, Mar. 7, 1983; the Washington Post Company's diversification activities discussed in the *Wall Street Journal*, July 28, 1983.

69   This description indebted to Christopher Evans's discussion of "chip" books in *The Micro Millennium* (New York: Viking, 1979), pp. 106–10.

74   Data for numbers of telephones in use in the world from United Nations Statistical Office, *1982 Statistical Yearbook* (New York: United Nations, 1985), Table 181, p. 1018.

74   The increase in INTELSAT transmissions from information office of INTELSAT.

78   Lloyd Cutler's comment in an interview on C-Span, the Public Affairs Cable TV Channel, reported in the *New York Times*, July 7, 1983.

78   Reuven Frank's comment from a speech to the Radio and TV News Directors Association, Dec. 4, 1980, printed in *Vital Speeches*, Mar. 1981.

78   Statistics on the credibility of news media since 1959 cumulated in *Public Opinion*, Aug/Sept. 1979, pp. 30–31. Quote regarding reliance on news sources from the report "Future Trends in Broadcast Journalism" by Frank N. Magid Associates reported in the *New York Times*, Sept. 1, 1984.

79   Research on computer communications undertaken at Carnegie-Mellon University, reported in the *New York Times*, Oct. 2, 1984.

80   John Maynard Keynes, *Essays in Persuasion* (New York: Harcourt, Brace, 1932), pp. 365–66.

80   Fernand Braudel, *Civilization and Capitalism*, vol. 1, *The Structures of Everyday Life* (New York: Harper & Row, 1981), p. 561.

83   Estimates for gross national product and population at the end of the eighteenth century discussed in Herman Kahn, William Brown, and Leon Martel, *The Next 200 Years* (New York: William Morrow, 1976), chaps. 1 and 2.

84   Data for sectoral distribution of product and employment for European countries given in B. R. Mitchell, *European Historical Statistics*, 2nd rev. ed. (New York: Facts on File, 1980), sections c and k.

84   Data on long-term growth rates for industrializing nations during the nineteenth and twentieth centuries given in Simon Kuznets, *Economic Growth of Nations* (Cambridge: Harvard University Press, 1971), pp. 11–19.

85   Death rates for England from B. R. Mitchell and Phyllis Deane, *Abstract of British Historical Statistics* (Cambridge: Cambridge Univ. Press, 1962), pp. 36–37; infant mortality rates from *European Historical Statistics*, pp. 137, 139, 141. U.S. data from U.S. Bureau of the Census, *Historical Statistics of the United States, Colonial Times to 1970*, Vol. 1 (Washington, D.C., 1976), pp. 57–59.

86   Figures on human development, given in *World Development*

Report 1981 (New York: Oxford University Press for the World Bank, 1981), p. 6.

86 The "triage classification" discussed in William and Paul Paddock, *Famine 1975!* (Boston: Little, Brown, 1967), chap. 9; William K. Stevens describes the new weight problems of Indians in the *New York Times*, Jan. 23, 1984; Joan Holmes's discussion of India's food production from the *New York Times*, Oct. 20, 1983.

86–87 Statistics for Indian development from *World Development Report 1984*, pp. 218, 220, 222, 256, 262, 266 and *World Development Report 1986*, pp. 180, 182, 184, 230, 232, 236.

86 Figures for sectoral distribution of employment and production, and for rates of growth, for middle-income and low-income countries from *World Development Report 1985*, Annex Tables 21, 3, 2, and 1, pp. 214–15, 178–79, 176–77, 174–75 and *World Development Report 1986*, Annex Tables 30 and 3, pp. 238, 184; factors of human development given in *World Development Report 1985*, Annex Tables 20, 23, and 24, pp. 212–13, 218–19, 220–21, and in *World Development Report 1986*, Annex Table 27, p. 232. Figures on adult literacy from *World Development Report 1983*, Annex Table 25, pp. 196–97.

90 Richard Critchfield, *Villages* (Garden City, N.Y.: Anchor Press/Doubleday, 1981); quotation from p. 336.

91 Rates of growth of gross domestic product shown in *World Development Report 1986*, p. 24.

91 Rates of productivity of performing artists and other similar examples examined in William J. Baumol and William C. Bowen, *Performing Arts: The Economic Dilemma* (New York: Twentieth Century Fund, 1966), chap. 7.

92–93 The hypothesis that economic development involves a shift in employment from extractive to manufacturing to service activities was first fully explicated by Colin Clark in *The Conditions of Economic Progress* (London: Macmillan, 1940), especially chap. 5 for the flow of labor to tertiary or service activities.

93 The seminal work on the rise and growing importance of service sector activities is Victor R. Fuchs, *The Service Economy* (New York: National Bureau of Economic Research, distributed by Columbia University Press, 1968).

93–94 Figures for sectoral distributions among services for recent years can be calculated from U.S. Bureau of Labor Statistics, "Handbook of Labor Statistics," Bulletin 2217, June 1985, especially Table 63, p. 175; an interesting discussion of these distributions, which also contains data for earlier years, is presented in Thomas M. Stanback, Jr., et al., *Services: The New Economy* (Totowa, N.J.: Allanheld Osmun, 1981).

96–97 These factors are discussed in greater detail in Leon C.

Martel, "The Growth of Growth," *Futures,* Apr. 1977, pp. 94–102; data showing productivity growth by economic sector, including slower growth in services, for sixteen industrial nations are given in Angus Madision, "Long Run Dynamics of Productivity Growth," *Banca Nazionale del Lavoro Quarterly Review,* No. 128 (Mar. 1979), pp. 3–43.

98 The need for new measures of productivity for services discussed in Victor R. Fuchs, "The Growing Importance of the Service Industries," *Journal of Business,* Oct. 1965, pp. 344–373.

98 Rankings by rate of growth given in Herbert Block, *The Planetary Product in 1980: A Creative Pause* (Washington, D.C., U.S. Department of State, Aug. 1981), Appendix Table B, p. 119.

98 Growth rates for different sectors of U.S. economy from *World Development Report 1984,* Annex Table 2, p. 221.

99 Success of steel mini-mills described in the *New York Times,* Feb. 24, 1984, and in *Wall Street Journal,* Jan. 8, 1987; the Brown Group discussed in *Forbes,* July 19, 1982, p. 50.

101 Data showing far smaller rises in unemployment in service-producing than goods-producing industries during the 1981–82 recession given in the *New York Times,* Oct. 10, 1982; an interesting analysis showing that the 1981–82 recession was actually more moderate than previous ones is presented by Alfred L. Malabre, Jr., in the *Wall Street Journal,* Jan. 24, 1983.

102 Data on U.S. exports and on increase in trade and services from the *New York Times,* July 3, 1983, and Oct. 24, 1984, and U.S. Department of Commerce, *Business America,* Mar. 4, 1985.

102 Albert Bressand, "Mastering the World Economy," *Foreign Affairs,* Spring 1983, p. 745.

103 Surpassing of exports of primary products by developing nations noted in the World Bank, *Annual Report 1982* (Washington, D.C., 1982), p. 27.

103 Peter F. Drucker, *Managing in Turbulent Times* (New York: Harper & Row), pp. 95–100.

104 Expansion of world trade faster than world product calculated from data in Joint Economic Committee, Congress of the United States, "U.S. Long-Term Economic Growth: Entering a New Era" (Washington, D.C.: U.S. Government Printing Office, 1978), p. 9, and the *Wall Street Journal,* May 28, 1981, p. 50; change in direction of trade in mid-1970s discussed in "The Hudson Letter" (Paris: Hudson Europe, Oct. 8, 1979); tendency of developed countries to increase trade shown in Simon Kuznets, *Modern Economic Growth* (New Haven, Conn.: Yale University Press, 1966), chap. 6.

105   External liabilities of developing countries tabulated in *World Development Report 1984*, Box Table 2.2A, p. 23.

105–106   Increase of bond issues and investments across national lines reported in the *New York Times*, Jan. 26 and Mar. 11, 1985; projections of purchases through 1987 from *Wall Street Journal*, Jan. 2, 1987.

107–108   Projections of world population growth rates and total numbers from United Nations, "World Population Prospects as Assessed in 1980," *Population Studies*, No. 78, 1981. Life expectancy figures from Population Reference Bureau, "1985 World Population Data Sheet," Apr. 1985.

111   Total fertility rates for market and nonmarket economies given in *World Development Report 1985*, Annex Table 20, p. 13; returns from World Fertility Survey, conducted under the supervision of the International Statistical Institute, discussed in the *New York Times*, July 15, 1980; *Euroform*, Sept. 3, 1979, p. 5.

111–112   The influence of fertility on population growth discussed by Charles F. Westoff in "Marriage and Fertility in the Developed Countries," *Scientific American*, Dec. 1978, pp. 51–57; recent estimates for the United States given in U.S. Bureau of the Census, "Projections of the Population of the United States by Age, Sex and Race: 1983 to 2080," *Current Population Reports*, series P-25, no. 952, 1984; planning by American women for fewer children is discussed in U.S. Bureau of the Census, "Fertility of American Women," *Current Population Reports*, series P-20, no. 378, 1983.

112–113   Mexico's national family planning program and its early results discussed in John S. Nagel, "Mexico's Population Turnaround," *Population Bulletin*, Dec. 1978, and in *Population Today*, Sept. 1984, p. 12; reports of China's population control programs given in the *Wall Street Journal*, July 6, 1983, and the *New York Times*, Oct. 28, 1983, and May 12, 1985; India's progress discussed in the *New York Times*, Dec. 28, 1983. Population growth figures and demographic indicators for the low-income countries given in *World Development Report 1986*, Annex Tables 25 and 26, pp. 228–31.

114   Figures for life expectancy at specified ages in Massachusetts given in *Historical Statistics of the U.S.*, Series B 126–135, p. 56.

114   Life expectancy figures from *World Development Report 1986*, Annex Tables 1 and 30, pp. 180, 233; death rates for selected causes from *Historical Statistics of the U.S.*, Series B 149–166, and National Center for Health Statistics, *Monthly Vital Statistics Report*, Mar. 26, 1985, pp. 8–9.

114   Age-adjusted death rates, given in U.S. Bureau of the Census, *Statistical Abstract of the United States: 1986* (Washing-

ton, D.C., 1985), p. 73; Dr. Thomas quoted in the *New York Times*, Feb. 20, 1984.

117 Survival rates for different types of cancer are given by Dr. Vincent T. DeVita, Director, National Cancer Institute, in an interview in *U.S. News and World Report*, Sept. 20, 1982, pp. 72–74; the American Cancer Society's survival estimate reported in the *New York Times*, Mar. 9, 1984.

119 Life expectancy indicators given in *World Development Report 1985*, Annex Table 23, pp. 218–19; their course in developing nations discussed by Davidson R. Gwatkin and Sarah K. Brandel, "Life Expectancy and Population Growth in the Third World," *Scientific American*, May 1982, pp. 57–65.

120 Research on aging and "active life expectancy" reported in *the New England Journal of Medicine*, Nov. 1983, pp. 1218–24, and discussed in the *New York Times*, July 16, 1982, and Feb. 21, 1984. Interesting anecdotal evidence of changing attitudes toward old age is found in comparing two series of articles on the elderly run in the *Wall Street Journal*: the first, in Oct. 1979, tends to emphasize the trials of old age, while the second, in Feb. 1983, speaks of the "more active" years of the elderly.

120 The U.N. projection for Europe depicted in Westoff, "Marriage and Fertility in the Developed Countries," p. 53.

120–121 Developed and developing countries' population projections from Population Reference Bureau, "1985 World Population Data Sheet," Apr. 1985; changing rates of growth of urban populations from *World Development Report 1984*, Annex Table 22, pp. 260–61.

121 Labor force growth rates given in World Bank, *IDA in Retrospect* (New York; Oxford University Press, 1982), Annex Table 22, pp. 126–27.

121 1981 and 1983 estimates by the United Nations Fund for Population Activities reported in the *New York Times*, June 15, 1981, and June 19, 1983; 1987 figure from telephone conversation with U.N. demographer Dr. Rao, Jan. 23, 1987.

122 Population projections for minority groups derived from Center for Continuing Study of the California Economy, "Projections of Hispanic Population for the U.S. 1990–2000, with Projections of Non-Hispanic, White, Black, Asian and Other Population Groups," Palo Alto, Calif., July 1982.

123 The changing population growth rates of the USSR's nationalities are discussed in Murray Feshbach, "The Soviet Union: Population Trends and Dilemmas," *Population Bulletin*, Aug. 1982.

124–126 Percentages for population age groups for 1970 given in World Bank Group, *Trends in Developing Countries* (Washington, D.C.: World Bank, 1973), Chart 2.2.

127 Projections of Americans sixty-five and over and eighty-five

and over made by the U.S. Bureau of the Census and reported in the *Wall Street Journal*, Sept. 30, 1983.

131 Drucker's essay, "Unmaking the Nineteenth Century," reprinted in Peter F. Drucker, *The Changing World of the Executive* (New York: Truman Talley Books, 1982), pp. 147–53.

131–132 Data for mothers in the workforce, given in Elizabeth Weldman, "Labor Force Statistics from a Family Perspective," *Monthly Labor Review*, Dec. 1983, pp. 16–20, and "Handbook of Labor Statistics," June 1985, Table 54, p. 123; poll data on valuation of jobs reported in the *New York Times*, Dec. 4, 1983; number of female mayors given in U.S. Conference of Mayors, "Female Mayors of Major U.S. Cities," Oct. 3, 1984.

133 Projections of rates of growth of labor forces for developed and developing nations given in *World Development Report 1985*, Annex Table 21, pp. 214–15.

133–134 Growth rates of U.S. labor force through 1982, and projections to 1995, given in Howard N. Fullerton, Jr., and John Tschetter, "The 1995 Labor Force: A Second Look," *Monthly Labor Review*, Nov. 1983, pp. 3–7; data for 1983 reported in the *Wall Street Journal*, Jan. 4, 1984.

134–135 Rates of change in employment by major sectors from Valerie A. Personick, "The Job Outlook Through 1995: Industry Output and Employment Projections," *Monthly Labor Review*, Nov. 1983, p. 26, and Michael Urquhart, "The Employment Shift to Services: Where Did It Come From?" *Monthly Labor Review*, Apr. 1984, p. 70.

135 U.S. employment/population ratios for 1960 through June 1985 are given in *Statistical Abstract: 1986*, Table 658, p. 390.

136–137 Projections of new jobs through 1995 made by George T. Silvestri et al., "Occupational Employment Projections Through 1995," *Monthly Labor Review*, Nov. 1983, pp. 37–48; estimates of percent of technical positions in high-tech industries by Dr. Henry Levin, Director of Institute for Research on Education and Governance at Stanford University, quoted in the *New York Times*, Apr. 4, 1984.

138 Data on white males in U.S. workforce reported in the *New York Times*, July 31, 1984.

139 Percentages of workforce in unions from Larry T. Adams, "Changing Employment Patterns of Organized Workers," *Monthly Labor Review*, Feb. 1985, p. 26; figures for income distribution from U.S. Bureau of the Census, *Current Population Reports*, Series P-60, Nos. 142 and 145, 1984, and Statistical Abstract: 1986, Table 754, p. 452.

140 Attitude changes in Pittsburgh and other urban centers due to shift from industrial to service-type economic activities described in the *Wall Street Journal*, Aug. 21, 1984.

141 Productivity gains of Control Data described in the *Wall Street Journal*, May 3, 1983; Alvin Toffler gives work at home prominent attention in chap. 16 ("The Electronic Cottage") of *The Third Wave* (New York: Morrow, 1980), and Jack Nilles, Director of Information Technology at the University of Southern California's Center for Futures Research, predicts that "by the end of the century, you could have as much as 20 percent of the workforce telecommunicating part-time." *(New York Times Magazine*, Nov. 14, 1982, p. 157). Cetron was quoted in *People* magazine, Jan. 12, 1987.

142 Citibank's credit card operations center discussed in the *Wall Street Journal*, Mar. 31, 1983; examples of Satellite Data Corporation and Swedish fire department mentioned in the *New York Times*, Oct. 3, 1982.

144–145 Data on percentages of workforce on flexitime and part-time schedules from U.S. Bureau of Labor Statistics, as reported in the *New York Times*, Aug. 14, 1983, and Dec. 30, 1986.

145 American Can's flexible benefit plan described in the *New York Times*, Apr. 17, 1982; performance-related benefit plans of Lincoln Electric and Electro Scientific Industries discussed in the *Wall Street Journal*, Aug. 12, 1983, and the *New York Times*, May 6, 1984.

148 Rates of growth of gross product, population, and GNP per capita from *World Development Report 1985*, Annex Tables 19, 2, and 1, pp. 210–11, 174–75, 176–77, and World Development Report 1986, Annex Table 1, pp. 180–81.

148–149 Data on rise of personal income in U.S. from 1929 to 1970 are given in *Historical Statistics of the U.S.*, Series F 262–286, p. 241. Rates of growth of total real disposable income are given in *Statistical Abstract: 1984*, Table 759, p. 455.

149–150 Examples of media reportage of declining median family income in *U.S. News and World Report*, Aug. 31, 1981, p. 6, and Aug. 23, 1984, p. 8, and the *New York Times*, Oct. 10, 1982, and May 21, 1984. Percentage increase in nonfamily households calculated from *Statistical Abstract: 1984*, Table 75, p. 55, and Table 754, p. 459.

150–152 Data on employer benefits given in *Statistical Abstract: 1986*, Tables 724, 707, and 708, pp. 436, 421; figures for European countries reported in *U.S. News and World Report*, July 9, 1984, p. 75.

152 The increased role of government transfer payments in incomes is discussed in Wassily W. Leontieff, "The Distribution of Work and Income," *Scientific American*, Sept. 1982, pp. 188–204; figures from U.S. Bureau of the Census' new statistical series, *Survey of Income and Program Participation*, reported in the *New York Times*, Apr. 17, 1985; data on federal, state, and local government transfer payments from

Statistical Abstract: 1986, Tables 597, 598, 632, 202, 593, pp. 356, 357, 373, 153, 354.

153–154   Hudson Institute Report HI-3101/3-P (draft), "Planning for the 80's," Dec. 1979, contains a brief but comprehensive discussion of income and demand generated by personal assets. Data on financial assets of U.S. households from *Statistical Abstract: 1986*, Table 815, p. 489.

154   Data for value of different kinds of assets for all persons for 1962 to 1976 given in *Statistical Abstract: 1985*, Table 775, p. 463.

154–155   Data on changes in median income for different age groups from U.S. Bureau of the Census, reported in the *New York Times*, Oct. 31, 1982.

155   Figures for farm workers' productivity cited in the *Wall Street Journal*, Jul. 29, 1982. Percentages of "needs" for 1930 and 1950 calculated from *Historical Statistics of the U.S.*, Series G 416–469, pp. 318–319; for 1982 from *Statistical Abstract: 1986*, Table 728, p. 435.

156   Changing shares of per capita personal consumption expenditures shown in U.S. Bureau of the Census, *Social Indicators III* (Washington, D.C., 1980), Chart 9/11, p. 432, and calculated from *Statistical Abstract: 1986*, Table 723, p. 433.

156–157   The role of economic security in influencing goals is developed —though in a different sense than here—in Ronald Inglehart, "The Silent Revolution in Europe: Intergenerational Change in Post-Industrial Societies," *American Political Science Review*, Dec. 1971, pp. 991–1017; "societal levers" were first discussed by Herman Kahn and B. Bruce-Briggs in *Things to Come: Thinking About the 70's and 80's* (New York: Macmillan, 1972), pp. 77–78.

157–158   The evolution of new values in Japan in recent years has been observed by many astute Western scholars of that country, including Herbert Passin ("Changing Values: Work and Growth in Japan," *Asian Survey*, Oct. 1975, pp. 821–50) and Robert C. Christopher ("Changing Face of Japan," *New York Times Magazine*, Mar. 27, 1983, pp. 40ff).

159   Data on family and nonfamily households from *Statistical Abstract: 1986*, Table 54, p. 39, and Andrew Hacker, ed., *U/S: A Statistical Portrait of the American People* (New York: Viking, 1983), p. 92.

159   Census figures concerning divorce and remarriage reported in the *New York Times*, Feb. 7, 1985.

159   Data on women and men enrolled in college from *Statistical Abstract: 1986*, Table 251, p. 149; numbers of women and men joining the labor force from *Handbook of Labor Statistics*, June 1985, Table 1, pp. 6–7.

160   Alan Bloom, "Our Listless Universities," *National Review*, Dec. 10, 1982, pp. 1537ff.

160 Data on increasing percentage of one-parent families with children from U.S. Bureau of the Census, *Current Population Reports*, series P-20, no. 398, 1985.

162 Report of new products discussed in the *New York Times*, Jan. 21, 1983.

162–163 Figures on increase in grocery store items supplied by library of *Progressive Grocer* magazine, Stamford, Conn.; correlation of food expenditures (including food away from home) with income and education discussed by Anthony E. Gallo and William T. Boehm, "Food Expenditures by Income Group," *National Food Review*, June 1978, pp. 21–23, and Judith Jones Putnam and Michael G. Van Dress, "Changes Ahead for Eating Out," *National Food Review*, No. 26 (Spring 1984).

163 Data on changing percentages in leisure expenditures, attributed to Sandra Shaber of Chase Econometrics, discussed in *Forbes*, Sept. 28, 1981, p. 9.

164–165 The varieties of automobile types available from manufacturers discussed in the *Wall Street Journal*, Dec. 15, 1983.

165 Surveys and studies showing increasing public concern about quality and value presented in *The Harris Survey*, Dec. 21, 1978, and *World Opinion Update*, Jan. 1979, p. 8, and discussed in the *Wall Street Journal*, Oct. 15, 1981, and July 5, 1984.

165–166 Howard Johnson's and Marriott's shifting strategies, and Revlon's plight, discussed in the *New York Times*, June 24, 1983, and May 31, 1984.

166 Data on percentage of population moving are from U.S. Bureau of the Census, *Current Population Reports*, series P-20, no. 393, 1984.

167 Exclusionary and no-growth zoning examined in Michelle J. White, "Self-Interest in the Suburbs: The Trend Toward No-Growth Zoning," *Policy Analysis*, Spring 1978, pp. 185–203.

167–168 A comprehensive discussion of growth and no-growth programs appears in the *New York Times*, Apr. 20, 1979; the struggle of the villagers in Crested Butte is described in Roger N. Williams, "A Tiny Town Battles a Mining Giant," *New York Times Magazine*, Mar. 4, 1979, pp. 17ff.

168–169 Charles A. Reich, *The Greening of America* (New York: Random House, 1970).

169 Results of 1978 survey (conducted by Bureau of Social Science Research and Roper Organization) reported in *Public Opinion*, Aug./Sept. 1979, p. 23; 1983 survey (New York Times, CBS News Poll) reported in the *New York Times*, Apr. 17, 1983.

170 Survey on risk of technologies reported in Paul Slovic et al,

"Risky Assumptions," *Psychology Today*, June 1980, pp. 44–48.

171   Changes in consumption of alcoholic beverages and certain foods reported in the *New York Times*, Sept. 17 and Dec. 9, 1984, and July 31, 1985.

171   Wheat Industry Council, "Food, Nutrition and Dieting: A Comprehensive Study of American Attitudes, Habits, Perceptions and Myths," Oct. 1983.

173   Statistics on migration to Arizona from Paul Bracken, "Arizona Tomorrow: A Precursor of Post-Industrial America," Hudson Institute Discussion Paper HI-2882-RR, July 1978, chap. 2; The growth of rural population in American is discussed in Larry Long and Diana DeAre, "The Slowing of Urbanization in the U.S., *Scientific American*, July 1983, pp. 334ff. American Association of Retired Persons studies and U.S. Bureau of the Census data on migration of retirees are reported in the *New York Times*, Dec. 4, 1983.

CHAPTER 4

175–176   Weiner offered his own explanation of cybernetics for the lay reader in Norbert Weiner, *The Human Use of Human Beings: Cybernetics and Society* (Garden City: Doubleday Anchor Books, 1954); an interesting application of cybernetics in explaining one aspect of human behavior is given by John D. Steinbruner, *The Cybernetic Theory of Decision: New Dimensions of Political Analysis* (Princeton, N.J.: Princeton University Press, 1974).

177   Mitchell's oft-quoted remark appears in his pioneer study of the subject, *Business Cycles* (Berkeley, Calif.: University of California Press, 1913), p. 449; the occurrence and duration of recessions and recoveries in the United States since 1790 is shown graphically in Conference Board, "Economic Change: A Bicentennial Perspective," and, more recently, in Center for International Business Cycle Research, *International Economic Indicators*, June 1984, app. A.

178   Kuznets cycles are discussed in Nathaniel J. Maas, *Economic Cycles: An Analysis of Underlying Causes* (Cambridge, Mass.: Wright-Allen Press, 1975), pp. 106–13.

179   Schumpeter's interpretation of Kondratiev waves is in *Business Cycles: A Theoretical, Historical, and Statistical Analysis of the Capitalist Process*, 2 vols. (New York: McGraw-Hill, 1939), vol. 1, chap. 4. Rostow's is given in "The Developing World in the Fifth Kondratieff Upswing," *Annals of the American Academy*, 1975, pp. 111–24. Forrester's is summarized in "Changing Economic Patterns," *Technology Review*, Aug./ Sept. 1978, pp. 46–53.

180   Data on percent changes in industrial production, total em-

ployment, and business investment during business cycles given in Victor Zarnowitz and Geoffrey H. Moore, "Major Changes in Cyclical Behavior," Working Paper No. 1395, National Bureau of Economic Research, July 1984, and in columns by Alfred L. Malabre, Jr., in the *Wall Street Journal*, Jan. 24 and Apr. 5, 1983.

180   Business cycle durations given in Geoffrey H. Moore, "Business Cycles, Panics and Depressions," *Encyclopedia of American Economic History*, vol. I (New York: Charles Scribner, 1980), p. 152, and Zarnowitz and Moore, "Major Changes in Cyclical Behavior."

182   The slower decline of employment in service sector activities in the United States during its recent recessions shown in U.S. Bureau of Labor Statistics, *Employment and Earnings*, vols. 21, 22, 28, and 29 (1974, 1975, 1981, and 1982).

184   The variation in high-technology factory shipments from different areas of the United States graphically shown in *Forbes*, June 20, 1983, pp. 132ff; the slowing migration to Sunbelt states and the reversal of migration from those in the Snowbelt is discussed in Peter A. Rogerson and David A. Plane, "Monitoring Migration Trends," *American Demographics*, Feb. 1985, pp. 27ff.

194–195   Data on increasing volatility in value of hard assets compiled by investment banking firm of Salomon Brothers and reported in the *New York Times*, June 27, 1982.

198, 200   Changes in the volume and volatility of trading in the New York Stock Exchange discussed in the *New York Times*, Nov. 30, 1982, Feb. 10, 1984, and Mar. 13, 1984; Tobin's views discussed in Peter Passell's "Editorial Notebook" column in the same newspaper, July 23, 1984.

203   Data on declining U.S. agricultural exports reported in the *New York Times*, Feb. 1, 1985, and the *Wall Street Journal*, Mar. 25, 1985.

206–207   The Paley Report, named after the commission's chairman, William S. Paley, was the President's Material Policy Commission, *Resources for Freedom*, 5 vols. (Washington, D.C.: U.S. Government Printing Office, 1952); data on use of scrap copper and aluminum from the *New York Times*, Oct. 9, 1983.

207   Declining per capita consumption of a number of resources discussed in Marc Ross and Arthur H. Purcell, "Decline of Materials Intensiveness: The U.S. Pulp and Paper Industry," *Resources Policy*, Dec. 1981.

208   The story of Qaddafi's success with Occidental Petroleum is told in Jack Anderson with James Boyd, *Fiasco* (New York: Times Books, 1983).

209   Canada's oil price projection and its support of companies

exploring the High Arctic is described in the *New York Times*, Mar. 3, 1983.

210 Fuel efficiency figures from *Monthly Energy Review*, Aug. 1986, p. 15; gasoline consumption data from the *Wall Street Journal*, June 28, 1984. Percentages of U.S. dependency on imported oil from *Monthly Energy Review*, Aug. 1986, p. 13.

212–213 Figures for low school enrollments and applications from the *New York Times*, Feb. 10, 1985, and the *Wall Street Journal*, Feb. 22, 1985.

213 Data on college graduates in education reported in the *New York Times*, June 24, 1984.

214–215 Data on science and engineering degrees from National Science Foundation, *Science and Engineering Degrees: 1950–1980. A Source Book*. Special Report NSF 82–307 (Washington, D.C.: U.S. Government Printing Office, Jan. 1982).

217 The fascinating history of the periodic reorganizations of the CPSU has been recounted by Merle Fainsod in *How Russia Is Ruled*, rev. ed. (Cambridge, Mass.: Harvard University Press, 1967), chap. 6.

217–218 Analysis of the adaptive behavior of business organizations is presented in Richard M. Cyert and James G. March, *A Behavioral Theory of the Firm* (Englewood Cliffs, N.J.: Prentice-Hall, 1963), especially pp. 99–101; a summary of arguments for centralization and decentralization is given in Douglas Basil and Curtis W. Cook, *The Management of Change* (London and New York: McGraw-Hill, 1974), pp. 91–95.

218–219 Brief descriptions of reorganizations by G.E., U.S. Steel, and Sears Roebuck given in Alfred D. Chandler, Jr., "Management Decentralization: An Historical Analysis," chap. 8 of James P. Baugman, ed., *The History of American Management* (Englewood Cliffs, N.J.: Prentice-Hall, 1969).

219–220 Beatrice's reorganization and subsequent acquisition of Esmark discussed in detail in the *Wall Street Journal*, Sep. 23, 1983, and Dec. 24, 1984; its 1984 earnings reported in the *New York Times*, Apr. 24, 1985.

220–221 Henry David Thoreau, *The Journal of Henry David Thoreau*, ed. by Bradford Torrey and Francis H. Allen (Boston: Houghton-Mifflin, 1949), vol. XII, Mar. 2, 1859–Nov. 30, 1859, pp. 317–18; John Stuart Mill, *Principles of Political Economy*, vol. II (New York: Appleton, 1864), p. 397.

221–222 Schlesinger's essay, "Tides of American Politics," first appeared in the *Yale Review*, Dec. 1939, pp. 217–30; the updated version is chap. 4 of *Paths to the Present* (New York: Macmillan, 1949). Quotations from pp. 85, 90, 91.

223 Karl W. Deutsch, *The Nerves of Government: Models of Political Communication and Control* (New York: Free Press of Glencoe, 1963), especially chaps. 5 and 11.

225   Decision by the Federal Communications Commission reported in the *New York Times,* Aug. 9, 1984.

225   Quincy Wright, *A Study of War,* vol. I (Chicago: University of Chicago Press, 1942), appendix 20, and J. David Singer and Melvin Small, *The Wages of War, 1916–1965: A Statistical Handbook* (New York: John Wiley, 1972), table 4.1, p. 59; both war lists summarized in David Wilkinson, *Deadly Quarrels: Lewis F. Richardson and the Statistical Study of War* (Berkeley: University of California Press, 1980), appendices 1 and 2.

226   Frank H. Denton and Warren Phillips, "Some Patterns in the History of Violence," *Journal of Conflict Resolution,* June 1968, pp. 182–195, and Singer and Small, *The Wages of War,* chap. 9 and chart on endpapers.

226–227   George Modelski, "The Long Cycle of Global Politics and the Nation-State," *Comparative Studies in Society and History,* Apr. 1978, pp. 214–35.

227   Data on periods of enmity and friendship for pairs of nations summarized and discussed in Singer and Small, *The Wages of War,* chap. 13.

230   The idea of a "pariah" policy to deal with nuclear weapon users was a frequent theme in the strategic writings of the late Herman Kahn. It is explored in further detail, though in a somewhat different version than here, in Herman Kahn and Leon C. Martel, "Nuclear Proliferation and U.S. Declaratory Policy," Hudson Institute Discussion Paper HI-2394-DP, Nov. 8, 1978.

231–233   A comprehensive display of changes in patriotism and other attitudes and values throughout the course of U.S. history is presented in B. Bruce-Briggs, "Changing Values and Attitudes in U.S. History," Hudson Institute Chart Collection HI-2006/ 2-CC, Aug. 30, 1974.

233–234   Jane Richardson and A. L. Krober, *Three Centuries of Women's Dress Fashions,* University of California Publications in Anthropological Records, vol. 5, no. 2 (Berkeley: University of California Press, 1940); quotations from pp. 148–49.

236   Data on new food products from the *Wall Street Journal,* Aug. 17, 1984, and Dec. 19, 1986.

237   Quotation from the *Wall Street Journal,* from column by Benjamin Stein, Apr. 16, 1984; Family Service America report described in the *New York Times,* Oct. 6, 1984.

238   Marriage rate statistics for Finland, Sweden, the United Kingdom, and France from Mitchell, *European Historical Statistics,* pp. 114, 115, 117, 119, 122, 123, 125, 129–31, 133, 134.

238–239   Average annual increases in marriage and birth rates from *Statistical Abstract: 1984,* pp. xix and 63.

239   Divorce rate for 1984 from *Monthly Vital Statistics Report,* Jan. 29, 1985, p. 2.

241   Pictogram in *U.S. News and World Report* issue of Dec. 7, 1981, p. 53.

243   Ted Robert Gurr, "Historical Trends in Violent Crime: A Critical Review of the Evidence," in Michael Tonry and Norval Morris, eds., *Crime and Justice: An Annual Review of Research* (Chicago: University of Chicago Press, 1981/82), vol. 3, pp. 295–353.

243–244   Property crime rates for years 1957 to 1970 from *Historical Statistics of the U.S.*, p. 413; rates for 1973 through 1984 depicted in *Statistical Abstract: 1986*, Fig. 6.1, p. 162 and Table 279, p. 166.

243   Gurr, "Historical Trends in Violent Crime," pp. 344–45.

244   Statistics for crime rates by type and area of residence in *Statistical Abstract: 1985*, Table 276, p. 166.

244–245   Smith quoted in the *New York Times*, Apr. 20, 1984.

245–246   Findings of the Lichters reported in the *New York Times*, Feb. 28, 1983.

246   Gurr, "Historical Trends in Violent Crime," p. 312.

CHAPTER 5

248   Story of the Warren Featherbone Co. told in the *Wall Street Journal*, Oct. 11, 1982.

249   White quoted in *Forbes*, Aug. 30, 1982, p. 184; Napoleon's reply quoted in *The Saturday Review*, Dec. 1979, p. 36; Keuffel and Esser study described in the *New York Times*, Jan. 3, 1982.

251   John Naisbitt, *Megatrends* (New York: Warner Books, 1982), p. 2; *Global 2000 Report*, p. 1.

253   Possibility of OPEC-like actions by other cartels discussed by C. Fred Bergsten in "The World May Have to Live with Shortages," *New York Times*, Jan. 27, 1974.

254   Plight of the Pacific Northwest timber industry described in the *Wall Street Journal*, June 19, 1984; MacMillan Bloedel vice-president quoted in *Business Week*, Dec. 20, 1982, p. 37.

255   Excess iron ore capacity in the steel industry, losses by California farmers, and the troubles of Scullin Steel reported in the *Wall Street Journal*, Aug. 29, 1983, Sept. 21, 1984, and Sept. 29, 1981.

255   Atari's fall described in Everett M. Rogers and Judith K. Larson, *Silicon Valley Fever: Growth of High Technology Culture* (New York: Basic Books, 1984), especially pp. 261–64; Tandy's difficulties examined in the *New York Times*, Aug. 19, 1984.

259   Developments in steel and plastic panels for automobiles discussed in the *New York Times*, Feb. 8, 1983, and July 2, 1984.

260   Alan Altshuler, et al., *The Future of the Automobile: The*

Report of MIT's International Automobile Program (Cambridge, Mass.: MIT Press, 1984), chap. 2.

260   Automobile supermarkets and other innovations in car dealerships discussed in the *New York Times*, Apr. 15, 1985 and the *Wall Street Journal*, July 1, 1985; figures on change in the Hertz fleet from the *New York Times*, Sept. 5, 1982.

261–262   G.M.'s problems with its downsized premium cars discussed in the *New York Times*, Jan. 1, 1987.

263–264   Automobile preferences based on personality discussed in the *Wall Street Journal*, Dec. 13, 1983. and Sept. 27, 1984.

263–264   A comprehensive examination of changes affecting the dental profession can be found in American Dental Association, "Interim Report of the American Dental Association's Special Committee on the Future of Dentistry," Chicago, Sept. 1982.

268   Lyell's teaching regarding future change discussed in J. D. Bernal, *The World, the Flesh and the Devil*, 2nd ed. (Bloomington: Indiana University Press, 1969), chap. 1.

270   Rise then slowing of technological change following scientific breakthroughs discussed in Peter F. Drucker, *Managing in Turbulent Times* (New York: Harper & Row, 1980), pp. 48–60.

272   Female labor force participation rates given in *Historical Statistics of the U.S.*, pp. 131–32 and U.S. Bureau of Labor Statistics, "Handbook of Labor Statistics," June 1985, p. 19.

275   Judge Hand's argument about discounting improbability found in *United States v. Dennis*, 183 F 2nd 201, p. 212 (2d Cir. 1950).

282–283   Hershey Foods Corporation profiled in the *New York Times*, July 22, 1984, and *Fortune*, July 8, 1985, pp. 53 ff.

283–284   Story of Pop-In's maid service from the *New York Times*, Jan. 20, 1985.

284   Ford's Flat Rock plant, RCA's videodiscs, and NCR's cash registers discussed in the *Wall Street Journal*, Sept. 16, 1981, Apr. 5, 1984, and May 2, 1983, and the *New York Times*, May 31, 1985; Vickers' and Lockheed's turboprops mentioned in Basil and Cook, *The Management of Change*, p. 215.

285   Entrepreneurial units supported or established by Tektronix, Security Pacific, and other companies described in the *Wall Street Journal*, Sept. 13, 14, 18, 1984.

286   Daniel J. Boorstin, *The Discoverers* (New York: Random House, 1983), pp. 64–65.

286   Satellite telecommunications and satellite business systems discussed in the *Wall Street Journal*, May 3, 1984.

287   Use of automation by General Electric, Black & Decker, American Textile Makers, and General Motors discussed in the *Wall Street Journal*, Apr. 4, 1983, Feb. 18, 1983, Sept. 14, 1984, and May 14, 1984.

288 Newmont Mining, Kiewit, Singer, Brother Industries, and Mead discussed in the *New York Times*, Dec. 6, 1984, July 13, 1984, July 12, 1984, May 3, 1983, and Apr. 23, 1984; Schlumberger's troubles reported in the *Wall Street Journal*, Aug. 26, 1983.

289 Cities Service and Monsanto's actions described in the *New York Times*, Feb. 20, 1984 and July 28, 1985; Dow Chemical's objective quoted from its *1983 Annual Report*, p. 4.

289 Shifts in emphasis and new service activities of Data General, American Can, and Sears Roebuck detailed in the *New York Times*, June 26, 1983, May 8, 1984, and Feb. 12, 1984.

290 Tandon's expansion overseas discussed in the *New York Times*, Mar. 25, 1984; changes LeBlond Makino and the machine tool industry described in the *Wall Street Journal*, Sept. 4, 1984.

291 General Mills' problems with Izod and its decision to sell off its fashion business discussed in the *New York Times*, Nov. 15, 1984, and Mar. 27, 1985.

292 Ryder System's management described in *Forbes*, Dec. 20, 1983, pp. 50, 55; Northwest Airlines in the *Wall Street Journal*, Oct. 3, 1983; Merrill-Lynch's hirings and announced layoffs reported in the *Wall Street Journal*, Feb. 3, 1984, and the *New York Times*, June 28, 1984.

293 Changes in prime rate cited in the *New York Times*, Oct. 28, 1984; John Thackray, "The Reign of the Finance Men," *Planning Review*, Jan. 1983, pp. 36–38.

294 Marriott discussed in *Forbes*, Mar. 2, 1981, p. 111, and *Business Week*, Oct. 1, 1964, pp. 60–62; DuPont in the *Wall Street Journal*, Nov. 26, 1982 and *Business Week*, May 30, 1983, pp. 73–74.

295–296 Statistics on U.S. wine consumption and descriptions of the plight of California winegrowers given in *U.S. News and World Report*, Oct. 17, 1983, pp. 82–83, and the *New York Times*, Oct. 25, 1984.

296 Ups and downs in the semiconductor business reported in the *New York Times*, June 29, 1983, Oct. 27, 1984, and Dec. 8, 1984.

297 Losses by casualty insurers for 1984 reported in the *Wall Street Journal*, Dec. 31, 1984.

CHAPTER 6

300 Mettler quoted in *Forbes*, July 18, 1983, pp. 102–14, which profiles the change and expansion of TRW.

304 Drucker, *Managing in Turbulent Times*, p. 24.

306–307 Peter Medawar, *Pluto's Republic* (New York: Oxford University Press, 1982), p. 190.

Index